TOKYO FIREWALL

Elizabeth Wilkerson

Arigato!
—em

Philadelphia, PA

First paperback edition November 2018

Cover design by Rafael Andres

Print and ebook layout by booknook.biz

Names: Wilkerson, Elizabeth (Elizabeth S.), author.

Title: Tokyo firewall / Elizabeth Wilkerson.

Description: First paperback edition. | Philadelphia, PA : Contrafish Media, LLC, [2018]

Identifiers: ISBN: 978-0-9994329-0-7 (paperback) | 978-0-9994329-1-4 (ebook) | LCCN: 2018910577

Subjects: LCSH: Americans—Japan—Tokyo—Fiction. | African American women—Japan—Fiction. | Hackers—Fiction. | Online chat groups—Fiction. | Cyberstalking—Fiction. | Cyberterrorism— Fiction. | Online sexual predators—Fiction. | Computer crimes—Fiction. | Data encryption (Computer science)—Fiction. | Fugitives from justice—Fiction. | Japan—Fiction. | Romance fiction. | Suspense fiction. | LCGFT: Thrillers (Fiction) | Detective and mystery fiction. | Romance fiction. | BISAC: FICTION / African American / Mystery & Detective. | FICTION / Mystery & Detective / International Mystery & Crime. | FICTION / Thrillers / Technological. | FICTION / Thrillers / Suspense. | FICTION / Mystery & Detective / Women Sleuths.

Classification: LCC: PS3623.I5458 T65 2018 | DDC: 813.6—dc23

www.elizabethwilkerson.com

For Tetsuki, who asked me to do it.

And told me that I could.

The ’90s

1

The calliope carnival tones of Tokyo's five o'clock song burst from the public address system and bounced through the streets of Akihabara.

Shit. He was really late. They'd be starting without him.

The icy bite of the late-autumn evening air prompted him to pick up his pace. Head lowered against the wind, he hugged the oil-treated paper bag close to his chest and elbowed his way past the pack of bargain-hungry *gaijin* tourists rummaging through electronic parts crammed into the sidewalk arcade.

Akihabara. Stall upon stall, row upon row, street upon street of computer parts, accessories, peripherals and pieces. A high-tech candy land of overwhelming proportions. Akihabara's alleyways were a black market of guts for the computer industry those Americans had long ago lost control of. He was sure there was nothing to rival Akihabara in Silicon Valley.

Damn foreigners in their baseball caps and T-shirts — they infested Akihabara like roaches, looking for discounts on electronics they could show off to their friends. Idiot Americans. Happy to pay full retail price for last year's junk. Didn't realize that Akihabara was the one place in Tokyo where you could — where you were expected to — haggle over prices. Explained why the Americans were always on the losing end of the trade imbalance.

A hulking linebacker blocked the passageway in front of him. Guy looked as oblivious as a dumb cow grazing. American meat was so full of hormones and steroids, it was no wonder they grew to the size of obese cattle. Even he had gained over five kilos during the semester he was in school in Boston.

He prodded the cow in the back as he made his way through the blockade. The big guy yelled "Hey!" and stared. Too slow. Steroids must have gotten to his brain. Moo.

He edged past the hawker giving away tissue packs with an ad for a new phone sex service. Trotted past the pawn shop that still held one of his server computers hostage until he paid up. Fuck them. Ducked into a *nezumi-dori*, a rat street, the footpath that ran behind a discount ticket broker and was the shortcut back to his "mansion" apartment.

Train tracks overhead formed a ceiling and trapped the smell of urine in the back-street corridor. With a slight adjustment of his earplugs, the deafening clatter from the trains was reduced to a muffled annoyance.

If he hurried, he'd be home in twenty minutes. His small apartment was conveniently located near the Akihabara district, but off the beaten path enough to be affordable for him. Affordable with a little help he'd had to squeeze out of his dear old dad. Those tightwads at the post-production house where he worked had refused to lend him the *reikin* key money and *shikikin* deposit money. Seven months' rent, upfront and in cash. Just for the privilege of moving in.

His apartment was far from swanky, but at least it was quiet. So quiet that he could sometimes do rough edits of the sound tracks for his commercials from home. Or he used to be able to before that obnoxious couple with their shrieking baby moved in upstairs. The soundproofing he'd installed helped.

He turned onto his street and raced down the block. His apartment's bamboo window blinds, closed tight, offered no hint of what was inside. He waved at the motion-activated surveillance camera he'd hidden above the windows, opened his door and entered his apartment without turning on the lights.

The blue glow beacon from a 27-inch Sony monitor guided his way as he removed his earplugs, loosened his tie and walked across the tatami mat, stepping over the shoebox-size plastic bins labeled with their contents: coax cables, circuit boards, RAM cards, anything else he could get his hands on to go into the next box he'd build.

A bank of five server computers weighed down a metal table in the middle of his apartment. Without stopping to see who was on his Bulletin Board Service or what whining email complaints they had sent to him as SysOp, the system operator for the BBS, he pulled out a chair and logged onto World NetLink using an anonymous backdoor connection he'd hacked.

Luv2Blow, DaikonDik, SweatySue, RodSukr. The regular gang had already gathered in the "It Really Happened to Me" sex fantasy chat room. Tonight's chat was already underway.

```
SWEATYSUE>>: The cockpit is filled with glowing
instrument panels. I sit down in the jump seat and
the pilot fastens a shoulder harness restraint
around me really tight. He's says it's in case of
unexpected turbulence.
LUV2BLOW>>: Safety first!
SWEATYSUE>>: The pilot says he has to check the
harness straps and he reaches under my blouse and
rubs against my tits. My body trembles at his touch.
He unfastens his belt and pulls out his Boeing.
LUV2BLOW>>: So that's why they call it the *cock*
pit ;-)
```

He slid his hand into the paper bag he'd brought home, pulled out the bundle and untied the silk casing that protected his new gun. His gun. The Yakuza guy he met online had sold it to him cheap. Who cared if it could even shoot straight? He liked the way the gun felt in his hand, its commanding weightiness. When he held the gun, its cold metallic song energized his whole body.

He watched DaikonDik and RodSukr leave the group and enter their own private chat room. Just the two of them. As the SysOp, he was undetectable, looking on while their virtual foreplay antics scrolled by silently on his screen.

He unzipped his tight pants. One hand on his crotch, the other hand stroking the cool smoothness of the pistol, he sat back and watched the online chat.

The screen flashed, announcing the arrival of a newcomer in the main group chat room. YokohamaMama. The SysOp fingered her and learned she was a foreign woman logging in from Japan. Perfect.

He'd make his approach, slow at first, then reel her in. Who should he be tonight? Why not Kawasaki8?

Kawasaki8 sent an instant online message to YokohamaMama:

"HELLO YOKOHAMAMAMA. ARE YOU CALLING FROM JAPAN?"

"Yes. I'm in Yokohama. I bet you guessed that, huh?"

"HAVE YOU BEEN IN JAPAN LONG?"

"I moved here from Vancouver two years ago. How about you, Kawasaki8?"

"I'M FROM NAGOYA. WHAT DO YOU DO IN YOKOHAMA?"

"I teach English to high school kids. How about you?"

"I WORK WITH COMPUTERS. LET'S GET A ROOM."

"OK."

With a simple, friendly online chat, an unsuspecting YokohamaMama had taken the bait. The foreign women always did.

2

"Who is that man?"

"*Sono hito wa dare desu ka*?" Alison repeated the language lesson along with the voice on the tape.

"Who is that man over there?"

"*Ano hito wa dare desu ka*?"

"I don't give a damn who that man is over there." Alison stopped on the sidewalk, snatched the headset from her ears and turned off her Walkman. She massaged the stiff muscles in her lower back. She hadn't wanted to be late for the interview, so she'd skipped her usual morning stretches. What a waste. The interview had been a disaster, she had a long hike back to the train station and now her back hurt.

The help wanted ad had said the language school was looking for a part-time English teacher. Native speakers only. The school could even sponsor work visas. Alison had thought her chances were pretty good, and a bona fide work visa was hard to come by in Japan, as she had quickly learned from her job hunt. So she'd donned her power-lawyer suit, complete with pumps and pantyhose.

But when Alison met the school's director, he didn't say a word of greeting or even look at her résumé. While Alison stood, ready to shake hands or answer questions, the director gnawed on his lip and inspected her gray eyes, curly auburn hair and olive-brown complexion. Her cheeks burned as his glance moved over her body as if she were a dog show entrant of questionable pedigree. A shelter mutt trying to sneak into the Westminster Kennel Club show.

After this painstaking examination, the director leaned in toward Alison and accused as much as asked, “Are you from Brazil?”

Alison knew that she didn’t look like the stereotypical blue-eyed, blonde American, an image created by Hollywood and exported around the world faster than supersized fries and Coke. But just by looking at her, the director had assumed her English wasn’t good enough — wasn’t native enough — for his crummy language school. Their help wanted ad had failed to mention one thing: Only Whites Need Apply.

She dropped some coins in the vending machine and bought a train ticket. Why had she thought it would be easy to find a job? Or, more to the point, find a job before her money ran out. The American law firms she’d approached had politely declined even to meet with her, claiming that her background wasn’t quite what they were looking for. Alison could read between those lines: they wanted an Ivy League corporate legal drone and not a graduate of Golden Gate Law’s night program.

She slid her ticket through the wicket’s automatic feeder and paused before the shifting labyrinth of escalators climbing up and staircases cascading down. Whistles screeched and conductors shouted. The unrelenting din engulfed Alison, and she felt light-headed as her eyes darted in search of a sign in English pointing her to the Tokyo-bound train platform.

Charles had told her that if she ever needed directions, she should ask a teenager since English classes were compulsory in Japanese schools. Searching the swarm of passengers, Alison targeted two girls who looked to be about sixteen years old. Dressed in the black public school uniforms that reminded Alison of Buster Brown sailor suits, the girls wore white anklets, scuffed-up black shoes and carried the ubiquitous dark leather book bag.

Alison waved. The girls looked at each other and stopped. She approached them and spoke slowly. “*Sumimasen.* Where do I catch the express train to Tokyo?” Alison prayed they understood her. “Tokyo train,” she repeated.

The girls giggled behind hands raised to their mouths. “*Ehh to…,*” volunteered one of the girls. She closed her eyes in deep concentration before responding. "Bitch. Fuck you."

The girls burst out laughing and sauntered off.

Alison stood, dumbfounded. Had she heard what she thought she'd heard? She tried to breathe in a deep yoga cleansing breath to calm herself, but after a few ragged inhalations, Alison still felt an urge to chase down the snotty-ass kid and punch her out.

And what the hell kind of compulsory English class was the girl studying? The lesson plan seemed to come from one of those misogynistic rap music videos broadcast across the planet. "Lesson #1: A Black Woman Is Referred to as a 'Bitch' or a 'Ho.'" And the kid had evidently been paying attention in class: her pronunciation was perfect.

Without venturing to ask any other students of the English language for help, Alison spied a sign for the train she hoped was the Tokyo-bound express and rode the escalator up to the platform. Judging from the small number of waiting passengers, Alison guessed that the train's arrival wasn't imminent. She stopped at the kiosk to buy the afternoon edition of the English language Yomiuri newspaper, some chocolate-covered almonds and an Asahi beer. Sitting down on a bench, she levered open the can and chugged the beer so fast that she choked.

Alison opened the newspaper and skimmed the headlines. A Canadian English teacher from Yokohama was missing. A native of Vancouver, lived with a roommate, twenty-four years old, had only five more months on her teaching contract, then she was planning to return to Canada.

Missing women all over the planet. How high a priority would the Yokohama police give to a foreign woman's disappearance? Probably not red-hot urgent. So sad.

Another short article caught her eye. A local environmental group, Green Space, was protesting a real estate development plan that would destroy an endangered coral found only off the coast of Japan.

"Go get 'em guys!" Alison pulled a pen out of her purse and circled the story. Next she turned to her required reading, the help wanted ads. English teachers. Once more unto the breach? Alison drew a star next to the ad. Hostess at a bar, guaranteed 5,000 yen an hour. What did you have to serve up for fifty bucks an hour? Pass. She wasn't that desperate. Yet. On the bottom of the last page of classifieds was a small listing for a 24-hour English help line. "Call us anytime about anything. We're your line of help."

Help. She needed help all right. Help remembering why the hell she had thought it would be a good idea to drop her law practice and follow her boyfriend to Japan. She drew a star next to the help line's phone number.

Clusters of people were forming at strategic locations on the platform. Hoping to be able to snag a seat, Alison got up and joined the end of the nearest line, straight and orderly and already twenty people deep.

She tried to imagine New Yorkers queuing up to get on the uptown IRT. What a concept. "After you. Oh no, you were here first. Please, after you." She laughed out loud imagining the scene, and the people standing near her turned to stare at the *gaijin* foreigner draining a can of Asahi.

The train arrived, and the orderliness of the line disintegrated into a frenzied mob jostling to get on board. Strangers' bodies pressed against her from every direction. Alison found a space on a strap to clutch for support. She grabbed high enough up so that she didn't have to touch anyone else's hand. Until the fourth straphanger added himself to her hold. He wrapped his clammy fingers on top of Alison's, and she cringed at the feel of skin on skin.

She closed her eyes and tried to visualize herself in a happy, open space before her claustrophobia got the best of her. While the train thundered back into town, Alison was enjoying the view of Lake Tahoe from the top of Heavenly Mountain.

The train's brakes squealed, and the undertow of passengers scrambling to push out of the train dragged Alison along and swept her out the doors. End of the line.

Back at home, Alison kicked off her shoes in the entry foyer and dropped her purse on the floor. She peeled off her snagged pantyhose, wadded them in a ball and threw them in the burnable trash bin. Her worn-out insulated slippers from L.L. Bean were a welcome change from her dress-for-success pumps.

The house that Morgan Sachs & Co. was renting for Charles felt deceptively American with its living room, dining room, study, three bedrooms plus Charles' office. But even at a whopping $25,000 a month rent, the house didn't have the one American luxury Alison was homesick for on a chilly evening like tonight: central heating.

She turned on the remote thermostat control for the heated carpeting and stretched out. The warmth from the floor seeped into her back and loosened up her tight muscles.

Another day wasted trying to get a job she wouldn't want to include on her résumé. This wasn't how she imagined it would be, wasn't what she'd planned. Not with Charles, and not with her career. Alison got up, went into the kitchen and poured herself a tall glass of merlot.

Maybe it was time to call it quits, to go back home. Go to a place where people didn't stare at her, a place where she was literate. A place where she could get a goddamn job.

She wished she had somebody to talk to. But who? Her brother wouldn't understand. He'd never been a fan of Charles. And her old roommate Jennifer had thought Alison was a fool for dropping her enviable job at Save-A-Tree and moving halfway around the world to be with Charles. Especially since Charles had a little problem with the "C" word. Commitment wasn't in his vocabulary.

Maybe Alison had been a fool, but she didn't want to give up so soon. She'd only been in Japan a couple of months. And she didn't want to have to hear the "I told you so's," not from Jennifer and not from her brother. She didn't want to crawl back to Save-A-Tree and ask for her old job back. And she certainly didn't want to have to admit that maybe she had been the proverbial fool for love.

Alison opened her purse, took out the newspaper she'd bought and stared at the ad. English Help Line.

Talking to an anonymous voice over the phone about her most intimate problems? She didn't think so. She could work things out herself. Somehow.

Alison flipped over the paper and saw the news story she'd marked. What did she have to lose? She called the English language operator to get the phone number for the environmental group Green Space and dialed.

"*Moshi moshi. Dare ka — dare ka eigo* — does anyone there speak English?" If no one at Green Space spoke English, it would be a short conversation, indeed.

"Hello. I am Suzuki, and I can speak English. You can hear that, right?" The man on the phone chuckled.

"My name is Alison Crane, and I'm calling because I've been reading about Green Space in the newspaper, and I was wondering if I could come by your office and—"

"Excuse me, Miss Alison," Mr. Suzuki began, "but we are not able to meet with reporters right now."

"I'm not a reporter, Mr. Suzuki. I'm an—"

"I am sorry, but it is our policy not to hold interviews."

"No, what I'm trying to say is that I'm an attorney, Mr. Suzuki. An environmental lawyer. I used to be chief counsel for the Save-A-Tree Foundation—"

"*Ehh*? We know Save-A-Tree Foundation very well. Good work you do."

"Thanks. I was hoping to visit and learn more about your organization. I wouldn't take up much of your time, maybe a half an hour."

"Of course. We would be glad to meet you, Miss Alison. Are you available on Tuesday?"

"Tuesday's perfect."

"Good. Come to our office at twelve noon, *neh*."

Alison smiled as she hung up. If she played her cards right, if she finessed it and was lucky, maybe she could end up with a job, a real job, at an organization right up her alley.

3

Outside her window, Alison heard the cry of a street vendor selling roasted sweet potatoes, guaranteed to keep you warm on a crisp autumn evening. At least that's what Charles had told her the guy was saying. A lively ditty befitting a Good Humor ice cream truck blasted through the public address system and drowned out the potato vendor's pitch.

"Damn noise pollution." She looked at her watch. Five o'clock.

She hit the power button on the fuzzy logic JVC entertainment center. Referring to the translated labels Charles had taped over the remote control buttons, she turned on the television. A cooking show. Alison zapped to another channel. A rock music video shrieked. Zap. Evening news. Alison pressed a button and the female reporter's incomprehensible Japanese switched to the British-accented voice of a man delivering a choppy simultaneous English translation of the newscast.

"The missing foreign woman was last seen in Tokyo, and the police suspect foul play. The woman, a Canadian national, is approximately 155 centimeters tall and teaches English in a high school in Yokohama—" Keys clinked at the front door.

"*Tadaima*!" Charles stepped out of his shoes in the marble *genkan* foyer and slid into one of the pairs of house slippers lined up by the entryway.

"Hey, Charles! You're home already?"

He grinned at Alison. A tall, mocha-licious African-American man with a steel-trap mind and movie-star smile. Charles was model-gorgeous, and Alison loved that he loved her.

"These are for you." Charles produced from behind his back a bouquet of rust-colored parrot tulips mixed with yellow freesia.

Alison inhaled the delicate perfume of the freesia blossoms. "Where'd you find spring blooms this time of year?"

"My secret sources." Charles winked. "I'll never tell."

Alison took the flowers into the kitchen and called back to Charles. "I was watching the news. Did you hear about the foreign woman who disappeared?"

"Disappeared?"

"Yeah. An English teacher." Alison returned with the flowers in a brass vase and set the arrangement on the console table. "Only twenty-four years old."

Charles smirked. "Probably took off with some guy. Foreigners don't just disappear in Japan. She'll turn up."

"I wonder." Alison breathed in the fragrance of the freesia again. "Since you're home early, how about going to a movie?"

"Sorry, gotta raincheck it. A huge client invited me to his club, and I can't blow him off. I just stopped by to check something online."

Charles moved closer to Alison and planted a kiss on her neck before striding into his home office. He sat down at the keyboard and typed in some commands. Alison followed him inside the room.

"You need to unplug from the computer, Charles. Online all the time. Bad for your eyes, bad for your spine. Bad for your relationship."

Charles swiveled around in his ergonomic desk chair to face Alison head-on. He grabbed hold of her wrists, pulling one finger from her mouth where she was nibbling a cuticle. "I told you that my stint here was going to be intense, that maybe it wasn't a good time for you to come here."

"It's never a good time, Charles. There always seems to be something."

"The bank is expecting me to pull off some minor miracles to boost the Asia business. It's just for a few more months."

"A few more months and then what? We'll get married? We'd talked about kids, a family…"

Charles exhaled with impatience and spun around, turning his back on Alison. He tapped some commands at his computer keyboard.

"We used to have so much fun, Charles. You'd kidnap me and we'd go on those crazy getaways. You took me to that shooting range, once. Remember?"

"Yeah, I remember. For a novice, you sure had some kind of eye."

"And Tahoe. Remember Tahoe?" Alison sat down on the edge of Charles' desk.

He nodded. "Yeah, Tahoe was great."

"We could go on a ski trip here. I was reading about the Japan Alps—"

"Look, Alicats. Things are going to work out. Give it some more time."

"It feels like we're moving in different worlds. You're so busy with your job, and — and I can't even find one."

"So why don't you have some fun? Take flower-arranging classes. I make enough money to cover whatever you need, so—"

"We're not having that conversation again. We made a deal. Equitable split of all expenses. *Pari pasu.*"

"You always sound like a lawyer."

"I'm carrying my own weight with my own money. If we were married, well, it'd be different."

"We're not having *that* conversation again, Alison." Charles returned his attention to the computer screen.

Alison stood behind Charles and massaged his shoulders, working her way down his stomach. He turned around in his chair.

Without standing, he unbuttoned her jeans, unzipped the fly and nuzzled her belly button while exploring with his hands under her sweater.

Her hips moved in small circles, and she let her head fall back while Charles squeezed her nipples.

"Hold that thought until I get back tonight," Charles said.

"All we need is ten minutes now." Alison leaned over Charles and eased his chair away from the desk. Backing up, she tangled her foot in the computer's cables and pulled a cord out of the wall. The monitor hissed and went blank.

Charles leaped from his chair. "What are you doing, Alison?" The telltale vein on his forehead bulged out. "You'll screw up my network connection like that." Charles pushed Alison away from the computer, crawled under the desk and reconnected the cable. He stood and glared at Alison. "Don't touch my computer, OK?"

"It was an accident, Charles."

He shook his head. "The computer? It's off limits."

"Boys with their fucking toys." Alison zipped up her jeans, went to the kitchen, and examined the stock in the wine cabinet. She found a bottle of Charles' prized pinot noir specially imported from a boutique winery in Sonoma. The last bottle of the pinot noir he had. She opened it. And filled a wine glass up to the rim.

"Don't wait up," Charles shouted from the *genkan* foyer. The front door slammed closed.

As if she ever waited up.

Alison took a big swallow of wine. She might not be the most tech-savvy geek like some of those Silicon Valley nerds Charles went to school with at Stanford, but she wasn't an idiot. She'd even signed up for a World NetLink internet account before she left the States. Not that she needed to get online, but her brother, Rob, wouldn't shut up until she'd promised to get an account.

But the way Charles had said it: "Off limits." Like she was a clumsy child hell-bent on destruction.

Alison took her glass of wine into Charles' office and sat down at the keyboard. She grabbed the mouse, and the computer screen came to life. The Morgan Sachs pyramid logo glowed and pulsed impatiently on the monitor. All the pyramid needed for it to look just like the one on U.S. currency was a wide-open eye on the pinnacle. No one could fault Morgan Sachs for being subtle.

Alison tapped the computer's return key and was asked for her user ID. She typed "Charles Gordon," a safe bet.

She was prompted to input a password. What the hell would Charles' password be? She typed in "Alicats."

Invalid password. She tried "Baltimore," Charles' hometown. Invalid. Next she tried "Money," his favorite pursuit.

"Log on attempt timed out. Firewall Access Denied." The screen went dead.

Boys with their fucking toys.

4

A row of ginkgo trees with golden fan-shaped leaves stood in front of Green Space's office. Planted alongside the trees were two security guards, dressed in full military gear.

The raucous crowd congregated outside the entrance to Green Space didn't look dangerous, exactly. But even from across the street, Alison could tell that folks were plenty upset. Their apparent leader, a middle-aged man with thinning hair, shouted through a bullhorn while his followers, about thirty men and women wearing headbands imprinted with Japanese lettering, chanted and clapped.

The leader approached the security guards and blasted them full force in the face with an amplified tirade through the bullhorn. The gatherers responded with thunderous cheers and applause.

One guard's face reddened, and the other cracked his knuckles. The demonstrators gathered tighter around the guards, but the gatekeepers held fast to their positions. Was she witnessing the beginning of a riot?

But unless she wanted to miss her scheduled appointment with Suzuki and her chance at landing a good job with a kindred spirit organization, she was going to have to plow right into the heart of the ruckus.

Or could it be that she was at the wrong building? There was no signage for Green Space on the door. And the Japanese system for assigning addresses was creative at best. Maybe she had made a wrong turn. It wouldn't be the first time she'd gotten lost in Tokyo.

Alison looked at the map that Suzuki had faxed to her and double-checked the address. This was the place. Onward and upward.

Alison feigned a no-nonsense resolve, a tough all-business demeanor, and charged ahead across the street. She could feel her heart pounding as her fight-or-flight sensors assessed the probability of imminent physical violence. She marched on.

At Green Space's front door, Alison nodded at the security guards, but the horde, chanting in concert with the bullhorn-bearer, remained in place, standing between her and the door. And her chance at a job.

Instinctively sympathetic toward the underdog, Alison hated crossing through picket lines. Back in the States, she was usually on the organizing side of unruly demonstrations like this one. But this was Japan, and things were different. There weren't any cops around, no one had firearms — she hoped — and things hadn't spun out of control. Yet. This might be her only chance to bust through the line.

She braced herself for body blows as she dove between two of the demonstrators and strode up to Green Space's door. The guards didn't try to stop her, and the crowd didn't try to push her away. She grabbed the handle on the front door and gave it a tug. The door did not yield.

The mob's chanting and the blaring of the bullhorn grew louder. Alison wanted to tell the demonstrators that she was really on their side, that she was a good guy. But she felt them looking at her, their darting glances like so many small slaps of accusation.

Alison turned to one of the guards. "Can you help me? I have an appointment, and—" The guards didn't look at Alison, and they didn't offer any assistance. They remained stock still, as immovable as Buckingham Palace sentries. Not the warm welcome she had hoped for.

Alison spied a doorbell on the wall next to the entrance, and she pressed the button.

"*Dochira-sama desu ka*?" said a voice through an intercom in the building wall.

Alison couldn't hear what the voice said over the clamor of the demonstrators, but she broke into her pitch anyway. "Hello. It's Alison Crane," she yelled into the speaker. She hoped the demonstration wasn't drowning her out. "I have an appointment with Mr. Suzuki, and—" In the middle of Alison's introduction, the door buzzed. She tugged the front door again, and this time it opened. The protesters' shouts heightened to a roar.

Alison scurried into Green Space's *genkan* foyer. As the door closed behind her, the shrill shouting and chanting deadened to silence. She took a deep breath.

Why should Green Space, an environmental organization, need security in the middle of Tokyo? Alison hadn't seen guards like those at other office buildings. And that mob. Where were the cops? Why wasn't anything being done to restore peaceful Zen harmony?

Street shoes were lined up in the entrance. Alison stepped out of her pumps and put on one of the pairs of slippers set out for visitors to wear. She climbed the step into the office space and was greeted by a man who was already half-trotting toward the front office door.

"Miss Alison-san! Hello. My name is Suzuki." Mr. Suzuki shook Alison's hand while he bowed. He reached inside his coat jacket pocket and pulled out a *meishi* business card case crafted out of polished cherrywood. With another small bow, he extended both hands and presented his business card to Alison. Alison couldn't help but notice that he was missing the tip end of his little finger.

"Hello, Mr. Suzuki. Suzuki-san." Alison tried out the polite Japanese form of address. When in Rome … "It's a pleasure to meet you."

"Please excuse our entry. From time to time we must deal with, um—" Suzuki closed his eyes and turned his head to the side and rubbed his temple while sucking air through his teeth. "We have to take — what is the word?"

"Precautions?" offered Alison.

"Yes! We have to take precautions."

"Those people seemed pretty intense," Alison said. "Who are they?"

Suzuki blinked hard behind his glasses. "Times have changed in Japan. The police — the police do not help." Suzuki threw his hands in the air. "But you are not in danger. Please, come this way." He led Alison into the office.

Rows of desks topped with computer terminals were squeezed into the Green Space office. The furniture looked ultra-contemporary and ergonomic. It was lunchtime, and a few of the employees were eating at their workstations. Even though the workspace would be considered intolerably congested by American standards, the office had a nice feel to it, Alison decided. Inviting and collegial.

Suzuki escorted Alison on a brief tour. Green Space's facilities boasted a library, a digital audio-video center, an amphitheater-style conference area and an exercise room with weight machines. Trees and plants occupied every available space. Alison took a deep breath. The air in the office enjoyed an oxygenated richness, like after a thunderstorm. If only Save-A-Tree had digs like this, she mused.

Suzuki opened a door to a small conference room. A built-in aquarium stocked full of neon-colored tropical fish comprised one entire wall.

"Please, sit down." Suzuki pointed to the seats surrounding a low-slung black glass coffee table. Alison pulled out a chair — a Wassily, if she wasn't mistaken — and sat.

"I'm impressed, Suzuki-san. Such a beautiful office."

"We are grateful to have the support of the Taisho Shipbuilding Foundation."

"Shipbuilding?" Alison didn't understand the connection.

"Yes. Both Taisho and Green Space believe in protecting marine life. In fact, Yamada-san of the Taisho family started Green Space. She will try to meet us for lunch."

As if on cue, a woman wearing a steel-gray trench coat and toting a bright green Louis Vuitton attaché case pushed through the door. Suzuki straightened to attention when she entered the room. The woman was accompanied by a young man carrying a stack of red lacquer boxes decorated with gold leaf. The man placed the boxes on the table, bowed and exited.

The woman tossed her trench coat over the back of a chair, and Alison admired her deep ruby suit. Chanel, of course. Her careful haircut, her French-manicured fingers adorned with a variety of pearl and diamond rings, but most of all her demeanor, screamed "Serious Money."

"Hello. I'm Yamada Yuko." Ms. Yamada bowed and handed Alison a business card she pulled from a Vuitton card case in her attaché. Yuko Yamada looked to be about thirty years old but moved with the surety, the quiet grace, of someone much older, of someone who knew that she owned the joint.

With no business card to present, Alison felt like an ill-mannered bumpkin. "Alison Crane. It's a pleasure to meet you, Yamada-san." Alison took the business card and attempted a bow. The unfamiliar movement felt awkward. She was sure she wasn't doing it right. How long were you supposed to stay in a courteous bow, staring at your toes? After a few seconds bent at the waist feeling foolish, Alison stood.

"*Tabemasho*. Shall we eat?" Yamada gestured for everyone to take a seat. "Ms. Crane, do you speak Japanese?"

A logical question and not entirely unexpected. But it pained Alison to admit that she was functionally illiterate, with the vocabulary of a newborn. And yet here she was, trying to wrangle a job. Was she deluding herself? "I'm learning," Alison said and quickly sat down.

Mr. Suzuki passed the lacquer bento boxes around the table. "These bento are from our organic food cooperative in Nagano prefecture," Ms. Yamada-san said. "We work with the local farmers there."

Following Ms. Yamada's lead, Alison lifted the highly polished lid off of the bento box. Artfully arranged inside was a selection of steamed bamboo shoots, red beans, vinegared fish filets, marinated ginger root, vegetable tempura and a host of other foods Alison couldn't identify. A pair of lacquered *ohashi* chopsticks were tucked in the side of the bento.

Alison felt her stomach growling. Had anyone else heard? Beautiful as the bento presentation was to look at, Alison was ready to chow down.

Watching Ms. Yamada's graceful use of *ohashi,* Alison struggled with the chopsticks and dropped a few items en route to her mouth. She quickly scooped up the wayward morsels and hoped no one noticed.

"Would you like a fork?" Ms. Yamada asked.

"No, thank you. I'm fine." Alison felt like a less-evolved being, one step removed from grunting and eating with her fingers.

Ms. Yamada quizzed Alison about her work at Save-A-Tree, her opinions about Japan, the problems the American environmentalists were having with the EPA. Between mouthfuls, Alison did most of the talking while Mr. Suzuki sat smiling and nodding his head. Ms. Yamada shot rapid-fire questions, which Alison deftly answered. So far, so good.

When they were finished with their box lunches, the office assistant brought in a tray with steaming cups of tea that gave off a smoky aroma. Yamada nodded at Suzuki, and he and the assistant cleared the box lunches and left the room.

"You came here to learn about what we do, Ms. Crane. What can I tell you about Green Space?"

Showtime. The spotlight was on Alison to dazzle Yamada with her expertise and ooze professional confidence, all while not breaking a sweat. If everything went according to plan, she could parlay a casual lunch meeting into a job offer. A yen-paying job offer. Stranger things had been known to happen.

Feigning calm, Alison took a sip from her teacup but quickly set it back down after the screeching hot liquid seared her tongue. Yamada-san was drinking the tea, no problem. Maybe she didn't have normal pain receptors. Alison wanted to ask for an ice cube, but she smiled instead. "I've read lots of articles about Green Space. Environmental activism seems unusual here in Japan."

"News articles?" Ms. Yamada smiled, a controlled mirthless grin. "The news media does not understand the good work we do. You saw the guards outside?" Alison nodded. "Someone threw a bottle bomb into our office. And the reporters call *us* the crazy ones…" The muscles of Ms. Yamada's jaw repeatedly clenched then relaxed, as if she were chewing on granite.

During her time at Save-A-Tree, Alison had encountered numerous hostile detractors who wished they'd go away, but never had there been a bomb threat. Clearly, Alison needed to do more research on Green Space.

Ms. Yamada continued. “We are focusing on Iriomote Island near Okinawa. There is a bed of coral in that area, the only coral of its type in the world. And the developer — the Tropic Reef Development company — is planning a resort community that would completely destroy the coral.”

“So you’re trying to stop the development?” said Alison.

“The surrounding land is a national park. Tropic Reef can’t go forward without the cooperation of the government.”

“Good news for your side,” said Alison.

Ms. Yamada shrugged. “The government is in favor of the project. They think it will stimulate economic growth.”

“What about the local community?” asked Alison.

“The Okinawans are tired of their land being sacrificed by the Japanese government. But Tropic Reef is well-connected. When we speak up against the development, we get threatened, criticized in the press.”

Alison tried her tea again. It had cooled down. “I’m familiar with that kind of smear tactic. At Save-A-Tree we’d bring attention to American companies’ bad environmental practices in other parts of the world. Didn’t make us many friends.”

“Tropic Reef is developing resorts all across Asia. What they’re planning would be an environmental disaster.”

“It’s frustrating when you can see the destruction about to happen, but you can’t stop it.”

“Sometimes we can make trouble.” Yamada smiled and covered her mouth with a hand. “When we learn that a Japanese company is planning an activity in Asia that is bad for the environment, we set up offices.”

“Offices in the local country? So Green Space is an unexpected watchdog to make sure they do the right thing no matter where they go. Shrewd move.”

"Yes, but again, the Japanese government has not been supportive of our work."

"I know what you mean. The American government is slow to prosecute U.S. companies who dump toxic waste offshore."

"In our case, the Japanese government gives the business advance warning that Green Space is planning to open in a particular territory."

"No kidding?"

"It gives the business a chance to create negative publicity about us and make it hard for us to find what you call grass-roots support."

"But how does the government know your plans in advance? It's like they're tapping your phones."

Ms. Yamada shook her head. "It's the banks."

"Banks?" Alison didn't see a connection. She hoped Yamada-san wouldn't think she was slow on the uptake. No one wanted to hire a nitwit.

"Yes. When we open a new office abroad and send funds, the banks have to report our currency transfers to the Ministry of Finance. And there are a lot of people in powerful positions who are not our supporters."

"So when you transfer money to fund your new overseas office, the government knows where you're about to strike, and they alert the local businesses?"

"It is a challenge for us." Ms. Yamada poured more tea for Alison, leaving her own cup empty. Alison remembered what Charles had said, that the Japanese considered it rude and piggish to pour their own drinks. Alison lifted the tea pot and refilled Ms. Yamada's cup.

"*Sumimasen.*" Ms. Yamada tipped her head in thanks.

Thinking of Charles gave Alison a flash of inspiration. He could be the linchpin she needed to seal the deal. "Ms. Yamada. Yamada-san. I have an idea that might help you with your funding problems. You should talk to my fiancé."

"Your fiancé?"

So what if Alison improvised a little with her story. A dollop of wishful thinking with a dash of yeast. She and Charles had talked about marriage. Granted, she'd done most of the talking. But hopefully Charles would cooperate.

"His name is Charles. He works with an investment bank — Morgan Sachs' Tokyo office — and he's a financial whiz."

"Morgan Sachs?" Yamada-san waved her hand in front of her face as if she were fanning herself. "They are much too big for a small organization like ours."

"Charles says the bank often transfers funds in ways that aren't immediately apparent. For the clients' financial privacy. Of course, it's all legal."

Ms. Yamada set down her cup. "Of course."

Alison pulled her notepad from her bag and jotted down Charles' number. "Charles Gordon. He can tell you all the details. The best time to reach him is after the market has closed, about five o'clock."

Ms. Yamada took the slip of paper and put it in her bag without looking at it. "Thank you, Ms. Crane."

"Please call me Alison."

"Domo arigato, Alison."

Alison saw her chance to go for the close. If she could only convince Yamada-san that Green Space needed an environmental lawyer. That they needed her. "Yamada-san, when you open an office in another country, what are the legal restrictions on Green Space?"

"Legal restrictions?"

"In the States, nonprofits are highly regulated when it comes to sending funds to a foreign country. The money has to be used strictly for charitable purposes. Sometimes the receiving organization has to be approved by the U.S. government."

"Things are quite different in Asia."

"We had a project in Asia — we tried to send money to an environmental group in Burma that was protesting against logging in virgin forests. It was a legal nightmare because, for Americans, Burma is an embargoed country, like Cuba and North Korea."

"I had no idea." Yamada-san crossed her arms and sat back in her chair.

Alison could feel Yamada drifting away. Along with her chance at a job. Japanese people thought that Americans were pushy. Time for Alison to push. "Did you know a nonprofit can face criminal penalties for sending funds offshore? If the arrangement isn't vetted and airtight. We lawyers are kept busy."

Time to nail it, Crane. Alison cocked her head to the side, as if the notion had only now occurred to her. "You know, Yamada-san, I was thinking. Maybe I could work with Green Space to explore some of the legal issues involved in your international expansion. Environmental treaties and— "

Ms. Yamada covered her mouth with her hand as she laughed, an ever-so-polite girlish giggle. "Ms. Crane, our little foundation is not nearly as sophisticated as you think. We don't have so many difficult laws."

"Oh." Alison's chances of snagging a job with Green Space were looking as endangered as the spotted owl.

"Our biggest challenge — other than the government interference — is finding the right local partners in other countries," Yamada said.

Alison nodded. Despite her growing disappointment, she tried to stay focused. "So, how do you find your partners?"

"We are doing what we can to reach out across borders. One problem is that our website is in Japanese. Very few people can read it."

"I hadn't thought about that."

"We're creating an English-language website so that the international community can learn about us."

Ms. Yamada toyed with her rings. Her nonstop fidgeting was making Alison feel even more jittery. "Ms. Crane. There is a way you could help us. But I don't know if you would be interested."

"Sure, I'd love to help." Alison shifted in her chair at the prospect of employment. "What is it you need?"

"The company we hired to design the English site is a bit slow. And frankly, they don't understand the world of environmental issues the way you and I do."

"Yes, our world is often not understood by outsiders." Lay it on thick, Crane.

"So what I would like to ask is, can you help us with our English website? You do use computers."

"Computers? Why, yes, of course. All the time. No problem." Alison hoped Ms. Yamada couldn't read her bad poker face.

"Good. What we need isn't too complicated. Mainly links to articles online about groups doing environmental work in Asia. Do you think you could do that?" Ms. Yamada looked at Alison.

"I'd be glad to," Alison said. "And maybe later we could talk about a regular job with — "

"It will be tremendously helpful for Green Space. I'll have Suzuki give you the background material you need."

"It sounds really exciting, Yamada-san." Not quite a job, but a foot in the door. "Can I ask you about your timing? When do you need the information from me?" Alison didn't want to mention that she needed time to find a computer and figure out how to get online from Tokyo before she could even think about beginning her internet research.

Ms. Yamada absentmindedly tapped a mabe pearl ring against her teacup. "Oh, I should think one month. Does that sound all right?"

"One month is fine." She was screwed. Charles would never let her use his computer. How would she get online?

"It will be a big help for Green Space." Ms. Yamada adjusted the rings on her fingers as she leaned in closer and smiled. "Now, tell me about this fiancé of yours." Her eyes shined with the rapt attention of a hungry lioness spotting its prey.

Alison swallowed her tea. "Charles? He got transferred to the Tokyo office. For two years. He asked me to come with him, so here I am." Except that he hadn't asked her. In fact, he had discouraged her. But here she was anyway.

"Wonderful! How did you meet?"

Yamada's eyes still held that gleam. "We met at a party through a mutual friend. That was three years ago, and we've been together ever since."

"How nice. My parents have given up on my ever getting married. They say I'm too picky." Ms. Yamada laughed, covering her mouth with her hand.

"There certainly is no point in being with someone you don't really love. No point at all." Alison drank some more tea as if to wash away the irony of her own words.

Ms. Yamada's cell phone beeped. She answered and carried on a terse conversation, her iron jaw muscles twitching. While on the phone, Ms. Yamada bowed as if the caller could see her. Old habits die hard.

Ms. Yamada hung up her phone and turned her attention to Alison. "I'm so sorry, but I must go." Yamada reached into her Vuitton case and took out a thick envelope which she handed to Alison. "An advance payment for your work."

Alison gawked at the thickness and heft of the envelope. How much money was that? They hadn't discussed fees. Hell, Alison would do the research for free. And maybe she really shouldn't take the money, especially since she didn't know if she was capable of performing the internet research Ms. Yamada wanted. Alison had, undoubtedly, over-stated her proficiency with computers.

What would Emily Post say was the right etiquette in the situation? Should she take the money, the desperately needed money, or would it be impolite to refuse when offered in Japan? Exigency trumped manners. "Thank you, Yamada-san. Let me give you a receipt."

Ms. Yamada shook her head. "I don't need a receipt. We can't be a visa sponsor, so let this just be our understanding." Ms. Yamada closed her briefcase.

"Thank you, Yamada-san. I understand."

Ms. Yamada rose from the table. "I'm sure we will have a chance to speak again soon." She bowed, gathered her attaché and coat and pressed a buzzer on the wall. Mr. Suzuki materialized.

"Suzuki-san, Ms. Crane is going to be helping us with our English website. Make sure she gets the information she needs." Ms. Yamada turned back to Alison. "Goodbye, Ms. Crane. Alison. It was my pleasure."

"The pleasure was all mine. I hope that—" Alison said as the door shut in her face.

"She is very busy," Mr. Suzuki explained.

Escorting Alison toward the front door, Mr. Suzuki paused in the hallway. "Yamada-san wanted me to give you information about our website. Have you seen it?"

"No," Alison mumbled. Visiting a website to prep for a meeting? The thought hadn't even occurred to Alison. Green Space was certain to see her for the net neophyte she was. The envelope of money weighed heavy in Alison's bag.

"The website is bilingual Japanese and English, but we need to add more English. One moment." Mr. Suzuki scurried back to an assistant's desk, and the assistant wrote on a piece of paper.

Handing the paper to Alison, Mr. Suzuki said, "This is the internet address for our English website and the phone number for Green Net, our electronic bulletin board. You might need to use it."

"Thank you, Mr. Suzuki." Electronic bulletin board? What was he talking about? She was in so over her head.

Suzuki gave Alison a brochure in Japanese. "We are translating these materials into English. They should be ready next week."

"Great. Would you send me a copy when they're done? I don't have any business cards — any *meishi* — but here's my home address." Alison reached into her bag for a pen and paper.

"What is your email? I can email the brochure when it is finished."

"Email. Of course. I just got a new account on World NetLink, so —" Alison plumbed her brain trying to remember the user name she'd selected when she'd signed up for the service before heading for Japan. "My user name is TokyoAli. A-L-I. All one word. I think." Alison hadn't planned on using her email address and hadn't parked it in long-term memory. She was off to a stellar start in impressing Green Space with her computer savvy. "I'm sorry, Suzuki-san, I'm not sure. But I'll call you when—"

"World NetLink. I will finger you and find your address. Please one moment." Suzuki trotted off again.

Did he say he'd finger her? Sounded obscene.

Suzuki returned with a computer printout. "You are from San Francisco. I visited there once. Golden Gate Bridge."

"But how did you know I'm from San Francisco?"

"When I fingered you. World NetLink's server computer gives me information. Please check your email, Miss Alison-san. I will send our pamphlet."

"World NetLink's computer?"

Suzuki clasped his hands together. "Thank you for your coming to our office. I am glad you will be helping us with our website. Goodbye." Suzuki bowed low while Alison put on her shoes and exited.

Outside the Green Space office, Alison was relieved to see that the mob was gone and the street was quiet. She nodded at the security guards still posted outside.

Green Space must have some powerful enemies to warrant all of the protection. But it came with the territory when you were fighting the good fight.

5

Sitting on the living room floor, Alison pulled the money from the envelope Yamada-san had given her, held the thick wad of crisp 10,000-yen notes up to her nose and inhaled. Nothing like the sweet aroma of fresh paper money. And lots of it.

Unlike Charles, who could translate the world's currencies as fluently as he could translate Japanese, Alison didn't have a knack for understanding the value of yen. Japan's currency came in such a confusing assortment of denominations. There were the annoyingly useless one-yen coins, so insignificant that no one bothered to pick one up if they dropped it on the street. The massive 500-yen coins that weighed down your purse like lead shot. The 10,000-yen notes were the only type of cash that you could get from Japan's ATM machines.

Might as well be pesos or rupees or Monopoly money. All Alison knew was that her cash seemed to evaporate in Tokyo, and she was constantly surprised at how quickly she was broke.

But now Alison was holding her own money. A hefty amount of money. And it was time to count.

Pristine and virginal, the bank notes stuck together as Alison peeled them off the stack. Like a veteran bank teller, she licked her index finger and snapped each bill as she flipped it off the bankroll.

After she finished her tally, Alison checked the currency exchange rates in the morning newspaper, got out a pencil and did the math in the margin of the business section. Wow! Could that be right? She checked her calculations. The numbers were correct. Yamada-san had handed her over twelve thousand dollars! Jackpot!

Alison's initial frisson of delight gave way to a gut-wrenching dread. Twelve thousand dollars. For that kind of money, Yamada-san would be expecting a bang-up, first-rate job. Alison took professional pride in her work, but computers weren't exactly her strong suit.

It wasn't too late to return the money. She could tell Yamada that she didn't have time to help out with the website. But if Alison backed out now, she'd probably blow any chance of a future job with Green Space.

Twelve thousand dollars. Some new clothes. A bit of breathing room until she found regular work. Financial independence from Charles.

She slid five of the bills into her wallet, and tucked the rest in her suitcase in the closet. She'd keep the money, and somehow figure out how to do the internet research.

It was time to earn her pay, and she needed help. Fast. Alison reached for the cordless phone and dialed her brother.

"Hey, Rob, it's me."

"Hey, kiddo, I was asleep."

"Asleep? What time is it there?"

"Four in the fucking a.m."

"Sorry. Anyway, how are you? How's the dissertation going?"

"Don't even ask. My adviser isn't for shit. How about you? Still in culture shock?"

"The proverbial stranger in a strange land."

"You find a job?"

"That's why I called. I'm doing some computer research for a green group out here."

"Computer research? You?"

"Yeah, well, the truth is, I might have bitten off more than I can chew. I don't have a computer here, and they expect me to be cruising the internet—"

"What about Prince Charles? He's gotta have a computer."

"Yeah, but he told me not to touch it. Doesn't want me to mess up some modem connection to his New York office."

"When are you gonna cut that guy loose, kiddo?"

"Don't start, Rob."

Rob exhaled audibly. "Anyway. For starters, kiddo, you need a computer. Go to a Kinkos or whatever rent-a-box place they have there."

"No, I don't want to do that. It can get expensive renting machines."

"Okay. You know that disk I sent you? You can run that software on Charles' box without fucking up His Highness' stuff."

"I tried to get online on Charles' Mac, but I got stopped by a firewall."

"You can get past that. Just run your software in the background. You set up an account on World NetLink, right?"

"Yeah."

"Good. Take a look at the stuff I faxed you about getting online from overseas. It explains everything. How to get onto NetLink from a dedicated line, how to override an always-on connection, how to dial into a BBS."

"A what?"

"BBS. Bulletin board system. Like when you dial up direct to another computer. You have to switch the modem settings if Charles is networked. Read the article." Rob yawned while he spoke.

"Thanks a lot. Go back to sleep."

"Good luck, kiddo. Email me. Let me know how it goes."

Alison went to the study and sifted through the folder of items she'd collected to help her adjust to life in Tokyo. Pamphlets, maps, letters, help wanted ads. She found Rob's fax, a *MacUniverse* article with a screaming banner headline: "GETTING ONLINE ON THE ROAD: EVERYTHING YOU EVER WANTED TO KNOW BUT WERE TOO STUPID TO ASK!!!" Rob had given her a World NetLink floppy disk to encourage her to get online.

Alison sat at the dining room table and smoothed the pages of the fax out in front of her. Bent over the article, she marked critical information with a fluorescent yellow highlighter.

Alison looked up from the papers. Even though she was home alone, she tiptoed as she prowled back to Charles' office. The flashing screen of the computer, her competition for Charles' time and fascination, danced and blinked seductively. She pulled out the chair in front of the keyboard, spread the how-to article out next to Charles' beloved computer, cracked her fingers, and tapped the computer's return key.

The computer screen sprang to life at her touch. The Morgan Sachs pyramid logo glowed with an expectant rhythm.

Alison glanced down to confirm the article's step-by-step instructions, then slipped the World NetLink disk into the computer's drive. She hit the combination of computer keys to toggle between applications without shutting down, inched the computer's mouse over to the WNL graphic and clicked.

A computer voice said, "Welcome to World NetLink!"

Alison grinned. "Thank you," she replied. No problem, she could do this. She entered her user name and set sail.

Cruising online through World NetLink was easier than Alison had thought it would be. TokyoAli, née Alison Crane, discovered weather reports, travel recommendations and even an online casino. She searched for information about environmental groups and issues, but found nothing. The Green Space research assignment was going to be tricky. Alison pushed on.

After hours of tracking down disappointing research leads, Alison decided to visit another part of the network, the community chat rooms. Maybe she could hook up with some like-minded environmentalists there.

She tried to maneuver to the chat area, but the network computer informed her that it was "For Adults Only."

Alison clicked on a box to affirm that she was over the age of eighteen, way over, and entered the restricted-access area.

The list of active rooms read like the personals section from an alternative newspaper. Men looking for women, men looking for men, couples looking to swap mates, even S&M devotees. These weren't the kindred spirits she was looking for to help with her Green Space work, but what the hell. With a tinge of voyeuristic guilt, Alison crept into the sex fantasy chat room.

Ten chat participants with descriptive screen names inhabited the room. LipLik was flirting with the other users as he — she? Alison wasn't sure — shed his/her clothes. The chat room inhabitants egged LipLik on with electronic whistles, hoots and applause, which sounded through Charles' computer speakers.

Alison's eyes were wide, her mouth agape in astonishment. How had she never heard about amusements like interactive computer porn?

A silent spectator, she jumped when the computer beeped at her announcing that she had an online instant message from ByteMe:

"Hey TokyoAli. You want to eat my sushi? It's really raw!!"

Alison sat in horror. She had assumed that she was invisible as long as she stayed out of the fray. But now she had to do something, to get into it. Or out of it. She typed "No thanks!" and beat it out of the chat room, launching herself into a distant area of the World NetLink network.

Once safely out of the electronic orgy she'd happened upon, Alison laughed. This could really be a lot of fun.

The computer beeped again.

"You've got a message from Kiyoshi346."

Now what to do? She wasn't supposed to even be using Charles' computer let alone communicating with other people. But what the hell. She hit the Reply button.

"Hello."

Kiyoshi346 came right back at her with a message.

"Hello, TokyoAli. Are you in Japan?

"Yes. I'm in Tokyo."

"Have you been in Japan long?"

"No, I moved from San Francisco a few months ago. Where are you from?"

"I'm from Kobe. Let's get a room."

Get a room? What was he talking about?

"What do you mean get a room?"

"I mean a private chat room."

Oh, of course. Alison knew that. Sort of. It sounded a little sleazy, but she replied.

"OK."

"I will create a chat room called Kobe. Meet me there."

Kiyoshi346's message broke off and Alison was left staring at the screen. She was enjoying herself online even though she didn't completely understand what was going on. But what could be the harm? She entered the newly created private chat room.

Kiyoshi was waiting for her and messaged:

"Hello, TokyoAli. I have been stuck in meetings all day. It's good to talk to someone new."

"What kind of work do you do?"

"I work in marketing. And you?"

"I'm an attorney."

"A *bengoshi*-sensei. Like Perry Mason."

"No, I'm an environmental lawyer."

"How do you like Tokyo?"

"It's so gray. I can't get a breath of fresh air."

"There are many beautiful places in Japan. As beautiful as Big Sur."

"You know Big Sur?"

"I studied at UCLA."

"Small world."

"TokyoAli, I must get back to work. Can we talk again tomorrow at 5 o'clock?"

"Sounds great. See you then, so to speak."

"SEE YOU I CAN SEE YOU!!! CAN YOU SEE ME SEE ME BECAUSE I CAN SEE YOU TOO YOU TWO??"

"I don't understand. How can I see you?"

Alison sent the message, but Kiyoshi had already left the chat room.

Who was that guy she'd met? And why had he suddenly switched to all capital letters in his message? Even Alison knew that all caps was considered rude. She was curious to know more about him, but she couldn't exactly ask. Mr. Suzuki had easily been able to get personal data about her online. Why couldn't she explore online to learn about her new acquaintance.

Alison entered the Member Profile area of the board where users could provide information about themselves and typed in a profile request for the screen name Kiyoshi346.

The computer responded:

```
"There is no user with that screen name."
```

Odd. He sounded interesting, but who was that man?

She arranged the screen just the way it had been when she sat down and positioned the mouse back to where it had been stored. She could do her research for Green Space online and Charles would never guess.

01001110 01100001 01110010 01101001 01110100 01100001

TokyoAli. Better known as Alison Crane. That much he had figured out easily. But what does she like to do? Where does she like to go?

Maybe she was married and having a little online fun and games on the side. A virtual affair. The online chat was innocent enough. For now, anyway. It hadn't started getting juicy yet. Not like the steamy online chat with YokohamaMama.

The *gaijin* women were such easy-going sluts, always ready for a virtual fuck. No inhibitions. So trusting, so stupid. As if a computer keyboard was all the cyber condom they needed for protection.

Didn't they realize that they were easily traceable? And trackable? They assumed that their foreignness made them better, made them untouchable, made them invincible.

His mishap in Boston had taught him well. Maybe he didn't get the Berklee music degree he'd dreamed of, but that didn't mean he hadn't gotten an education. He'd learned everything he needed to know about foreign women. How those big-eyed cunts will tease you with their blond *gaijin* pussy hair. Come on to you, suck you dry. And then nonchalantly destroy your future.

But with education came power, and now things were different.

After Boston, he'd learned how to control the foreign bitches. How to bend them and break them. He always made sure that they enjoyed it. Until it was too late for them.

TokyoAli, you have a new admirer. He set up a user trace on his network so that he could monitor TokyoAli's online moves.

Adjusting the gun in his lap, he settled back in his chair, and entered the Adults-Only area. He created a new public chat room, "Looking for Love in Tokyo," and sat and waited.

6

Charles' eyes volleyed back and forth between the quotes on the screens at his desk. He had one phone tucked under his right ear and another phone held up to his left. Into the right phone he barked instructions in English, into the left phone he placed an order in Japanese.

Charles slammed down both phones and threw his fists up over his head. Victory.

"Cleared our position in CMOs with Bankers. Less than thirty seconds to close."

"You got balls, man," said Osborne.

"That's why they pay me the mega-bucks, my friend. I just hope those fucks in the head office don't go limp again."

Charles pushed back the telephones and computer monitors in his work area, reached into the bottom drawer of his desk and poured himself a generous shot of Lagavulin. His hands stopped shaking as the buttery burn of the Scotch slid down his gullet.

Osborne held out a cigar, which Charles took. "You going back to New York after your assignment here?" Osborne asked.

"Haven't decided." Charles bit the end off the cigar, lit up and sucked hard. "Tokyo agrees with me."

Charles peered out of the trading floor window and looked down on the gray-suited foreigners scuttling below on the streets of Otemachi, Japan's Wall Street outpost.

He remembered his arrival on Wall Street. He had been one of the anointed ones from Stanford Business School who'd landed a summer position with the Corporate Finance department at the Morgan Sachs investment bank. At the end of a summer of ego-inflated MBAs jockeying for entry into the most elite of I-bank clubs, Charles had been summoned into the office of the Managing Director of the Corporate Finance department.

Charles had tried to look relaxed and worry-free as he'd entered the inner sanctum of lucre, but the starched collar of his monogrammed Turnbull & Asser shirt bound at the neck by an Hèrmes tie — an I-Bank uniform he had noted and copied — felt like a garrote choking off his oxygen.

"Sit down, Gordon."

Charles obeyed.

"Scotch?" The MD pushed the crystal decanter across the desk. Charles took a tumbler from the tray and poured himself a glass. But he didn't dare drink. Not yet. Not when his future was about to be unveiled.

"Charles, you've had a terrific summer. We've all been highly impressed by your performance."

"Thanks, Scott, I've had a great time, and—"

"Congratulations. We'd like you to come aboard."

"Awesome, Scott. The Corporate Finance department's—"

"However, we think that you'd feel more comfortable in a slightly different position, a position where your skills and talents could really shine."

"Oh?" Charles felt his heartbeat quicken, and he had a sip of Scotch. The firm had even bigger plans in store for him.

"Yes. We'd like you to join us on the floor, to give it a go as a trader."

"The floor? A trader on the floor?" Charles' shoulders sagged against the chair. "But Corporate Finance is what—"

"Charles, to be perfectly candid—" The MD put down his drink and locked Charles in his sights. "With your background and skill set, you'd be better leveraged on the floor. You don't bring the value-add we're looking for in Corporate Finance."

Value-add? Charles understood what the partner was really saying — that Charles didn't have the requisite family pedigree and country club network to cut it in the rarefied Corporate Finance department, where personal connections were everything.

But Charles had been realistic. He knew that his contacts were more blue collar than blue chip. And when he was being painfully honest with himself, he knew that Morgan Sachs wasn't ready to be represented before its bread-and-butter Fortune 500 clientele by a Black man.

So Charles had taken the position he'd been offered. A trader. And found that the down-and-dirty world of the trading room floor, where the most daring pitted their wits against the world, suited him to a T.

He was good, and the money was good. Damn good. Better than what'd he'd pull down in Corporate Finance. But even so, Charles still bristled to think that as much money as he was making, the firm was making even more money off of his smarts, his instincts, his street sense. His fucking value-add.

Osborne interrupted Charles' thoughts. "Listen, some of us are grabbing a drink at the Pool Cue tonight. You in?"

An OL, a so-called "office lady," a young woman hired at the bank to serve tea and, unofficially, to find a husband, walked by in the uniform blue vest and hip-clinging blue skirt. She stopped at Charles' desk and refilled his glass of Scotch. The OL took a sip from Charles' glass, licked her lips and pushed the glass over to Charles. Without a word, she headed toward the door.

"Chieko'll be there." Osborne winked.

Charles' eyes followed Chieko's ass down the length of the trading floor. Big butt for a Japanese woman. He liked that.

"Yeah, I'm free."

7

“It’s never good news when a person’s been missing this long.”

“The Canadian Embassy is doing its own investigation.”

“I’m scared to go out at night.”

Alison had finished her Green Space research for the day and was reading the day’s entries on WNL’s “Tokyo — Love It or Leave It” message board when the municipal PA system began its broadcast. Five o’clock. Time to talk to her new friend.

She paged Kiyoshi346 online, but there was no reply. She searched the list of users logged on to the network. Kiyoshi346 wasn’t among them.

Disappointed, she sent him an email.

Dear Kiyoshi – I was looking for you this afternoon.

Just wanted to say hello.

Regards, TokyoAli

What to do next? As she was thinking, her computer announced, “You’ve got mail!”

Kiyoshi was online. She opened the message.

TOKYOALI, ARE YOU LOOKING FOR SOMEONE??

There was no name attached to the message, no way to reply. It had been transmitted anonymously.

What kind of joke was Kiyoshi playing? She paged him again, but there was no answer. Weird. Maybe there was some mistake.

Since she was online, she decided to drop Rob a little note.

My dear little brother:

Look who's online now? There goes the virtual neighborhood!

love, Ali

Alison was about to log off when her computer again announced: "You've got mail!"

Kiyoshi must be online. She opened her new mail. It had been posted by an anonymous sender.

DON'T WORRY ALI ALI ALI. HE'LL BE BACK TOMORROW. ME TOO!!!

The message faded on the computer monitor and the screen flashed a strobe of Day-Glo colors. A woman's breathy voice announced, "I'm coming. I'm coming. Three, two, one." The voice screamed and the screen went dark.

What was that? Alison punched in commands at the keyboard, but the computer had crashed.

Shit. How could she explain to Charles that his computer had just up and died? Would he believe her if she said she hadn't touched it? Not likely. It was time for self-help.

She dug out a computer magazine she'd bought and read how to reboot Charles' Mac. The computer came back alive, auto-dialed into

Morgan Sachs' intranet and the pulsing pyramid reestablished itself. All looked normal.

But what the hell had happened? Such odd, perverse messages. And it wasn't random spew being hurled her way. The sender knew her name. Her World NetLink user name, anyway. But it probably was some teenage hacker wannabe getting his rocks off. Bothersome, but relatively harmless hijinks.

01000011 01101001 01110100 01111001

He didn't want to make it too easy for her at first. Didn't want to be too predictable. He knew from his experience with the others that once she had a taste of the attention, she'd crave more, come back for more. Junkies needed their fix.

But this one was turning out to be almost too easy. She was already lowing, grazing, looking for him. The slut. Where was the sport in that?

He preferred it when they were a challenge, when they resisted, put up a fight. Because then when they finally came around, they really wanted it and would do anything for it. Those were the ones it was sweetest to break.

8

Her legs burned as she trudged uphill after heartbreak hill. The physical exertion felt good and was a welcome distraction from the gloom she felt in her heart.

How could she get any work done if the computer kept crashing on her? And always after she got those weird messages. Was that guy Kiyoshi such a freak, or was it something — somebody — else? She needed to clear her head, and there was nothing like a good run.

Reaching the summit, she began the steep descent. Her left knee was getting sore. Which meant it was going to rain soon. A barometric reminder of her accident at Tahoe when Charles had fallen off the chair-lift and dragged her down with him. Her knee hadn't hurt much at the time. Little did she know that years later, it would still act up.

A speeding Jeep, too big for the narrow road, zoomed by too fast, too close. Alison leaped to the edge of the street and pressed herself against the stone barrier wall. Would it be asking too much for the Japanese to build some sidewalks? Lest she become a hit-and-run victim, she decided to get off the road and cut through the park.

A cold rawness pierced the wind, but bright late afternoon sunshine illuminated the maple trees' fiery crimson foliage. Alison ran past a young mother pushing a baby carriage.

Kids needed fresh air. When she had kids, she'd tuck them into one of those jogging strollers and take them running with her. *When she had kids.* Charles said he wanted kids, lots of kids. But at the rate things were going with their relationship, kids would be a fertility clinic miracle. Surely Charles understood that time's a-wasting. Or at least her time was.

Alison passed a group of little boys — four, maybe five years old? — all wearing the shortest of shorts, inadequately covering their bare legs. The boys' cheeks, ears and knees were bright red with cold. How could their mothers dress them up with so little concern for their warmth? Alison filed it under "cultural differences" and kept on running.

She rounded a corner to head home and collided with a man on a bicycle who surprised her coming from the left side of the path through the park. Her knee broke the impact as she landed hard on the ground.

Alison had been walking on the right side — which in Japan was the wrong side — of the path. When would she remember that foot traffic followed the same flow as cars? Driving on the left side, walking on the left side.

She tried to apologize to the guy in English, in Japanese, in gestures, but the man, apparently unhurt but inconvenienced, yelled at her as he mounted his bicycle and sped off. The only word Alison could understand was *gaijin*. He turned around spat the word over his shoulder as if it were the filthiest of insults. Alison knew that *gaijin* meant "foreigner," but Charles had tried to explain how *gaijin* carried a certain pejorative sense that was hard to explain exactly. Whatever. She'd been hailed with enough pejoratives at home in the States that it didn't bother her much. Or at least not too much.

What did bother her was her knee. Her left knee. She stretched and tested it out to see if she could make it home, but her knee buckled underneath her.

A woman came trotting toward her from a nearby park bench. "Are you all right?" The petite woman with blonde hair going gray spoke with a thick Australian accent. She carried a tennis racket case over her shoulder.

Alison shook her head. "I'll be fine. Just a bit surprised, is all."

"You're bleeding." The woman pointed to Alison's hand. Her knee had been rubbed raw in the fall and was sprouting rivulets of blood.

"You need to bandage that up. My clubhouse is right behind the courts. Let's get you some sticking plasters and fix you up."

Alison limped along with the woman as they entered the warmth of the athletic club's front room. "She's with me," the Australian woman said to the attendant at the front desk. "Just one moment, dear." The woman went into a side room and returned with bandages, cotton balls and alcohol wipes. "Try these," she said, handing Alison the supplies. "The loo is the second door on the right." The woman pointed. "By the way, my name is Rachel."

"Hi, Rachel. I'm Alison."

"So nice to meet you. Now you go get yourself straight, and I'll get us a nice cup of tea."

When Alison returned from washing off her wounds, Rachel was sitting at a small table and had set out teacups and saucers along with a thermos of hot water. Next to the thermos was a small cut-glass bottle of Suntory whiskey. Rachel put an Earl Grey tea bag in each of the cups and filled them with water.

Rachel poured milk in her cup, added a healthy splash of whiskey and took a sip. "So, Alison, what brings you to Japan?"

Alison tore open a paper tube of sugar and poured it into her cup. The tea tasted good, but she was glad to add some whiskey to take the edge off of the pain that she was beginning to feel creep from her knee into her lower back. "My fiancé got transferred here for work, and I came along with him."

"Do you have a job, too?"

"I'm doing a little legal research."

"You're a solicitor?"

Why did everyone look so surprised when they learned she was an attorney? "I'm an environmental lawyer."

"Oh, my. How nice." Rachel had more tea. Alison could see the gears in Rachel's brain trying to process the fact that Alison was a lawyer. By the way Rachel was biting the side of her cheek, the cogitation must have hurt. She set down her teacup and smiled at Alison. "So how do you like Japan?"

"Most of the time I feel like I'm stumbling around in culture shock."

"Do you speak Japanese?"

"No, but my boyfriend is fluent. He helps me get around."

"That's makes it easier."

"Yes, but it's still hard doing the most basic things. Reading a map, taking the subway, grocery shopping. And Charles — that's my boyfriend — fiancé — he's always so busy. Too busy to spend much time with me." Alison closed her eyes hard against the threat of tears. She found some Kleenex she'd tucked up her sleeve and wiped her nose.

"Sounds like culture shock, all right," Rachel said. She added more whiskey to Alison's cup.

Alison had a deep drink. She wasn't used to drinking hard liquor. But it put things in a pleasant haze. "I thought that Charles and I would get closer if we were actually living together." Why was she telling a stranger all this? Must be the whiskey talking.

"You weren't together before?"

"We lived together in San Francisco, but then he got transferred to New York. And then transferred again to Japan."

"Most businessmen who get transferred to Japan leave their wives behind. Alone in Tokyo and living the expense account life of an ex-pat bachelor. A different Japanese girl every night."

"Charles isn't like that." Was he?

Rachel snorted. "Well, now. Do you have any friends here besides your boyfriend?"

"Not close friends." Not any friends. Alison took a big swallow. A splash of tea dribbled down her chin. "There is a guy I talk to on the internet."

"You met someone online? Be careful. Some Japanese men have a special fetish for foreign women. You heard about that Canadian girl who disappeared?"

"I'm completely safe. It's all online."

Rachel shook her head in dismissal. "I've lived in Japan for eight years, and everyone goes through an adjustment period. Get out, meet some new people, you'll be fine."

"I'm sure you're right," said Alison. "Thanks for listening. I'm not usually so fragile."

"No worries." Rachel poured more whiskey into her own teacup and drained it. "Alison, may I ask you a question? It's rather personal."

"Of course. Shoot."

Rachel leaned forward in her chair. "Are you just a little bit — colored?"

Alison blinked. Colored? What century was this? "Yes, you could say I am. One hundred percent Black."

"Oh—I… But your skin is still pretty." Rachel glanced at her watch and did a bad double take, furrowing her brow. "Look at the time. I have to go. Please stay, finish your tea. Perhaps we'll meet again." Rachel grabbed her racket case and started for the door.

Alison stood. Pain radiated from her coccyx to her knee. But thanks to the whiskey, the soreness didn't register as intensely as it might. "Yes, perhaps we will." When pigs fly.

Alison watched the door close behind Rachel. So much about life in Japan felt exotic and odd. And yet so much felt altogether too familiar.

9

Home alone the next morning, Alison appropriated Charles' desk and took control of the computer mouse. Like a seasoned pilot, she strapped herself in, adjusted the flight controls, and ran through the sequence of commands that would transport her off into cyberspace. Alison started up the engines, got the propellers going, and then lifted off into the freedom, the soaring ecstasy, of flight through virtual space and time.

The computer recognized her commands and greeted her. She was in.

Her Green Space research was moving forward slowly, and she worried that she had an embarrassingly small amount of information on Indonesia. Through a stroke of luck, also known as bumbling, she came across a website that promised to be a motherlode of information: an online newsletter about Asian environmental activism. Alison cruised to the site and scanned the headlines.

One title grabbed her attention: "Green Space Donates $500,000 for Indonesian Copper Cleanup." Alison read how Green Space had pledged funds to set up an advisory group in Indonesia that would counsel indigenous people on how to counter the effects of toxic by-products left behind by foreign mining companies. Hiro Yamada was leading the effort and would be working closely with Green Space in Tokyo.

Hiro Yamada. Maybe he was related to Yuko Yamada. Alison added the URL to her research report and made a mental note to ask Ms. Yamada about the advisory group.

Alison was about to move on when the computer announced she had a message from Kiyoshi.

"Hiya, Kiyoshi. What a surprise to catch you online at this hour."

"I'm on the road."

"Where are you?"

"I was in Seoul, now I'm in Shanghai."

"Do you travel a lot for work?"

"I used to go to the U.S. a lot, but now that I'm based in Kobe, I usually just travel in Asia."

"You said that you worked in marketing. Tell me about it."

"I'm in the international division of Tai Tsu, Pacific Communications. We help foreign companies doing business in Asia."

"Do you enjoy it?"

"Yes. Most of my clients are from the U.S., and I like working with Americans. I've answered your Perry Mason questions. Now it's your turn. How did you decide to be a lawyer?"

"It runs in the family. Dad was a tax attorney, and Mom was a judge in family court, so I had it in my blood."

"No lawyer jokes from me."

"Despite the bad publicity we lawyers get, we

can have a positive social impact. Especially environmental lawyers."

"And what do environmental lawyers do?"

"I worked as a staff attorney for an organization devoted to preserving virgin forests. We were kind of controversial in our tactics. It was fun."

"Sounds fascinating."

"It was, but I gave up my job when I moved here. I can go back, but for now I am, as they say, 'between jobs.'"

"You have time to enjoy yourself."

Alison's computer screen flashed, accompanied by the sound of a woman's voice moaning in orgasmic ecstasy.

"I ENJOY MYSELF ALL BY MYSELF!!!"

Alison was bewildered.

"What was that, Kiyoshi?"

"I was about to ask you the same thing. Did your computer just send a message?"

"Yes. I thought it was from you."

"No, not me. Maybe some telephone lines got crossed."

"NO CROSSED LINES!!!"

There was the message again, the orgasmic voice again.

"Kiyoshi, really, is that you?"

"Absolutely not me. Let's get a different room and see if we can get some privacy. I'll meet you in the KIY-ALI room, OK?"

"See you there!"

Alison entered the commands to move to a different private chat room.

"Let's hope we're alone now."

"I think so, Kiyoshi. You know, the strangest thing happened to me when I was online the other day. I kept getting these weird messages being sent anonymously. Kind of like today."

"Did you report it to the SysOp?"

"The what?"

"The System Operator. They manage the network."

"Good idea. I'll do that."

"HELLO AGAIN!!!"

This time the posting was accompanied by a trumpet fanfare.

"Kiyoshi, did you see that?"

"Yes. What a bother."

"This feels kind of creepy. How about if we meet tomorrow at our usual time."

"OK. Meanwhile, I've got some news I'll email to you."

"I look forward to it. Cheers!"

"Goodbye."

They broke their chat connection and went their separate ways on the network.

Still agitated by the gall of that online intruder who wouldn't leave her and Kiyoshi alone, Alison sent an email message.

To the Netlink System Operator:

I have been harassed online by an anonymous person sending me irritating messages and interrupting private chats. Please advise me as to what I can do to stop this annoyance.

– TokyoAli

Alison was preparing to log off when the computer announced incoming email. Another message from the weirdo? She hesitated before she opened the email.

Hello, TokyoAli!

I hope we can get rid of our online visitor but at least we can talk through email even if it takes longer.

My news is that I will be coming to Tokyo for business. May I invite you to dinner next Thursday

```
evening? I would like to meet you in person. I hope
you feel the same way.

Yours truly,
Kiyoshi
```

That Australian woman Rachel might be an atavistic piece of work, but she was right about one thing — Alison needed to get out and meet some new people, make some friends. And Kiyoshi was her first friend in Japan. Her only friend in Japan. And even though they hadn't had a proper introduction, if she met him in a public place, if she kept her wits about her, and if she lined up an exit route, what could be the harm in getting together? She sent Kiyoshi a note back accepting his invitation.

After posting the email message, Alison noticed that her online mailbox icon was still blinking. She had mail waiting from the NetLink System Operator.

```
Dear TokyoAli:

Thank you for your message. Occasionally we get
news of online users abusing the network. Please
be assured that we are investigating your problem.
In the meantime, we suggest you change your pass-
word often and make sure it is a non-obvious word.
Foreign words or passwords containing numbers are
recommended.

Happy to help you.
```

Alison was unimpressed. Yeah, big help. Translation: They're clueless. But at least she and Kiyoshi could send each other confidential email even if they couldn't chat directly without interference. That way their online rendezvous would be solely their affair. "Freudian slip, Alison," she warned herself.

Kiyoshi, formerly Kiyoshi346. With a face-to-face engagement imminent, he began to take on real human proportions. She wished she had gotten some of the nitty-gritty details about the man. What did he look like? How old was he? Was he married? Did it matter? She was with Charles, and that wasn't stopping her from having dinner with Kiyoshi. It was only dinner, no big deal.

01101001 01110011 00100000 01100001

He hadn't decided yet what the come-on would be. He needed to get a better sense of her personality, of her likes and dislikes. And her weaknesses. They all had weaknesses. And they all had their vulnerabilities. He'd find hers. He had to pay attention, to read between the lines, and he was halfway there.

He knew she was from California. Meant she was probably athletic, outdoorsy, had a hot body. Probably was blonde. All Californians seemed to be. Maybe she was even one of those beach volleyball babes with their skimpy bikini uniforms, like he'd seen in the Olympics.

But she said she was some kind of lawyer. So she must be smart. That was good — he liked them that way. The brainy ones always assumed they could outsmart him. So they put up more of a fight. Which meant more fun for him, watching them struggle with their disdain and their desire.

But the details didn't really matter in the end. Once their panties were wet and their nipples were hard, the foreign women were all alike. And TokyoAli, like all the others, would come crawling to him with her pussy throbbing. And she would spread her legs wide open and beg for it. One more stupid cow foreign bitch to add to his collection.

10

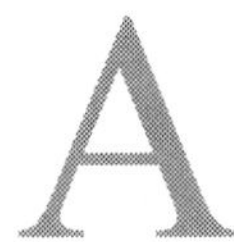s dependable as the five o'clock song, Kiyoshi was online the next evening and invited Alison into a chat room.

"Shall we get our usual room, madame? Or is it mademoiselle?"

Oh, he's smooth.

"It's mademoiselle, and I'll meet you there!"

She moved over to the chat room they created for themselves, Ki&Al.

"Are you still traveling? Or back home with your family in Kobe?"

She could be smooth, too.

"I'm going back home to Kobe. But I live alone."

Alison grinned and grabbed the air with her fist. "Yes!"

"I'm glad you can have dinner with me, Alison. I'm looking forward to finally meeting you."

"Me too. Where should we meet?"

"I'll be at the Compu-Expo Land convention in Akihabara. Is it all right if we meet at the Digital Pavilion at 7 o'clock?"

A public place. Lots of other people around. Safety in numbers. Sounded good to Alison.

"OK, but where is it?"

"Akihabara. Do you know the area?"

"I'm sure I can find it. How will I know you?"

"I'll have a rose behind my ear."

"Very funny."

"Seriously, I'm about 180 centimeters, my hair is *goma-shio*, what you call salt and pepper, and I don't wear glasses. How will I know you?"

"I'm easy to spot. I'm about five feet six, curly brown hair, shoulder length, gray eyes. I'm African-American, but people here in Japan tell me I look Brazilian. Whatever that means."

"YOU CAN DANCE A BRAZIL SAMBA IN MY LAP! A SAMBA LAP DANCE!!!"

The computer message was accompanied by the sound of a woman's squeals.

"It looks like he's back, Kiyoshi."

"Let's just say – *ja ne*!"

"What?"

"*Ja ne*. It is like 'bye' rather than 'goodbye.' Friends use it with friends."

"Well, then, *ja ne*."

"You learn quickly, Ms. Alison. See you Thursday."

"I'LL BE BACK!" warned the voice of the Terminator.

Damn that jerk who kept busting in on them. What a no-life creep.

There had to be some way she could get her privacy back. She decided to call Rob. If anyone knew what she could do to defend herself online, it would be her techno-geek brother.

Reaching for the phone, Alison paused. What time was it in Chicago? Counting on her fingers, she calculated that it was 2:30 in the morning. Better to send Rob an email.

SOS, Rob: There's some weirdo online stalker who keeps bothering me with freaky messages and busting into my chats. What can I do to stop it? Help!

Alison sent the email and sat back in the chair.

Daydreams about Kiyoshi, the mysterious Japanese stranger, floated through her mind. A smile tugged at the corners of her mouth. She pulled herself up short.

You're heading for a fall, Crane. She knew nothing about the guy. And how did he know her name was Alison? She never told him. Maybe it was a lucky guess, but maybe he's an ax murderer. That poor Canadian woman who disappeared might've been out on an internet date, meeting a guy like Kiyoshi. Going out with Kiyoshi was like responding to a personals ad. The blindest kind of blind date.

And you have a boyfriend. What about Charles? So what about Charles? He didn't need to know every detail of her life. He went out with lots of people without ever telling her. And Kiyoshi was just her online friend. He lived hundreds of miles away. It was only a meal. Charles didn't need to know all the particulars. Neither did Kiyoshi, for that matter.

When it became a problem, if it became a problem, then she'd deal with it. It was premature to make any decisions. It's like they say in the law: The matter was not ripe for deciding.

11

The bell over the door jingled as he stepped inside the dimly lit jazz coffee shop. He nodded to the mama-san and headed for his favorite table in the corner, directly under the heater. The only other customer, a college kid, was parked at a small table, with his head resting on his crossed forearms. With eyes closed and burning cigarette unattended, the kid looked like he'd fallen asleep. Only his tapping toe revealed that he was wide awake and deep in concentration.

The mama-san brought over a steaming cup of black coffee. He loosened his tie and pulled out his earplugs.

Giant Steps. He whistled along almost inaudibly. Even with his perfect pitch, it was hard to hit some of those wild leaping intervals dead on. How had Coltrane strung together such an improbable sequence of notes and keys and turned it into a brilliant melodic line? Genius.

He'd tried to underscore some Coltrane into the TV commercial he was editing. Idiot producer had said that he wanted to hear something smoother. What could be smoother than Trane? Fucking TV producer. He'd had to re-edit the soundtrack eight times before the asshole was satisfied. Goddamn tin ears.

He finished his coffee and let his chin drop to his chest. "A Love Supreme." This tune he could easily follow. Four notes. Four sublime notes. "A Love Supreme."

He'd had a love supreme. During his freshman year at Berklee College of Music. Wide-eyed with hope and excitement to be in America, he'd finally been studying at the school he'd dreamed about his whole life.

A Love Supreme. She had freckles and reddish blond hair. He didn't care that she was taller than he was. Big deal. They were in music history class together, and she'd asked him about Japanese pop.

He didn't have many friends at Berklee. Americans talked so fast he had trouble keeping up. But he could understand her eyes. Jade green like the waters of Tokyo Bay, they flashed when she looked at him. Those green eyes had fixed on him and invited him into her dorm room. Sure, he'd come. How could he say no? A Love Supreme.

She had wallpapered her room with yellow plaid sheets. She showed him how she'd stapled sound insulation underneath the sheets so her neighbors wouldn't complain about her oboe practice. She'd been so proud of those damn sheets.

And she smelled like strawberries. Maybe it was her shampoo or her deodorant. Even her room smelled like strawberries. He'd always liked strawberries.

He sat down in her desk chair, and she offered him a glass of cognac. To warm up. After two glasses, he'd pretty much forgotten Boston's winter chill.

She lit a candle, turned off the lights in the room. And put on Coltrane. How could a chick like that listen to Trane? But she did.

She moved close to him and massaged his shoulders. Pulled off his sweater and took his shirt out from under his belt. She loosened his pants and stroked his already hard dick. He hoped he could hold back and restrain himself.

She refilled his glass and told him she wanted to show him something. She peeled off her jeans and stripped off her sweater. No shyness, no hesitation. Just that brash confidence so typical of Americans. She stood in front of him in her lacy green bra and matching panties. Her panties were the color of her eyes. Eyes that dared him not to worship her.

She took off her bra and revealed two round breasts. In the candlelight, he could see her nipples standing firm. Firm and pink. Not plum-colored like a Japanese girl's. His dick throbbed, and his breathing was rapid and shallow. He felt lightheaded and giddy, like he was in the middle of a pleasantly surreal dream.

She dipped her finger in his cognac, then dribbled the cognac on her nipples. Lick it off, she said. Lick me dry.

And he did. She tasted so sweet. Like strawberries. And cognac. But more intoxicating.

He began to take off his jeans, but she said, no. There was more that she wanted to show him.

She leaned back on her futon bed and opened her legs wide. With cupped hands, she rubbed her pussy with one hand while reaching into the nightstand next to her bed with her other hand. She pulled a huge *kokeshi* out of the drawer — a purple rubber dildo as big as his dick. Bigger. She stared at him and grinned before squirming out of her panties. Her pussy hair wasn't black — it was blonde. Foreign girls were so different.

She asked if he wanted to watch.

He couldn't find his voice to answer. His heartbeat skittered in his chest, and his dick itched and pulsed at the same time.

She licked the dildo and eased it into her cunt. Her body shivered as she slid it in and out. In the candlelight, the dildo glistened with her pussy juice. Head thrown back, she'd moaned with pleasure.

With green eyes glittering, she asked him if he liked what he saw.

He kicked off his jeans and jumped on top of her. She had practically asked him to come fuck her. Had practically invited him to. It was her idea, not his.

So why was he the one who'd gotten thrown out of school? She didn't even bring official charges. Went running straight to the dorm proctor with her tears and accusations.

But it was enough to get him an instant one-way plane ticket back to Japan. Enough to stop his music studies cold. A Love Supreme. The little cunt.

American girls. Carefree seducers and indifferent destroyers with their teasing round eyes and toothpaste smiles. In the States, he hadn't known how to defend against their siren song. But in Japan, it was a different story. A different tune altogether.

And if the *gaijin* bitches wanted to get to know a Japanese man, wanted to get to know the natives, they'd better be prepared for what they might find. And let *them* struggle to understand the cultural differences. Let *them* try to understand how yes meant no, and no meant yes. Let them be humiliated and confused and off balance, like he had been. Let their dreams be shattered. And let them go sniveling home. A Love Supreme.

12

Dressed, coifed, perfumed, and with a Japanese-English dictionary tucked in her evening bag, Alison was ready to go. She stepped down into the *genkan* foyer and selected some Jimmy Choo pumps from the shoe closet. Charles called them her hooker heels. The shoes would be torturous to wear, but she hoped the effect on Kiyoshi would be worth it. Question was, would he be worth it? Alison tried not to have any hopes, any expectations about the man, about the friendship. But she tried in vain. She was excited about meeting him and had needed to run twice her usual distance in the morning to calm her nerves.

As Alison was squeezing into the heels, the phone rang. She stepped out of the shoes and ran into the living room to catch the phone before the answering machine picked up.

"Hey, Alicats!"

"Hi, Charles, what's up?" She tried to coax some gaiety into her voice. "I was on my way out the door to meet Ruth."

"Who?"

"Remember, I told you. My friend Ruth from law school's in town, and we're getting together for dinner."

"Oh, right," said Charles.

"Anyway, I'm on my way out, so I'll see you when I get back."

"The guys here decided not to go out tonight, so how about I join you?"

Think fast Alison. "Charles, it'd be great if you could come, but — I know Ruth wants to talk to me about some problems she's having with her husband. She's only in town for tonight, and I don't know if she'd feel comfortable with—"

"Got it. Ladies Night Out. So, where're you going?"

Why was Charles suddenly getting so interested, so inquisitive? "We'll probably go to Spago. I'm on my way to her hotel now."

"Where's she staying?"

"At the Imperial. Look, darling, I gotta go. See you when I get home."

Alison hung up the phone. Why was she suddenly lying to Charles? She hadn't planned to. But neither had she intended to tell him she was off to meet another man for dinner, a man she'd met online, no less. Charles wouldn't understand that it was just a dinner. Was it just a dinner?

Now that she'd embarked on weaving a tangled web of deception, she'd have to be careful. Would Charles notice the new outfit? Would he wonder why she was dressed like this to meet a girlfriend? Maybe she should reserve a room at the Imperial in Ruth's name if Charles called. Just in case.

Alison reined herself in for a reality check. There was really no reason to get paranoid. Charles never kept such close tabs on her. She had that in her favor tonight. Alison put on her heels again and stepped out.

The filled-beyond-capacity train stopped at Akihabara station and spat out the disembarking passengers.

"Akihabara: The Electric City," boasted the neon signs on the train platform. Alison fought her way out to the door of the train. She struggled against the phalanx of shoppers battling onboard using their newly purchased boxes of electronics as battering rams.

Alison looked at a map of Akihabara station to try to find her way to the conference center where she was meeting Kiyoshi. Countless train, subway and streetcar lines all intertwined in a convoluted muddle at the station. Where was the orderliness Japan was so famous for?

Too much noise, too many people. The familiar tightness grew in her skull as her brain deliberated whether to shift into claustrophobic panic attack mode, or not. She had to flee the clattering racket of the station. Now. Any door, any exit, would do. She pushed through crowds and escaped to the street. A huge banner stretched across the avenue: "Welcome Compu-Expo Land!" Hallelujah.

Dumb luck guided Alison to the conference center, a collection of ultra-modern buildings, each seemingly cantilevered out of the next. Conference attendees streamed in and out of every door. Carrying canvas bags with the Compu-Expo Land logo, they looked as happy as kids in a toy store on Christmas Eve. She was in the right place, but finding Kiyoshi amidst the sea of digital devotees would be a challenge.

Alison checked her time. She was five minutes late. All was going as planned. Not too early, and not late enough to be considered rude in a time-obsessed society like Japan.

Standing outside, smack in the middle of the main entrance to the conference, she struck what she hoped looked like a casual, relaxed pose. She'd be hard for Kiyoshi to miss. Especially because there were hardly any women in sight. Or foreigners. She alternated between arms crossed over her chest, to one hand on her hip. She wanted to look available, but not like a working girl. And in the dress she was wearing with the stiletto heels, it might be a tough call.

Piercing gusts blew through the plaza in front of the conference center. Alison hugged her thin, cotton swing coat around her. The coat was more for fashion than for warmth, and her legs felt wind-whipped and numb.

A digital billboard flashed the time and temperature, 7:45 p.m. and 11 degrees Celsius. Alison couldn't convert the temperature into Fahrenheit in her head, but 11 degrees Celsius sure felt fucking cold. And she didn't have to calculate any numbers to know that Kiyoshi was forty-five minutes late.

Maybe he'd gotten held up in traffic. Maybe he'd had business meetings that had run over. Maybe, maybe. Or maybe he had shown up, taken a look at her and decided he wasn't interested. She'd come this far, she'd give him another few minutes.

She rocked from one leg to the other, giving each foot a momentary rest from the pain of her shoes. Alison looked for a place where she could sit down while still keeping an eye out for Kiyoshi. He was almost an hour late, and she was cold. What had she been thinking?

Throngs of conventioneers swept past her and into the hall. Alison's gaze followed them inside. Nerdy men in suits, jam-packed together. Excited and enthusiastic. It had to be warm in there. The close proximity of too many bodies had freaked her out on the train. But now, with toes and fingers gone numb, Alison welcomed the idea of sharing the body heat of strangers. It sure beat hypothermia.

Her gut tightened with disappointment tinged with anger with the realization that she'd been stood up. Kiyoshi — or whatever his name really was — was proving to be a jerk. Better to know sooner rather than later. But he'd seemed like such a nice guy. And he was her only friend in Japan. She rubbed her hands together to get the blood moving. Maybe he had a good excuse. Or maybe she was pathetic. She'd go inside, thaw out, then head home.

Walking into the convention center was like entering a psychedelic circus tent. Three billboard-size high-definition television screens flanked the walls of the center and simultaneously projected a music video of a tone-deaf girl group jerking through labored choreography. Fighting for airtime, a recording of Beethoven's Ninth piped through stereo speakers showcased on a stage in the center of the hall. Overhead, laser light shows beamed advertisements through the ethers.

Alison's gaze bounced around the hubbub as she searched for a place to sit down, warm up and rest her abused and aching feet. Stumbling past the exhibition booths whose enthusiastic merchants bombarded her with offers of pens, key chains, T-shirts and magazines, she spotted a booth where a vendor was passing out samples of sake in square wooden cups.

An answer to her unspoken prayers. Sake was just the thing to defrost her bones. Alison snagged a sample, downed it, and had another.

The fresh, sweet fragrance of the cup's unfinished wood — some type of cedar, Alison guessed — blended perfectly with the sake. She had one more cup for good measure then started for the door.

"Hello! Hello!" called a voice. It must be Kiyoshi. Alison turned. From across the convention hall floor, a man seated behind a computer monitor waved at Alison. On top of the computer monitor sat a gizmo that looked like a baseball with a big lens in the middle. Alison smiled and waved back. The man pointed the baseball device in Alison's direction, and the ball flashed a red light.

Alison climbed through the crowds and walked over to the man. "Kiyoshi, it's so good to meet you at last!" She extended her hand. He didn't rise from his chair.

"Kiyoshi? It's me, Alison. I'm glad we found each other."

His face was an expressionless mask, eyes as milky and lifeless as the eyes of a dead fish.

Alison glanced at his computer monitor and stopped. On the screen was an image of a bikini-clad woman worthy of a centerfold. It took Alison a moment before she realized that the centerfold's face was familiar. It was hers.

"What the hell are you doing!?" She pointed at the monitor.

"Sorry, I do not speak English," the man said. He dropped his head and busied himself at the keyboard.

"What the hell right do you have to do this?" Alison poked at the image on the monitor. She looked around. The roar of the expo floor had deadened to a silence. All eyes turned to gaze at the scene Alison was making.

"Some other man call to you. Not me."

Alison felt a tap on her shoulder and she reared around, ready to fight.

"Can I help you, ma'am?" A petite man in a Compu-Expo jacket stood behind Alison. When she turned, he gave a shallow bow, gaze lowered, hands folded in front of him.

"Yeah, you can help me. This guy here," Alison moved to point out the paparazzi, but he had taken off when her back was turned. Alison sighed. "Forget it," she said. "Look, is there any way to leave a message for somebody here?"

"Yes, ma'am." The man gestured to a bank of keyboards lined up beneath small monitors. "You can leave an email with the party's name on it, and they can check messages."

"Thanks." Alison waited in line for a keyboard to free up, all the while keeping one eye on the convention hall entrance. Kiyoshi might turn up, and she didn't want to miss him. When she got to the front of the queue, she despaired to see that the keyboards were in Japanese. What a night.

She spun on her heel to head out when she noticed next to the keyboards stood a good old-fashioned, analog, three-dimensional bulletin board bearing a sign — in English — reading "Messages." Folded pieces of paper were pinned to the board, and a small table held pens and Compu-Expo scratch pads.

Alison tore a piece of paper from a pad and wrote a note. "Waited for you. Did we get our signals crossed? What happened? — T. Ali." She folded the paper in half, wrote Kiyoshi on the front and pinned it to the board. When Kiyoshi came to the convention center — if Kiyoshi came to the convention center — he would probably go looking for her, just as she had looked for him. And he would see the message on the board. Her note was the only one written in English. It stood out. Like her.

Alison decided to call it a night. She regretted that she and Kiyoshi hadn't exchanged cell phone numbers, but he was, after all, an unknown guy she'd only met through the internet. And she knew that a prudent woman was supposed to meet an unknown stranger in a public place, and that said prudent woman didn't give out her cell phone number to said stranger. Just in case.

But the bottom line was that she was all dressed up with no place to go but back home. But not before downing two more glasses of sake. For the road.

Alison bought her subway ticket and joined the line waiting for the next train. She was near the front of the queue and would be certain to get a seat and relief for her throbbing feet. Her pumps definitely weren't made for walking, let alone standing any length of time. She felt herself swaying. Too much sake on an empty stomach. She focused on a sign on the far side of the platform to ground herself.

Alison heard the train coming before she could see it. A recorded message warned passengers to step back behind the white line, or at least that's what Charles had said the message meant. But rather than draw back away from the arriving train, the line of waiting passengers compressed itself in anticipation of the fight to get on board.

The train light was in view. Alison stood ready to push on while at the same time trying to brace herself in her tottering heels as the train neared. The sake didn't help her sense of balance.

On unsteady legs, Alison felt a sharp shove between her shoulder blades. She lurched in her stiletto heels and screamed as she fell onto the tracks between the rails.

The train horn blasted. A man yelled. Alison scrambled to stand, to haul herself up onto the platform.

"Help! Somebody help me, please!" She cried out to the waiting passengers, but those nearest to her slid away.

Alison jumped at the platform ledge and clawed for a handhold. Her fingers grasped at air, and she fell back onto the tracks. Again, she tried to boost herself up. Again, she fell short.

The oncoming train's horn screeched. Alison turned to look at the train. Its bright light, unstopping and inevitable. She observed the light with an awareness that felt disembodied from the woman trapped on the tracks. The light was getting bigger. And the woman wasn't moving.

A burning pulse of adrenaline slapped Alison back to reality and demanded that she take immediate action.

Alison pounded the edge of the platform walls with her hands. "Please help me!" she wailed. "Somebody!"

A faceless pair of strong hands grabbed Alison by the elbows and lifted her, depositing her on the cold cement of the platform. Alison looked up to thank her Good Samaritan, but the do-gooder had disappeared into the crowd.

The train pulled into the station. Right on schedule. The doors opened. Passengers got out. The doors shut. The train departed. Not one moment late, not one second lost. Business as usual.

On the rough pavement of the station's floor, Alison sat. Blood trickled from her scraped palms, and she had lost one of her treacherous pumps. Her nose was running with tears she hadn't shed. She wiped her face with the back of her hand. What a fucked-up night.

Still, Alison reminded herself, it could've been worse. If it hadn't been for her savior. If that anonymous stranger hadn't snatched her up… Alison shuddered. The evening news story wouldn't be about a missing Canadian woman — it would probably be about her.

01101000 01101001 01100100 01100100 01100101 01101110

Sitting on the train, he took her note from his pocket, unfolded it and read it again. "Did we get our signals crossed?"

No, he hadn't. He knew exactly where and when to meet her. And she was easy to spot in the crowd. He wasn't the only man looking at her tits in that tight dress. And legs. Foreigners had long legs, but hers were like a model's. She must work out, legs like that. He couldn't wait to feel those legs. To inch his fingers up those legs to her hot cunt. While he sucked on those tits. She'd really like it.

He put the note back in his pocket and moved the Compu-Expo Land bag onto his lap to hide his hard-on.

He wanted her, and he would have her, but he had patience. And in the meantime, he would do all he could to get to know her better. Study her, tease her. Wait until she was panting, drooling, wet for him. It really wasn't a wait at all, but rather a tantalizing crescendo building up to an orgasmic fortissimo climax. Foreigners were always in such a hurry. But he could wait.

He was off to a good start. He was sure he'd made a memorable first impression, had gotten a good digital image of her. When he got home, he could upload her picture to his computer network and share his artistry with the world.

She was right — she did look Brazilian.

13

"Where were you, Kiyoshi? I waited over an hour!"

"I was right next to the DVD display in the entrance. You didn't hear your name being paged? I thought you changed your mind about meeting me."

"I didn't hear any page. All I could hear was Beethoven's Ninth. They blasted it through the speakers the entire time."

"Alison, that was the SOUND Pavilion. Not the Digital Pavilion. I think you were at the wrong place."

"Oh."

"Sorry about the confusion."

"At least I had some really good sake while waiting."

Too much sake. Alison didn't want to tell Kiyoshi that she'd guzzled so much sake that she'd stumbled in her stilettos and fallen into the path of an oncoming train.

Or that maybe she'd been pushed onto the tracks.

In the sober light of morning, she still wasn't exactly sure what had happened. She'd been tired, drunk and pissed off after being stood up.

She hadn't felt up to filing a police report. Not in the state she'd been in. And not now. She'd lucked out that Charles wasn't home when she'd gotten back. Charles didn't need to know any of the details of her misadventures on the train track, that she hadn't been out meeting Ruth from law school.

And there wasn't any need to mention the incident to Kiyoshi, either. He might think that she was a paranoid nutcase.

"I'll be back in Tokyo soon. We can try again."

"I'm really sorry, Kiyoshi. Let me know when you're heading back here. Meanwhile, I'm a modem call away."

"I AM EVEN CLOSER THAN THAT!!! CLOSER THAN YOU THINK. CLOSER THAN YOU KNOW."

A bossa nova beat lilted in the background while the sound of a woman's voice panted hard.

"Our friend has returned, Alison."

"I sent an email to my brother. He might have some ideas of what we can do to lose him."

"I hope so. Same time tomorrow, Attorney Crane?"

"Of course. *Ja ne*."

Alison had jumped to the wrong conclusion about Kiyoshi. She had been ready to come out with guns of accusation blazing, but he hadn't stood her up. She should have guessed that her ineptitude with the language was the cause of their screwed-up meeting. And he'd taken her no-show well. Kiyoshi was an OK guy.

But "Attorney Crane"? How had he known her last name? Alison was sure she hadn't mentioned it. She'd decided earlier that there wasn't any need for him to know. Just in case. Yet somehow Kiyoshi had known. And she'd forgotten even to ask him his last name. Regardless of what Kiyoshi thought, she didn't have Perry Mason's knack for interrogation.

01100111 01100101 01101101

Idiot Americans. So trusting, so blind. Why the hell can't they go back home and stay there? They aren't welcome in Japan. Never were. *Sayonara*, Commodore Perry. *Domo arigato*, General MacArthur.

Dumb Yanks tried to castrate a warrior culture. To demilitarize Japan. Instead, the dim-witted foreigners created a fierce industrial powerhouse. And now those self-proclaimed conquerors were eating stale raw fish in Kansas, jerking off with their Nintendo and dreaming of one day being able to afford a Lexus. Jiu jitsu this, MacArthur motherfucker.

14

Charles checked his Rolex. Yuko was late. The towering buildings of Ebisu Garden Place created a wind tunnel whipping nighttime gusts through the deserted urban canyon. He blew into his hands to generate some heat and sat on a bench. He'd give her five more minutes.

A keening whine echoed through the multilevel courtyard. Charles jumped up, looking for the source of the sound. At the top of a long staircase stood two white wolves, their fur glowing in the light from the street lamps. They howled again and raced each other down the steps to the ground-floor level toward Charles.

What the hell were wolves doing in the middle of Tokyo? He leaped onto the bench for tactical cover and was considering his defense strategy when he heard a shrill whistle. The charging wolves stopped cold and sat.

A petite woman laughed and bounded down the stairs. She knelt to pet the wolves. Her white fur vest coordinated with the creatures' pelts. She looked like a member of the pack. The alpha dog.

The woman tied a leash around each of the wolves' collars and strolled into the middle of the courtyard. As she approached, Charles realized that the woman was Yuko Yamada. She waved when she spotted Charles and headed his way with beasts in tow.

"It's good to see you again, Charles. Thank you for meeting me here."

"Hi, Yuko. You brought some friends." The animals nudged Charles' legs, depositing clumps of white fur on his trousers. He backed up a few paces and made a mental note to send his pants to the dry cleaners.

Yuko smiled. "Meet Luna and Susie. They're sweet but very spoiled girls." Yuko rubbed their heads. "This is their favorite place to go for a walk. Very dog-friendly."

"Dogs? What kind of dog?" Charles had never heard a dog howl the way those creatures had. They sounded — and looked — like wolves under a full moon in Transylvania.

"Samoyeds. Don't be afraid. They're trained to not bite."

Charles had never been a dog person, but he knew you could never be sure what a dog would do. Especially when they looked as dangerous as these mutant wolves. He would keep his distance.

"You said you wanted to talk to me about something, Yuko. A financial problem?"

She nodded. "Let's walk while we talk. Do you want to take one of the dogs?"

Charles waved his hands to decline. "I'm sure you've got them under control." He prayed she did.

They covered the length of the courtyard, climbed the stairs on the opposite end, and toured the second level of the garden space. Charles noticed how well the she-wolves heeled and obeyed their owner's subtle commands.

Charles spotted other dog walkers prowling around. With big dogs. He wasn't used to seeing dogs in Tokyo. Not like San Francisco, where dogs had their own parks, and people would take their pooches to restaurants, inflicting them on the other diners. Japan was different that way, thank God. But how could people in tiny Tokyo apartments live with such large dogs? It must be some sort of status symbol. A big dog meant a big house.

Yuko slowed to look at Charles. "What I want to talk to you about, I didn't want to discuss on the phone. It has to do with — with private matters."

"I'm used to handling private matters. It's all part of my job." Charles had one eye on the dogs.

Yuko stopped and the dogs sat on their haunches. "This involves something that would be — how should I say? It would be different from your usual work. Because it's highly confidential. Do you understand what I am saying?"

"I deal with confidential information every day. Keeping secret things secret goes with the territory." Charles braved taking a step closer to Yuko.

"It involves international finance. Large amounts of money." The dogs stirred, and Yuko reached down to quiet them.

"That's what I do." Charles tentatively reached one hand out toward the dogs, but quickly withdrew it when they snarled and bared their teeth. Fangs, really. He didn't care what Yuko said. Those were wolves.

"I have a problem," Yuko said.

"Tell me more. I'm good at making problems go away."

15

Asia was big. And there was a surprising amount of environmental work going on. Alison had to remind herself that green activism was a good thing even if it did mean she had a continent of data to dig through for her research.

Indonesia. Done. Singapore. Check. Alison refocused her eyes as she ticked countries off her list. She promised herself a stretch break and a glass of wine as soon as she finished investigating marine pollution in India.

She typed in another internet search and unearthed an article about Green Space making a $1 million contribution to an environmental outfit working to protect the beaches in Goa. Hiro Yamada was the chairman.

Again, Hiro Yamada. He was a busy man. Like a green Santa Claus, traveling around Asia delivering gifts of cash to needy environmentalists.

Could Green Space take donations and spend the money however it wanted? Ms. Yamada had certainly been blasé enough with the yen she had advanced to Alison. "No need for a receipt," Yamada had said.

At Save-A-Tree, despite all the brash acts of environmental derring-do they embarked upon, the organization was never so brazen as to spend its money in violation of its bylaws. They could risk losing their precious nonprofit status and even face criminal sanctions.

In Japan, there must be some restrictions on how charitable organizations could use their funds. Or at least, didn't the organization have to answer to its donors? Ms. Yamada had said that most of Green Space's contributors were private individuals. And in Japan, the benefactors didn't get any tax break for their donations — just warm fuzzy feelings.

Save-a-Tree had an entire department devoted to hunting down deep-pocketed do-gooders in need of some warm fuzzies. And once found, those golden-egg-laying geese were coddled and pampered. They were the organization's financial lifeblood. And yet Green Space seemed to be throwing its money at all manner of offshore groups.

Something didn't sit right with Alison's lawyerly instincts, but she couldn't pinpoint what. She understood that the rules for charitable organizations might be very different in Japan. But did the organizations have no accountability? No government oversight of their spending?

Alison needed to learn more about Green Space. And what she wanted to know, she wasn't going to find through World NetLink. It was time to call in the Marines.

16

"Picture identification, please, ma'am."

A burly Marine with the beginning of a spare tire rolling over his belt buckle stood in the American Center's doorway and blocked Alison's entry to the library of the United States Information Service. Or was it the United States Information Agency? Alison could never remember which one was the CIA organization and which one was the front. Regardless, she suspected both the USIS and the USIA had defense-budget dollars at work collecting all sorts of worldwide factoids about people, places and things. Today she would access some of those factoids, and by the afternoon, she'd know as much about the Green Space group as any government functionary.

Alison dug in her handbag and flashed her passport.

"Leave everything in the locker." The gatekeeper pointed a finger in the direction of a wall of lockers, most of which had keys stuck in the locks. "You can take a pencil, note paper, your wallet."

Heaven forbid she should carry any potentially dangerous materials — like a ballpoint pen — into the precious CIA information reserve. She dropped her purse in a locker and took the key.

Thus unencumbered, Alison pondered where to start. She pulled up a chair in front of the bank of research terminals. Looked pretty straightforward. She followed the commands as they appeared on the monitor.

"Enter 'Subject ='" the terminal prompted her. Easy. She typed "Subject = Green Space" and pressed the Enter key.

The computer screen was instantly filled with newspaper and magazine article citations. *The Japan Times*, the Asian *Wall Street Journal*, *Japan Business Today*, *EnviroNews* and more. Over forty hits altogether. Alison printed out all of the cites.

Waiting for the printer to plod through the list, her mind drifted. While she was at it, no harm in seeing if there was something in the archives about Kiyoshi's company. What was the name of his company? Something generic. She remembered: Pacific Communications.

Alison entered the company name, and received a handful of hits which she also printed out.

Alison took the pages of cites over to the CD-ROM reader. Cross-checking against her printout, Alison picked the corresponding CD-ROMs that contained information about Green Space. And about Pacific Communications.

She sat down at the CD-ROM reader, inserted the first disk and typed in the page number cited. The screen displayed a long article about a run-in the Green Space people had with some real estate developers who wanted to build a resort by the coral reef off of Iriomote Island in Okinawa. Green Space maintained that development of the resort golf course would poison the groundwater and affect the coral. Apparently there had been quite a few arrests during the altercation, and the development company had received some not-so-anonymous phone threats.

The writer made Green Space sound borderline fanatic. Alison discounted a lot of the media hype because she knew from her own experience at Save-A-Tree that the press was often less than sympathetic to movements they dismissed as the work of extremists. She read on.

The next article reported an incident in which Green Space closed down the operations of the Japanese subsidiary of an American chemical conglomerate. Toxic waste disposal that the EPA had prohibited in the States was being shipped offshore by the subsidiary. Green Space exposed the practice, and an international shit storm ensued. The State Department and the Commerce Department hurried to Tokyo for all-around damage control.

Good one. She liked Green Space's style.

Global Giving ran a piece about Green Space's advisory group in Vietnam. Local donors claimed that Green Space had raised money to clean up waterways polluted by Japanese steel manufacturers, but in fact, was colluding with the steel companies. The donors called for a government investigation.

At Save-A-Tree, Alison had been in the uncomfortable position of having to field phone calls from cranky, but vocal, contributors. People thought that because they had written a twenty-five-dollar check, they could dictate Save-A-Tree's policies. Pissing off donors was not something green organizations could indulge in.

And the Green Space donors in Vietnam had called for a government inquiry. Maybe Green Space needed lawyers more than they realized.

After reviewing all of the articles, Alison felt that she had a good grasp on the group's activities and the controversies they were facing. From what she could glean, they were fighting the good fight, and fending off the predictable media mud and naysayers. She had some questions, but they seemed like her kind of folk. And they were paying her kind of money.

Alison printed out the articles. Now, for the juicy stuff.

She pulled out the stack of CDs with information about Kiyoshi's company, Pacific Communications. An article from the *New York Times* explained a joint venture between Taiheiyo Tsushin, known as Pacific Communications in the U.S., and a computer game software company in Silicon Valley. Pacific Communications had developed the game software and now it was being licensed to the U.S. Department of Defense for military applications.

Alison vaguely remembered hearing about the deal, about the legal questions it raised when the American military built classified defense software based on a foreign company's technology. So that was Kiyoshi's company. Interesting stuff. If you're a technology lawyer. Alison preferred to stick to trees.

Next was a color piece from *Advertising World.* An executive of

Pacific Communications discussed the lucrative deals for American talent, mostly movie stars, making television commercials in Japan. The artist contracts stipulated tight constraints on publicity so that the image of the star would not be tarnished in the U.S. The report outed foreign stars and the products they represented in Japan. Arnold Schwarzenegger hawked instant ramen noodles, while Madonna peddled beer. Some of the stars got paid over $1 million for a few hours' work.

Alison understood. She wasn't the only on with a yen for yen.

The last article was a lengthy interview with Pacific Communications' chairman and founder, Sadao Hisaka. Hisaka described his experiences growing up in American-occupied Kobe, and how, as a boy, he'd washed dishes at one of the military bases. He learned English from the American soldiers and was influenced by seeing firsthand the vitality of American people. Hisaka had subsequently grown Pacific Communications into one of the world's largest advertising and media companies. His oldest son, Kiyoshi Hisaka, had attended university in the U.S.

So, Kiyoshi was a ringer. The son of an international media mogul. Alison laughed as she pushed back from the computer. Boy, could she pick 'em.

17

Alison raced to open the front door and catch the ringing phone.

"*Moshi moshi*," she said. Why did she bother answering the phone in Japanese when *moshi moshi* — "hello" — comprised a large percentage of her conversational vocabulary?

"Hey, Alicats. The guys from the office are getting together for a pub crawl tonight. You want to tag along?"

Tag along? It made her sound like some damn puppy dog. "Charles, every time I've gone out with your office buddies, you talk shop. In Japanese."

"No, really, it'll be fun tonight. Lots of the other ex-pats are coming, so English will be the preferred language. And if you get sick of it, we can blow it off and go home. What do you say?"

Alison felt, maybe out of her own sense of guilt from her covert attempted date with Kiyoshi, that she'd better say yes. "Well, OK, I guess."

"Great. Can you get here in an hour?"

"Sure, see you."

Alison hung up the phone. Maybe the evening wouldn't be so bad. She'd give it the old college try, hope to make the best of the situation. She owed that much to Charles. And she still had some time before she needed to head out.

She logged into NetLink, and there was mail waiting for her. From Rob.

Ali–

Glad you're finally online. You might become a world-class hacker if you're not careful. <ggg>

Chicago's cold as a bad fuck. Had 6 inches of snow yesterday. Why didn't I go to Cal Tech?

That shithead busting in on you sounds like some phone phreak getting kicks. Probably a pimply faced adolescent jerking off. What might help is encryption software called FYEO (For Your Eyes Only). If you run the software, your messages are automatically encoded. When you send a message to somebody else, they can decrypt if they have your pass key. I've seen FYEO in operation. It's pretty snazzy. You can download it from elite BBS in Palo Alto called SwampLand at 415-555-2346. The NUP is Acidjazz. That's the NUP this week only, so if you don't d/l this now, I'll have to get the new NUP. Good luck. You know how to d/l, right?

Your prompt-to-reply bro, Rob 0:-)

PS: If they want to know who sent you, say Fright-Night at FantomCity. Don't ask…

18

A tide of salarymen and OLs surged out of their Otemachi offices. It was Friday, and the twenty-fifth — the twenty-fifth being payday for virtually every worker in the nation — so the employees were in high spirits. And when payday fell on a Friday, all was right with the world.

Alison battled against the undertow of streaming bodies, swam through to the lobby's elevator banks and pressed the button for the top floor. She emerged in the reception area for Morgan Sachs.

The firm's entrance for receiving visitors was impressively plush. Silk Persian carpets lounged in the hallway from the elevator to the waiting area. Gilded Japanese screens with paintings of green-eyed tigers adorned the waiting room. How appropriate that Morgan Sachs would feature carnivorous beasts of prey in their office reception.

She walked to the lobby desk, which was unoccupied. So much for the tight security of the Morgan Sachs trading floor. She waited a few minutes then decided to go hunt down Charles.

Alison poked her head through the door to the trading room floor. Charles' voice boomed in Japanese followed by whoops of laughter. She was more than mildly dismayed to see an Office Lady — couldn't be a day over 22 — sitting on Charles' lap, laughing her head off with a group of men in shirtsleeves joining in the joke. Charles had his arms around Miss Lap Dog and seemed to be enjoying himself.

Play it cool, Crane, Alison told herself. It's just some office fun. She tried to plant a warm smile on her face, but it felt more like a grimace.

"Hello, Charles," Alison said, holding open the trading room door with one hand.

"Alison! Good! You're here!" Stating the obvious, Charles stood, and the OL scampered off.

"There wasn't anyone at reception, so I came looking for you, and—"

"No problem. The gang's all here. Time to mobilize! Don't forget to hold hands and stay together, children! We don't want anyone to disappear on us."

"Yeah, one Canadian is enough!" yelled one of Charles' compatriots.

With much hooting and laughter, the group of seven American men and four Japanese women, including Charles' lap dog, grabbed their coats and bags. Charles took the lead in organizing the ranks.

"Attention, attention, everyone. This is our game plan for the much-anticipated and soon to be regretted Hana Kin, the Flower of Friday carousing and debauchery!" The troops whistled and cheered. "But remember: we have to keep this clean and respectable. We're Morgan Sachs."

"Morgan sucks? Who?" hollered one of the boys.

"Morgan sucks your dick, Lester. Keep it up, and I'll have you cut off your little finger," Charles said.

Alison looked on in amazement at the Charles she rarely saw. Energized, rousing. A bad boy impervious to the consequences. Male bonding at its most testosterone-esque. Must remind him of his beer-chugging frat days at Dartmouth.

"Tonight, our mission is to explore every respectable — and some not so respectable — *nomiya* in Shimbashi. If they hang a red lantern, we will come. We will come, we will drink, and we will conquer! To the taxis!" More whoops and hollers as the battalion mobilized. Alison hoped she'd be able to last the evening.

Night was coming on fast, and by the time the commandeered taxis arrived in the heart of Shimbashi, the red lanterns hanging in front of the *nomiya* drinking pubs were all alit. Equally aglow were drunken salarymen already staggering through the small streets crowded with taverns.

Alison and Charles squeezed with three others in the backseat of a taxi. "Charles, what was that crack you made about the little finger?"

Charles looked at Alison. "What? Oh. You know, when a yakuza shames his gangster boss, the guy'll cut off the tip of his little finger to apologize for fucking up. I was just kidding, Alicats."

Alison remembered her visit to Green Space, Suzuki holding his hands out to present his business card. Hands that were missing a digit of the little finger. Couldn't be. Suzuki? Alison shook the ridiculous idea out of her head and rededicated herself to having a good time with Charles' friends. No matter how painful it would be.

The taxi stopped in front of the *nomiya* Charles had designated as their first target. Alison followed the others as they ducked under the *noren* curtain hanging in the entrance. The place was packed with rambunctious customers, hell-bent on having a good time.

The *nomiya's* manager led the group to a room upstairs that was not as crowded as the first floor, but no less noisy. Alison blinked hard to give her eyes a little relief from the sting of the thick cigarette smoke that filled the air. I will survive, I will survive, she silently repeated as a mantra to get through the night.

Removing their shoes, the group gathered around a low table on the tatami mat floor. Alison sat down next to Charles, and Miss Lap Dog sat directly across from him. Charles ordered five large bottles of Ebisu beer for the table, crispy cooked river shrimp, sticks of yakitori chicken with green onions, and boiled soybeans. All his favorite dishes, Alison observed.

The bottles arrived, and the customary pouring of beer into everyone else's glass began. No one noticed that Alison's glass was empty. She was forced to be rude and get her own damn beer.

"Does everyone here know my friend Alison?" Charles asked. Quick introductions were made to the people Alison didn't already know, which was just about everyone.

It hadn't gone unnoticed by Alison that Charles hadn't introduced her as his fiancée. Not even his girlfriend. She was his Friend. My Friend Alison. She'd deal with that one later. In the meantime, Alison tried to engage in some chitchat with the guy sitting next to her.

"Hi, I'm sorry I didn't catch your name," she started.

"Guy Taylor. You're Alison, right?"

"Right."

"Been in Japan long?"

"Just a few months," replied Alison.

"How do you like it here?"

"It's not too bad, I suppose. How about you, have you been here long?" Alison could hear the condescension in her own voice talking to this kid. The guy, sitting there in his boxy Brooks Brothers suit, looked like he had barely started shaving.

"No, I got transferred from New York two months ago. But during my undergrad at Princeton I spent a semester in Kyoto, so I know my way around."

Alison noticed Guy's attention drifting toward the conversation going on at the other end of the table. But at least he was trying to be polite to her. And she was doing her part to drag the dead horse on home.

Guy turned his attention back to Alison. "So, what brings you to Japan? Teaching English?"

Alison bristled. His question dripped with an investment banker's typical egocentrism. If you were a foreigner in Japan and you weren't an overpaid I-Banker, one could safely assume that you were a member of a lesser caste, the lowly English teacher. The little twerp was still popping zits and yet he was going to patronize her. She'd set him straight.

"Actually, I'm an attorney, and I—"

"And they bought them for two points over prime!" Guy shouted over Alison's head to someone at the far side of the table. With that comment, the group burst into uproarious laughter for reasons Alison couldn't surmise. This was going to be one helluva long night …

With no one to talk to, Alison drank too much. First beer, then sake, then some rot-gut corn mash drink. Gave her something to do. But as she and Charles were heading home in the cab, each turn and swerve added to Alison's discomfort. She hung onto the door handle and endured. Pain pounding in her head, she knew the morning would deliver a nasty hangover.

It wasn't an opportune time, but Alison couldn't stop herself. "Charles, why did you introduce me as your friend?"

"Huh?" Charles was unfocused and couldn't appreciate the real question being posed.

"Why didn't you introduce me as your fiancée?"

"Friend, fiancée, what's the difference? Those people don't care, and it's none of their damn business." He rubbed his eyes.

"What's the difference? There's a huge difference! And it sure would send a message to that Cheeko—"

"Her name is Chieko."

"That Cheeko who had her ass glued to your lap." The conversation wasn't going anywhere good, especially at two in the morning. But she couldn't let it go. "Those Japanese women treat you and your buddies like little pashas. It's nauseating. I thought you were more of a feminist, Charles. The least you could do is acknowledge in front of those—"

Charles sat up and, with narrowed eyes, studied Alison with an intensity that burned through her alcohol haze. "I'm not talking about this," he proclaimed and sank back down on his side of the cab seat. They rode the rest of the way home in silence. Alison's cheeks burned with contained rage.

They had entered the front door and walked into the *genkan* when she cracked. "Are you sleeping with her?"

Charles wheeled around. "What the hell are you talking about?"

"Cheeko. Chi-e-ko. Are you fucking her?"

Charles glared at Alison, his face a mixture of exasperation and contempt. "Jesus, you're drunk." He threw his coat on the couch and stormed into the bedroom.

Alison collapsed on the *genkan* step. Hugging herself, she sobbed, gulping hard for air. She wasn't too drunk to notice that Charles hadn't said, "No."

19

"Gone out. Back late."

Alison snatched Charles' note off of the refrigerator, crumpled the paper and threw it in the trash can. Charles' response to their fight was typical — withdraw and disappear. If Charles was going to be gone all day, then she'd get on his computer, ride it hard and put it away wet.

Alison popped some aspirin, thankful that her hangover wasn't too bad. She spread out on the living room floor with her coffee and a pile of computer magazines she had bought at an English-language bookstore.

With a whole day home alone on the computer, she had a chance to get that software Rob had told her about so that she could encrypt files online. That way, she and Kiyoshi could have their privacy and not be dogged by that wacko. All she had to do was download the software.

Downloading, downloading. Where had she seen something about downloading? She leafed through her collection of computer magazines until she found the article she was looking for. A how-to article about downloading software, how a user could connect to another computer system and retrieve files from its directory. Once the file was located, the download process began. But the receiving computer had to be set to a receive mode which was compatible with the host system, and on and on and on.

Alison's eyes glazed over as the article discussed stop-bits, flow control and AT codes. Why not give it a shot?

With magazine in hand and her email note from Rob, Alison sat down at the computer. She adjusted the modem settings to bypass Charles' network connection, and typed in the phone number for the BBS in Palo Alto, crossing her fingers.

Either it works, or it doesn't. But it better work.

The modem beeped away, digitally dialing. The computer emitted a different set of tones and the computer screen changed to a picture of two hands shaking. Alison guessed that meant she was in. That was easy.

Then the screen went blank. Nothing. Not knowing what to do, Alison hit the computer's Return key a few times, as her magazine article suggested would sometimes establish a connection with a remote computer.

The screen changed again.

```
Welcome to SwampLand. Enter your handle or the NUP.
```

Alison didn't understand what the hell was going on, but she had Rob's instructions. NUP? Okay, no problem. Alison typed in "Acidjazz." The computer immediately came back at her:

```
That is an unrecognized name. Enter your handle or
the NUP.
```

Alison typed in "Acidjazz" again. The computer flew back:

```
Illegal logon attempt.
```

The screen cleared, and Alison heard a dial tone. The damn remote computer had hung up on her.

She'd try it again. Alison went through the same steps, the same dialing sequence, got a handshake with the other system, but in the end the remote computer dumped her again.

"Fuck you, too," she said. Asshole computer. She knew she shouldn't be taking it personally, but she was being told she wasn't worthy — by a damn machine!

Or maybe the NUP was no good. Rob said the NUP changed from week to week. She'd give Rob a call. Maybe he knew something.

She picked up the phone handset at the computer and called Rob. Miraculously, he was at home. And having a party, judging from the throb of George Clinton's funk music pounding in the background.

"Hey, it's me," Alison said.

"Hey, kiddo! Wazzup?"

He definitely was partying. "It sounds like you're having a great Friday night."

"All work and no play. You know how that goes."

Alison laughed. "I won't keep you, but I'm trying to get into the bulletin board you told me about. Problem is, I keep getting thrown out. I think that the N-U-P—"

"That's NUP like 'noop.' You know, New User Password."

"Oh! Right. Anyway, I think the password has expired, or something, and I was wondering if you could get me the new one."

"Ali, I doubt it's old. I got that three days ago. There's some more six-packs on the fire escape."

"Huh?"

"Sorry. You sure you're inputting the password right?"

"Give me a little credit, Rob."

"The system might be case-sensitive."

"Come again?"

"You know, it might read upper case and lower case differently. Try again, and type in all caps, and all lower case, and variations on that, OK? Look I gotta go. Send me an email and let me know what happens."

"Okay. Thanks, Rob," she said to a dead phone line.

All right. Case-sensitive. Alison felt a rush at the challenge of getting into the remote computer that had so ungraciously snubbed her.

"I've got you now, you little twit computer. I'm busting in," she said. "Nobody and no thing is keeping me out."

She hit the redial key on the computer, and the modem obligingly beeped out the series of tones to connect her to the BBS.

```
Welcome to SwampLand. Enter your handle or the NUP.
```

I'm ready for you this time, she thought. Alison input the password with all capital letters. ACIDJAZZ.

```
That is an unrecognized name. Enter your handle or
the NUP.
```

This time she'd try all lowercase letters. Alison typed "acidjazz." The screen chirped at her, and the graphic image of a bubbling swamp filled her screen. Bloopy, gurgling noises provided online background music.

"Weird. Very weird," Alison said. The screen welcomed her to SwampLand.

She was instructed to enter her name. Easy enough. She typed in "Alison Crane." And her handle. That must mean her screen name. Alison typed in "AliCat." Next, a password. How about *bengoshi*, Japanese for "lawyer," a hard-to-guess foreign word, like that worthless customer service rep at World NetLink had recommended.

The screen scrolled with text laying out the bulletin boards' Terms of Service. Among the other items, all users had to attest to the fact that they were in no way, shape or form employed by, connected to, or affiliated with any law enforcement agency.

Does being a member of the State Bar of California count? Who cared, just a bunch of boilerplate legalese. Alison entered her agreement to abide by the Terms of Service.

The SwampLand BBS computer asked for her phone number for

verification before her membership would be complete. That was a problem. Alison didn't want anyone calling her at home in Tokyo. Maybe she should put in Rob's phone number. No, that wouldn't work. The BBS said that the phone verification was immediate. After she typed in her phone number, the computer would call her right back to confirm.

Tokyo home phone number it was. Boy, would they be surprised to get have an overseas call-back for a new BBS member.

She input her home phone number in Tokyo. The computer shot back at her:

```
Welcome, AliCat. You are now a registered member of
SwampLand, subject to phone verification. We will
now disconnect and call you back. Please leave your
modem on.
```

The modem connection was broken, and the screen turned gray. As promised.

Within one minute the phone rang. The computer modem picked up automatically, restarting the monitor. The handshake graphic appeared again. Her screen informed her:

```
SwampLand membership complete. Welcome, AliCat. When
you call back, you will have full access and online
privileges.
```

Then the modem connection was broken again.

Alison redialed the SwampLand BBS yet again, entered her handle and password as instructed. Her password was accepted. She was in the club. And from all the hoops she'd had to jump through to join the club — referrals, passwords, verifications — she felt like she'd been accepted into an exclusive secret society like Skull & Bones or the Masons.

The computer screen flashed an exhaustive directory of files she could access. But where would the encryption software be? The "Mac Files" area sounded promising, so she entered and saw a lengthy list of files available for downloading.

SwampLand maintained quite a catalog. The word processing sub-directory included Microsoft Word, WordPerfect. In the business area she saw Works, Excel, PageMaker.

She remembered seeing those same programs for sale at a computer shop in Akihabara. For sale at a hefty price. But here at SwampLand could she download the programs for free? Or maybe you had to give a credit card number. Or maybe it was there for the taking … Not her concern. See no evil, hear no evil. She was looking for her encryption software, so she moved along.

Alison browsed through the file directory but could not find her program. In the midst of her fumbling around, her computer screen beeped, and, letter by letter, a message appeared.

```
"Hey there, AliCat. You're new and it looks like
you're having some trouble. Can I help?"
```

What or who was that? She typed back:

```
"Who are you?"
"I'm one of the SysOps for the board. RoadKill's my
name. I happened to be here and saw you join up.
What're you trying to do?"
"I'm looking for a file to download. I can't seem to
find it in the directory."
"What's the file called?"
"FYEO. An encryption program."
```

"Cool, we got it. You want to send someone some GIFs, or something? It's really good for that."

"What?"

"Some JPEGs, GIFs, you know, pictures. Forget it. Since I'm here, I'll just shoot the file over to you."

"Sounds great."

"OK, all you need to do is set your computer ready to download, and I'll send it over. Ready?"

"Yes. Thanks, Roadkill."

"De nada. Here we go. Just lie back, spread 'em, and enjoy it."

Alison watched as her computer screen flipped to a picture of an hourglass.

File download: FYEO, 156.8 MB.

She watched as little computer-generated grains of sand fell through the hour glass, filling it up.

Receiving an unknown file from an unknown man. She assumed he was a man. Her computer was wide open and receiving whatever wad he was shooting her way. Waiting for the hourglass to fill, she felt like she was having unsafe sex with a stranger. "Lie back, spread 'em and enjoy it," he'd said. He didn't have to be so crude.

But she needed the file. Having the software meant she could keep that online creep out of her life. So, she would lie back and spread 'em. Just this once. Boys with their fucking toys.

After a few minutes of staring at falling sands, Alison got on the floor to do some yoga stretches. In the middle of the cobra pose, the computer spoke.

```
File received.
```

Alison smiled. Good job, Crane. You have the makings of an official techno-nerd.

20

Alison was itching to install the FYEO encryption software she'd downloaded, but she had to wait until Monday before she had access to Charles' computer again. Sitting at the monitor to his computer, she caught sight of the installation icon for the encryption software. Had Charles noticed it? He hadn't mentioned anything. But once she installed the software on Charles' computer, would he know it was there, that it was running on his machine? How could she hide it?

What a bother trying to cover up her tracks and slink around in her own home. She was a grown woman. She could get her own damn computer. And she wouldn't have to give a hoot what Charles had to say about how untouchable and off-limits his exclusive toys were.

Computers were expensive, but it would be a tax-deductible expense. And having her own computer would certainly make it easier for her to finish her research for Green Space.

Alison made up her mind to get with the times and buy her own laptop. If the Gods of Plastic were willing.

She combed through her purse, pulled out her wallet and dialed the emergency number on the back of her Visa card. When quizzed by the customer service agent, she rattled off her account number, mother's maiden name and the last four digits of her social security number. Yes, she was Alison Crane.

"I want to check my available credit. I'm in Tokyo, and I need to know how much room I have—"

"Ms. Crane, we haven't gotten a payment from you in the past two months."

Alison swallowed. An everyday detail she'd overlooked while trying to adjust to her new life in Japan. "I'm sorry. I'd meant to set up my account to automatically pay out of my savings account, but I guess I forgot."

"There's a hold on your card, Ms. Crane. You can't use it until you make the minimum payment past due. With late fees with accrued interest." The card service rep seemed to enjoy berating Alison in his nasally whine.

"I'll fax you the authorization form. You can see I've got some money in my savings account. Can't you transfer the money out of my savings account?" Alison kicked herself for forgetting to send in that damn form.

"Your account is delinquent, Ms. Crane."

Alison was getting nowhere with the pissant's red tape. "May I speak to your supervisor, please?"

"One moment." Alison was subjected to golden oldies on-hold music while Visa dug up another body to stand between her and her money. Or, rather, her lack of money.

"This is Ms. Wright. How can I help you, Ms. Crane?"

"I'm in Tokyo, and I was trying to figure out how much money I had on my Visa card, and I completely forgot to fax back to you the auto-payment authorization, so I'm behind in my payments." The words tumbled out as Alison tried to appeal to the supervisor.

"We haven't received any payment for the past two billing cycles."

"I know but I'd like you to pull the funds out of my savings account to bring me back up to date. And you can check my savings account balance with your bank. I have enough to cover it."

"There's nothing I can do without written authorization. If you send us the form, it will only take three or four business days."

Four business days in the States. That translated to maybe a week in Japan, given the time difference. Getting her credit card rehabilitated with enough capacity to buy even a cheap computer wasn't going to happen anytime soon. And she wanted her own computer now.

But how much would a computer cost? Especially with the added inflation of buying anything in Tokyo. Alison steeled herself and raided her stash of Green Space retainer money. She counted out twenty 10,000 yen bills and stuffed the cash in her wallet. Heaven help her if Ms. Yamada wasn't satisfied with her work product and wanted the money back.

01101110 01100101 01100001 01110010

Kinokuniya. Tokyo's answer to Barnes & Noble, Borders and the local library. A high-rise bookstore that was chronically crowded with ravenous eyeballs hunting for new reading material to devour.

Alison was amazed by the amount of printed matter the Japanese consumed. A nation of readers. Standing on the train, waiting for the bus, between slurps in the noodle shop. Everyone traveled with something to read.

Charles had told her that Japanese kids studied from first grade to senior year in high school to learn the 1,800 basic Chinese kanji characters they'd need to know just to be able to read the daily newspaper. Yet with a literary rate of 99 percent, virtually everyone in Japan could read. How did things go so wrong in the States?

She and about ten other people fought their way onto Kinokuniya's elevator. Alison was thankful that she could read the only part of the store's floor directory written in English. Seventh floor, English-language books, magazines and newspapers. Ah, literacy.

The door opened on the seventh floor, and Alison joined the homesick foreigners trying to stay current with local U.S. newspapers air-delivered to Tokyo, Japanese wanting to read classic English novels, and students of the Japanese language who were adding to their collection of books, tapes and kanji dictionaries.

Alison snagged a shopping basket and cruised by the shelves packed with Japanese language study materials. One text that promised she could "Read Kanji Today!" Alison rolled her eyes. Hollow promises.

If only she could read written Japanese kanji today or any day. Alison was still plowing through the two other phonetic alphabets that comprised modern Japanese — hiragana and katakana. Still, no matter how she cut it, she was functionally illiterate. And after a few months in Tokyo — not being able to read product labels in the grocery store, having no idea what train she was getting on — she understood too well the frustration and vulnerability of illiteracy.

Holding the kanji text, she thought of all of the language instruction materials she had purchased with the highest of intentions yet they remained virtually untouched on her shelf. Alison shrugged and added the kanji book to her shopping basket. Buying a new textbook was almost as good as actually learning the language.

Alison browsed through the bookstore shelves until she came to an area dedicated to computers. She leafed through a wide assortment of books about the internet and computer networks. Whereas just a few weeks ago, all of these book topics would have been Greek to her — or perhaps, more accurately, would be like kanji to her — now she could peruse the tables of contents and understand, at least conceptually, what the discussion was about.

She scanned book covers looking for information on online privacy protection, internet security systems, anything that might help her keep that creep out of her life. Not finding a single relevant book, she reminded herself that she had come to the bookstore to get information about how to buy a computer. She walked on to the magazine area.

Customers reading magazines crowded the periodicals row. In Japan no one cared if you stood and read an entire magazine without buying it. The economics didn't make sense to Alison, but she enjoyed being able to dip in and out of the latest issue of *Newsweek* without paying the shocking price of a periodical that had been flown halfway across the planet.

Alison put back the *Vogue* she'd been leafing through and found what she had come for — a Macintosh computer buyer's guide. Megahertz comparisons, RAM upgrades. What the hell were they talking about? She just wanted a nice little computer, something cheap and small. She mentally ballparked a yen conversion for the dollar prices quoted in the magazine. Ouch. She'd definitely be tapping the Green Space booty to finance a purchase.

While thumbing through the magazine, she spotted a little flyer taped to the magazine rack. The flyer announced a Macintosh User Group meeting — "All Welcome" — at 8 o'clock Thursday night at the Omote-Sando Kaikan. English.

A Mac User Group? That could be interesting. She pulled a notepad from her purse and copied down the information.

"Don't waste your time with that MUG."

Startled, Alison looked up from her notepad. A young guy in a wheelchair parked in front of the magazines next to her. With long limbs, the gangly guy had a rubber-banded ponytail tucked into the collar of his army combat jacket. Stickers with skulls and lightning bolts plastered his chair.

"Waste time with what?" Alison asked.

"That user group. Don't bother. A bunch of fresh-off-the-plane types whining about the bad internet connections from Tokyo. Newbies who don't know shit." He continued reading his magazine.

"So you're a Mac hotshot, huh?"

"Wouldn't touch anything else."

"Maybe you can help me."

The guy whirled his wheelchair around, looked at Alison and grinned. A dimple appeared in his right cheek. "I'm here to help," he said.

Alison smiled back. "I'm shopping for a Mac. On a budget. I'm not looking for anything fancy. I just need something to get online. Do you know a place where I can get a good price?"

"Hey, you're asking the right guy. Would you be interested in an experienced machine?"

"Experienced?"

"Yeah, used. I can help you get a good deal on a gently used Mac. No problem." The guy smiled at Alison and looked genuinely interested in trying to be of assistance.

"I just started getting online — I guess that makes me a newbie, right?"

The guy made a face. "No offense," he said.

"None taken. Anyway, I've been borrowing my friend's Mac to get on World NetLink. Do you know it?"

The guy clicked his tongue in disdain. "NutLink? Of course I know it. Do I use it? Hell the fuck no. A rip-off, it holds your hand if you're nervous on the net."

"You're looking at Nervous Nellie."

The guy's face lit up with his lopsided dimpled grin. He might be kind of cute. If he combed his hair, shaved, got some new clothes. Some clean clothes. The Sixties are over, man.

"I'll tell you what I got," the displaced hippie guy began. "She's a rebuilt laptop, got an OK hard drive, but she's loaded with RAM. Plus, and here's the beauty part, she's got a built-in modem."

"Meaning..."

"You plug in your cable and get online."

Lots of RAM was good, Alison had learned from her reading. But what would she do with a built-in modem, whatever that meant? "Sounds OK, but how much are you asking?" Alison braced herself.

"Go man."

Alison counted to herself in Japanese. "That's fifty thousand yen, right?"

Jed nodded. "A steal."

Alison mentally calculated the dollar conversion. "Sounds too cheap to be true. This didn't fall off the back of a truck, or anything ..."

The guy snorted. "I can have her here in half an hour, show her to you, put her through her paces. You don't like, you don't buy."

"Yeah, but—"

"Meet me in the *kissaten* downstairs in half an hour, have the money in case you're interested, and we can go from there."

The guy looked honest enough. And he was letting her test drive the computer before she had to part with her precious cash. What did she have to lose?

"By the way, I'm Alison. I didn't catch your name."

"Just call me Jed. Short for Jedi. That's my handle," he explained.

"All right then. Jed," Alison laughed, going along with it. Whatever.

"See you in thirty," Jed said and rolled to the elevator.

Alison paid for the basketful of texts and magazines and waited while the store clerk wrapped each book with a Kinokuniya-branded paper cover. Was the additional cover meant to protect the book or to keep out prying eyes? Maybe both.

She rode down to the first basement and ordered an American coffee at the *kissaten* coffee shop. Alison found it amusing that the Japanese called "American coffee" the watered-down version of the caffeinated battery acid they considered a regular cup o' joe. She found an empty table relatively far away from a pack of teenage girls fouling the air with their cigarette smoke.

Two cups of American coffee later, Jed appeared. He pulled a PowerBook computer out of the Maruzen bookstore bag in his lap. The computer's plastic case bore a skull sticker. "Jimi Lives!" Jed booted up the Mac. "Check out this speed. She really rips."

The computer booted up and icons marched across the bottom of the screen.

"What's that?" Alison pointed to the lineup of the logos.

"Software. She's fully loaded. Latest versions, too. There's FileMaker, Photoshop, SimCity. Check it out." Jed showed off the Mac's bells and whistles, most of which Alison didn't grasp. But she clearly understood the computer's most important feature. 50,000 yen and it was all hers.

"How much for the software?"

"Huh?"

"You said fifty thousand for the Mac, but how much for the software?"

"Why don't you pay me what I paid for it."

"So how much total?"

"Fifty thousand."

"But then—"

"Like I said, you pay what I paid."

Alison decided to drop it. She didn't want to know the details. She ran her hand over the laptop's sleek gray glossiness. "Hello, my little friend. I think we're going to get along just fine."

"So it's a deal," Jed asked.

"Yes, indeed." Alison counted out five 10,000 yen notes from her wallet. She'd have to raid her Green Space stash again soon, but this computer was a steal. Maybe a literal steal… Alison tried not to dwell on it. "Can I get a receipt?" she asked. "For taxes."

"A receipt?" Jed shifted in his chair. "Sure, I guess. What do you want it to say?"

"Here, I'll write it." Alison pulled a notepad from her bag and jotted down something she hoped would satisfy the IRS. She handed the receipt over to Jed and he signed it. "J. Knight." Alison hoped the document wouldn't have to withstand an IRS audit. She put the receipt in her wallet.

"Thanks, Jed. There's one other thing you might be able to help me with."

"Shoot."

"I've been getting all these obnoxious messages sent to me online. Anonymous messages. It's really a pain, and the network administrators say there's nothing I can do since I don't know who the sender is."

Jed smirked. "Network admins aren't for shit."

"I downloaded some encryption software, but the guy still lobs these messages at me. Sometimes it makes my computer crash."

"That's so fucked. But there's lots you can do to protect yourself. Depends on how far you want to go."

"What do you mean?"

Jed cracked each knuckle of each hand, pulling his fingers so far backward it was obvious that he was double-jointed. "There's a guy who sends you messages over the net, and you don't know who he is."

"Right, but somehow he seems to know things about me."

"Okay, so let's say this guy has access to some equipment. When he sends messages, are there any tags on them?"

"Tags?"

"You know, routing info about how it got to you?"

"No, there's nothing. Just the message."

"Shit." Jed started knuckle-cracking again. "Okay, we can go at it another way. Have you done a trace on your phone system? This guy might be accessing from NutLink, but he could be jacking in from another net altogether. Or even be doing a live feed if he's close enough."

The thought of some person taking such pains to pry into her personal life sent a shiver through Alison. Not so much a shiver of fear as of anger.

"Please translate that into English, OK," she said. "Assume I know nothing, and you'd be pretty close to right."

Jed laughed. "Okay, no problem. It's like this: A lot of computer networks are connected together. And even if they aren't exactly connected, people who know how — the real bitheads — can get into one system from another."

"Like the hackers, right?"

"Yeah," Jed nodded. "That's one way your buddy could be talking to you without leaving a trail. But here's another way. He might be busting into your modem communications. Kind of like a phone tap."

"You mean he could bug my computer line?" asked Alison.

"Kind of like that. And, if he's really good, he could even send messages undetected."

"Wow. How could he do that?"

Jed shrugged. "Listen in on the noise — the electromagnetic noise

— from the monitor. Patch in that way. But he'd have to be real close to do it. I mean, close to your computer."

"How close are we talking about?" Alison sat back. It had never occurred to her that her internet stalker could be physically close to her. Her lip curled with distaste.

"Depends, but they'd have to be within, say, about a hundred meters of your computer."

"So you mean the guy harassing me might be one of my neighbors?"

"Might be. Or he could have a portable remote location. You know, transmitting from a car, a cell phone. Wouldn't matter so long as he was close to your computer."

Her stalker could be right next door? Too creepy. "Does this guy know where I live?"

Jed's head was lowered in thought. "You don't have to sit there and take it," he said. "There are countermoves you can make." The way Jed was abusing his digits, Alison predicted arthritis in his future.

"Countermoves?" The idea of empowerment, of not being a defenseless target, excited her. "What would I have to do?"

"You'll need to invest in some hardware. First, you can get a little box called a Tracer. It'll tell you if anyone is listening in on your modem line."

"How's that?"

"If the guy is doing a near-range feed, a light will go on. You'll know someone's busting your EM noise."

"I have no clue what you're talking about, but OK. What else?"

"With the Tracer, you'll know if someone's listening in. But what you really want to know is who's calling you, where they're calling from, right?"

"Right."

"So you can run some software that'll tell you the access point for any message sent to you."

"And that means—"

"That means you could tell how the phreak — spelled with a 'ph' — was cutting into the network. You'd know where he was calling from."

Blankness registered on Alison's face. She shook her head and shrugged with palms up. Jed kept at it. "You've heard of Caller ID, right?"

"Sure. If you have Caller ID on your phone, it tells you what phone number is calling you." Alison was glad to be back on terra firma.

"This software works on the same principle. It can give you a handshake ID of the computer calling you. Just like Caller ID. Problem is, for the software to be able to analyze the handshake data, you have to be receiving a direct message from the caller, not just email. You with me?"

"Yeah, I think so." Alison was somewhere, but not "with him," that was for damn sure.

"With the software running, you'll be able to know the phreak's phone number if he's calling in directly, or at least the IP address of his computer network. Now your guy sounds a little bit sophisticated, your basic wirehead. So I'm guessing he's calling in from another network, not direct from his own phone number or from NutLink."

"And so—"

"If he's calling from another system, that system computer would have a node user log of who was online and which number they'd called into at any time of day or night. So you'd know where the guy had called from and what time. Then if you get the system node user logs, you know what the guy's phone number or IP address is. Then, all—"

Alison raised her hand to ask a question. "Hold on, Jed. I need to write all this down." She pulled the notepad and pen from her purse. "You said something about logs?"

"Yeah, the node user logs. If the guy is calling from outside."

Alison jotted in her notebook. "Got it. But what if he's not calling from outside?"

"If he's calling direct from NutLink, even better. The software will tell you his phone number, and you could get an ID that way. Assuming you want to play it out that way." Jed's fingers twitched.

"I don't understand this completely, but at least it looks like there's a glimmer of hope," Alison said. "So what should I do first? What's my next move?"

"You gotta gear up. The Tracer hardware you can get in Akihabara. Lots of places. Just plug it into your computer and the wall. When the red light goes on, you've got company."

Alison took notes. "Sounds straightforward enough," said Alison. "What about the software?"

"I'd go with PeepHole."

"PeepHole? That's software?"

"Yeah."

"Great. Where do I get it?"

Jed pulled at his goatee. "Now that's a little harder."

"Why's that?"

"Let's just say that certain interests don't want to see it freely distributed." Jed wiggled his eyebrows.

Alison set down her notepad. "You mean it's hacker software?"

"You might say that."

Alison shook her head and laughed. "I can't picture myself as a hacker. Not this newbie. I'll find some solution, something this side of the law. But thanks a lot, Jed. You saved me a bundle."

"No problem. Always ready to help out a fellow *gaijin.*" He pulled a card out of his jacket. "Here's my *meishi*. Email me, let me know how it goes."

Alison returned home, happily toting her new purchase. A better bargain couldn't be had. She hoped she hadn't been had, either.

With her user's guide open, Alison plugged in her laptop computer and read how to copy the FYEO file from Charles' computer hard drive onto her new laptop. She dragged the FYEO icon on Charles' computer desktop to the trash. Gone without a trace.

Alison loaded the disk containing the FYEO software onto her computer. She'd be ready to take off as soon as she found a phone jack. She searched for a suitable work space and found a jack right by the dining room table. It would do perfectly. She cleared a space on the table and set up shop.

Alison booted up her network communication software and punched in the access number for World NetLink. The computer's modem sounded a dial tone, then emitted a series of beeps. Music to her ears.

Her little PowerBook lit up with the NetLink welcome screen. She entered her user name and password, and was greeted as a recognized member. She was one of the cool kids.

Next was uploading the FYEO encryption software. She navigated over to the software area of the network, and read the online instructions for sending software to another user by email. Sending the encryption file to Kiyoshi, she attached a little note:

> Hi, Kiyoshi: This software should solve our problems with the Peeping Tom. I made a key for our messages and uploaded it for you. If you run the software and use the key, no one will be able to read our messages. See you at 5.

Alison caressed her PowerBook in her lap. Things were going to work out all right.

21

"Are you a complete fucking idiot? You short it, you buy it, you transfer it. Leave the rest to me. Make sure to use the goddamn street name. Got it? The Hang Sen is closed on Tuesday, so run it through SIMEX. Check the Singapore calendar."

Charles slammed down the phone. "Damned fool," he muttered.

Charles' shouting had awakened Alison. She looked at the clock: 5:15 a.m. It must be New York. She couldn't imagine what was going on to get Charles so worked up, but it certainly wasn't the first time.

01010100 01101111 01101011 01111001 01101111 00101110

"Sorry I was late today."

"No problem. How've you been?"

"Busy researching environmental organizations in Asia."

"Are there a lot of them?"

"Yeah, I was surprised. The other day I visited a group right here in Tokyo. Green Space. Have you heard of them?"

"I don't know very much about the group, but I know the founder's family."

“Yamada-san? I had lunch with her.”

“Yamada Yuko and I were at high school together. The international school in Kobe.”

“No kidding? Small world.”

“Kobe is a big port city. Taisho is the Yamada family business. They build ships. And other things.”

“Yuko Yamada asked me to help with their website. She’s impressive.”

“Please go slow before getting involved with them. There is more to the Yamada organization than you might realize.”

“You’re sounding very mysterious, Kiyoshi. What’s the deal?”

“They are not popular with everyone.”

Alison thought of the guards posted outside the entrance to Green Space. All kinds of groups doing the right thing needed security. Planned Parenthood, Greenpeace, NAACP, for starters.

“What do you mean, Kiyoshi?”

“Just don’t move too quickly with them.”

Why was Kiyoshi so put off by Yamada’s group? Maybe Yuko had broken his poor little high school heart when they were kids in Kobe.

“I FOUND YOU! THERE’S NO HIDING FROM ME!!!!!”

“Alison, did you see that?”

“Yes. He’s back.”

"It looks that way."

"But you know, I don't think he can read our messages since they're encrypted. He probably can only tell that we're online, but he can't read what we're saying."

"You think so?"

"Hello, you weirdo creep. Can you read this? Is our encryption software working? Are you there? I don't think he can read this, Kiyoshi."

"Let's hope you're right, Alison."

"ALISON ALI ALISON. DO YOU MISS ME? I VISIT NISHI AZABU. YOU LIVE IN NISHI AZABU. I SEE YOU."

A woman's voice sounded through the computer speakers. "No. Don't! Stop!"

"Kiyoshi, I'm getting spooked by this. Let's log off, OK? I want to contact the system operators here, see if there's anything else to do."

"Of course. See you tomorrow."

Alison entered the World NetLink tech support area and initiated a real-time online chat with a network administrator. It wasn't as good as a phone call, but it would have to do. She could type fast.

"I have been having constant problems with annoying, anonymous messages and communications being sent to me. I tried changing my screen name, encoding my messages, but still the harassment persists."

The network administrator replied.

"Hello, TokyoAli. I'm sorry about the problems you're having. If you know the user name of the person sending you the messages, you can block email transmissions from them. Good luck!"

Good luck?! What was this, a lottery? Alison fired back.

"I have zero idea of who this guy is. That's my problem. This creep seems to know what I look like, even where I live. Do you release personal information about your online users?"

"Not at all. As explained in the Terms of Service, all of the membership information you provide when you join World NetLink is considered confidential. But occasionally we provide members' profiles to a select group of marketing companies."

Alison had spent too much time in law school not to recognize legalese double-talk.

"You mean you sell personal information about WNL users to outside companies?"

"It helps keep down user costs."

"What kind of information?"

"Names, addresses, clickstreams usually."

"Clickstreams? What's that?"

"The path the user navigates through the network, the areas they like to visit on WNL as they click on the mouse. If a user doesn't want to participate in our marketing program, they can opt out of it."

Yeah, if they even know about the program.

"Consider me opted out."

She exited the chat.

What nerve World NetLink had selling personal information. WNL had details about its users that more than marketing companies would be eager to know. Mr. Smith spends five hours each week in the gay men's chat room. Ms. Jones regularly posts questions in the substance abusers message center. Mrs. Doe posts to the battered spouse help board every month. All of it was nobody's business but their own.

Alison was sure the online users assumed they were as anonymous as they wanted to be. Now she knew better. But the damage had been done. The creepy freak knew her name, knew what she looked like, knew where she lived. But she still hadn't the foggiest idea who he was.

01000101 01101101 01100001 01101001 01101100

Bent over his computer keyboard, his two index fingers pounded in commands. He sat up, looked at his monitor and examined the results. *Kuso*! Shit! He was having more trouble than usual breaking into this software.

None of his favorites in his digital bag of tricks was doing the job. His picklock programs, his de-encryption programs, his key code emulators, and his link-level decryptors all failed at breaching the FYEO encryption software that American bitch was using for her messages.

Kuso! Did she think she could outsmart him? Stupid foreign cow. She'd learn.

This little roadblock she'd set up was making things even more interesting. Teased his anticipation. But, of course, in the end, he'd take her down. She'd join his collection, just like all the others. It was inevitable. But he appreciated a good challenge. She was working hard to play the game, make it fun for him. He liked her spirit. Just a little roadblock.

He closed his eyes and sat back in his chair, scanning his brain for another way in. There had to be a way to get in. If he could completely sidestep the encryption process, if he could intercept her transmissions direct from the terminal, that would solve all of his problems. But how the fuck could he do that? Think. Think.

Frustrated by this rare experience of being shut out by a computer, he decided to call his favorite phone-sex line. A good jerking-off would take his mind off of things until he figured out a way to hack the encryption program.

He rooted under a pile of discarded Styrofoam instant ramen noodle bowls that had been tossed short of his trash can and dug out a cell phone. He hit the speed dial, and the phone-sex line's computerized operator offered him a menu of people eager to talk with him. Nymphomaniac housewives. High school girls sitting on the toilet. Naked elementary school girls in their bedrooms. Quite the smorgasbord.

When prompted, he punched in a credit card number — some dumb fuck's stolen JCB card number — and entered the code to be connected to an English-speaking foreign woman under thirty years old. Nothing was as relaxing as hearing a foreign bitch tell him how badly she wanted to lick his balls and rub his sticky *zamen* on her cunt.

"Hello, there," a woman said. "I'm Cassidy." Her breathy voice sounded like a teenager's. A young Marilyn Monroe. This would be great. He cradled the phone between his shoulder and ear while he unzipped his trousers. "How can I make you feel good?" Cassidy asked.

"You can suck my dick, taste my come." He reached across his desk and slid a box of tissues closer.

"You got it. Lie back. Close your eyes. Can you feel my tongue circling, exploring your—"

The phone line went dead.

Kuso! Shit. Had that bitch hung up on him? When he was spending as much money as he was on her services? Somebody's money, anyway.

He redialed the phone sex line. His cell phone didn't connect to Cassidy's erection-saving purr, but instead to the muffled voices of two men.

Kuso! The fucking phone was always picking up somebody's connection. He repeatedly poked the redial button, but he couldn't get rid of the two guys. It was getting impossible to get a clear line in Tokyo. Too many cell phones, too much electronic noise in the air.

He jumped from his chair. "*Atta*!" he shouted. "That's it! Got you, you bitch." He had found his way in.

22

Flue-gas desulfurization in Laos.

Alison yawned, added the article to her list for Green Space's website and pushed back from the computer. She flopped onto the living room sofa and turned on the TV.

The Japanese newscasters' noisy badinage blared through the room. Alison picked up the remote and switched sound bands. An English-language interpreter delivered the newscast in an efficient, but slightly stilted, manner.

Japan's governing body, the Diet, announced campaign reform. An agricultural trade mission from the U.S. would arrive next week. The police were widening their search for the missing English teacher from Canada, and the teacher's school was offering a reward for information. Iranian workers camped out in Ueno Park were being deported for overstaying their visa.

Alison stiffened as if she had been shocked by a live electrical wire. She sprang from the sofa, dashed into the bedroom, and dug out her passport from the nightstand drawer. The pages seem to stick together as she flipped through the pages looking for the entry permit into Japan. Shit. Her visa had expired two weeks earlier.

How the hell could she have been so forgetful? Lawyers knew better than to miss deadlines. Was she losing her edge already?

She'd been absorbed in her work for Green Space. And that online creep had been a major distraction. Kiyoshi had been a distraction, too. A good kind of distraction.

But those Iranian workers had overstayed their visas, and now they were being deported. What would happen to her?

Things in Japan weren't exactly going the way she'd hoped, but she wasn't ready to leave yet. Especially not because of some legal technicality.

And she had to complete the research assignment for Yamada-san. Professional ethics dictated she finish the work she'd been paid to do, work that her client was relying on her for. Or return the money. Except that Alison had already spent a huge chunk of her advance on that computer.

Alison's stomach felt heavy, as if she had eaten a lead ball. She was fucked. What to do?

Charles would be able to help her. He would know how people dealt with overstaying their visa. Surely it wasn't uncommon. Not such a big deal. She called Charles at his office.

"Charles, it's me."

"I'm really busy right now. Can this wait?"

"I'm being deported!" Maybe overstating it a bit, but she needed to get Charles' attention.

"What?"

"I mean, my visa's expired, and I—"

"You didn't write the date on a calendar? Not a smart move."

"I thought I'd call the embassy, and—"

"The embassy can't help you. You're going to have to go down to the immigration office, fall on your sword, beg for mercy. Did you get a re-entry permit stamp back in the States like I told you?"

"I called the consulate in San Francisco, and they said that Americans don't need visa stamps anymore. Just a passport."

"You don't need a stamp, but if you have a re-entry permit, you can renew it and extend the time you can stay. You're going to have to go to immigration."

The leaden weight in Alison's stomach felt heavier, like gravity bearing down against escape velocity. Another hoop to jump through to justify her existence in Japan. "Will you go with me? I don't know about the laws here, and you can speak Japanese."

Charles hesitated. "Look, I can't get away from the floor. Besides everyone at immigration speaks English. Just explain to them what happened."

"Okay," Alison said, disappointed that she was being left to fend for herself and that Charles didn't seem too concerned. "They deported some Iranians. They won't arrest me or deport me, will they?"

Charles laughed. "No way. You're an American. They won't be booting you out."

"Are you sure you can't get away to meet me there?" Alison hated the whining tone she heard in her own voice, but the image of the Iranian visa violators being hauled off by the police stuck in her head.

"You'll be fine. I promise. And I'll take you out to dinner after, OK?"

"All right," Alison grumbled. Pouting didn't become her, but she couldn't help herself.

"We can have some people over this weekend," Charles said. "Nothing elaborate, just a little get-together. Take your mind off of this visa mess. What do you say?"

Alison was still sulking over feeling abandoned in her time of need. "I don't know, Charles. How many people are you talking about?"

"Small. Around fifteen people."

"When do you want to have this soirée?"

"What about Saturday? Short notice, but it'll be casual, like an open house."

"Oh, all right, what the hell. But I don't want everybody to be from your office. I want to invite some of my friends, too."

"But you don't have any — I mean, sure, invite whoever you want. Gotta go. Talk to you tonight."

Alison hated the thought of having to entertain all of Charles' work colleagues. If Charles wanted a party, she'd be damned if she wasn't going to enjoy it, too. She'd invite everyone she knew in Tokyo. She'd invite Ms. Yamada. She'd even invite Jed. And why not invite Kiyoshi, she mused devilishly. Running through her own mental guest list made her feel better.

She could straighten out her visa trouble tomorrow. And if she had any problems at immigration, she'd go to the American Embassy. They could help her. It wasn't like she was a criminal or anything.

23

Alison woke up early and taxied to the immigration office in Otemachi. It was first thing in the morning, but already a United Nations of languages and peoples spilled out of the huge complex. Despite the wide variety of nationalities represented, everyone's face wore the same expression. Worried concern tinged with fear.

Alison maneuvered her way inside to an information counter staffed by an older Japanese man. His mouth looked pinched with the taste of impatience, as if he were barely able to endure the remaining days until his retirement.

"Hello," Alison began, "I need to speak to someone about a visa problem, and—"

"Room 7," the man snapped. He waved to summon the next person in line.

Alison knew when she'd been dismissed. She moved to the side to consider the next step in the visa scavenger hunt. Room 7.

She walked further into the lobby of the immigration office and saw a map. Room 7 was on the second floor, in the rear. She looked up the stairwell. A jumbled mass of people snaked along the hallway and crowded down the stairs.

Was that her line, the line to room 7? Couldn't be. Alison climbed up the steps, excusing herself as she pushed through the wall of waiting people.

Halfway up the staircase, Alison spied a twenty-something-year-old woman wearing Birkenstock sandals. The navy-blue passport stuffed in the back pocket of the woman's jeans was Alison's beacon. Chin to chest, the woman was engrossed in a paperback wrapped in Kinokuniya's signature paper.

Alison approached her. "Excuse me, are you an American?" Asking the obvious.

The young woman looked up and smiled broadly. "Born and bred!" A silver stud adorned her tongue.

Alison appreciated the Haight-Ashbury chic. "I'm trying to renew my visa and they told me to get in this line," Alison said. "Is this the right place?"

The woman laughed. Her stud glinted in the light. "If you're not here by eight o'clock, count on spending the day. Once I got here at nine and still didn't get through. Had to come back the next day and start all over again. Japanese efficiency, *neh*?"

"This is some kind of hell," Alison moaned.

"Hey, you want to get it done without coming back tomorrow, stand in line with me." The woman tugged Alison's sleeve and encouraged her to join the line. "I got here at a little after eight, so we should make it through." The woman held up crossed fingers and smiled at Alison. Did that stud in her tongue hurt?

Alison felt only a moment of guilt before cutting in the line to join her new friend.

"I really appreciate this. By the way, I'm Alison. Alison Crane."

"Hey. Zoe Brown. Originally from Albuquerque, now on my third year in Ogikubo."

"Nice to meet you, Zoe. Looks like we're going to be fast friends before the day is through."

Time crawled. A young Filipino woman stood behind Alison and Zoe. The woman carried an infant who wouldn't stop wailing. Alison prayed for someone to produce a pacifier to shut the kid up. Or an aspirin to give her nerves some relief.

The man in front of her lit up a cigarette, filling the already stuffy air with noxious tobacco fumes. Didn't he see the "No Smoking" signs?

Alison tapped the man on the shoulder. He turned his head and scowled. Pointing to the sign, Alison spoke slowly. "No smoking." She was sure the guy understood her, but he clicked through his teeth and went back to his nicotine. Asshole. Alison hoped a sadistic bureaucrat would snatch the cigarette out of his mouth and send him to the back of the line. Would serve him right.

Another hour dragged by, and the line barely inched forward. Alison felt sorry for the women whose small children were now fussy with boredom, hungry or had to go to the bathroom. Alison was all three. She stewed while the morning wore on.

At the stroke of noon the visa processing came to a complete halt. Lunch time.

Hundreds of anxious people had been standing, waiting for hours. No chairs, no break. Why couldn't the immigration office come up with extra workers to keep the line moving during lunch?

Alison tried to keep her temper in check. Charles had cautioned her to keep it together, be polite with the immigration officers no matter what. They held all the cards, controlled her fate. But she was getting hungry. And angry.

"I'm going to grab something to eat," Alison said to Zoe. "You want anything?"

Zoe shook her head. "I'm cool. Brought some *onigiri*. Want one?"

"Onigiri?"

"Rice balls. I got a shrimp and mayo and one with fish eggs."

Alison was hungry, but the combination of shrimp, mayo and cigarette smoke sounded like a recipe for nausea. "Thanks, but I'll see what I can find."

Zoe held Alison's place in line while Alison foraged for grub at the vending machines on the first floor. Lunch selections ranged from hot canned coffee to something labeled Pocari Sweat. Alison didn't even want to speculate as to what Pocari Sweat was. She dropped in coins and pressed the button for coffee. A delicious and nutritious meal.

Back in line, Alison said, "I'm going nuts here. I would've brought something to read if I'd known it'd take all day."

"I've got another book," Zoe said, reaching into her knapsack. "I haven't started it yet, but it looks pretty good."

"Thanks," Alison said. Embossed and gilded letters on the paperback's cover promised an epic story of true romance. Not Alison's usual reading material. She wished she had a Kinokuniya cover to hide the book jacket. Nevertheless, Alison was soon absorbed in the star-crossed exploits of the lowly but proud hero and the raven-haired patrician beauty. Anything to break the tedium.

By 3:15, Alison was shifting from foot to foot like a prizefighter getting ready to enter the ring. Her nerves were a hot jangle and she vowed never to fuck up and end up in visa trouble again. "I've got to get some air, Zoe. I'll be back in a few minutes."

"Sure, OK. But don't pull a disappearing act like that girl from Canada. You don't want to miss your place when we get to the front of the line."

"Don't worry, I'll be back."

Zoe pointed down the stairs to the most recent arrivals in line who were dripping wet. "Looks like you're gonna need an umbrella." Zoe pulled a collapsible plastic umbrella out of her knapsack and handed it to Alison.

"Thanks. You certainly came prepared."

Zoe laughed. "Hey, it's not my first time. Don't take too long."

With the prospect of being able to breathe fresh air, Alison practically skipped down the stairs. She fought her way through the waiting crowds and outside.

The outdoor air was chilly and wet but infinitely more pleasant than the smoke-and desperation-filled atmosphere of the immigration office. Alison opened the umbrella and took a tour around the neighborhood.

Gray sky, gray concrete sidewalks, gray raindrops pounding heavy enough to make you run for cover. Gray faces of office workers in gray suits ducked under umbrellas as they burst out of gray buildings. The white-noise blanket of falling rain muffled the traffic sounds on the rain-slicked streets.

Otemachi. The business center of Tokyo. So joyless, so grim. And the trees. How did they manage to grow? They looked like they were weary, tired of trying to be green. And without any nourishment or encouragement from the earth or the sky. Displaced and displayed for the convenience of people who barely noticed the trees trying so hard. Surviving in an inhospitable landscape, despite all. So much like her.

Snap out of it, Crane.

Alison took a deep breath in and blew it out hard. The melodrama of Zoe's paperback must have rubbed off on her. She stretched her arms wide and held her face to the sky. Dirty raindrops landed on her nose and dribbled between her lips. Communing with nature. Tokyo-style. It was time to go back.

Soggy but refreshed, Alison ducked under the umbrella and marched back to the immigration office.

The line of visa penitents had zipped forward while Alison was out hugging trees. She looked up the steps to the front of the line where Zoe was waving frantically, gesturing for Alison to hurry.

Alison joined Zoe at the front of the line and returned the umbrella. "Thanks for looking out for me," Alison said.

"We gotta hang together." Zoe reached into her knapsack and handed Alison her *meishi*. "Give me a call. If you're still in the country, that is." Seeing the frozen expression on Alison's face, Zoe added, "Just kidding."

"Right," Alison said, off-balance but recovering. "I don't have any business cards — any *meishi* — but I'll be in touch."

A light in the doorway of Room 7 flashed. The immigration officers were ready for their next supplicant. "See ya, Alison! Good luck!" Zoe marched down the row of counters and stopped at the booth of the officer whose light was flashing.

The signal in front of another counter flashed. It was Alison's turn to run the gauntlet. Alison's lucky draw was a heavy-set Japanese man who had bureaucrat stamped on his dour face.

"Passport." The immigration officer barely looked up from his desk area. Alison presented her passport, cleared her throat and launched into her saga.

"I seem to have a little problem here. You see, I inadvertently overstayed my visa. Only a few days. This is my first time in Japan, and I didn't get a visa stamp in the States because the consulate told me—"

"Your entry permit has expired. You are now in Japan in violation of our immigration laws."

"Yes, but as I was saying, I only just realized that—"

"What is it that you doing here?" The officer looked down on her past his ponderous jowls.

Alison hadn't anticipated that question. "Well, I — I'm here with a friend."

"You are a tourist?"

"Yes, that's right."

"How much money do you have with you?"

What the hell business was it of his? "I have enough to meet my needs." Alison was getting irritated at the inquisition. "I'd like to get an extension on my visa for a few more—"

"Are you looking for a job? English teacher? Hostess?"

Alison didn't know how to answer that question. She *was* looking for work, had in fact arguably taken work if you count the Green Space research assignment. But it wasn't a *job* job. She used a technique she had learned in law school: When you don't want to answer a question, don't answer the question.

"I'm an attorney." She stood up straighter. "I have money, and I'm here visiting a friend. I came here today in good faith to renew my visa. If you can't help me, I'd like to speak to your supervisor."

"Do you have an airplane ticket back to America?"

"I have an open ticket to San Francisco."

"Show it to me. And your bank statement."

What gall this guy had. "I didn't bring any of those documents with me. I can't see how that's relevant. I'd like to speak to your supervisor."

"You have violated the terms of your visa," the official said. He opened Alison's passport and stamped it. He handed her back her passport, turned on his counter light, and sat back with arms crossed, waiting for the next person in line.

Alison sighed loudly and snatched her passport up. Stepping away from the counter, she opened her passport to see what the officer had stamped in it. The jerk had given her five more days in Japan. And, with a bureaucratic coup de grace, he had stamped in fat red letters, "FINAL EXTENSION."

24

Alison stood dazed in the crowded hall of the office. She had to be out of the country in five days. The reality, surreal though it be, started to sink in.

She couldn't pick up and leave. Not in five days. Where would she go? She had work to do for Green Space. Surely there was a mistake. If she could speak to a supervisor. And why couldn't Charles be there when she really needed him. But she was on her own, and she needed help.

She mulled over her limited options and decided to try the people at the information desk downstairs.

Descending the staircase, Alison was appalled to see the line for Room 7 was as long as it had been when she first arrived. These folks will be back tomorrow. She sympathized with the late arrivals at the end of the line. Alison would've been among them if Zoe hadn't helped her out.

A young woman was on duty at the information desk. She looked fresh, not yet suffering from job burn-out. Alison did her best to look pleasant.

"I was wondering if you could help me," she said. "I've been trying to speak to someone about my visa problem, and—"

"Room 7," the woman responded with a touch of automaton in her voice. She couldn't have been on the job long enough to have turned into a bureaucratic robot already.

"I just got an extension on my visa, but there seems to be a mistake,"

Alison said. "I need to speak to a supervisor for the visa department. For Americans." Alison knew that the U.S. and Japan had a longtime love-hate relationship. But as allies, it would seem that Americans would get some kind of special dispensation when it came to visa infractions. Or was everyone treated with equal efficiency and given the boot, like the Iranian workers?

"There are no supervisors for visas. Please call your embassy if you need assistance." The woman reached under the information desk and handed Alison a sheet with a multilingual list of embassy addresses and telephone numbers.

"Thanks for all your help." Alison pocketed the sheet and stomped out of the building. At least it had stopped raining.

It wasn't 4:30 yet. If she called now, she could probably reach someone at the U.S. Embassy.

Alison stopped on the sidewalk, dug around in her purse, and pulled out her cell phone. She dialed the embassy number listed on the sheet of paper.

"United States Embassy," a woman's voice answered.

"Hello, I'm trying to get some help with a visa problem. I'm here in—"

"One moment please," the voice said, and Alison was switched over to background music, "Home on the Range." Alison could feel her neck muscles tightening and took a few deep yoga breaths.

"Lauren Lipton," announced a new woman on the phone. "How can I help you?"

The woman spoke with a punched staccato delivery. Alison recognized the type. A champion of cut-through-the-bullshit efficiency. The kind of person Alison needed to get her out of the visa mess.

Alison explained how her tourist visa had just expired, and that the immigration office wanted her out of the country within five days.

Ms. Lipton was silent. Alison was wondering if the call has been disconnected when Ms. Lipton said, "Is leaving the country a problem? Do you have a return airfare to the States?"

"Yes, but I was hoping to stay longer in Japan. My fiancé is here, and…" And she still had a shit load of work to do for Green Space, and she and Charles needed more time together.

Ms. Lipton continued. "The bad news. The U.S. Embassy has no jurisdiction to intercede in a case like yours. Happens all the time, and, frankly, there's nothing we can do. The good news is that usually visa violators have 48 hours to depart Japan, so consider yourself lucky."

"Funny, I don't feel lucky."

"My suggestion is leave the country, go someplace close like Seoul, Guam, Hong Kong. Visit the Japanese Embassy or consulate and apply for a short-term business visa. It's similar to a tourist visa, but easier to renew.

"When you come back to Japan, carry some documents related to business meetings or appointments you have scheduled. Also, have a round-trip ticket out of Japan and cash to show. It might sound excessive, but the immigration officers are predictably unpredictable. Good luck, Ms. Crane."

Alison switched off her cell phone. Looked like she had better pack her traveling shoes.

25

The wind outside of Seibu department store lashed Alison's bare legs numb with cold. Slight miscalculation on how wintry the nights were getting. She was relieved to spot Charles' purposeful stride, his head bobbing amidst a sea of passersby. Alison waved, and Charles flashed a thumbs-up.

"Hey, Alicats." He reached out and squeezed her arm. Alison still wasn't used to how undemonstrative Charles was in public in Japan. He said he didn't want to attract attention. Not that being an African-American foreigner, at six feet two, wasn't attraction enough. "How'd it go at immigration?" he asked.

"Not so good. I'm getting kicked out."

"No way. Did you call the embassy?"

"They told me to leave the country, get a short-term business visa, and then come back."

"Shit. But it could've been worse, you know."

"If it could've been worse, why didn't you come to the immigration office with me?"

Charles shook his head. "When do you have to leave?"

"They gave me five days."

"Think of it as an impromptu vacation. A weekend getaway to Seoul or Hong Kong."

"Can you come? We could use a romantic escape."

"Can't. I'm swamped at the office. You go, do some sightseeing, come right back. It'll be fun."

"But—"

Charles put his arm around Alison's shoulders. "Let's talk about this after we get some sake in us. I was at this really great *oden-ya* a couple weeks ago with Ueda-san from the office."

"What's an *oden-ya*?"

"*Oden*? It's the antidote to a cold blustery night. Hot broth with fish, tofu, seaweed. Guaranteed to warm your innards. It's down this way."

They walked along the main boulevard of Harumi-dori for a few blocks before cutting over to a side street. A carved wooden sign hung above the entrance door.

"This is it." Charles held the door open for Alison.

Two chefs working at the counter measured out bowls of steaming soup for the handful of customers seated at the bar. When the chefs weren't dishing out food, they drank sake and watched a sumo tournament on the television behind the counter.

A chunky Japanese man struggled to his feet from the stool where he was seated by the door. "We're full," he said in English. Alison and Charles looked at each other. As tiny as the restaurant was, with only six customers, the place was nearly empty.

Charles spoke to the man in Japanese. "*Sumimasen ga aite iru seki wa yoyaku desu ka? Dekireba koko no oden wa oishii kara, seki wo tote hoshii no desu ga …*"

"Sorry, full," replied the man in English.

Charles' Japanese took on a decidedly different tone which even Alison could understand, though she couldn't follow the conversation. "*Isshukan mae ni kita toki ni oku no heya ga arimashita neh. Soko mo ippai desu ka*?"

"We are full. Please go now," said the man. He opened the door for Charles and Alison to leave. Just as the door opened, in walked a Japanese couple. The restaurant manager greeted them warmly and directed them to seats at the counter where the *oden* chefs were at work.

The vein on Charles' forehead pulsed. He was danger-zone pissed.

Alison reached for Charles' arm. "Let's go." She gently tried to pull him toward the door.

"You say you're full?" Charles yelled to the restaurant manager in English. "You're full of shit, that's what!" Charles kicked the door.

The restaurant patrons turned to look at the scene.

Charles' blood-rushed face was fiery. "I ate here last week, asshole. You'll hear about this. You refused the wrong fucking *gaijin*." Charles stormed toward the door. "Come on," he said to Alison. Two more couples entered the restaurant as Charles and Alison left. Alison could hear the manager welcoming the newcomers.

"Dammit! Sometimes I can't get over these racist yellow sons of bitches!" Charles said.

"Forget about it, Charles. How about Spago? We always like it there."

"Yeah, why the hell not. At least we can get in the damn door." They hailed a taxi and headed off for American food, Japanese style.

The enthusiastic reception by the maître d' at Spago was a welcome contrast to the animosity of the *oden-ya*'s gatekeeper. Alison and Charles were seated at a prime table even though the restaurant was crowded and they didn't have reservations. Inquiring heads turned to check her and Charles out, wondering if they were Somebodies. Or maybe they were just checking out Charles.

He was good-looking — gorgeous, really — but it still surprised her when women flirted with him right in front of her. And he never seemed to discourage the attention.

Alison looked over her menu. How Tokyo could feel so much like California was an amazement to her. Not only did the waitstaff speak fluent English, but the menu, in English, of course, with Japanese translations, featured a full wine list. Of California's finest. The place was a complete cut-and-paste from the States. A balm for the homesick Californian.

"I need a drink, Charles. What a day." Charles summoned over the waiter and sent him in search of a bottle of Mumm's.

Alison gulped the champagne. Its festive bubbles burned her throat. "Maybe this is a sign."

"A sign?" Charles asked.

"That I should leave Japan. Go back to the States."

"Your call, but you've hardly given it a go."

"I can't find a real job. My money's tight."

"I told you. I got you covered."

"And I told you. I don't want to be a kept woman. I'm a trained professional. At the peak of my career. But I can't even get a job as a goddamn proofreader."

Charles reached across the table to caress Alison's hand. "Give it time, Alicats."

"I'm dependent on you for every little thing. I can't speak the language, can't read the language. Maybe I should go back home."

"Do you want to go back?"

"I can't find my place here. We'd talked about getting married, and—"

"You talked about marriage. I said why don't we live together, see how it goes."

Alison had another slug of champagne. "Charles, if this relationship isn't what you want, tell me. I'm packed and gone. Say the word." Alison stared across the table, daring Charles to commit, one way or the other.

"I don't want to rush things. Not while I'm here, not while I'm building out the firm's Asian business. Can we drop this now and just enjoy the meal?" Charles refilled Alison's glass. "Tell me about that green group you were talking about. Green Peace?"

"Green Space. I'm still hoping to wangle a full-time job out of them. Did their president call you? Yuko Yamada?"

"Why would she call me?"

"They're having some problems with international finance. I thought maybe you could help." Alison didn't want to admit to Charles that his help might help her land the job. Not after her big speech about being an independent woman.

The server presented Alison's meal. Sheep cheese pizza with a side of linguine in squid ink sauce. After her marathon day at the immigration office, she deserved some carbo-loading.

"Take a break, Alicats. Go to Guam, lie on the beach. Or check out Hong Kong. You'd like it. Unbelievable shopping."

"Charles. My Visa card couldn't handle a pleasure trip. I have five days left in Japan and a ticket back to San Francisco. Maybe it's a sign."

Charles reached inside the breast pocket of his suit jacket and took out his cell phone. He punched in three numbers and waited.

"Charles Gordon, Tokyo office. I need an open round-trip to Hong Kong … Charge it to Business development … Crane. Alison Crane. And leave an account at the Mandarin." Charles slipped his phone in his jacket pocket and grinned.

"What did you do, Charles?"

"My bon voyage present. Sorry I can't make it with you, Alicats, but enjoy Hong Kong."

"Charles, I can't let you pay. I — it's too expensive."

Charles snorted. "Rounding error in my expense reports. No argument, it's done."

Alison had heard that the shopping in Hong Kong was legendary. Maybe she could find some shoes in her size. A woman's size 9 shoes were a rare sighting in Tokyo's stores.

She still had cash from the advance she'd gotten from Yuko Yamada for website research. Research Alison had yet to complete. But if she stayed on a tight budget and hauled ass on Green Space work when she got back to Japan, why not take a quick trip to Hong Kong?

"That's really sweet of you, Charles. I think I'll take you up on your offer."

"Good. Stay out of trouble."

"Is Hong Kong dangerous? God, where in the world is it safe for women?"

"Figure of speech. You'll be fine."

They finished their meal and walked arm in arm down the street looking for a taxi. After a few unoccupied cabs whizzed right by them, a taxi not averse to picking up foreigners stopped. They climbed in the backseat, and Charles barked out their address.

Charles reached around Alison's shoulders and pulled her close. Traffic crawled through the crowded streets of Roppongi. They weren't going anywhere fast. Charles felt inside Alison's overcoat and rubbed his hand up and down her thigh. "No pantyhose," he said, innocently staring straight ahead in the cab's back seat while his hand was busy exploring up her leg and under her skirt.

"Charles!" Alison closed her overcoat around her legs.

"Yes?" He moved his hand higher up her leg until his fingers were playing at the top of her inner thigh.

"Really, Charles!"

His fingers slipped under her panties, and he lightly stroked Alison's clitoris. Her vagina responded with a pleasurable fluttering, and she was instantly wet. Charles massaged her skillfully, and Alison gasped, trying to suppress an orgasm.

"What were you saying, Alison?" Charles asked sweetly, the face of an angel.

Alison closed her eyes in surrender. "Nothing, Charles." She opened her legs wide in the backseat. "Nothing at all."

26

"I have to leave Japan, Kiyoshi."

"What happened?"

"I overstayed my visa."

"Can you come back?"

"Yeah. But can't a person make an honest mistake in this country?"

"We try to avoid such things."

"I'm going to Hong Kong to get a new visa. Have you ever been there?"

"Many times. My company has an office there."

"Any recommendations?"

"Stay at the Regent. It's got a great harbor view."

"What about shopping? Restaurants?"

"I'll put together a list for you. When do you leave?"

"In two days."

"OK. Let me know where you're staying and I'll fax the list to you in Hong Kong."

"Thanks, Kiyo."

```
"It looks like our friend is leaving us alone
tonight."
"Looks like it. I want to track that little creep
down and expose him."
"Let's hope he's gone."
```

They ended their chat, and Alison sat looking at her blinking screen. Kiyoshi was such a nice guy. A really nice guy.

Alison stopped by the travel section of the World NetLink network to get information about Hong Kong. Maybe a few sights to see, shopping tips. A little history of the island would be nice. She cruised around the Hong Kong forum for a while, but then she remembered the party.

If she didn't start inviting people, she'd be stuck playing hostess to Charles' merry band of investment-banking boys. Heaven help her.

Alison shuffled through her stack of accumulated *meishi*, looking for potential party guests. She paused when she got to Yamada Yuko's card. Printed on hand-pressed washi paper with a natural fiber edge, threads of wood pulp added texture. Yamada's *meishi* oozed refined elegance. Rubbing her thumb along the uneven surface of the card, Alison noticed her torn nail.

Alison could introduce Charles and Yamada at the party. And Charles, ever the dazzler, would solve Green Space's international finance problems. And in gratitude, Yamada would offer Alison a bona fide job. And they would all live happily ever after. It could happen.

Alison picked up the phone but paused before dialing. How would she explain to Yamada that her internet research was coming to a screeching halt because of technical difficulties? Like getting booted out of the country.

Maybe a party invitation would defuse Yamada-san from getting angry over Alison's slow research progress.

She dialed the Green Space office and caught up with Ms. Yamada.

"It is good to hear from you, Alison. How is the website project going?"

"Actually, Yamada-san. I've had a little hiccup. With my visa. Nothing big, but I have to dash off to Hong Kong for a few days."

"Is everything all right?"

"Yes, but I might need a little more time to finish the research."

"Is it going well?"

"It's coming together." Sort of. Alison was going to have to produce huge results quick or return the money. What was left of it. "But the reason I'm calling is because my fiancé and I are having some people over for drinks on Saturday, and I was hoping you could join us." Alison held her breath. Yamada-san couldn't be too angry if she accepted Alison's party invitation.

"Saturday? That sounds wonderful."

Alison exhaled. "Around eight o'clock. We're in Nishi-Azabu. I'll fax you a map.

"By the way, have you had a chance to speak to Charles—" Alison began, but the phone had already gone dead in her ear.

Ms. Yamada seemed like a decent person. She didn't sound mad when Alison told her about the delay in her work. Why had Kiyoshi expressed those vague cautions about his old high school chum and her organization? The most diligent green groups worked hard to protect the environment, and all they got for gratitude was bad press on the front page. Kiyoshi shouldn't believe everything he read.

Alison emailed an invitation to Jed, and, for the hell of it because she was so off the beam, left an answering machine message for Zoe. She plumbed her brain trying to think of people to invite, anyone, to save her from the boredom that would otherwise be in store for her. But the one person she most wanted to invite was the one person she couldn't invite. How could she explain Kiyoshi to Charles? Or Charles to Kiyoshi.

With her whirlwind invitations issued, Alison stood and unkinked her neck and shoulders. Movement outside the bay window caught her eye. Someone was prowling in the bushes across the street. Or maybe it was tree branches caught in a gust. But maybe not.

Alison turned off the lights in the living room. She crouched down and crawled up close to the bay window to have another look across the street. Shadows from the tree limbs and bushes flickered in the dark. But there wasn't anybody there.

You're getting paranoid, Crane. Get a grip.

01101101 01100101 00100000 01101001 01100110

He found the perfect perch in the *kinmokusei* olive trees in the yard of the house across the street. The trees' dense leaves gave good coverage, yet didn't interfere with his reception much at all. He could squat down with his cell phone connected to his laptop and pick up the electromagnetic transmissions leaking from across the street. Sometimes he got interference from the satellite television dish behind him, but this evening his computer feed was crystal clear.

He'd hit the jackpot tonight. She was sending out email messages that weren't encrypted. A party? It'd been a while since he'd been to a party other than for the idiots he worked with. A party would be amusing. He could finally meet her. Really meet her. So much easier than online. And she couldn't refuse him, not at her party. Couldn't keep him out.

And she'd like him, he knew she would. Just like all the other *gaijin* women. Stupid cows. He could be charming when he wanted to. And he could have who he wanted. When he wanted.

A taxi pulled up in front of the house. He snapped his computer case shut and retreated farther back into the cover of shadows behind the trees. A tall Black guy got out of the taxi, walked up to the front door, pulled keys from his pocket, opened the front door.

The front door closed behind the Black guy. A lamp turned on in the house.

He was sure that no one had seen him standing in the trees. Even so, he counted. Waited. And waited some more until moving out of the dark and returning to his surveillance position.

Through his binoculars, he saw the Black guy walk up to that bitch and wrap his arms around her. She smiled and tilted her head up to kiss him. He massaged her stomach, then her breasts, while she kissed him. She stopped. Pointed to the window. The Black guy walked across the room, pulled a cord to rotate the blinds and returned to her.

The blinds were only partially closed, and he still had a good view from his position behind the tree branches.

The Black guy lifted her up and carried her to the couch. He peeled off her sweater, then her pants. Her naked body glowed in the lamplight. The Black guy sat next to her on the couch. He clutched her shoulders and shoved her on her stomach, across his knees. He spanked her ass hard with one hand while he groped her pussy with the other.

From his stakeout in the bushes, he couldn't hear her. Couldn't hear if she was moaning, crying or screaming. But from the way her body squirmed, he guessed that she was enjoying it.

Slutty freak. She liked to be spanked. He'd enjoy getting her alone, teaching her some tricks. Making her respond. Like all the other *gaijin* women. They said they wanted to have fun, and he'd made damn sure they had a time they'd never forget.

She turned herself over and unzipped the Black guy's pants. Licked his dick like it was a fucking Meiji chocolate bar. She arranged her legs and descended. He saw her smile as she straddled him on the couch.

The Black guy pinched her nipples, tugged on her tits. Head thrown back, she exposed the long line of her neck as she rode him, slow and teasing.

He let his binoculars hang by the neck strap, loosened his pants. Why hadn't he brought his digital camera? He could've recorded the scene. Relived it. Studied it.

Now the woman pumped hard, her head bobbing up and down with an unmistakable rhythm and urgency.

He kneaded his rigid penis, synchronizing the timing with the undulation of her hips and the Black guy's thrusts.

She twitched in spasm. The Black guy's body shivered and went still.

He snatched a tissue from his jeans pocket but was too late to catch the squirting stream of semen. He wiped off his dick and tossed the soggy tissue in the bushes.

Those two knew how to put on a show. They didn't realize it was a *ménage a trois*.

He loaded up his computer gear and stowed the binoculars in his jacket pocket. In moments, he was another man walking down the streets of Nishi-Azabu.

Next time, he'd bring the digital camera.

27

Alison mixed another batch of margaritas at the bar counter. Had she known that Charles' intimate little gathering of "around fifteen people" would draw over ten times that many, she would have arranged for help. Or skipped out.

She sampled her concoction, added more triple sec, and hit the frappé button. The noise of the blender competed with the stereo speakers' blasting David Byrne's "Burning Down the House."

Burning down the house? Didn't sound like such a bad idea, Alison decided. She topped off her own glass with the frozen drink then filled the pitcher.

Alison wandered among the clusters of guests, offering refreshments. A hostess smile smeared across her face. The room full of chattering strangers floated in front of her eyes.

"Hey, Maxwell, you're Canadian. Why don't you call in the motherfucking Mounties! They'll find her disappearing Canuck ass." A drunken loudmouth and rip-roaring laughter.

Who were these people she was entertaining? The men in their dark suits, the women in their tight-fitting bodycon dresses. Where had they come from?

And where was Ms. Yamada? And Jed? No one Alison invited had shown up. Eyes blurry, she listened to conversations in Japanese and laughed at the words she divined to be the punch line. And drifted on. Charles really owed her.

Floating past the study, she glanced in to see a few revelers in various degrees of stupor. The distinctively sweet aroma of marijuana wafted from the room.

Those idiots had the nerve, the brazen stupidity, to smoke dope in Japan. And in her house. Correction. Charles' house. Didn't they know they could get deported? But she was the one that Immigration was booting out of the country. Alison snorted bitterly at the irony.

She left the half-empty pitcher of margaritas on the dining room table. The partygoers could fend for themselves.

Back in the kitchen, Alison popped open a bottle of Perrier-Jouët. With her finger, she traced the spiraling white flowers painted on the champagne bottle. Charles had said that they were Japanese anemones, but how would he know? Then again, Charles seemed to know everything.

She poured herself a glass and roosted on the living room couch. Her efforts at mingling had worn her out. She preferred sitting on the sofa and trying not to look miserable. But not trying too hard.

Alison heard a familiar voice and turned to see Yuko Yamada stepping into the *genkan*. Ms. Yamada looked stunning in a black and red silk sheath patterned with a jacquard design. A pearl barrette adorned her slicked-back hair.

Thank God Charles was on duty playing host. He shared a belly laugh with Yamada-san who handed him a package intricately wrapped in cloth.

Alison struggled to rise to her feet and greet her guest, the only one she had invited who had actually shown up. The floor shifted slightly. She paused to regain her balance — and to sober up — before going to welcome Ms. Yamada.

Standing in the *genkan* foyer, Alison reached out to shake Ms. Yamada's hand, but quickly caught herself. This was Japan. People didn't shake hands in greeting. A California-style hug was definitely out, so she smiled at Ms. Yamada and bowed.

"I'm so glad you could come, Yamada-san." Alison touched Charles' elbow. "Let me introduce you to my fiancé. Yamada-san, this is Charles Gor—"

"We've already met," Charles said. He and Ms. Yamada exchanged a glance.

"Oh. I didn't know. Well, then. Good. Let me get you a margarita."

Alison returned from the kitchen and found Charles and Ms. Yamada deep in conversation. It was sweet of Charles to chitchat with Ms. Yamada, to help grease the skids for her to get a job at Green Space.

"Here you go." Alison extended the margarita to Ms. Yamada. Charles left to hang up Ms. Yamada's coat.

Ms. Yamada took the glass. "You're off to Hong Kong. Have you been before?"

"No, this is my first time."

"If you have a chance, you might want to visit the Green Space office there."

"I didn't realize you had an office in Hong Kong. I'd love to stop by."

Ms. Yamada reached in her bag — tonight it was Prada — and pulled out a business card with the Hong Kong office's address. "I'll let them know you might be visiting."

"Thank you, Yamada-san. I'll make a point of dropping by." Yamada-san was showing interest in her. She'd come to the party. Alison's mood lightened as her probability of employment increased.

"But there is one thing," Yamada-san said. "If it's not too much of a bother for you."

"Not at all, what is it?"

"If you visit the Hong Kong office, would you mind ever so much dropping something off for me? You see, I was planning to go to Hong Kong myself, but things came up, and—"

"I'd be delighted to." Alison was more than happy to do anything that would move her one step closer to a job with Green Space.

"If you could just drop this off." Ms. Yamada took a small padded envelope from her purse. She lifted the envelope flap to show Alison a computer disk inside.

Alison took the envelope.

"I know it's an inconvenience, but if it weren't so important—"

"Consider it delivered. When I was staff counsel at Save-A-Tree, I often hand-carried critical documents. You can't be too careful."

"I'm glad you understand."

"And you know, Yamada-san—"

"Please call me Yuko."

"Yuko. I'm eager to work with you, with Green Space, however I can best help. When I get back from Hong Kong, perhaps we can meet and—"

"Yes, please call my office. When you get back. And thank you, Alison. You're helping us more than you know."

The party roared on behind her as Alison escaped into her bedroom to put Ms. Yamada's envelope away in a safe place. The beat of the music shook the bedroom walls.

Alison stored the disk in her wheeling suitcase. Hong Kong might be fun. She'd deliver the disk to Green Space, do a little sightseeing, some window shopping, and when she came back to Japan, a grateful Yamada-san — Yuko — would have the perfect job all lined up for her.

Alison returned to the party only to see Charles teaching Yamada a line dance. Alison smirked. Yamada might look as elegant and polished as a *Vogue* cover girl, but she moved like a rusty robot. Charles put his hands on Yamada's hips and guided her through the steps. Wasn't it presumptuous of Charles to make body contact in a culture where people went to lengths to avoid touching each other? Yamada, smiling broadly, didn't seem to take offense. Thank goodness.

With a guest to attend to, Alison resumed her hostess duties. She felt almost Martha Stewart–like as she mixed more margaritas, refilled trays with chips and salsa, and freshened drinks.

Pitcher empty yet again, Alison returned to the living room where she saw Charles clutching a fat joint in his hand. He took a long hit and held the smoke in, trying to get the maximum effect from the high.

She'd have to talk to Charles about the legalization of dope in Japan. Or lack thereof. Even Paul McCartney had gotten booted out of Japan because he'd been busted for drugs. Did Charles and his ex-pat pals assume they were above the law?

Charles held the joint out, offering it to Alison as she walked by, but she shook her head to decline. As Alison walked away, Charles tapped her on the shoulder. She turned around and he exhaled smoke in her face. Just what she needed — a contact high.

"What, Charles?"

"Did you see your friend?" He took another hit on the joint and held his breath. His lazily focused eyes glowed like smoldering red embers. Alison could see that Charles was lit.

"My friend?" she asked. "Yamada-san? Don't you remember? I introduced you." The marijuana was affecting Charles' memory.

He blew out another smoky breath. "No, not Yuko. The guy. The Japanese guy. The dude wearing earplugs."

"Who're you talking about, Charles? Are you wasted?"

"No, no. He said he was—" Charles chuckled. "Maybe I am."

"You're what, Charles?"

"Wasted."

Alison rolled her eyes. "Have you seen Yuko?"

"Had to take off. She said to tell you bon voyage."

Alison dropped the pitcher off in the kitchen., Alison's interest in partying had walked out the door with Ms. Yamada's departure.

She glanced at the wall clock. Almost two o'clock in the morning. When were these people going to go home? Someone had found the classic Motown CDs and suddenly everyone was a dancing Blues Brother. Like an out-of-control train headed downhill, the party was picking up momentum.

She had an early flight to Hong Kong and wanted to get some sleep.

Or pass out. Whichever, blissfully, came first. Charles could be the gracious host to his houseful of party guests. She needed a time-out.

Alison went to her bedroom, kicked off her slippers, killed the lights and stretched out on the futon bed. After a quiet moment to rest her eyes, she'd be ready for another round of hospitality.

She must have dozed a bit, but she had a feeling, a sixth sense, that she was being watched, that there was someone in the bedroom with her.

"Hey, Charles." She sat up in bed in time to see a man's head duck out of the door. The bedroom door slammed shut. The man wasn't Charles.

Who the hell was that? Some freak voyeur in her own home? Maybe she dreamed it, but she didn't think so. Was it just some drunken sot looking for a bathroom?

Alison got out of bed and turned on the lights. On top of the futon, next to where Alison had been resting, was an envelope. Alison tore open the envelope. Inside was a picture postcard of Hong Kong harbor at night.

Alison smiled. How sweet of Charles to leave her a note. For Charles, a postcard was tantamount to an effusive love letter. He was missing her already. She turned the postcard over to read his message.

Glued to the back of the card was a slapdash, digital composite image. Alison's face had been pasted onto the naked body of a woman, bound by her wrists and ankles to the poles of a four-poster bed. A coiled bullwhip lay between her spread-eagled legs. Scribbled on the bottom of the card was a handwritten message. "Have a good trip, TokyoAli!!! I will be waiting for you!!!"

28

It was him. In her house. The damn freak had been in her bedroom. A scream rocketed from Alison's gut and exploded out of her mouth.

She threw the postcard on the floor and thundered into the living room.

"Charles!" She yelled but the music drowned her out. The partygoers were caught up in their own highs, their own drunkenness. Alison scanned the glazed faces. Was one of them her stalker?

Where was Charles? If he knew that some twisted psychopath had crashed his party. Had ventured into his bedroom hunting his girlfriend. Charles would handle it. Would handle him. But where was Charles?

Alison raced to the first-floor guest room, pushed open the door. No one. She ran down the back hall and saw Miss Lap Dog scurrying from the study. Miss Dog was pulling down her very bodycon dress. Shrink-wrap would have been a looser fit.

"Have you seen Charles?" Alison asked.

Without answering, Miss Lap Dog trotted down the hall.

Alison opened the study door. The lights were off, but Alison could see Charles on the couch, his profile reflected against the glow of the street light on the window.

"I've been looking everywhere for you, Charles. There's some freako nut in the house."

"What're you talking about?"

Alison switched on the table lamp. Charles blinked at the sudden brightness. Shirt half-unbuttoned, he leaned heavily on his elbow for support staying upright.

"There was some guy here. I don't know who. I was resting on the bed, and he left a postcard right next to me. A bon voyage card."

"Yeah, so. That's nice."

"No. It was really perverted. And he knew I'm going to Hong Kong."

"I didn't realize it was a state secret."

"I was alone in the bedroom with some deranged lunatic."

Charles dropped his chin to his chest and massaged his eyelids. "You were dreaming, Alison. You've been hitting the sauce pretty hard tonight — tequila, champagne. Makes a person imagine things."

"Imagine things? That postcard isn't a dream. It's a threat. Can't you do something? Throw everybody out? Party's over."

Charles stood up with an air of impatient resignation. "Show it to me."

Alison led Charles to the bedroom, but the postcard was gone.

Charles raised his eyebrows and looked down at Alison like she was a poor, misguided child. She hated that look. It was his supercilious way of saying I told you so.

"Get some sleep, Alison. And if the postcard-writing boogeyman comes back, I'm here to protect you." Charles snorted.

"Protect me? I was frantically searching for you, and you were back there in the dark with that lap dog bimbo."

"Get off it, Alison. You're imagining things. All kinds of things." Charles rubbed the backs of his eyelids. "We got any eye drops? Visine?"

Alison stared at Charles. His red-rimmed eyes gazed at Alison as if from a faraway distance. She wanted to scream all over again. He'd been smoking dope all night, and yet she was imagining things.

"I'll tell you what I saw, Charles. Sworn testimony. An eyewitness account." Alison held her palm in the air. "I saw her. That lap dog bitch. I saw you, too. And I saw a postcard. Humiliating, degrading. All of it."

"You've been drinking."

Why did she have to convince him of anything? Why couldn't he just believe her? Believe in her. "I'm tired of being sober."

Alison stopped by the living room and snagged an open bottle of champagne. The bottle, almost full, was still chilled. She retreated to the bedroom and locked the door. Visiting hours were over.

"Open the door." Charles' pounding shook the door in its frame.

"Go back to your party."

Charles kicked the door. "Dammit, Alison! What's the matter with you?"

"There was a strange man leaving me obscene messages in my bedroom while you were fucking around with some bimbo in my own house." Alison laughed. "In *your* house. But you know, you're right. I must have imagined the entire thing."

Alison had a big guzzle of champagne straight from the bottle. The bottle was heavier than she realized and champagne sloshed out of her mouth and dribbled down her chin.

She dragged herself into the bathroom to find an Actifed. Allergy medicine with an alcohol chaser was the closest thing she had to a sleeping pill.

"Fuck it, Alison. Go to Hong Kong. Do what you have to do. But when you get back, you need to talk to a shrink. Someone who'll help you be more rational."

Alison popped the Actifed into her mouth and washed it down with a swig of champagne.

"That's the problem, Charles. I'm completely rational now."

01111001 01101111 01110101

Alison cracked open an eye to squint at the bleeping clock on the nightstand: 5:30 a.m. She had fallen asleep in her party clothes and her morning mouth tasted like dried shit, a remembrance of last night's festivities.

It was way too early, and she'd barely dozed off. But remembering the blowout with Charles, she was ready to pull herself together and hit the road. All she needed was a hot shower, cool mint toothpaste and coffee. She'd be good to go.

Alison called the contact number Charles had given her for Morgan Sachs' travel department. She switched her hotel reservations at the Mandarin and booked a deluxe single at the Regent, the hotel Kiyoshi had recommended. Let Charles explain the expense to his firm. If they even noticed, which she doubted they would.

Alison emailed Kiyoshi telling him where she was staying so that he could fax her the list of his recommendations in Hong Kong. Then she packed her bag.

Passport, business suit, briefcase. She snatched up the pile of business cards she had collected, a pack of American Express traveler's checks and her return ticket to the States. All the trappings that Ms. Lipton at the embassy had suggested she offer up to satisfy Japanese immigration enough to grant her a business visa.

What other evidence could she present to plead her case? She scanned the bedroom. Just in case, she took some Green Space material as proof of her business meetings. And she double-checked that the disk Ms. Yamada had entrusted to her was securely stored in her purse.

That should do it. As an afterthought, she pulled out her computer and attached it to the strap on her rolling suitcase. She didn't want Charles to stumble upon her Mac.

Alison couldn't resist looking in on Charles and found him splayed out on top of the guest bed, fast asleep in his clothes. She leaned down to give him a light kiss on the cheek, but then realized that she didn't feel like bothering.

Hong Kong would be a good break for her. A chance to get clear about her relationship with Charles. The trip would be a welcome escape.

She closed the guest bedroom door, grabbed her suitcase and rolled out onto the street.

29

The jet taxied to a halt in the middle of the tarmac at Kai Tak airport, and Alison relaxed her death grip on the armrest. Landings at her hometown SFO airport were scary enough. It always looked like the plane was going to crash into the bay until at the very last minute a runway would miraculously appear. But the descent into Hong Kong offered a heart-pounding thrillfest when the 747 banked precipitously and zoomed uncomfortably close between skyscrapers.

The passengers deplaned and were shepherded onto buses to take them to the terminal. Alison wasn't expecting the mild breeze that greeted her on the ground in Hong Kong. She immediately liked Hong Kong's moderate climate in contrast to Tokyo's chilling winds.

Still bleary from lack of sleep, Alison shuffled along with the crowds through immigration and customs. She changed a little money at the currency exchange counter before climbing into a cab.

Her car pulled up in front of the Regent Hotel. Unsure if tipping was standard practice in Hong Kong, Alison paid the driver and threw in an extra 20 percent to be safe. An eager doorman assisted her out of the cab, and Alison had to fight to keep him from taking her suitcase. She checked in at the registration desk and received her electronic room key.

"By any chance did a fax come for me?" Alison hoped Kiyoshi might have already gotten her email message and faxed his list of recommended sights.

"No, but if we get one, we will turn on the message light on in your room."

Alison tapped the card key against her cheek. Maybe she should let Charles know where she was staying in Hong Kong. Just in case.

Alison asked the man at the front desk for a fax cover, and he passed her a sheet printed with the hotel's name and logo. She scribbled a short note and handed the paper back.

```
Charles – I'm at the Regent in Kowloon.
—Alison
```

Brief, but that's all he needed to know. Alison waved off the bellhop who wanted to take her bag and rolled her suitcase over to the lobby gift shop. She bought a guidebook about Hong Kong and rode the elevator up to her floor.

The room felt comfortably modern with a big-screen television, surround-sound radio, and water kettle with a variety of imported teas, coffees and packets labeled "tisane" — whatever a tisane was. All the luxury amenities an elite clientele would expect at a hotel that catered to their kind.

As a budget-conscious traveler who was stashing away the freebies, Alison was sure she wasn't the typical Regent customer. But she would do her best to suffer her fate in the lap of luxury.

She moved on to the bathroom to see what loot awaited her. Score. A hefty bar of French milled soap rested on the edge of a marble soaking tub. She picked up the soap without removing the wrapper and held it to her nose. Lavender with a touch of verbena. Yeah, she could definitely get used to this.

Alison ran water for a bath. Waiting for the tub to fill, she unpacked her lawyerly all-purpose, all-season dark blue Donna Karan suit and hung it up in the bathroom to steam out the wrinkles. All this bother and preparation for a damn visa stamp. But then again, she'd blown it. She'd overstayed her visa. If the Japanese consulate wanted a dog-and-pony show, she wouldn't disappoint.

Alison stripped and eased into the bath. The deep tub was small, and there was no place to sit on a stool for a prewash before hopping in. She realized how quickly she'd become accustomed to the Japanese way of bathing and the spacious *ofuro* in her house. She let her mind drift and her muscles relax while the warm water invited her to nap.

Waking herself up, Alison dried off and slipped on a plush hotel robe. Embroidered with the Regent's name and logo and lined with terry cloth soft as velvet, the robe might have found its way into her suitcase, if she weren't such a straight-up, true-blue Girl Scout. And if the hotel didn't have her credit card number. Or, rather, Morgan Sachs' account number. She certainly didn't want to get Charles in trouble over a stolen hotel robe.

Bundled up and getting hungry, Alison went in search of a room service menu. Looking in the drawer of the nightstand — no Gideon's Bible, she noted — she found a binder describing the hotel's services. The in-room dining options sounded delicious, and her stomach growled in agreement.

She used her calculator to convert the room service prices to U.S. dollars and decided what to eat. The cheapest thing on the menu.

A child's meal of a hamburger and fries was promptly delivered on a linen-draped rolling cart. Maybe they wouldn't notice there weren't any kids staying in the room. Alison scarfed down the food and picked up the phone to have housekeeping remove the cart. The telephone's red message light was on.

Alison smiled in anticipation of reading Kiyoshi's fax. Or, she realized with a thud back to reality, it could just as easily be a message from Charles. She dialed the front desk.

"A fax arrived for you, Miss Crane. Shall we have someone bring it up?"

"Yes, please."

Within moments — had somebody been waiting outside of her room? — an envelope was slipped under the door.

The fax was from Kiyoshi, sent to her by way of World NetLink.

```
Dear Alison,

I hope you had a good flight. I am sorry if this list
is late reaching you. Here are my suggestions.

- Dim Sum at Diamond Restaurant

- Drunken prawns at any restaurant

- A ride on the Star Ferry

- The Jade Market

- Victoria Peak

- Also, I highly recommend drinks at the lobby bar
at your hotel. Sunset is the best time.

I wish I could be there to show you these sights,
but maybe the list will be helpful.

Yours truly,

Kiyoshi Hisaka
```

Alison read the note and beamed. "I wish I could be there to show you these sights." She wished he could be here, too. She hung her motion-activated travel burglar alarm on the hotel door and fell into a deep, dreamless sleep.

30

Alison's wake-up call jarred her out of sleep. She ordered coffee and toast from room service and began her morning stretches. Minutes later, the room service man arrived with her breakfast. He set the tray on the table in front of the window and pulled open her curtains.

As he prepared to leave, he said, "This fax came for you during the night, Miss Crane," and handed her an envelope.

"Thank you." Alison scrounged in her purse for some coins and handed them over. The huge grin on the man's face made her think perhaps she didn't have an understanding of the value of the Hong Kong dollar.

She sat down at the table and poured her coffee, appreciating that the hotel had provided a side pot of hot milk. She sipped her coffee, putting off the inevitable. She didn't want to read the fax, undoubtedly an abject, groveling apology from Charles.

What the hell, she opened the envelope.

DO YOU MISS ME ALISON????? MISS MISSS MISS ME MISS ALI???? I MISS YOU. THANK YOU FOR THE PARTY!!!!! I HAD FUN. WHY NOT YOU??? LET'S MEET AT HONKON!!

Dumbfounded, Alison stared at the fax page. No doubt who it was from. But how did that bastard know where she was?

She had sent Kiyoshi an email telling him where she was staying, but all of their messages were encrypted. So that must mean the techno-creep had been able to break the code.

"I had fun. Why not you?" Damn him! Like a tick that had burrowed under her skin, this freak had invaded her life and wouldn't be shaken loose.

The anger she had felt when she knew that the guy had violated her bedroom, her most intimate personal space, returned and lodged in her stomach. Even though she'd only had coffee and toast, Alison felt queasy, like she was going to be sick. She took some calming yoga breaths and waited for the nausea to pass.

She looked at Kiyoshi's fax again. Kiyoshi had sent the fax through World NetLink's fax service. Could the cybernut pick up faxes sent through the computer network? Why not? It was all digitized information being hurled through the ethers, there for the intercepting.

But the creep couldn't actually be coming to Hong Kong. No way. Just a bluff to unnerve her. Nevertheless, the guy was way too close for comfort.

Alison phoned the front desk. "This is Alison Crane, and I'd like you to hold all my phone calls. And if I get any faxes, please throw them away."

"I'm not sure I understand, ma'am," the operator said. "You would like for us to discard faxes we receive for you?"

"That's right. No incoming communication. I'd appreciate your help." Alison hung up. She was going offline, underground, incognito. She'd be damned if that cyberfreak was going to ruin her trip.

She showered and donned her lawyer gear. It was time to plead her case.

01110111 01100001 01101110 01101110 01100001

Leaving the consulate, Alison sighed with relief. There was no telling when it came to the Japanese immigration office. She'd had to pay fines for overstaying her visa, and they'd even made her write a damn letter of apology. But she'd gotten a new visa, so all was good. Except for now she was stuck wearing a monkey suit and carrying a heavy briefcase. She hailed a cab back to her hotel.

Alison changed into her favorite no-iron travel pants and blazer. Businesslike enough to make a good impression at Green Space's branch office but comfortable enough for sightseeing. She spread out on the hotel bed with her guidebook and Kiyoshi's list of must-see places and planned her day.

First, she would stop by Green Space's office, deliver the disk, chat a bit with the locals who would love her and tell Ms. Yamada that she had to give Alison a job. Or something like that.

After Green Space, she'd take in the sights of Hong Kong. She could visit the Tiger Balm Gardens or Victoria Peak, or — go shopping. Given her budget, she'd better stick to window shopping. But one never knew.

According to the guidebook, Hong Kong offered not-to-be-missed shopping bargains from clothes to cameras. The Silvercord Building housed nothing but computer stores selling hardware and software at rock-bottom prices.

Silvercord sounded interesting, but so did the backstreet clothing warehouses that abounded in Hong Kong. Alison decided to ride the Star Ferry across Victoria Harbor. The ferry departed from Kowloon Peninsula not far from her hotel and landed at Hong Kong Island. The short voyage would fulfill her self-imposed minimum sightseeing requirement, then she'd see what shopping adventures called to her.

Impatient passengers waiting to board crowded the entrance to the ferry on the Kowloon side of the harbor. At the ticket window, Alison opted to go first class — for less than twenty-five cents U.S. No wonder the room service guy had been full of smiles for her. She'd tipped him enough to buy at least thirty first-class round-trip tickets. Alison joined the odd mix of tourists, local people and business types all waiting for the ferry to start loading.

Finally, the gates opened to allow the first-class compartment passengers to board. A swell of bodies carried Alison forward like a piece of flotsam.

The ferry pushed off from the Kowloon peninsula with a heave and began its short voyage to the island of Hong Kong. Alison stood on the deck and watched as tiny fishing boats and a huge Chinese junk decked out with dramatic orange sails all plied the waterway with equal authority. A parade of centuries of seagoing history floated by.

Hong Kong was a working harbor. Not a coastal area that had been relegated to sightseeing and tourist attractions like San Francisco, but a harbor that was about serious trade and transportation. So what if the water looked a tad polluted, even gave off a trace odor of gasoline. People on the water had business to conduct and ports to call on.

In less than fifteen minutes, the ferry pulled into its berth on the Hong Kong Island side of the harbor. Caught in the riptide of people surging out of the ferry terminal, Alison paused on the street to take in her surroundings.

There was a palpable buzz in the air. With the regularity of a metronome, a steady stream of Mercedes limousines pulled up to towering international bank buildings and deposited business executives. Elegant Tai-Tai ladies toting shopping bags from Fendi, Dior and Valentino marched to the music. It was the buzz that infected Wall Street, the hum that was unmistakable in midtown Manhattan, the same vibration that was practically an undertone in Tokyo. The sound of money. Of money being made and money being sold. The music of commerce. Getting and spending. Alison could feel it animating the island like a heartbeat. Money. Money. Money.

She walked over to an array of bank booths displaying currency exchange windows. The money booths were as unremarkable as fast-food windows in a suburban shopping mall in the States. Yet here, at these windows, the world's coin was being bought and sold at rates that flashed on screens in front of Alison's eyes. Rates that changed with each monetary transaction in the financial centers of the world.

Being in this milieu made her think of Charles. Alison could feel the rush, feel what he must feel, knowing that he was one of the market makers in this international orgy of finance. *This is the energy, almost a sexual energy, that Charles gets off on in his job.*

She didn't want to think about Charles now. This was her time, a chance to get her affairs in order. She'd straightened out her visa problem, and now she'd visit Green Space's local office and deliver the disk.

She consulted the business card Yuko Yamada had given her and studied her map. Green Space's office was seven blocks up the hill and five blocks over. Alison began the steep ascent and regretted not thinking ahead to bring her walking shoes.

At the top of the hill, she turned the corner and headed down two blocks. The retail business exteriors gave way to warehouses and manufacturing plants. Hardly a soul on the street. Where was the crush of humanity she'd experienced everywhere in Hong Kong and Kowloon?

Was she on the wrong street? Alison reconfirmed the address on the card. No, she was standing in front of the address where the branch office should be. But it wasn't there. Nothing was there. The street numbers jumped over the Green Space address completely.

Alison examined the computer disk in the envelope from Ms. Yamada to see if there was an address. The disk's label was blank. Alison chided herself for not having asked the concierge for directions, for not having had a cab drop her off. In Hong Kong, she was back in an English-speaking territory, on relatively solid ground compared to Tokyo, and had set out with a certainty that she'd find the place, no problem. Wrong.

She would try one more block. Her frustrating experiences getting lost in Japan had taught her that addresses in Tokyo were at best creative suggestions as to what general area you wanted to go to. Maybe Hong Kong streets were equally jumbled.

She continued to tread down the broken sidewalk. Alison could hear footsteps behind her. Good, she could ask the person where the Green Space address was.

She turned around. A young guy, maybe twenty-five years old, in jeans and a Chicago Bulls T-shirt, was walking her way. Alison waved.

"Excuse me." The man advanced but did not respond. Alison held up her map. "Can you help me find an address? I'm looking—"

The man picked up speed and torpedoed right for her. Alison stood immobile. Too stunned to react quickly, too surprised to move. The man tackled her to the ground, grabbed the envelope she was carrying for Yuko Yamada and fled down the street.

31

"I told you. It was a CD. A disk for a computer." Could the cop really be as dim-witted as he seemed?

There wasn't much hope of recovering the disk, but it would be prudent to get a police report in case Ms. Yamada needed one. Alison had wanted to impress Yamada, but now she'd managed to lose the computer disk she'd been entrusted with. Ms. Yamada would be impressed, all right. Impressed by Alison's ineptitude.

"What kind of data was on the disk?" The young policeman's uniform looked too clean, too new, too unsullied. And what was with that beret posed on the side of his head? Altogether too jaunty. Then Alison recalled Tiananmen, remembered what the Chinese police could do if challenged. But this was Hong Kong. It wasn't exactly China. Yet.

"I don't know. I was carrying it for a friend." Alison massaged her knee.

"You don't know what was on the computer disk?" The ferret-faced policeman taking down the report all but blew his cigarette smoke in Alison's face. Alison waved the air in front of her and gave a little cough. Maybe the jerk would get the message.

"Like I said, I was dropping the disk off."

"Where is your copy of the disk?"

"I don't have a copy. I'll say it again. I was walking down the street, looking for the address for Green—" Oh. Now she got it. She was the dim-witted one. *Dense, Alison, dense.* Ms. Yamada had said that Green Space had enemies around the world, that sometimes the government was working against Green Space. Maybe it hadn't been such a good idea to come running to the police.

"The address for who?" The cop puffed on his cigarette while he stared at Alison through narrowed eyes.

"I'm sorry, what were you asking me?"

"Who were you looking for? Where were you going with the disk?"

"I'm afraid I've wasted your time, officer. I'm sure it was just a mistake." Alison stood up to go.

"Sit down, miss."

The policeman's tone surprised Alison. She sat.

"I asked you who were you going to meet?"

"A friend. A friend from law school." Maybe the cop would back off if he knew she was a lawyer, on his side. Sort of. "A friend of mine from law school is visiting Hong Kong. From Australia. And we thought we could meet, catch up. Before her plane took off. I'm sure she's already gone by now. The disk was for her." Alison wished she were more skilled at making up convincing lies on the fly.

"What was on the disk?"

"Vacation pictures, I think. I'm sure it's nothing important. Sorry to bother you."

Alison got up. This time the cop didn't try to stop her. She took the opportunity to bolt out of the police station. They couldn't arrest her, could they? She was the one who had come in looking for their help. Even so, she checked behind her to make sure no one was following her as she hurried down the street.

32

Alison caught the Star Ferry to the Kowloon side of the harbor and returned to her hotel room. Reflexively, she glanced at the telephone's message light, but there was no red light flashing. The hotel operator apparently was on the case doing as she had directed, holding all calls and faxes to her room.

Charles still hadn't called. Even if the hotel operator had blocked his call, he knew her cell number. Maybe he was giving her time to clear her head. Maybe he was waiting for her to make the first move and apologize. He could wait. She didn't feel like revisiting old, depressing issues. Especially while on vacation in an exotic new city.

She hunted through the business cards in her wallet and used her cell phone to call Ms. Yamada at Green Space in Tokyo. Alison gnawed on her cuticle while the long-distance call rang. How could she explain to Yamada that her precious cargo hadn't made it to its destination without blowing her chances of getting a job with Green Space?

The phone clicked into a recorded message. The electronic voice of a woman blathered on about something or another in Japanese, Alison had no idea what. While she was waiting for the phone to beep so that she could leave a message, the call disconnected.

Maybe the office was closed. She'd try again tomorrow. Alison wasn't in any big hurry to pass on the bad news of her botched delivery attempt.

She stripped off her dirty clothes, noticing that she'd torn a hole in the knee of her pants when that punk knocked her down. And she'd really liked those pants. The jerk. She took a hot shower to revive herself.

Rays from the setting sun beamed low in Alison's hotel room window. Now was the optimal time to visit the hotel's cocktail lounge. Kiyoshi had said that its view was not to be missed.

She changed into a cobalt blue Issey Miyake pantsuit, an architectural accordion of pleats that defied wrinkling, pinned up her hair, and slipped on sandals. Into her evening bag went Kiyoshi's list of restaurant recommendations and her guidebook, hidden behind a paper cover. She didn't want to look too much like the tourist she was.

Alison rode the elevator to the lobby and walked to the lounge. Not seeing any host, she seated herself at a small table next to the soaring floor-to-ceiling wall of windows, which presented a panoramic view of Hong Kong.

The cityscape had captivated Alison during her Star Ferry voyage to get her visa. But now, at dusk, the skyscrapers' sparkling lights danced against a shadowy backdrop of mountains and cast a watery reflection in the sea. Even at this hour, vessels large and small traversed the harbor.

The view of San Francisco from Sausalito was picturesque. On a clear day. When there wasn't any fog. But this larger-than-life IMAX display of the Hong Kong harbor was spectacular. Alison took mental pictures so that she wouldn't forget. Maybe she'd even break down and buy some postcards. Just like a tourist.

"Excuse me, ma'am." A waiter materialized beside Alison's table and jolted her from her reverie. He was holding a cordless phone. "Are you Miss Alison Crane?"

"What is this about?" The muscles in her stomach tightened as she glared at the handset.

"The concierge has forwarded a call for you." The waiter placed the phone on Alison's table and departed before she could stop him.

She was settling in to enjoy an evening by herself, but barely a moment had passed before it started again. He started again. The intrusions, the unrelenting assaults. But maybe it wasn't the freak. Not all the way here. It might be Charles. There was only one way to know. She steeled herself and picked up the handset.

"Hello." There was no sound from the other end of the phone. "Who is this?" Silence. Alison hung up the phone and gestured for the waiter. "Would you please remind the front desk that I don't want any phone calls. None. Not in my room, not in the lobby. No calls. Can you do that?"

"I'm very sorry, ma'am." The waiter removed the handset. He stood staring at his feet, looking dejected. "May I get you something to drink, ma'am?"

All Alison had wanted was to relax, enjoy herself and not think about the shit she'd been dealing with in Tokyo. But she didn't need to unload her anger on this guy who was just doing his job. She'd leave him a good tip.

"Thank you. What kind of champagne do you have by the glass?"

"We have Dom Perignon, Perrier-Jouët, Mumm's, Krug—"

"A glass of Perrier-Jouët, please."

In a few minutes, the waiter set a champagne flute in front of Alison, popped the cork on a bottle of Perrier-Jouët and poured a sample. Alison tasted the champagne and nodded her approval. The waiter pulled up an ice-filled bucket on a tall stand and parked the bottle of champagne in it. He turned to walk off.

"Excuse me," Alison called after him. "I just wanted one glass of champagne, not a—"

"The gentleman ordered a bottle for the table." The waiter bowed and retreated toward the kitchen.

Gentleman? What gentleman? Alison's teeth clenched. She remembered yet another reason why she didn't like drinking alone in hotel bars. Unsolicited offers were an annoyance.

An even more worrisome thought entered her mind. Could it be that techno-geek who was hounding her? He had said in his fax, "Let's meet in Hong Kong."

She looked around to see who might be the man who had her in his crosshairs. With a scowl to ward off any potential hopefuls, she scanned the lobby bar.

Several couples enjoyed the harbor view. A smattering of tourists laughed. No one was looking her way, no one at all. What the hell. After the day she'd had, she needed a drink. Or drinks.

Alison lifted the delicate crystal flute to her lips and drained the glass. The waiter was nowhere in sight for a refill, so she reached into the ice bucket to retrieve the bottle.

A man's hand locked over Alison's. "I'll get that," he said.

33

Alison swung around, ready to fight. "I don't need any—"

In front of her stood a quietly attractive Japanese man, tall, athletic build. Black hair shot with silver. The man smiled. His eyes looked like they were accustomed to laughing.

"*Hajimemashite*, Alison-san. I'm Kiyoshi."

Alison sat, speechless.

"From online?"

Alison laughed. "Kiyoshi? Really? What are you doing here?" She held out her hand, and he shook it firmly. She liked his grip, the warmth of his skin.

"Do you mind if I join you?"

"Of course not. Sit."

Alison was unexpectedly tongue-tied. She hadn't recovered from how much she was immediately attracted to this man. His stylish charcoal gray suit — Armani? Brioni? — showed off his broad shoulders. And in his face, she saw an earnestness as well as an openness that she found disarming. Altogether a one-two knockout punch.

"I was sitting at my desk in Kobe, and I thought that better than faxing you a list of places to visit in Hong Kong, I could show them to you. If it's all right …"

"Of course it's all right. I'm mildly shocked, is all. You scared me." Alison gestured to the waiter. He brought over a champagne flute for Kiyoshi and filled it.

"Scared?" Kiyoshi asked. "How did I scare you?"

Alison shook her head as if to erase her words. She'd had plenty of scares that day. The threatening fax. The mugging on the street. The mysterious phone call.

But now, all she wanted was to enjoy meeting her new friend. Her handsome, online friend. And in such a magical setting, she didn't want to think about her mishaps. And she certainly didn't want to think about Charles.

"How long have you been here?" she asked.

"I got in this afternoon."

"I hope this doesn't screw up your work schedule."

"No, nothing I can't handle. Have you been to the consulate?"

"I went this morning. Breezed in, got my visa, and breezed out. No problem."

Alison and Kiyoshi clinked champagne glasses and settled back in their chairs, watching the sun set while the lights came up over the harbor.

After a few moments of silence, Alison said, "This view is mesmerizing. Thanks for the recommendation."

"It's one of my favorite spots," Kiyoshi said. "So, what about dinner? Do you have plans, or can I take you on an adventure?"

"I don't have any plans, but I don't know if I'm ready for an adventure." She didn't want to tell Kiyoshi that the jerk from online was providing all the adventure she could stomach.

"What's the matter, Alison? Don't you trust me?" Kiyoshi laughed, one part chuckle and one part cough.

She laughed along with him. "Of course I trust you. Adventure away."

"Give me a moment while I make a call." He excused himself and walked back into the hotel lobby.

Alison drank her champagne and watched the boats float by. She was so glad that Kiyoshi had surprised her like this. Better than seeing Hong Kong with a guidebook was seeing Hong Kong with a friend.

A friend. She realized that Kiyoshi was getting to be a good friend, perhaps her only friend in Japan, even though they'd only just met. The unreality of this setting in Hong Kong made her life with Charles seem equally unreal, remote, almost dreamlike. Or nightmarish.

She was going to enjoy the hell out of her time here. This would be her party, the party she didn't have two nights ago.

Kiyoshi returned, paid the bill, and the two set out.

"Where are we going?" Alison asked.

"You'll see. You said you trusted me, right?" Kiyoshi steered Alison to the front of the line of waiting taxis and gave the driver directions.

The cab raced through an underwater tunnel to Hong Kong. Alison hadn't realized that there was an alternative to taking a boat to the island. The tunnel was faster for sure, but not nearly as scenic as the water route.

The taxi driver dropped them at a bay filled with flat-bottom sampan boats. Fishermen gutted their catches off the side of the smaller vessels. The larger boats, decorated with strings of Christmas lights, served drinks and meals to the tourists aboard the floating parties. Their pocket camera flashes lit up the night.

Kiyoshi and Alison walked along a pier jutting out into the water. An elder Chinese man scrambled out of his boat with a nimbleness that belied his apparent age.

"Hello, sir. Hello, sir," the old man waved and bowed to greet Kiyoshi. When the man straightened, a gap-toothed smile cracked his wrinkled face.

"How've you been, Chen?" Kiyoshi asked.

"Good sir, good. Please this way. This way, madam." With a knobby finger, he pointed toward a dinghy. Kiyoshi helped Alison step down onto the boat then followed her aboard. The boat sat low in the water, and Alison didn't see any life preservers.

She chose to not worry about things. Tonight, she'd let go and enjoy the sensation of the misty sea breeze on her face. She was a strong swimmer. She'd be OK.

Chen cranked up the dinghy's motor, and after a false start and a sputter, the motor kicked in. He backed the boat up through the crowded confusion of sampans and houseboats and eased out into the harbor proper.

Clear of the logjam, Chen revved the engine, and the dinghy sped off toward the far side of the island. Alison watched the boats behind them rocking in the wake they kicked up.

Alison turned to Kiyoshi, who was staring at the watery night horizon with a thoughtful face. The boat's noisy motor made conversation impossible, and Alison wondered what Kiyoshi was looking at, what he was thinking about.

After several minutes of flying at top dinghy speed, Chen cut down the motor. The dinghy neared a larger boat — actually a small yacht — that was anchored inconspicuously in a cove. The old man expertly steered the dinghy next to the yacht and tied up alongside.

Kiyoshi climbed out of the dinghy and assisted Alison aboard the yacht. The dinghy's engines stuttered and came alive. Chen sped off.

Alone on a boat in an isolated inlet with a guy she'd just met. Alison had wanted to relax and have a good time, but that didn't mean being foolhardy. She'd keep your wits about her.

Alison looked around. The yacht was about forty-five-feet long, she guessed, judging from a pleasure boat her parents had when she was a kid. The yacht's intricately carved teak decks shone in the moonlight. An exquisite craft. Alison had to remind herself that rainforests were endangered because of extravagances like this boat.

Candlelight flickered on a table set for two and sparkled against the plates, wine glasses and champagne flutes. Chopsticks rested on a polished stone stand. Next to the chopsticks lay Western cutlery, wrapped in indigo towels. Alison guessed that the knife and fork were there for her benefit, if she couldn't handle the chopsticks and needed to bail. Good call.

A pudgy Chinese man in a white chef's uniform complete with a ten-inch-tall white toque popped up from below deck. All Alison could think of was how much the man looked like the Pillsbury doughboy. She liked him instantly.

He pumped Kiyoshi's hand with gusto. "Hisaka-san! *Hisashiburi de gozaimasu*," the doughboy said.

Kiyoshi answered him in English. "It has been a long time. How are you, Zhong-san?"

"Good, sir, *okagesama de*. And how is your father? I am sure he's happy that you are visiting the boat." Zhong gave Alison a sidelong glance and smiled.

"I'll tell my father that you asked about him."

Zhong nodded and clasped his hands together. "Dinner will be ready soon now. But first you sit and begin with a small something."

Zhong brought out a plate of pickled sashimi and uncorked the chilled champagne. After filling Alison's and Kiyoshi's glasses, he returned below deck.

"This is your boat? It's gorgeous," Alison said.

Kiyoshi looked in his lap. "It's my father's. His company's boat." Kiyoshi poured more champagne into Alison's already-full glass, overflowing the sides. He took his napkin and patted at the tablecloth in front of Alison. "Sorry," he said.

"It's OK, Kiyoshi."

Mr. Zhong announced dinner and set out the first dishes. "Please enjoy," he said.

Alison sampled white fish topped with ginger, green onions and sesame oil. Somehow the ginger tasted fresher, hotter, spicier than the ginger she'd had back at home, or even in Tokyo, for that matter. The fish was followed by crab steamed in black-bean sauce.

She eyed small bread rounds topped with some brown mystery meat. Did they eat dog in China? She wasn't sure. After another glass of champagne, she wouldn't care.

Kiyoshi saw Alison hesitating over the dish. "That's golden coin chicken. It's chicken liver."

Alison picked up a coin and popped it in her mouth. Crunchy, creamy, with a smoky roasted finish. She closed her eyes to taste more clearly. "Delicious," she said. Definitely not Fido.

After the first few dishes, Alison stopped asking what she was eating and just enjoyed the masterful blend of flavors and textures. Zhong appreciated Alison's appetite and, when the meal was over, he even gave her a little wink when Kiyoshi wasn't looking.

Her stomach full beyond capacity, Alison was grateful that her Issey Miyake outfit had an elastic waistband. She stood with Kiyoshi on the side of the gently rocking yacht, enjoying her tea. Its perfume-laced aroma suggested a jasmine blend and made the perfect finish to a delectable feast.

Soon, the engines started. The boat emerged from its hideaway headed back across the bay. Far off in the distance, the lights from mainland China twinkled.

"This is wonderful, Kiyoshi," said Alison. She shivered in the sea air.

"Are you cold?" Kiyoshi asked.

"No, not really," she said. "Maybe a little bit, but I'm OK."

"Here." He took off his jacket and draped it over Alison's shoulders. Alison began to protest, but she liked feeling the weight of Kiyoshi's jacket on her, the intimacy of a coat warmed by his body. She moved in to be closer to him.

"Kiyoshi?"

"*Hai.*"

"You said online that you were divorced. Isn't divorce unusual in Japan?"

For a moment she could sense a guarded hesitance in Kiyoshi. "I suppose it is unusual. But it's a growing trend. They say Japanese like to imitate American culture." He chuckled. Alison was grateful for the lighthearted retort.

"Sorry for bringing it up. It's just that—"

"It feels like a long time ago. Almost two years now."

"That's good to hear." What was she talking about? Stupid comment, Alison. Undaunted, she pressed on. "Do you have any kids?" She held her breath. As if it were any of her business. As if it mattered.

"No, we didn't have any. I suppose that's a good thing, given what happened."

"Yes, a good thing," Alison was quick to agree.

"Asking questions, like Perry Mason." Kiyoshi chuckled that laughing cough. "What about you?"

The tables were turned. What could she say? That no, she wasn't married, that she was in a frustrating relationship with a guy she'd followed around the world thinking that he would finally be able to commit, that her boyfriend was probably cheating on her, and she was fed up and confused? But most of all that she didn't want to think about him tonight, didn't want to spoil the evening?

"Oh, me? I don't have any kids either." Asked and answered, that's what Perry Mason would say. "I've never been married."

Kiyoshi put his arm around Alison, pulling her in closer. Alison thought she would ignite at his intimate touch. They looked out over the water as the yacht plowed through the harbor waves.

Unfortunately, but inevitably, they reached land on the Kowloon side. A dock crew met them and helped them tie up at the pier. Alison could see the lights from the Regent Hotel. Thanking Zhong, Kiyoshi helped Alison onto land. The two strolled toward the Regent Hotel arm in arm along the Victoria Harbor waterfront.

Salisbury Road bustled with shops, outdoor markets, restaurants, and crowds — always crowds — even at this late hour. When did people sleep?

"Getting tired?" Kiyoshi asked.

"No, not at all." Alison felt more wired than she had in a long time. How could a person be tired amidst so many bodies, so many lights, so much motion? It was the adrenaline charge she experienced when she visited Times Square at night.

"Do you like music? I know a jazz club not too far from here. Nothing fancy, but they usually have good bands."

"Let's go."

They hailed a cab and were let out in front of a lonely warehouse in a bleak part of town. The isolation of the area reminded Alison of her misadventures earlier in the day when she had gone looking for Green Space's office. Maybe it wasn't such a good idea to go out at night with a stranger. And no one knew where she was, including her.

But Kiyoshi was such a nice guy, he wasn't really a stranger. Was he?

Alison saw nothing but boarded-up buildings around them. "Are you sure this is the spot?" she asked.

"It's down this way," Kiyoshi said. He led her around a corner and into a dark passageway. As they continued, the neighborhood grew more desolate. No other people walked on the streets. No cars passed by. Off at a distance hovered the shell of a burned-out building. It was almost spooky, so marked was the contrast between this deserted area and the nightlife hub they had left. It wasn't the kind of neighborhood where you wanted to be walking at any hour, and especially not at night. Sure, she was with Kiyoshi, but how well did she really know him?

As soon as they crossed the corner, two couples emerged from an unmarked doorway. The muted tones of a jazz band issued from behind the door. Relieved to see other people, Alison followed Kiyoshi down a steep staircase into the basement jazz club.

A man with weighty under-eye circles sat at a booth at the door. He collected their cover fee from Kiyoshi. "Two-drink minimum," the man said.

Cigarette smoke hung thick in the air, and Alison's eyes burned as soon as she entered the club. The space was jam-packed with tables, most of which were occupied by foreigners — Brits, Australians and Americans, Alison surmised from the bits of conversation she overheard. She and Kiyoshi sat down at a wobbly linoleum table. A concrete pillar obstructed their view of the stage.

The band, a three-piece combo, plodded through some old jazz standards, uninspired renditions of "Someone to Watch Over Me" followed by "Smoke Gets in Your Eyes." How appropriate.

A harried waitress came to their table and took their drink orders. They drank in silence, listening to the jazz band labor through "Autumn Leaves."

Kiyoshi must have picked up on Alison's mood because he suggested, "Let's get out of here."

"I'm right behind you," Alison said. She reached for her handbag, but the bag was gone.

"Wait a second, Kiyoshi. I can't find my purse. I left it right here on this chair." Alison looked under the chair next to where she had been sitting and under the table. Kiyoshi joined in the search. They called over their waitress who also helped look, if somewhat unenthusiastically.

"Shit. Shit. Shit," Alison muttered, anticipating all the hassle she'd have to deal with. Losing the credit cards and cash was an unfortunate inconvenience, but she dreaded having to work through the bureaucratic paperwork to get a new passport. And yet another visa.

After twenty minutes, they declared the search futile and gave up looking. On the way out, Alison made one last inquiry, stopping to ask the sour old man manning the entrance desk.

"I lost my bag here tonight. It's a silver mesh bag, about this big," she held up her hands to indicate the size. "If anyone finds it, would you call me at my hotel? I'm staying at the—"

"This it?" The man reached under his desk and pulled out a handbag.

"Yes. Thank you so much. Here, this is for your trouble." She opened her bag to give the man something. Her wallet was there, but the cash was all gone.

"Oh. Let me get your name, and I'll send you—"

Kiyoshi handed the man some bills, and he and Alison climbed the stairs to the street. The fresh air was a welcome change.

"Sorry about the excitement, Alison. But at least you got your bag back. Did you check to make sure everything else is there?"

"Let me take a quick look."

They walked under a bright street light on the main boulevard so that Alison could see better. She felt around inside her bag. Her credit cards seemed to all be there, and, thank God, her passport.

"Looks like all they took was the cash," she said.

"Maybe we should call it a night, then," Kiyoshi said.

"You're probably right."

Within a few blocks they were able to find a cab back to the Regent. The doorman helped them out of the taxi.

Alison turned to Kiyoshi. "It was wonderful to meet you. Finally. And such a surprise. Thanks so much for dinner." Should she bow? Give him a hug? She extended her arm and shook his hand.

"It was my pleasure, Alison." He kissed Alison on the side of her head. Very continental.

"Will I see you tomorrow?" she asked. *Yes, yes, please say yes.*

"I hope so. I'm staying here, too," he added with a smile. "Company apartment."

"Really? Great. Well. I'll say good night then." The awkwardness continued.

"Let's talk in the morning, all right?"

"Of course." Alison leaned forward and kissed Kiyoshi on the cheek. Her lips prickled with pleasure at the scratchy warmth of his skin. She needed to extract herself before she did something she might regret. With a gawky schoolgirl's utter lack of cool, Alison dashed to the elevator.

What a night. No, what a day and what a night.

Standing outside her door, she reached in her bag for her room card key. It wasn't there. Had she left the card key in the room? Or maybe the two-bit thief who had snatched her purse at the jazz club and stolen her cash had also made off with the room key.

But why would someone steal a room key if they didn't know who she was, where she was staying? It didn't make sense. A daunting realization pressed down on her. It wouldn't make sense to steal a room key unless someone knew exactly who she was and exactly where she was staying. Like that psycho cyber creep who managed to know exactly everything about her.

The sensible thing to do would be to get a new room key with a new access code. Just in case.

She took the elevator down to the lobby and explained her problem to the front desk clerk.

"We can issue you a new key right away, Miss Crane." The clerk, a young woman, went into an office and in a few moments returned with a card key.

"This is your new key and the code has been changed. So even if you do find your old key you won't be able to use it."

"Thanks so much," Alison said. She took the card key and headed for the elevator.

"Miss Crane, one moment, please," the clerk called after her. She handed Alison a piece of paper. "This arrived for you a few minutes ago."

Alison gazed at the paper. A fax. She'd given the front desk explicit instructions to destroy any fax that came for her. Why couldn't they understand a simple request? Before she could stop herself, she read the message.

SORRY I CAN'T BE IN HONKON. DID YOU MEET MY FRIENDS? THEY WANT TO SHARE YOUR SOFTWARE TOO. DO NOT MAKE IT HARD FOR THEM AGAIN!!! YOU ARE MY TARGET NOW!!

On the bottom of the fax was a picture of Alison. Hand-drawn concentric circles delineated a target covering her body. The bull's-eye was centered on her forehead.

Alison's stomach knotted with rage. That bastard. That unrelenting, sick bastard. She didn't know how, she didn't know when, but she was going to nail him for fucking around with her like this. She was resourceful. She was smart. She would figure out some way. He was messing with the wrong woman.

Alison turned on the young woman at the front desk. "Excuse me, but I have a problem."

"Yes, ma'am?" The clerk blinked repeatedly as she looked up at Alison.

"I left instructions. Very simple instructions. I'm to receive no phone calls and no faxes." Alison held up the paper, crumpled it into a ball, and dropped it in front of the clerk. "Especially no faxes."

34

Alison unlocked her hotel room door with the new card key. She couldn't wait to get out of her smoky clothes, take a shower and replay in her head the unexpected date with Kiyoshi, the highlight of a day otherwise plagued by mayhem.

She stepped through the door and halted at the sight of her clothes strewn across the floor and her open suitcase flipped upside-down on the bed. Papers from her briefcase lay scattered around the room. A yellow puddle that stunk of urine had soaked into the carpeting.

Alison recovered her rolling bag from the bed and stood the luggage upright on the floor. She examined the bag. Her computer case was still attached, but now the case was hooked on backward. And the lock had been removed.

Either housekeeping was doing a lousy job, or someone had been looking for something. In any event, she was getting out of there.

Alison walked over to the bedside phone, called the operator and asked for hotel security. A guard soon knocked on her door. Accompanying him was a member of the police. Alison recognized the cop's uniform from her misguided visit to the police station. She let the men in and gestured inside.

"As you can see, my room has been vandalized. I was out for dinner, and—"

"May I see your passport, ma'am?" asked the policeman.

"Of course." Alison pulled her passport from her purse.

The cop took down some information and handed Alison's passport back to her. He then pulled out a cell phone and uttered a succession of quick grunts into the phone. After disconnecting the call, he turned to Alison.

"You were at the Western District police station earlier today. About a stolen computer disk. But you did not want to file a report."

"Yes. I mean, no. I went to the station, but there was a mistake. At any rate, I doubt this damage to my room is related to that." Or was it? Could the same goon who had mugged her on the way to Green Space have broken into her room? With a room key he pilfered from the jazz club? Alison closed her eyes and took a deep cleansing yoga breath to calm and center herself. It didn't help.

"What is missing from your room?"

"I'm not sure. I looked at the mess and called security. Everything seems to be here, I'm not sure." Alison caught the two men exchanging a look. "You can see somebody trashed my things," she said. "And they definitely were monkeying around with my computer."

The cop poised his pen over his pad of paper. "Do you want to file a report. This time?"

Alison didn't appreciate his sarcastic tone. "Yes, I do. My handbag was stolen earlier tonight. Stolen from a jazz club near here. I don't know the name of the club, but I can find out."

"And what was in the bag? What was stolen?"

"They took my money — about one hundred dollars. U.S. dollars. But I got the bag back."

The two men looked at each other again. The cop stopped writing on his pad.

Alison pressed on. "But that's not all. They also took my room key. I had to get a replacement at the front desk. The front desk will have a record of that." Why did she feel like she had to defend herself?

The cop rubbed the bridge of his nose. "So you are saying that someone stole a computer disk from you earlier today, but that was a mistake. Then your handbag was stolen, only nothing was taken and you got your handbag back."

"I told you my room key was taken. And my money."

"That is right. Your room key was taken. And cash." The cop snorted. "And someone entered your room, disturbed your computer, but nothing is missing."

"Well, yes. I suppose that's technically correct. But look what they did to my clothes, my papers. They even urinated on the floor." Alison pointed to the damp spot on the carpeting.

"Right. We will call you when we have more information about this — incident." The cop snapped shut his notebook and departed.

The security guard said to Alison, "The hotel would invite you to please move to a different room, as our courtesy to you. Of course, we are sorry, and there will be no charge for the room."

A free room? A nice gesture, but Charles' firm was already footing the bill. And if she stayed at the Regent, whoever had trashed her room would know where to find her. And how to get to her. They'd proven quite adept at it.

"Thank you, but I'm going to check out. Would you have the front desk recommend another hotel for me? Something reasonably priced." Alison hoped that they understood that "reasonably priced" meant a cheap little fleabag. Charles' five-star expense account wouldn't be underwriting her one-star room, but at least she'd be safely ensconced, whereabouts unknown to that freak and his friends.

But maybe she should let someone know that she was leaving. Just in case.

She called the operator and asked to be put through to Kiyoshi Hisaka's room.

"*Moshi moshi.*"

"Hi, Kiyoshi, it's Alison. Someone was in my room tonight, going through my things. I can't imagine what they were looking for, but the place was ransacked."

She wanted to tell Kiyoshi about how she'd gotten mugged on the way to the Hong Kong office of Green Space. But she knew how Kiyoshi felt about Yuko Yamada. And Alison didn't want to go making waves unnecessarily and screw up her best chance of getting a good, full-time job in Tokyo. The mugger was probably some street kid, anyway. The cops didn't seem too concerned.

Kiyoshi asked, "Did you call security?"

"Yes, but I've decided to go to another hotel. I wanted to let you know, since we were planning to meet tomorrow, and—"

"Come stay with me. It's a big corporate suite, and there's lots of room."

Alison hesitated. Alone in a hotel room with Kiyoshi? Innocent enough. Sure, she'd met him online, but she knew him, trusted him. Was she being dumb? Maybe.

"Thanks, but it's OK. The front desk is finding another hotel for me now. I'll call you after I've moved. But I hope we can get together tomorrow. If you still want to, that is."

"Of course I do. Call me. You know where I am."

Alison was stuffing her belongings in her suitcase when the phone rang. "Miss Crane? This is the concierge, and I'm terribly sorry to say that I have called several other hotels, and they all have no space available. The nearest available room is about one hour away by train. So would you consider moving into another room here, compliments of the hotel?"

"Thank you," Alison replied, "but I'd rather not."

Alison dug out her Hong Kong travel guide and started phoning hotels herself. She called eight locations, all with no luck. How could an entire city be sold out of rooms? She knew from experience that San Francisco was notorious for running out of hotel space, but Hong Kong?

Alison picked up the phone. "It's me, Kiyoshi. I don't want to put you out, but I can't find another hotel. If it's OK, can I move to your room? I mean, to your suite? If it's not a problem."

"Not at all. You can have your own bedroom, bathroom. Like I said, there's lots of space."

Her own bedroom. She could lock the door. And she had her burglar alarm to hang on the doorknob. She'd be OK. And Kiyoshi seemed like a nice guy. What could be the harm? "Thanks, Kiyoshi. It's just for tonight. I'll find someplace to go."

"I'll call the bell captain to get your luggage."

"Not necessary. I have one small bag. I'll go check out of the hotel, then I'll come by your room."

She would check out of the hotel and disappear. No one would know where she was. Not those punks who'd trashed her room. And not Charles.

35

Kiyoshi held open the suite's French doors and invited Alison in. Contemporary paintings hung on the walls of the foyer and cloisonné vases overflowing with cut flowers scented the air. The suite's key selling point, however, was the vista from a long balcony that looked out on the harbor and Hong Kong.

"Make yourself at home," Kiyoshi said. He led Alison on a quick tour of the corporate apartment and rolled Alison's bag into an empty bedroom.

"Thanks so much, Kiyoshi. I don't want to be in your hair, but—"

"Nonsense."

Alison returned to the living room and crumpled into a chair. Finally, a quiet moment of peace in a secure place. No obscene faxes, no muggers, no stolen purse, no burglars. The events of the day caught up with her, and, face buried in her palms, she cried softly. Kiyoshi might think she was a nut, but she couldn't stop the tears.

"What's the matter?" Kiyoshi walked over to her chair.

Alison looked up, hugging her arms around her chest. Kiyoshi reached out and took her hand. "You're safe here," he said. "We'll straighten everything out tomorrow." He handed Alison a handkerchief from his back pocket. She took the handkerchief, crisp and ironed, dabbed at her eyes and handed it back.

Kiyoshi didn't seem to mind that his handkerchief was now streaked with mascara. He said, "I have a great idea. It'll help you relax. How about a midnight Jacuzzi?" He gestured with his head to the spa on the balcony.

Alison smiled. Why the hell not? A dip in a spa tub would be just the thing to soothe her nerves, which were strung tight as a violin's bow. "Sounds perfect," she said.

"Meet you outside, then."

Meet her outside? The two of them? Alison had assumed she was taking a dip solo. She didn't have a swimsuit. But then, again, Japanese people didn't wear suits in outdoor baths. Did they? After the fucked-up day she'd had, she didn't much care about social proprieties. "Okay," she said. "Meet you outside."

Alison showered, washed her hair and wrapped herself in one of the luscious hotel robes. She padded out to the balcony where Kiyoshi was already in the hot tub. A bottle of champagne and two flutes stood on a tray alongside a bud vase holding an orchid.

How had Kiyoshi put together such a sweet arrangement so fast? As if she hadn't already exceeded her quota of champagne that night. Was that part of Kiyoshi's plan? Alison didn't care. She was exhausted trying to second-guess people, to worry about their motives. She reminded herself that she had set out to have fun that night, that she was on vacation.

Alison shrugged off her robe and slid into the water next to Kiyoshi. The cool night air on her face contrasted with the warmth of the water to create a delicious sensation of total and instant relaxation.

Kiyoshi opened the champagne bottle and poured the glasses. "*Kampai*!" They took deep swallows as they leaned back and watched the lights of the watery cityscape through the rising mists of the hot tub. The setting felt surreal, pleasant and dreamlike. The gurgling of the spa jets provided a soothing serenade, and all the pain and frustration of the day seeped out of Alison's body.

After several trancelike minutes in the swirling hot water, Alison grew lightheaded and wanted to cool down. She climbed out of tub, and Kiyoshi turned to face away from her as she stood. "Kiyoshi, it's OK.

I'm not shy." Alison sat on the ledge of the spa with her calves dangling in the water.

"It's funny how you don't feel chilly at all after you've been in a hot tub," she said. "It's like you get heated through and through. It's great out here. Open air, night skies."

Awkward and lounging naked in front of Kiyoshi, Alison jabbered away. She wasn't shy. But here, now, she felt like an exhibitionist. And even more worrisome, she admitted to herself, was that she liked the idea that maybe Kiyoshi was checking her out.

Increasingly self-conscious, she decided to slip back in the water. Besides, her Lady Godiva act was starting to get cold.

Alison sank down to her chin in the tub, closed her eyes and enjoyed the water's soft heat on her body. When she opened her eyes, she saw Kiyoshi staring at her. She returned his gaze, holding the contact a little too long. Shaking herself out of the dangerous mood, Alison reached for the champagne glass only to discover it was empty.

Kiyoshi refilled her flute, Alison drank.

"Heaven," she said softly.

"Excuse me?" Kiyoshi turned to her.

Alison set down her glass and gave Kiyoshi a wet champagne kiss. His luscious lips enticed and exhilarated. Alison explored his mouth, unfamiliar yet inviting. It had only been Charles for so long. For too long.

Kiyoshi kissed her neck and shoulders while stroking up the side of her thighs to her ribs. He reached to pull her face toward his, and his hand brushed her nipple. The contact sent shock waves reverberating throughout Alison's body down to her toes.

She took Kiyoshi's hand and pressed it against her chest. "Can you feel my heart racing?"

Kiyoshi plunged his tongue between Alison's lips while he rubbed her nipple with his thumb. Alison dropped her hand to her side, and Kiyoshi twirled and pinched her nipple between his fingers.

Alison's pulse pounded in her temples and throbbed between her legs. She didn't know if it was the heat of the Jacuzzi — or Kiyoshi's hand, which tortured her with its tenderness as it ventured around her electrified body —but she was sure she was going to faint. And the letting-go would feel so good.

"You're in hot water," Kiyoshi said. "Let me help you out."

36

The coffee's smoky aroma tantalized Alison awake. Kiyoshi sat on the edge of the bed and offered her a cup.

"Good morning." She sat up in bed and took a sip. "How did you know I drink coffee?"

"You're an American, aren't you?" he joked.

"Kiyoshi, last night was — was," Alison hesitated, not wanting to sound trite or corny. "You're pretty wonderful," is how she decided to leave it.

He bent over and gave her a quick kiss. "Come out to the deck. See the city waking up."

"I'll be there in a second," Alison said. She finished the coffee, put on her hotel robe and walked to her room. Her unopened suitcase sat next to the bed that was still made up. Alison smiled. Sometimes things don't go according to plan. In a marble bathroom, even grander than the one she had vacated, she opened a complimentary hotel toothbrush, brushed her teeth and splashed cold water on her face.

Alison grinned at her reflection in the mirror. *You've got afterglow, Crane.* She hadn't felt those first-date jitters — the shy curiosity, the excitement of meeting someone new and being immediately attracted to them — in a long, long time. Good thing Charles wasn't around to see her telltale face.

She pushed to the back of her mind the bothersome inconvenience of living with Charles while being smitten with Kiyoshi. The matter was not ripe for deciding.

Just thinking about Charles made Alison realize how far removed from her he was, how separate their lives were. That phone phreak probably knew more about her everyday life than Charles did. But she was reminded that she had unfinished business. There still was a Charles in her life.

"I'm ordering room service," Kiyoshi called from the living room. "Do you want anything?"

"Just some fresh fruit." Alison tamed her bedhead hair with a damp hand towel and declared herself morning-after presentable.

She entered the living room and halted. "Oh my God, Kiyoshi. The message light—" Her trembling finger pointed to the phone. How had that damn techno geek known that she was staying at Kiyoshi's corporate suite?

Kiyoshi looked up from the *Nihon Keizai* newspaper he was reading in the armchair. "What's the matter?"

"Is there a message for me?" Alison's grip on her coffee cup loosened, and Kiyoshi set it on the table before it slipped out of her hand.

"I'll find out what it is." He picked up the phone and spoke to the front desk. "Everything's fine, Alison. It's just a fax. The office gets worried when I'm out of the country."

"I need some air." Alison wandered onto the balcony and stared blankly out on the harbor. Even the port's early-morning clamor and organized chaos couldn't penetrate her anesthetizing sense of anxiety. She bit down on a hardened nail cuticle.

How had she let herself get so overwrought? When a hotel has a message for a guest, they turn a message light on. It didn't mean that the guest was in imminent danger of bodily harm. Kiyoshi must think she was a nutjob.

Room service arrived, and the delivery guy handed Kiyoshi an envelope. "Your fax, sir."

Alison returned to the living room and sank down at the dining table. From over the top of his paper, Kiyoshi watched her pick at melon slices on her fruit plate.

"What's going on, Alison? You look so frightened. I know it was upsetting that someone broke into your hotel room, but you're OK now."

"That's not it. It's—" Alison poked a piece of lychee. "I didn't want to tell you last night."

"Tell me what?"

"I didn't want to ruin things. But that guy sent me a fax yesterday. A fax here at the hotel."

"Who?"

"That weird freak who's been bothering us online."

Kiyoshi set his newspaper aside and opened the envelope that room service had brought. He read its contents. His eyes, usually dancing and animated, now flared. He folded up the fax, creased its edges with the nail of his thumb and sat across from Alison.

"How did the guy know you were here?" Kiyoshi's eyes pierced her with a probing focus.

"Really stupid of me. I sent you an email saying where I was going to stay in Hong Kong."

"But he couldn't have read it. Our messages are encrypted."

"It looks like he figured out the code. Or he somehow read the fax you sent me. Maybe he's even picking up the messages from near my house."

"Near your house? What do you mean?"

"I met someone who told me about a computer program for tracing anonymous email messages."

"Yes, and —?"

"The guy who told me about it — Jed's his name — he said that the creep online might be tapping into my computer line."

"So what if he does have the line tapped. All he'd pick up is modem noise."

"Not according to Jed. If the guy's close to my house running this intercept software, he can see everything my computer is sending or receiving by modem. Kind of like eavesdropping, computer-style."

"So you think this guy might be picking up your computer messages with a bugging device?"

"I don't know how the hell he's doing it, but he's back in the game."

"Looks like he is," Kiyoshi said. "And he knew you were going to be at this hotel. I wonder if he's the one who broke into your hotel room."

"The fax he sent said that his friends had done it."

"I wish you'd told me," Kiyoshi said.

"I'm so damn sick of this guy. He's amusing himself by spying on my life. I'm his puppet. He torments me, pulls my strings, watches me dance."

"We'll find him, Alison." Kiyoshi moved behind her chair and massaged her neck. "We'll stop him."

Alison relaxed beneath the firm pressure of his touch. With a grin, she remembered how just last night those same fingers had launched her into mind-blowing orgasmic ecstasy. But now, in the reality of morning light, her problems were still present, and she recalled what else Jed had told her.

"There's some device I could install to tell if that freak is tapping my computer line. At least that's what Jed said."

"A device? Like a bug detector?"

"Some kind of hardware you run through your computer. If the modem line is being busted into, a light goes on."

"And then?"

"And then you know you've got company close by."

"If he's close by intercepting your email, it means it'll be easier for us to catch him. He's probably just some lonely guy."

"Excuse me if I don't feel the least bit sympathetic. I've had it with his taunting and teasing. And I didn't tell you, but I think he was in my house."

Kiyoshi walked around to stand directly in front of her. "In your house? You saw him in your house?" Kiyoshi's face was stern, his voice hard-edged. Alison felt like she was being interrogated yet again.

"I don't know. I mean, I'm not sure, it's just — like he was there watching me when I was in bed. And when he left there was this threatening note addressed to TokyoAli. Only people I've met on the internet call me that."

Kiyoshi closed his eyes and, after a few seconds, nodded his head as if in agreement with a thought he was having. "The guy's crossed the line, Alison. He could be dangerous. So this is what we'll do. First, we'll call the police in Tokyo to tell them the about the guy, and then—"

"I don't want to get the Japanese police involved. Not yet, anyway. I just cleared up this mess with my visa status, and I don't want them asking me more questions about what I'm doing in Japan. I'll talk to them, but not right now."

"But the police — "

"I want to deal with this myself first, Kiyo. And then I'll turn the guy over to the cops. Okay?"

Kiyoshi sighed, shaking his head. "I can't force you, but you have no idea who you're dealing with."

"You're damn right about that," Alison said.

Kiyoshi sat at the dining table. "There are other ways to handle this problem." He poured himself some green tea. "I know some people who will make sure the guy doesn't bother you anymore."

"I said I want to handle it. My way. Agreed?"

Without answering, Kiyoshi finished his green tea and reached across the table, covering Alison's hand with his. "Listen to me. I've got to stop by the local office. I want you to stay here, keep the door locked. Don't order room service or anything. You can watch TV, read, there's lots to eat in the refrigerator. I'll be back this afternoon. We'll figure out our next step then. Will you be all right?"

"I'm not a child. I can amuse myself."

"It's just that I'm worried, Alison."

"I'll be here when you get back."

"And try not to think about that guy. We'll get him. I promise."

She'd had to rely on Charles to help her with everyday life in Japan where her inability to communicate kept her as isolated as a bird in a gilded cage. And now Kiyoshi was telling her to lock herself up, cut off all contact with the outside world, and wait until he returned to make everything all right.

She didn't think so. She was a lawyer. A highly trained professional. And no one was trained like lawyers were trained on how to figure out solutions to messy problems. It was time for her to clean up the mess.

37

Confession time. Alison dreaded having to explain how she'd managed to lose the disk that Yamada-san had entrusted her with. Would Yamada understand that getting mugged wasn't the same as being careless?

Alison tried again to call Green Space from the taxi. The phone rang, and the same recorded message played. What was going on? Why wasn't anyone answering the office's phones?

Alison put away her cell. She'd have to try again later. She wished she could get it over with. No one liked to be the bearer of bad news. Especially if it might cost them a job.

The cab pulled up in front of the Silvercord building. The trip was shorter than Alison had expected. She could've easily walked to her destination. But having once miscalculated the complexity of Hong Kong's bewildering streets, she'd decided that taking a taxi was the way to go. Plus, if the nut who'd broken into her room was stalking her, a cab might offer her some protection.

Alison entered the multistoried Silvercord shopping center. What her guidebook promised was dead on. The building, with scores of electronics shops, was a computer nerd's Mecca. But where to start?

She wandered the hallways on the first floor and spotted a store with an Apple computer sign hanging in its window. A chubby-cheeked young white guy greeted her at the door. He wore a wrinkled short-sleeve shirt and a necktie that stopped a good six inches shy of his belt.

"Y'all need some help?" he asked.

Amid all the strangeness of Hong Kong and the indecipherable foreignness of the computer hardware in the shops surrounding her, here was an American. Someone she could talk to. Someone who could translate for her.

"Yes, I'm looking for a device to attach to my computer," she said. "It tells you if your modem line is being bugged. I think it's called a Tracer."

"Wow, yeah. I heard about those. Shoot, where did I hear about those gizmos?" The clerk tapped his forehead. Alison had to suppress a chuckle at hearing such a thick Southern accent in the middle of Hong Kong.

The clerk gave up on trying to thwack his brain into recollection. "Can't remember where, but you need anything else? I can give you a good price on the new Microsoft suite. Retails for over seven hundred dollars in the States, I'll let you have it for four-fifty Hong Kong. Comes with a manual. How 'bout it?" He grinned at Alison.

Stacks of photocopied computer manuals were piled up behind the counter. She'd heard about software piracy problems in China. Every company in Silicon Valley was bellyaching about the rampant counterfeiting. But to see it with her own eyes was different. Even the retailers were getting in on the action. A bit brazen.

"I'll pass," she said. "But there's some other software I'm looking for. It's called PeepHole. It's for—"

"Yeah, I heard of that one, too, but we don't carry that neither." The clerk leaned over the counter and lowered his voice. "I'll tell you what you want to do. The kind of stuff you're looking for, you want to go back outside, around to the back of this building. There's a yellow sign, a real big sucker, hard to miss. Says 'Happy Camera.' If anybody has the kind of stuff you're looking for, it's them."

Alison thanked the clerk and left. He'd shamelessly displayed bootleg software for sale, and yet when Alison asked him about PeepHole, he'd reacted as if she were trying to score some heroin. She shrugged it off and walked around to the rear of the building.

If the retail side of Silvercord celebrated unabashed piracy, the back alley was part street festival, part flea market. Men stood behind card tables doubling as impromptu sales counters. They were doing a brisk business selling software ranging from audio CDs to computer games to DVD pornography. The shoppers consisted of mostly young Chinese men and teenagers, but Alison could hear an occasional bit of Japanese.

Scofflaws. Alison picked her way past the miscreants and entered Happy Camera.

The store's walls, painted in taxicab yellow, intensified the glare of the fluorescent lights hanging overhead. Televisions, microwaves, refrigerators, all were scattered hurly-burly throughout the store. Alison couldn't figure out any rhyme or reason to the organization or lack thereof. It was as if a bomb blew up in Akihabara and they erected yellow walls around the wreckage.

After twice touring the perimeter and searching the aisles, she found a store directory. Third floor, computers. She boarded a rickety elevator and rode up.

On the computer floor, disciplined order governed the arrangement of items for sale. Here, the different areas of interest were clearly defined — monitors, printers, memory, PDAs — and each enjoyed its own little cubbyhole.

Unsure of which area to enter, Alison walked to a service island in the middle of the floor. A Chinese man, mid-twenties, in a sweatshirt and jeans, tended the counter.

"Excuse me," Alison said, "I'm looking for a device for my Macintosh. It's called a Tracer. Do you carry them?"

The man's eyes widened briefly. He gave Alison a not too subtle up-and-down scan before saying, "Back here."

Alison followed as the guy led her to a private door in the rear of the computer area. He directed her to sit down at the table in the back room.

"You want an EM Tracer?" the guy asked.

"Yes, if that's what it's called," said Alison. "Basically, I need a device to tell me if my modem line is being listened in on. If someone is trying to access my internet connection."

The guy blew out his cheeks. "Okay. Listening or accessing. That's two different things. The Tracer will tell you if your modem line's tapped. Like from another computer. If your EM waves are being picked up from outside, a light goes on."

"EM waves?" Alison asked.

"Yeah. All this stuff works by electromagnetic waves. Cell phones use security coding, but not modem nets. So computers can be listened in on. If you know what you're doing," the man said. His haughty expression suggested he didn't think Alison knew in the least what she was doing.

Not to be put off by the guy's obnoxious attitude, Alison asked, "Is there any way to scramble the EM waves so that they can't be picked up?"

The guy snickered. "Hey, I haven't heard of it, man. You tell me if you figure it out."

What an asshole.

The young guy continued. "If you need to stop someone from getting into your system, that's FireAx. Access protection. Which is it you want, lady? Listening to EM waves or access protection for your files?" Arms crossed, he eyeballed Alison.

"What do you mean about access protection? Someone at another computer can get inside my Mac and pull up my files?" Alison asked.

The guy sighed wearily as if Alison was his cross to bear. "If you and the other computer are both online through the same Web IP protocols — and you probably are — it's like you're standing out there naked. No protection at all. So you need to load software like FireAx to block access. Or," he paused, "you can run the software to give you access." He let the implication of what he was saying sink in.

Alison leaned in toward the guy. "Let me get this straight. By using the FireAx software, I could block someone from getting into my computer from online. Or use that same software to get into their system."

"Yeah, something like that."

Alison broke into a smile. A preemptive strike had never occurred to her. She could beat that cyberfreak stalker at his own game. She could get online and sneak into his computer. And she could figure out who the hell he was.

But first she had to confirm what she hoped she'd just heard. "Okay. What about this — I want to find out who's sending me anonymous messages. Could I use the software to do that?"

"Easy. It echoes back the source tag."

"Source tag?"

"Yeah, you know, basic stuff. Like user ID, name, phone number."

"That sounds like some software I heard of called PeepHole," Alison said.

"PeepHole?" The guy snorted. "We got PeepHole. But FireAx's much more powerful. PeepHole'll give you some trace data on who's busting into your system, but FireAx'll give you a whole directory of the other system. You can see everything that's on their computer and pull out any files they have on their hard drive. PeepHole can't do that," he sniffed. "But some people use 'em together."

She'd found the mother lode. One-stop shopping for hardware and software to keep that online creep out of her life. "I want it, I want all of it," she said. "The Tracer, the software, PeepHole, FireAx, everything." But. She thought of a threshold problem. "Do you have instruction manuals? In English?"

The computer guy burst out laughing. "English? You crazy, man? All this stuff's from the States. But I wouldn't call it no instruction manual. Just a how-to-do-it thing. Real easy."

"Load me up with the works." Simultaneously giddy and scared, Alison felt like she was buying a gun. She was arming herself against the enemy, and empowerment felt good.

The guy stood. "A Mac, right?"

"Yes, a PowerBook." Waiting alone in the room, Alison fantasized about retribution, about gaining her privacy back, getting her life back.

The clerk returned carrying a metal box not much bigger than a pack of cigarettes and a bunch of floppy disks.

"The Tracer." He handed Alison the small device. A cable dangled from a side port. He gave her a stack of three floppy disks bound together with a rubber band. "These'll load up the Tracer and PeepHole. This is FireAx," he said, passing over a larger stack of about six floppies also bound in a rubber band. "It'll give your system all the protection from the outside you need. But remember you can mix it up and go out looking around in other systems, too. Either way you want it. Got it?"

If Alison was sure of one thing, it was that she didn't "get it."

"Yes, I think I understand," she said. She hoped she could figure it out. "So how much is everything? The Tracer, PeepHole and the FireAx software?"

The man pulled a credit-card size calculator out of his back pocket and punched in some numbers. He turned the calculator around and slid it across the table toward Alison. She read the numbers and chewed on the inside of her cheek. Much more than she was hoping to pay. But she needed this stuff if she were going to mount a serious defense against that online bully.

Imitating a technique she had observed in her shopping expedition the day before, Alison took the calculator, entered a few numbers, positioned the calculator to face the store clerk and pushed it back across the table.

The guy frowned and thought for a moment. Then he punched in some more numbers and slid the calculator back over.

"Deal," Alison said. She paid for the hardware and software and left Happy Camera as a happy customer.

Walking down Salisbury Road on her way back to the hotel, Alison spotted Kiyoshi coming from the opposite direction. He spied her on the street before she had a chance to slip into the hotel.

Footloose on the boulevards of Hong Kong when she had promised to stay in the suite on lockdown, what could she say? She was busted, plain and simple.

Res ipsa loquitur. The matter speaks for itself. The legal term for when evidence of a fuck-up is so obvious that there was no need for an explanation.

And only now did Alison realize that her secretive excursion suffered from a fatal flaw— she didn't have a key to get back into the hotel room. In her job search, she'd be well-advised to rule out a career as an undercover agent.

Kiyoshi trapped her with his laser beam gaze. Alison might not be 007 material, but Kiyoshi, with that penetrating stare, would make an intimidating prosecutor.

"Hey, Kiyo!" Alison tried to distract Kiyoshi with a "say cheese," happy-go-lucky, just-out-for-a-stroll smile. If she had a parasol, she'd be twirling it.

"What are you doing out here, Alison? We agreed. You were going to stay in the room."

"I was bored, so I went souvenir shopping." She hugged her bag of computer supplies closer to her body. "I'm fine, everything's OK." Kiyoshi didn't need to know that she'd loaded up on hacker-grade artillery.

"You've got to be careful, Alison. Bad things have happened, but you've been lucky. So far."

So far she'd been lucky, and now she was going to be smart.

On the way to the room, Kiyoshi stopped at the front desk to pick up his messages. Alison waited by the lobby bar, never tiring of the moving-picture panoramic view of Hong Kong and the harbor. Kiyoshi spoke with the front desk clerk, and the two men turned to look at her.

Under such close scrutiny, Alison's cheeks warmed. She wasn't a hotel guest in her own right, but did the hotel staff think she was a prostitute? She held up her head higher. Who the hell cared what they thought? While she worked on mustering attitude, Kiyoshi walked over.

"Let's go up," he said.

They entered the suite, and Alison quickly put away her Happy Camera bag. In the living room, Kiyoshi was pouring a shot of bourbon into a glass. He held the bottle up to Alison, but she shook her head.

He reached into his lapel pocket and pulled out a folded piece of paper.

"This came for you," he said. "The front desk clerk said it arrived after you checked out, but since they saw you — well, here it is." He gave Alison the paper and tossed back his whiskey.

She took a deep breath before looking at the fax. That creep was not going to leave her alone. And the hotel's front desk couldn't seem to understand that she didn't want to receive faxes. Not when she had been a hotel guest and certainly not now when she wasn't even registered.

But being with Kiyoshi, she didn't feel as vulnerable. And the bag full of goodies she'd acquired at Happy Camera, with their promise of protection, bolstered her sense of empowerment. Whatever madman missive that online jerk might lob her way, she could handle it.

Resignedly, she opened the fax. But it wasn't from the cyber freak. It was a simple handwritten note. From Charles.

Alicats,

When are you coming home? I miss you. I'm going crazy here without you. Please come back soon. We can work it out.

Love you,
C

She quickly folded up the paper as if to make it disappear. Had Kiyoshi read the fax? How could he not have? She watched as he finished off his second drink. Her stomach felt both hollow and leaden.

"Kiyoshi," she started, not knowing what to say or how to say it. "About the fax."

"It's none of my business." He sat down on a chair overlooking the harbor.

"I know I should've said something, told you what was going on with me." Alison was tongue-tied and brain-tied. What did she say to explain something she didn't understand?

Kiyoshi looked at Alison who was still hovering near the door. "Come sit down," he said. Alison did as she was told. "I've known you were with someone, Alison. I've known for a while," he said.

Alison was dumbfounded. What did he know? How could he know? "Huh?" was all she managed to say.

"Our friend online is the one who told me. He sent me some interesting pictures, too."

Alison squinted her eyes closed and buried her face in her hands. Anger mixed with embarrassment. She winced imagining the sort of perverse images that the freak must have sent to Kiyoshi.

"Let me tell you what's going on so you can hear it straight from me." She took a deep breath. Might as well come out with it.

"In Tokyo, I live with someone. Charles is his name. We met in graduate school, years ago."

Kiyoshi sat straight in his chair, listening.

Alison plowed ahead. "He's an investment banker. He got transferred to his firm's Tokyo office, and I joined him. I thought it would be wonderful. But instead, things between us have been…strained."

"You don't have to tell me any of this. I never asked."

"No, I want to. It's only fair. Charles and I have been going through a rocky time. Right before I left for Hong Kong, we had a huge fight. I don't know if I even want to go back to be with him. We used to be so good together. Back when we were at school, it was so much fun and spontaneous and—" Alison stopped. Her rhapsodizing might not fall softly on Kiyoshi's ears. "Charles and I are trying to see where we stand, what's going on with our relationship."

Kiyoshi sat unblinking, his glassy gaze fixed on the harbor.

"I'm so sorry, Kiyoshi. I didn't mean to hurt you or mislead you. Being with you has been like a dream. So easy, so friendly, and so—" She looked away. "Can you understand what I'm trying to say?"

"Of course I can. When my ex-wife left me—" he began slowly.

"She left you?" Alison interrupted.

"Yes. There was someone else. Not with me, with her. Someone she met at a party. A party I took her to." Kiyoshi focused on a distant image. From the lines etching his eyes, Alison could see his pain at the recollection of the betrayal.

"I'm so sorry," she said.

Kiyoshi tried to smile. "We were having our problems, too." He moved next to Alison on the sofa. "I know it's not easy sometimes. I'm not putting any pressure on you."

Alison was the one who smiled now. "You're unbelievable, Kiyoshi. Thank you. I need some sorting out time. To figure out what's going on."

"Take all the time you need. Come to Kobe if you want a change from Tokyo. We've got company apartments, and—"

"Thanks, but I need to work it out with Charles, one way or the other. In fact, I should probably make some reservations back to Tokyo."

Alison went into a small sitting room in the suite, closing the door behind her. She called Cathay Pacific and was able to book a seat on a flight the following morning. Next came the harder call.

She dialed Charles' office. A secretary answered his phone and told Alison that he was in Osaka.

"Would you tell Mr. Gordon that Alison is coming back to Tokyo tomorrow?" Alison relayed her flight information and hung up the phone.

She returned to the living room where Kiyoshi was working on a notebook computer. "Everything all right?" he asked.

"I got a reservation on a flight tomorrow morning."

"That's good. I mean, that's terrible, but it's good."

"I know what you mean." She liked this man all over again. "Kiyoshi, how about we stay in for dinner, get room service?"

"A quiet evening sounds perfect."

"Who said anything about quiet?" Alison replied.

38

Before the plane began its descent, Alison locked herself in the restroom, beating the crowd. In the cramped space, she fought to brush out her curls and bind up her hair in a severe French twist. She smoothed the front of her silk blouse under the lapel of her suit and traded her comfy travel loafers for conservative pumps. A string of pearls and reading glasses finished the look.

Faster than you could say "Clark Kent," Alison's transformation was complete. She was now a no-nonsense international lawyer returning from a business trip to Hong Kong. She would play it as the woman at the U.S. Embassy had suggested — costume, props and all. Alison wouldn't have any problem clearing immigration now. And with her new visa, everything would go smooth as sake.

The "Return to Seat" light came on in the restroom as Alison was admiring her metamorphosis. She was ready for them. She returned to her seat, strapped in and prepared for reentry in Japan. Game on.

Putting on her lawyer's face, a mask of imperturbable composure with a touch of arrogance, Alison walked down the concourse and rounded the corner leading to the arriving-passenger checkpoint. Long queues of disheveled, jet-lagged travelers stood at the immigration windows, trying to enter Japan. Not certain that her bladder could hold out for an indefinite duration, Alison made a restroom pit stop so that she wouldn't have to break away from the line and lose her place.

She returned to the area for clearing "Alien" passports and moved slowly along the back wall. She wasn't looking for the shortest line. Or the line with the most U.S. passport holders, which Charles said tended to move along faster than lines with mostly Asian nationals. Instead she was looking for an immigration officer who appeared friendly. Someone she could connect with. Someone who would be sympathetic in return.

Alison sauntered along, studying each officer, looking for her pigeon. Window after window was manned by a bitter-faced functionary. Officious attitudes and job tedium oozed from their sagging faces. She could do better. She continued walking while trying to not draw any attention to herself.

Bingo. She spotted her guy. Late twenties, cheerful demeanor. He even smiled at a baby in the arms of a woman at his window. Definitely the right line. She wheeled her bag and joined the long queue.

After thirty minutes in the slow-moving line, it was Alison's turn to approach the window. She pulled up in front of the immigration officer and smiled.

"Passport, please," he said. Alison made a show of opening her all-business briefcase to get out her passport and immigration forms. The officer took the documents.

He flipped through her passport and stopped on a page. Alison imagined it must be the page with the damning stamp of "FINAL EXTENSION" calling attention to the fact that she had overstayed her visa. Why hadn't she just lost this passport and applied for a replacement at the U.S. consulate in Hong Kong? Too late now. On with the show.

"What is your reason for coming to Japan?" the officer inquired.

"I'm an attorney, and I have some business meetings in Tokyo." She put extra emphasis on "attorney" and "business meetings."

"*Soo ka*," the officer said. He held open the inside front cover of Alison's passport and cross-checked the number against a computer-generated list in a notebook. Alison caught his not-so-subtle glance up at her before he returned to examining her documentation.

With the back of a pen, he tapped each number in her passport. Tap

tap tap, pause, tap tap tap, pause, tap tap tap. He then referred to a line in his notebook and drummed out the same nine beat rhythm.

The officer looked up. He sucked air through his teeth, while rubbing the back of his head. His scrunched face looked pained, as if he felt a migraine coming on.

Alison would've offered him an ibuprofen, but it might be construed as bribery. And no way was she going to chance anything that might jeopardize her reentry into Japan.

"Wait here, please," he said. The officer left his booth, taking Alison's passport with him. He walked down the length of the immigration desks to a glass-enclosed office.

What was going on? Where was the guy going with her passport? Alison couldn't help but steal a glance in the direction of the office he entered. Her immigration guy was conferring with an older man sucking a cigarette. His face was so puckered it looked like it had been dehydrated.

Seeing her officer returning, Alison spun around to stare straight ahead. She attempted to muster a pleasant look, an unperturbed smile. She failed.

The immigration officer spoke to her, his eyes darting. "Please, go with this man." He gestured to a policeman who had materialized at Alison's side.

"Is there a problem, sir?" she asked. "And, I'd like my passport back, please." Alison didn't want to budge from the line, but she didn't want to appear uncooperative, either. She tried to swallow, but her mouth was dry.

The formerly cheery immigration officer's face was now red and flustered. "Go, please." He gestured for Alison to accompany the policeman who was now standing so close to her that she could smell his BO.

A cloud of confusion immersed Alison in déjà vu. Why was she being detained? She had her ticket out of the country and a roll of money to flash, everything the U.S. Embassy woman had suggested would facilitate smooth sailing with Japanese immigration.

At the consulate in Hong Kong she'd said her *mea culpas* and paid her fines for overstaying. Now what did they want — her first-born?

She wished Kiyoshi were there to help her. Or even Charles.

Alison adjusted her glasses. With wheeling bag in one hand and briefcase in the other, she accompanied the policeman who marched her toward the glass room.

The policeman held open the door to the office which, despite its see-through walls, was as claustrophobia-inducing as a two-person submarine. The prune-faced cigarette-smoking immigration official sat behind a metal desk. Alison's passport and immigration papers lay spread out in front of him. Her police escort retreated to position beside the office door.

Inquisitive passersby peered inside to catch a glimpse of something they were sure glad wasn't happening to them. Alison felt like an exotic specimen in a fish tank.

"Have a seat, Miss Crane," Prune Face said. He motioned for Alison to sit down in the empty chair in front of his desk. "I see you are arriving from Hong Kong. Did you enjoy your time there?" He smiled, revealing tobacco-stained teeth.

What was with the chitchat? Was he trying to lure her into a false sense of security through some sadistic cat-and-mouse game? She'd play along. She had no choice.

"The food was quite good and the harbor sights were amazing." She tried to match his breezy tone.

"Was it your first visit to Hong Kong?"

"Yes, it was." He could see that from her passport. Why the hell didn't he get to the point?

"What did you do in Hong Kong?" He sat forward in his chair and, through half-closed reptilian eyes, analyzed Alison. She felt that he was reading her every little gesture, her every eye movement.

Alison tilted her head and tried to look unruffled despite the fact that she could feel her silk blouse sticking to her sweaty armpits. "I did some sightseeing, rode on the Star Ferry." She hoped to sound like the innocent abroad. Hell, she was innocent.

"And I see you visited the Japan Consulate," he added, holding up her passport.

Alison nodded. "Since I'm in Japan on business, I thought I should have a proper business visa, not a tourist visa like I had before."

Prune Face silently smoked his cigarette, his eyes locked on Alison. Was he waiting for her to elaborate? To confess to her relatively minor visa infraction? Alison swallowed, her mouth dry.

"I miscounted the number of days I could stay here on a tourist visa. As soon as I realized my mistake, I immediately contacted the immigration office in Otemachi. And my embassy." Would mentioning the U.S. Embassy to this functionary encourage him to go easy on her? It was worth a try.

"I see." He didn't sound impressed by her diligence. "Is this the address where you plan to stay during your visit in Japan?" He pointed to her immigration papers. "Nishi-Azabu?"

"Yes, it is."

"That is a house, correct?"

"Yes, it is." She could behave like a well-trained witness testifying on the stand, offering only minimal answers. The less she said, the better. At least until she understood where he was going with his questioning and why she had been specially selected for the fish tank interrogation.

"Who owns the house?" the official persisted. He was all business. His breezy tone had blown away.

"Uh, it's my — it's rented by the firm a friend of mine works for."

"What is your friend's name?"

Alison didn't want to answer any of these questions. But she didn't see any alternative.

"His name is Charles Gordon."

"And his company?"

"Morgan Sachs." Alison hoped this wasn't going to make trouble for Charles at his job.

"I see. Did you make any special trips for Morgan Sachs during your stay in Hong Kong?"

"No. I don't understand what you mean. I was in Hong Kong for personal reasons."

Prune Face took a long drag on his cigarette before crushing it in the glass ashtray. "You stay in a house rented by Morgan Sachs, they paid for your airfare to Hong Kong as well as for your hotel accommodations. And yet you claim you went to Hong Kong for personal reasons?"

"I — my boyfriend, my fiancé, Charles, he offered to pay for the ticket. It was charged to his firm, but I'm going to pay him back."

"Miss Crane, your answers are — I will say — insufficient."

"It's the truth." Alison crossed her arms, wrinkling her power suit. She was off her game, shrinking and sweating and on the defensive.

What was the relevance of this new line of inquiry about where she was staying in Tokyo and who had paid for her hotel? It wasn't complicated. She'd fucking overstayed her fucking tourist visa.

Did she need a lawyer? Did she even have the right under Japanese law to request a lawyer? She swallowed again. Her throat was parched from answering so many questions.

"May I have some water, please?" she asked the immigration official. He tapped another cigarette out of the pack of Mild Sevens on his desk, lit up and enjoyed a protracted inhale, ignoring her request.

Fuck the old prune. He needed hydrating more than she did.

"Tell me. Why did you leave your plane and walk directly into the ladies' restroom, Miss Crane?"

Was this guy kidding? Alison wanted to come back with a smartass retort except for the fact that she was in a foreign country being interrogated. The joke would be on her. "I had to use the facilities," she said.

"A restroom can be a convenient place to rearrange cargo, wouldn't you agree, Miss Crane?"

"Cargo? No. I mean, I don't—"

"What are you carrying with you, Miss Crane?" Prune Face tapped the ash off of his cigarette and hit it yet again. Hadn't he heard anything about the dangers of smoking? Not to mention the effect of the secondhand smoke he was imposing on his detainees. But given the circumstances, Alison didn't feel compelled to object.

"I have my passport, plane ticket, documents, clothes. The usual things."

"What did you collect in Hong Kong that you're concealing now? What did Morgan Sachs arrange for you to transport?"

"Nothing. I don't know how you got the idea that I was trying to bring something into the country without—"

The official picked up his desk phone, snarled at the person on the other end, and hung up. Before the prune had a chance to suck on his cigarette, a pudgy woman with the downturned mouth of a catfish entered the office.

"We need to conduct a search, Miss Crane. Please go with Ikeda-san."

"A search? What are you talking about? I want to call the American Embassy. I have the right to call the United States Embassy."

"Certainly, you may call, Miss Crane. As soon as we finish." He nodded at Ikeda.

"Leave your bags and follow me," the woman said. She snapped on a pair of latex gloves as she led Alison into an adjoining room.

01101011 01101110 01101111 01110111

Standing naked in the bright room, bending over when told, submitting to being poked and probed, Alison squeezed her eyes shut so hard that she saw searing red-orange flames behind her lids. She bit her top lip to keep the tears at bay.

What the hell were they looking for? Why did they think she was concealing something in her privates? She was a lawyer, goddammit. Not some mule for a Golden Triangle drug dealer.

After inspecting Alison's every bodily crevice, the sadistic customs officer from hell told her she could get dressed. Alison quickly put back on her underwear, pantyhose and power suit. Evidently, her power suit wasn't powerful enough. She stepped into her pumps and exited the torture chamber.

The lizard-eyed old prune, still sitting at his desk, flashed his tobacco-browned teeth at Alison and held out her travel documents. Through a veil of smoke he said, "Welcome to Japan, Miss Crane."

"And what a warm welcome." Under her breath she added, "Prune-faced bastard." Alison snatched up her passport and immigration papers, retrieved her bags and bolted out of the glass prison.

Her body burned with the humiliation of the invasive search. What was with that inquest? Why had she been singled out for the special treatment? Walking down the stairs to the Customs area, she considered reporting her experience to the U.S. Embassy, but decided against it. When it came to immigration matters, she realized she was on her own. And one thing she was sure of, having learned the hard way, was that the Japanese take their immigration laws very seriously.

As a precaution against any future legal entanglements or latex-gloved strip searches, Alison stopped to examine her passport's new visa stamp. Everything looked good to go. She resolved to mark her visa expiration date on her calendar with a thick red circle. Nobody could call her a slow learner.

She joined the fatigued travelers pushing luggage carts and toting suitcases while waiting in line to clear customs, the final checkpoint on their entry into Japan. The green sign hanging overhead read "Aliens with Nothing to Declare."

39

Alison rummaged through her purse, examined every corner of her briefcase. Where were they? She was sure she'd packed them. What had she done with her house keys?

She dug through the pockets of her overcoat yet again. She remembered having the keys in Hong Kong, remembered removing them from her evening bag because of their bulkiness and weight. After that, she wasn't so clear.

Could the person who broke into her hotel room have taken her house keys? Why would they want them?

She took out her cell phone and called Charles' number at the office.

"Morgan Sachs."

"Charles Gordon, please. It's Alison Crane."

"Gordon's in Osaka. Hang on, I'll transfer you."

A tinkling Casio keyboard rendition of "Greensleeves" played while Alison was on hold. What was with Japanese telephones and "Greensleeves"? And "Home on the Range"?

"Morgan Sachs *de gozaimasu*," a Japanese operator said.

"Hello," Alison ventured in English, "I'd like to speak to Charles Gordon." Winning the arm-wrestle over the governing language for communication was the all-important first step.

"*Eh to* — Gordon-san is not here."

"Do you know how I can reach him?"

"Not here."

"Is there someone there who speaks English?"

"Thank you very much." The phone went dead.

"Dammit! Dammit!"

Alison pummeled her wheeling bag and slumped on the ledge of the front door step. All she wanted was to take a hot shower — no, a hot bath — and soak away all memory of prying fingers and exploring hands. Her abdomen contracted when she thought of the violation. Strip-searched. How demeaning. And now she was locked out of the damn house.

Who could she call to help her? Charles wasn't reachable, but she could try Yamada. She had the number at Green Space, and she needed to tell Yamada about her bungled disk delivery job.

Alison was certain to impress Yamada. In all the wrong ways. She imagined the call. Hello, Yamada-san, this is Alison Crane. I'm locked out of my house. Can you help me? And by the way, you remember that disk you entrusted me to deliver to your office in Hong Kong? Well, I have no idea where it is. It was guaranteed to be an awkward conversation, but Alison was out of options.

She dialed Green Space and heard the same exasperating answering-machine message. What the hell were they saying? In a flash of brilliance, Alison called the English information line and asked them to try the Green Space number for her. They could get through and translate the answering machine message.

Alison waited on the line while the operator called Green Space.

"Ma'am," the operator said. "The number you gave me, are you sure you have the correct phone number?"

"Yes, I'm quite sure."

"Excuse me, ma'am," the operator hesitated, "but the phone number has been disconnected. That is what the message on the recording said."

Disconnected? How could the Green Space number be disconnected? Alison still owed Yamada a lot of research work. Or she owed Yamada a lot of money for work not performed. What had started out as an extraordinarily shitty day was now taking a turn for the absurd.

If the Green Space phones weren't working, the only way Alison could reach Yamada would be to swing by their office. Their heavily guarded office. Alison wouldn't be surprised if they took their phones offline because of some nutcase threat. She'd follow up in the morning, after she'd had a chance to take a hot bath and things returned to normal.

"Thank you for trying, operator."

"My pleasure, ma'am."

"Oh, operator!" Alison had another flash of inspiration. Or inspired desperation. "I have a bit of a problem. I got locked out of my house. Do you have a number for a locksmith?"

"Yes, ma'am. I can call a lock company for you. What is your address?" Alison told the operator her *ku*, her block number and the lot number on the block in Nishi-Azabu. If only Japanese houses had real addresses like in the States. Definitely an idea worth importing.

"And your name, ma'am?" Alison told her, and the operator placed her back on hold.

The cement step she was sitting on felt like a block of ice. Alison's butt was going numb waiting for the operator to get back to her. Was Tokyo already so deep into winter, or was it just that she had gotten used to the gentler climate of Hong Kong?

She drifted back to thoughts about hot water, a hotter tub, and lavender verbena bath salts. She'd managed to "borrow" a few packets. Souvenirs. Kiyoshi had enjoyed their shared morning bath as much as she had. Maybe more. She'd made sure of it.

The operator's voice whiplashed Alison back to bone-chilling reality. "I'm sorry, ma'am. The lock company said that your name is not on the police registry. They are not allowed to replace the locks. Perhaps you could call a—"

"Thank you, operator. I'll figure something out."

The rules, the endless rules. When would she ever learn the interminable rules of life in Japan? Point her chopsticks to the left, not the right. Turn her shoes to face the door when she stepped up from a *genkan*. Wear slippers inside but take them off before walking onto a tatami mat. Don't pour her own sake, wait for someone to do it for her.

Kiyoshi had dutifully kept her champagne flute filled. Alison had assumed he was trying to nudge her toward the tipsy side of good judgment, but maybe he was just being polite, in keeping with Japanese custom. Perhaps the Japanese strictures didn't stem from robotic compliance with random rules, but rather an acknowledgment of basic courtesy.

It was obvious who she should call. Alison dialed Kiyoshi and waited. With each passing second of ringing, her hope of finding Kiyoshi waned and then died along with her cell phone battery.

Kiyoshi wasn't answering. Charles was unreachable. Her cell phone was out of juice, and her ass was anesthetized from the frigid steps.

The rule-bound lock company wouldn't change the bolt on the house, but that didn't mean she couldn't get in. There was always the utility room door in the backyard. Alison slapped her legs to get the blood flowing, stored away her computer, and wheeled her bag to the side of the house.

A dense thicket of towering bamboo blocked entrance to the backyard from the street. The grove had looked like a picturesque landscaping feature, a nod to the location of an ultra-contemporary Western house incongruously sited in Asia. But now the gargantuan grass was the enemy that denied Alison entry.

She fought through the bamboo, sidling between stems that grabbed her pantyhose and scratched her skin. Emerging from the grove, she examined her now bedraggled power suit. Finding a new interview outfit would be a challenge in Tokyo, where the clothing wasn't cut to accommodate her long arms, long legs and Black girl butt.

The setting sun and the falling temperature reminded her that she had more immediate concerns than worrying about her wardrobe. She needed to get into the house.

The backyard, a poured concrete deck edged with maple saplings staked to poles, offered no comforting nature energy, no welcoming urban sanctuary. But even this sterile patch of artificial outdoorsiness could provide the equipment she needed. A rock. If she wanted to get home, she'd have to break in.

Alison searched around the artfully stamped and acid-stained terrace, but came up empty-handed. Whoever heard of a backyard without a rock? She could find one if she raided a neighbor's yard. But if they spied her snooping in their bushes, they might call the cops. And she'd had more than her fill of dealing with cops.

Alison studied the house's exterior and saw the mission-critical problem with her comic-book heroine plan to smash through the utility room's window with a rock and scramble through the opening. The door was windowless.

She twisted the knob and yanked. The mechanism didn't yield. The solid door was locked tight as a bank vault. She wasn't Wonder Woman, and she wasn't getting in.

Alison tromped back through the bamboo, stood at the front door and pondered her options. If the alternatives were spending her own money to check into a hotel or sitting in the dark as night fell hard around her, she could do it. She had no choice.

Alison kicked off her shoe — her favorite lawyer dress-up Ferragamo pump — and examined its heel. A rock would definitely do the trick, but an Italian shoe? She hoped so.

Grabbing the shoe by its vamp and closing her eyes, Alison swung hard, aiming for the middle of front door's windowpane. The glass didn't break, but the heel of her pump did. Shit. Since she would be going to the cobbler anyway, no harm in trying again with the other shoe.

She stepped out of the pump and immediately realized her error. She didn't have proper grounding to swing the bat the first time. Yoga class 101. Solid grounding with the earth and proper breathing equals power. This time it would work.

Alison inhaled sharply feeling the connection of her pantyhosed feet on the cold steps. On a powerful exhale, she batted at the window with her remaining shoe. The pump bounced off the window intact. Those Italians knew how to make some sturdy footwear.

Barefoot and shivering, Alison reassessed her situation. Charles was MIA. Kiyoshi was who-knows-where. And the locksmith was not inclined to do her any special favors. Smashing through the window had seemed like the best course of action, but with no rock and no more shoes, she was at a loss. And the evidence had established that she was no Wonder Woman.

Alison rummaged through her suitcase for something with enough heft to break the glass. Lightweight travel clothes and hotel bath salts weren't going to cut it. She eyed her computer case. No way was she going to use her precious Mac as a battering ram. But maybe there was some other part she could sacrifice.

Alison opened the case and took out the computer's power adapter. A mini electronic brick, the device was small enough for her to get a good grip yet weighty enough to mean business. She might be able to lob it through the window. And if its delicate electronics broke into pieces on impact, she could always ask Jed to get a replacement.

Holding the power adapter with its dangling cord, she remembered a TV show on NHK about Olympic athletes preparing for competition in the hammer throw. The national Japanese network's programming could be dry viewing, but since they often simulcast in English, it was Alison's most-watched channel.

The hammer throw competitors had swung a big rock attached to a wire over their heads, lasso style, circling with increasing momentum before releasing the rock and hurling it into the distance.

Alison unwound the scarf from her neck. Silk fibers were supposed to be strong, and the scarf looked long enough. It was a crazy idea, but she was desperate. And no one was watching on her quiet residential street. It was worth a try.

She shrugged off her battle-scarred jacket, stretched her scarf out on the step and placed the power adapter on top. Right over left, left over right. Alison drew on knot lore acquired at summer camp to cinch one end of the scarf tight around the adapter.

Clutching the tail end of the scarf in both hands, she took a deep grounding breath before whipping her improvised hammer throw weight over her head. Around and around, the lassoed mass gained centrifugal force. Alison envisioned the pig-faced Customs woman who had invaded every inch of her personal space, and on the count of three, directed her payload toward the window.

The glass, designed to be earthquake-safe, shattered into tiny, harmless cubes. Alison reached through the smashed window and unlocked the door. Wonder Woman would approve.

She toted her belongings inside and hung the travel burglar alarm on the doorknob. At least she'd have an early warning if someone tried to surprise her. An early warning, and then what? She'd think about that later. Charles could get the window repaired. Once he reappeared.

Dropping her ruined pumps in the genkan, Alison stepped into slippers. It had only been a few days, but her own living room felt as unfamiliar and impersonal as a hotel room. Colorless, utilitarian, lacking in coziness. Vestiges of her fight with Charles hung thick in the air and pulled her back to the unresolved state of affairs. But he was absent now. And she had something to look forward to.

Alison opened her suitcase and removed the plastic laundry bag from the Regent Hotel. The loot she had scored at Happy Camera and deposited in the bag was waiting for her.

A prickle of paranoia made her glance at the closed blinds. Of course nobody was watching her, but still she felt on display. There was nothing flagrantly illegal — she hoped — about the goods she'd purchased in Hong Kong. But unloading her spoils in the private study would feel more comfortable.

Alison carried the bag to the secluded office and switched on the desk's reading light. The room was dark except for the pool of illumination spotlighting her gear.

Like a child on the afternoon of a bountiful Christmas morning, she reexamined her haul. The little Tracer box had a reassuring bulk and metallic hardness. She enjoyed the quaintness of the rubber bands bind-ing her stacks of unlabeled floppy disks. No instruction manual needed, the guy had said. He better be right.

Alison positioned her laptop on the desk. Her new supplies offered power, control, admittance to a cordoned-off community. She was kitted out with equipment that was possibly illicit, or at least of curious origin. Who cared? Whatever it took to reclaim her life, her own space, her own thoughts.

She'd begin with hooking up the Tracer box. The instructions for the Tracer were minimal. Alison mulled over references to SCSI chains and external terminators. What were they talking about? The instructions assumed that the user knew what he — she — was doing. An erroneous assumption. She hoped that the simplest way to hook up the box would be the right way. It was her only way.

Holding the cable that came with the Tracer, Alison poked around the ports in the back of her computer, looking for a match. The cable only fit snugly in one hole. Thank God for idiot-proof design. Alison connected the Tracer box's power cord to an electrical outlet. She was off to a good start.

Installing the PeepHole software on her computer was easy and uneventful. Bolstered by her success, Alison picked up the FireAx program designed to give her protection from snoops trying to break into her computer. Or enable her to nose around in their system, Alison remembered.

She removed the rubber bands from the stack of FireAx disks and, one by one, copied the contents onto her hard drive. Some of the disks loaded up easily, while others got spit out by her computer. Quality control, where's the quality control? Alison tried installing the last floppy three times before her computer would accept the disk. The entire operation took her nearly forty minutes. A slow start, but a successful install. A smile spread across her face. She was back in the game and ready to rock.

Alison booted up the new software and flipped on the Tracer box.

Nothing happened. She slapped her forehead. *Wake up, Crane!* Of course nothing was happening. She wasn't online.

She logged onto World NetLink. No mail was waiting for her. The little red light on the Tracer box didn't flash on. FireAx wasn't spitting out reports of attempted system break-ins.

She didn't know for sure what she had bought at Happy Camera. In her eagerness to fortify her defenses against the cyber freak, had she been rooked? A gullible tourist who'd been sold crap? Maybe so. Caveat emptor.

But until someone came at her online, she couldn't be certain that her gear was legit, so to speak. She'd have to make herself vulnerable to attack. Only then she could test just how powerful the software was, if the Tracer device was advanced microcircuitry or merely a box of wires.

Alison didn't relish the thought of hanging around online, waiting for someone to stroll by and try to break into her system. Not her idea of fun.

But it might hasten things along if she were to hold herself out as bait. She could test PeepHole by going to one of the more lively chat areas and getting approached.

Alison knew which chat areas got the biggest play — the seamier chat rooms. It felt kind of sleazy hanging out in an Adults-Only chat, but she wanted to know if the software worked. Maybe even the cyberjerk himself would make an appearance. She'd have to try.

TokyoAli logged out of World NetLink, and Alison created a new screen name for herself, just for the occasion, and logged back on. Tokyo Ali was now PartyAnimal. In her new persona, Alison cruised over to the Adults-Only section.

Checking out the active rooms, she decided to enter the "Looking for Love" chat area.

Alison was online only a minute before she got a direct message from KimDwong.

`"Hello, PartyAnimal. MOF?"`

"Pardon me?"

"Are you male or female?"

"Female."

"Do you cyber?"

"Yeah, sure." What the hell was he talking about?

"Let's do it!"

Alison hit the "OK" button and joined KimDwong in a private chat room. How long would she have to have a connection for the software to work?

"Tell me what you look like, Miss Animal."

"I'm five foot seven, I have long blond hair down to my curvaceous hips, and I've got huge tits like watermelons."

"You sound hot. I'm getting hard."

Yuck. How long did she have to keep this up?

"Tell me about yourself, Dwong."

"I'm six feet of studly manliness. My dick is rock hard now. Eight inches. Can you handle it?"

This has got to be enough.

"Sorry, Dwong. All of my men are one-footers."

She abruptly disconnected the chat.

Now, let me take a look at you through my PeepHole, KimDwong. She exited the network and opened the PeepHole log.

```
13:43
Recipient Name: PartyAnimal
Registered as: Alison Crane
User Computer Identification: Alison Crane
Logon Point: 8132345-2348
Sender Name: KimDwong
Registered as: Tei Dwoh-Kwan
User Computer Identification: Kaiwoo Electronics
Logon Point: 8862411-8546
```

Alison grinned as she read the well of information captured by PeepHole activity log. She recognized her phone number, but where was the phone number KimDwong was calling from? She consulted the English language phone book. Taiwan. Great. She'd been picked up by some horny Taiwanese electronic lounge lizard who was calling from his job, no less.

At least she knew that the PeepHole software was working. All she had to do now was wait for the cyber freak who'd been tormenting her to crawl along, and then she'd spring the trap. She had the means to expose his ass. He wouldn't be able to hide behind bullshit online anonymity.

Pleased with her progress so far, Alison booted up the FireAx program to get a feel for how it worked. She opened the text file, which warned her to ReadMeNow. The instructions might as well have been in Japanese for all she could glean from them. She decided to trust the program's professed intuitive interface to hold her hand while she stumbled through learning the software.

The FireAx boot-up screen offered Alison two set-up options, Basic or Power User, depending on the level of protection against intruders and search capabilities in accessing remote systems. The Power User option contained a perplexing array of customization. Alison opted for the basic settings. She was happy to swim in the shallow end. Or even just splash in the kiddie pool.

The program described how in the event a foreign system tried to access her computer, she would get an on-screen notification and a report of an attempted break-in. The report included the perpetrator's tag — their calling card, as the guy at Happy Camera had said — their phone-in access point, computer identification, plus the time of the attack.

Alison pushed up her sleeves. Time to get busy.

FireAx's defensive muscle was only half of its talent. The software could also make a proactive move and enter another system. To test out FireAx on the offense, Alison needed to call up another computer network and see if she could get inside. It wasn't like she was breaking any laws. She was only exploring, taking FireAx for a spin.

But which computer network to call? World NetLink was certain to have impenetrable protective barriers in place. And they had her phone number in their records. They could easily detect her trying to sneak in the back door. She needed another network.

A twinge of pain stabbed at Alison's shoulders, which had borne the burden of her amateur attempt at an Olympic hammer throw. Massaging her trap muscles, she wondered how she could find some other network. It wasn't like she could call the English language operator the way she had called for help in getting in touch with Green Space.

Of course, that was it. Suzuki-san had taken special pride in telling her about Green Space's electronic bulletin board, its BBS. Alison couldn't remember the name of the network, but Suzuki had written down the phone number. Buried in her pile of research documents was the paper Suzuki had given her with the network name jotted down. Green Net. She had her guinea pig.

All she had to do was see if she could get inside the Green Net system, take a quick look at the private file directory, and scoot back out. Then she'd know for sure that FireAx was working, that she had real protection against her cyber stalker.

With the timid excitement of a new driver taking her first solo spin, Alison entered the Green Net BBS phone number in the FireAx program. She reversed the direction of the program's arrow to indicate that she wanted to call into the location rather than monitor calls from the outside.

The built-in computer modem clicked and dialed. Alison's heartbeat reverberated in her stomach, and she unbuttoned the tight collar of her blouse.

A directory of files arranged in columns appeared on the monitor. Most of the text was gibberish — a random assortment of letters, symbols and numbers — but some were in English. File listings she could read included Press Releases, Int'l. Transfers, Acquisitions and Foreign Orgs.

She'd done it. She was looking at the inner workings of Green Space's computer network.

Alison clicked on the Press Releases heading. Nothing happened. She tried again. No response.

Alison sank back in the chair and rolled her shoulders. Who was she kidding? She didn't know what she was doing. She'd gotten overly excited and bought some software that was at best over her head and at worst a piece of shit. Maybe Jed could help her figure out which.

Scrolling to close up the press release column, she noticed that the releases were listed as item 17. Was that the problem? Was it as simple as that? She typed "17" on the keyboard. The screen momentarily blanked out then flashed a list of dates and titles:

```
08.05.94  Coral Reef Endangered in Japan
13.03.93  Golf Resort Pesticides in Philippine Drinking
Water
25.08.93  Malaysia Tropical Rain Forest Destroyed
```

The screen displayed three more pages of listings, and Alison skimmed some of the articles. Typical marketing hype touting the organization's work.

Since she was already poking around, she might as well see what else was on the network. Alison opened the Foreign Orgs category and scanned what appeared to be a list of accounts at financial institutions.

Account	Location	Transfer Agent
Kazan Fire Trust	Vanuatu	Pacific Bank & Trust
Lakefrost Holdings	Zurich	Fifth Trust Co.
Coral Waters Trust	Nauru	Bank of Samoa
Palmetto LP	Tonga	Banco de Vallarta
Sunlight Trust	Guernsey	Hangsen Bank Co.
Turtle Bay Holdings	Grand Cayman	Gulf Shore Bank

An otherwise random assortment of banks, but Alison recognized the locations from listening to her father, the tax attorney, during his riveting dinner conversation. Tonga, Guernsey, Nauru, the Caymans. All of the locations shared a common denominator — they didn't ask too many questions about the movement of foreign currency.

Ms. Yamada had said that Green Space was having problems transferring money to fund its international offices. No wonder they parked their cash in tax havens. Only made sense.

Alison was rolling the computer's trackball to close up the file directory when one particular entry jumped out.

Tropic Reef Development	Bahamas	Morgan Sachs

Tropic Reef? That was the real estate developer planning the resort near the endangered coral reef in Okinawa, the ones Green Space was having so much trouble with. So why was Tropic Reef listed as a Green Space account?

Alison clicked the entry to get more detailed information. The account had been set up three days ago. Established with a transfer of 700 million yen from Tokyo to a bank in the Bahamas for the account of Tropic Reef Development. And the Morgan Sachs agent handling the transaction was none other than Charles Gordon.

"I'll be damned." Alison stared slack-jawed at the screen. Shock and puzzlement stunned her, like the clueless guest of honor at a surprise party.

Charles hadn't mentioned that he was working with Yamada-san. Maybe he was bound by client confidentiality. But he made it seem like he and Yamada were meeting for the first time at the party. Or maybe Alison had just assumed as much. She remembered Charles' hands on Yamada's hips when he was leading her through a dance. He and Yamada certainly had looked chummy. A little too friendly for a first-time meeting.

She couldn't ask Charles about it. She wasn't even supposed to be seeing this stuff on Green Space's computers. And she could hardly confront Charles about a flirtation with Yamada. Not after her dalliance with Kiyoshi.

Nosing through the computer records was immoral if not illegal, and she'd already seen more than she'd anticipated. Alison closed the Green Space network connection and quit the program. FireAx was working just fine.

Through the cracks in the window blinds, Alison watched the outdoor light turn from a mousy brown to a muddy gray. Her mood mirrored the murkiness of the late evening sky. After her first foray in breaching a computer network, troublesome thoughts niggled at her. And none of them made sense.

An ear-shattering screech cut through her brooding. The burglar alarm. Alison scrambled for a weapon. All she could find was a staple remover. It would have to do.

She could call 911 — or was it 119? — for help. Where was her cell phone? In her eagerness to check out the new software, she'd broken into her own house, left a smashed window as an open invitation to the world, and forgotten to bring her cell phone with her. She'd left herself exposed and vulnerable, just for a chance to play with her new computer programs designed to keep her from being exposed and vulnerable.

It was too late for self-recriminations. The alarm's piercing shriek warned that someone was at the door. Was it Charles? Or the cyber freak. She needed a plan.

The squawking stopped. Silence.

"Alison?" Charles called out. "You home? Are you all right?"

Hearing Charles' voice, Alison's stomach tightened. She was glad it wasn't some lunatic invader, but Charles' arrival was an irritating disruption reminding her that the vacation was over.

He'd interrogate her to explain what she was doing with a computer. It was her computer, but he would be certain to needle her with questions. She wanted to keep some parts of her life private, even from Charles. Especially from Charles.

Alison swept all of her Happy Camera gear into the laundry bag and hid it, along with her computer, under the desk.

"Hey, Charles." Alison walked to the living room where Charles was exchanging his shoes for slippers.

"Glad you're back, Alicats. What happened to the window?" He hugged Alison while working his hands down to cup her ass.

He smelled like Charles, a faint trace of Lagerfeld. Was he wearing it for her? And he caressed her butt cheeks the same way that he always did. But Alison stiffened at the intimacy of his touch. Had she only been gone for just a few days?

"I lost my keys. It's a long story."

"I'll have the office fix the window. Glad you're home."

Alison peeled Charles' hands from her body and backed up to face him. "We've got to talk," she said, crossing her arms.

Charles nodded and walked toward the kitchen. "You want a drink?"

"Sure."

He returned with two Scotches and handed Alison her glass. They sat at the coffee table on opposite chairs.

"So, let's talk," Charles said. He knocked back some Scotch and leveled his gaze at Alison. This was her stage, her show.

Alison took a sip of Scotch. "Yeah, let's talk." Where to start, what to say? So much had happened since she'd been booted out of Japan.

"How was your trip?" Charles derailed her as she was marshaling her arguments about the countless things that were wrong with their relationship, why she didn't want to continue the way they were, and, oh, by the way, was he having an affair with Yuko Yamada?

"It was OK." Except for getting mugged on the street, having her hotel room broken into, and, to cap it all off, a strip-search welcome reception at Narita airport. Not to mention mind-blowing sex with her new lover she met online. She raised the glass to her mouth to cover the grin she couldn't control just thinking about Kiyoshi. "And I got my visa, no problem."

"Good job."

Alison downed more Scotch. It wasn't her drink of choice, it was Charles'. He had already established a home field advantage. "Look, Charles, you know that things between us have been kind of — well, not the best. Ever since I came to Japan."

"I've been damn busy. I told you not to move here right away, to give me some time to get my ducks in a row."

"I know, I know. You're right. I probably shouldn't have come so soon but I wanted to be with you. In the same city."

Charles drank his single malt. "Bottom line it. What's going on?" He stared at her through those eyes, as cold, metallic and hard as two ball bearings. Alison didn't see anything remotely resembling love reflecting back at her in those steel-alloyed eyes.

She set her glass on the table. "I'm wiped out from my trip, Charles. Let's do this another time. I came back, OK? I'm back."

Their lovemaking was slow and easygoing, comfortable and familiar. Alison didn't try to moralize about what she was doing or attempt to sort it out in her head. Her body had its own wisdom, its own authority, and her body responded to Charles as it invariably did. She could always count on her body to betray her that way.

40

Five Americans. Three Brits. He reviewed the collection of recordings in his iTunes library. One Peruvian. But she was Peruvian-Japanese, so she didn't really count. Two Australians. Those Aussie chicks were wild. The threesome had been their idea.

When he got to the Canadian, he paused. Maybe he should delete her. The recording was incomplete and the sound quality was shit. He'd had to record her in that flea-bag love hotel in an echo chamber of a room. The quality wasn't up to his standards.

Stupid bitch from Vancouver. Going to the love hotel had been her idea. She'd thought it was cool that he wanted to record her voice while she played with herself and while they fucked. She said the idea turned her on. But she'd insisted on doing it in a love hotel.

It would've been easy to get a decent recording at his apartment. His state-of-the-art equipment was ready to go, and his acoustics were fine-tuned. It would've been a hell of a lot cheaper, too. That damn love hotel charged by the hour. But she'd insisted, and he'd agreed. He didn't have any Canadians in his collection.

So he'd packed up his gear — a Shure wireless microphone, XLR cable, digital recorder — and reserved a room for a three-hour "rest" at a cheap love hotel in Yokohama. He'd have to set up his equipment, check his sound levels and get a good recording, all in three hours. Should be enough time, if her pussy was juicy and she was begging to fuck. He tossed a bottle of shochu liquor in his gear bag in case she needed warming up. At 40 percent alcohol, a couple of shots would help move things along.

The love hotel room wasn't a tacky fantasyland like most of the others he'd seen. Just shabby, plain and practical. If it weren't for the condom placed on top of the pillow, he might've thought he was in a seedy flop-house. It didn't matter. He wasn't there for romance. He was there to do a job. And he was on the clock.

In the gloomy room, he set up his equipment while she hummed Mariah Carey tunes, sipped shochu and undressed. She had a girlish voice, like that spacey chick from Iceland who warbled and growled when she sang.

The room's bouncy acoustics were a problem. He adjusted the input levels, wondering if he'd be able to capture the Canadian's vocal tone when she came. His apartment would have been so much better. He switched on the recorder and handed her the cordless mic. And a purple latex dildo. Showtime.

She was a natural actress, really enjoyed playing it up. Standing naked in front of him, she flicked his microphone against her tits and swung her hips. She stared direct at him, challenging him, while she leaned forward and drove the dildo into her cunt.

Her howl, primal and raw, made his dick throb in anticipation. Performer that she was, she held the microphone up to her lips the whole time. He hoped he'd get a decent recording of her, even in this shithole room with its fucked-up acoustics.

She pulled the dildo out and rubbed it over her lips, smearing her pussy juices across her face. "Come here," she'd said. She dropped to her knees, unzipped his jeans and sucked him so hard that he'd gasped and bit his lip. He had to fight not to lose it. Not yet, not too soon. He needed to hear her come first, get a good, clean recording of her out-of-control climax. Then he could enjoy himself.

He pushed her mouth off of his dick, said he had a surprise for her. Reached into his gear bag, took out his gun. Told her to take the gun, slide it into her cunt and fuck it. Promised her that the gun was hard and smooth and would feel so good in her pussy that she'd scream with pleasure.

And damn, did that dumb bitch scream. Not that anyone would notice in a love hotel, where a woman's screams were nothing unusual. But, eyes wide with terror and hands outreached, she shrieked and scrambled backward trying to get away from him.

Clumsy bitch. Tripped over her own damn feet and cracked her head on the table. Fell as hard as if she'd really been dropped by gunfire.

It wasn't his fault that she panicked. He wasn't going to use the gun. Didn't even have any bullets. He only wanted to hear how a tinge of fear changed the timbre of her voice. To get a sample. For his collection.

Sprawled face-up on the carpet, she was unconscious but still breathing. He could fuck her if he wanted to, she was laying there with her pussy open wide. But if he couldn't get a recording, what would be the point?

He considered skipping out, leaving her there for the cleaning crew to find. But the love hotel had his credit card number and could track him down.

And if they found her, a foreign woman stark naked and unconscious in the room he'd rented, it'd be her word against his. He hadn't done anything wrong. Hadn't made her do anything she didn't want to do. But they would believe the *gaijin* bitch's lies and exaggerations, just like they had when he got kicked out of school in Boston. They'd believe her, and he'd be the one who'd get fucked over.

He wasn't going to let a foreign whore mess him up. Not again. This time, he'd take care of things.

From his gear bag, he retrieved gaffer tape and sealed her mouth shut. Her blue eyes, partially open, made him feel like she could see him, was bearing witness. He taped her eyes closed.

The threadbare pillows were thin, so he grabbed two for the job. It took forever before the bitch's chest stopped fighting for air and her pulse quieted to nothingness. He glanced at the clock on the nightstand. Eighty minutes left on the reservation.

He ducked out of the room, stopped at a discount luggage shop and bought a nylon duffel bag. At the love hotel, he folded her knees to her tits and bound her body with gaffer tape before stuffing her in the bag. Good thing she was small. Some of those gaijin bitches were big as men.

With his gear bag slung over one shoulder and his new parcel weighing down the other, he pushed the button in the love hotel room, signaling that he was checking out. At a nearby construction site, he gathered some broken-up pieces of concrete and added them to the duffel bag. An isolated stretch of the bay provided a perfect spot. Yokohama was a big, busy port town. They wouldn't be finding her anytime soon.

She'd been his only Canadian. But the sound quality wasn't any good and the recording was incomplete. He deleted her. Another Canadian would come along.

Anyway, he was working on his new prospect, a Black chick. Everyone knew Black chicks were loud and loved to fuck. Pussies so big your dick could get lost inside. A Black *gaijin* would make a perfect addition to his collection.

He created a new folder in his library of recordings: "African-Americans." TokyoAli would be his first.

41

Alison pulled the pillow over her head to block out the persistent chirping of Charles' computer. The head office was trying to reach Charles before he left for work. Why didn't those idiots in New York cotton to the fact that there was a fourteen-hour time difference between Tokyo and The Center of the World?

The noise stopped. Peace and quiet. Alison turned over to get in a few more minutes of sleep when the computer began squawking again. She shot a mean glance at the bedside clock. It was already after eight. Charles had long been in the office.

"New York twits." She stumbled out of bed and plodded over to Charles' sacred computer shrine. His desktop computer, once forbidden to her, now looked massive and out of date compared to her sleek little laptop. With one eye still shut in sleep, Alison glared at the screen.

As she suspected. An instant chat message. Alison leaned forward to see the screen more clearly and was immediately wide awake. The chat request wasn't from Charles' office. It was from World NetLink. And it was addressed to her.

Damn that techno-freak. Not only had he woken her up, but he dared to contact her directly on the computer. On Charles' computer. She'd forgotten to uninstall World NetLink from his Mac. Lucky thing for her that Charles wasn't home to see the message.

Her stalker was back at his game, tormenting her from behind his mask of anonymity. But after her shopping spree in Hong Kong, she was no longer a helpless sitting duck. Digital defense systems shielded her and weapons stood ready in her arsenal.

If she could persuade the jerk to meet her online when she was at the controls of her fully loaded computer, she might be able to lure him into a little trap. Grateful that the gears of her coffee-denied morning brain were nevertheless turning over, she took the first step to exposing the identity of her cyberbully. Let the games begin, asshole. She accepted his chat invitation.

She groaned when she saw that the person paging her wasn't the cyber freak. It was her brother.

"Rob, I was dead asleep. Can't you call me on the phone and wake me up like everyone else does?"

"Sorry. But we need to talk."

"Then let's talk. I'm awake now. Thanks to you."

"We need to talk offline."

Why was Rob being so guarded?

"Call me collect. Or I'll call you. Are you at home?"

"Can't do it like that. We need to talk where no one can hear us."

"Is this a joke?"

"Do you have a fax machine? Not a fax modem, just a fax machine?"

"Yeah, you faxed me once before, remember?"

"Right. I forgot. Make sure the machine is on.

```
I’m going to be sending you a fax. It’ll explain
everything.”
“What’s this about? Why are you being stranger than
usual?”
“Just make sure the fax is on and that it’s ready to
receive. I’ll fax you in 30 minutes. OK?”
“Sure. Whatever.”
“Bye.”
“Rob, I’ll call you. Are you at home?”
```

She hit the return key but got a message that the chat connection was closed. What the hell was Rob talking about? She had to get some coffee.

A steaming mug of coffee and yoga stretches helped Alison get back on track. Rob had sounded so bizarre online. She could almost hear his desperation being transmitted down the modem line along with his electronic message. He’d pulled some elaborate pranks to get her, ribbing his big sister who he always said was too serious. But the tone of his online chat felt different. There was none of his usual smart-ass humor. Maybe the fax he was sending would be the punch line, and she would’ve fallen for yet another one of his practical jokes.

Unable to concentrate on her yoga breathing series, she got up and checked the fax machine. Fax turned on? Yes. Paper? Yes. There was nothing but the waiting. And waiting.

After sitting by an inert fax machine for nearly an hour first thing in the morning, waiting for some secretive message to be delivered, Alison realized that she’d been had. Again. It wasn’t one of his better pranks, but score yet another one for Rob.

Walking to the *ofuro* for her morning shower, Alison heard the fax line ring. She returned to the machine, now vibrating and spewing out its dispatch. The machine spat out a roll of fax paper, reminding her of Rob sticking out his tongue in his jokester's victory lap.

The fax cover sheet showed that Rob had sent the message from some pay-as-you-fax copy shop on campus. Two pages to follow. Not waiting for the entire document, Alison snatched the first sheet.

Rob had written the fax by hand in that tight, meticulous scrawl he had developed in elementary school and which had stuck with him all these years.

A–

I'm sending this fax at a public machine because I don't want any of this message traced. My fax modem is online so it's detectable, and I didn't want to send this over the usual email route because email can be intercepted as I know you know.

I got some bad news for you, kiddo. The feds shut down the SwampLand BBS. You said you got through and logged in as a user. That's why I'm faxing. The BBS got busted because the SysOp for the board had some weird fuck kiddy porn GIFs and stuff on their servers. The SysOp copped and is now working with the feds. Word is he's turning over the BBS user list to them. And a log of files each user uploaded and downloaded.

The feds really got it up their ass to bust boards these days, especially the ones with lots of bitheads. I know you weren't into any of that kiddy porn shit. Anyway, I'm sure a smart chick like you used an alias when you logged in, so they wouldn't be able to track you down right away. But I wanted to let you know in case. They're making arrests and talking about some kind of criminal conspiracy. I don't understand it exactly, but you're the lawyer.

So this might not be anything, but it might be something. And you're all the fucking way on the other side of the fucking planet. I don't even know if they could find you or would care.

Don't worry. I'm in your corner. Lay low. Don't call that BBS anymore. Stay in school. Don't do drugs. Look both ways before you cross. Don't talk to strangers. And have a good day.

—R.

Alison reread the fax. Rob must be overreacting. The Fed's closure of SwampLand couldn't possibly affect her. She wasn't a child pornography pervert.

Surely, a person couldn't be in violation of the law for making a phone call with a computer and a modem. But why had Rob said he hoped she'd logged in under an alias?

"Oh, hell," she moaned, remembering that when she joined SwampLand, not only had she supplied the BBS with her real name, but she'd given her phone number, as well. Or Charles' phone number. Or more accurately, the firm's phone number because the firm had rented the house and had leased the phone lines. Morgan Sachs wouldn't appreciate being a party to a porn conspiracy. Still, the thought of those self-important Wall Street demigods being charged as pornographers made Alison smirk.

The kiddie porn crackdown was unlikely to affect her. But the Feds were involved, and the Feds were unpredictable. Alison began to appreciate the gravity of her situation. Taking things too lightly would be unwise.

She brewed a second cup of coffee, grabbed a notebook and pen, and took a seat at the kitchen table. With professional detachment, as if she were interviewing a client, she assessed her legal position.

A threshold question was jurisdiction. When she'd joined the SwampLand BBS, she'd been in Japan, not the U.S. Could U.S. federal law reach her in Tokyo? Would U.S. law even apply to someone who wasn't in the States?

She'd accessed a BBS located in the U.S. through telephone lines regulated by the federal government. It could be argued that she had a virtual, if not physical, presence in the States. What's the relevant jurisdiction when you're in cyberspace? She wrote "Jurisdiction?" in her notebook.

Maybe she could rely on a First Amendment defense. The BBS was a repository of speech. BBS users had a fundamental right to say what they wanted to say, send messages, share files. It was their protected, Constitutional right. She added "1st Amdmt — Free Speech?" to her notes.

The government couldn't abridge First Amendment rights without a compelling interest. But Alison was pretty sure that kiddy porn fell outside of the realm of protected speech contemplated by the Founding Fathers. Way outside.

Rob's fax had mentioned the Feds bringing conspiracy charges. Alison vaguely remembered conspiracy theory from Crim Law in her first year of law school, how the laws made it easier for prosecutors to bring in all kinds of bad guys and their associates. It didn't matter if a person performed a specific illegal act or even knew that another co-conspirator was up to no good. Designed to be expedient, the conspiracy laws were swift, harsh, and a prosecutor's best friend.

She could argue that she didn't even know about the illegal kiddy porn on the BBS. She didn't have the conspirator's requisite "corrupt motive." And without the necessary *mens rea* state of mind, she couldn't be deemed part of the conspiracy. She jotted down "Conspiracy — no mens rea" in her notebook.

And the First Amendment gave her a Constitutional right to associate freely with whomever she pleased, including the other members of the BBS, whatever they were up to. She drew a star next to First Amendment and wrote "Freedom/Association."

On the other hand — one thing she'd learned in law school was to always consider the other hand — she'd agreed to the Terms of Service of the SwampLand BBS. She'd even affirmed that she wasn't affiliated with law enforcement. That click of her mouse could be considered an agreement between conspirators. And after seeing the wealth of bootlegged commercial software available for free downloading, it'd be hard to argue that she had no constructive knowledge of the BBS's questionable practices.

Face buried in her hands, Alison slumped at the table. The unthinkable threat of disbarment loomed. Disbarred and in prison all because of some damn computer network she knew nothing about.

Her heart fluttered and hammered in her chest. The second cup of coffee hadn't been such a good idea. Inhaling deep cleansing breaths to slow herself down, talk herself back from the edge of the precipice, Alison recalled a legal maxim: A lawyer who represents herself has a fool for a client. The smart thing for her to do would be to find an attorney.

But she wasn't convinced she'd done anything wrong, certainly nothing like committing a federal crime. Another legal adage came to mind: Ignorance of the law is no defense.

42

Alison gathered her wallet, pencil and paper, deposited her purse and coat at the front desk of the American Center, and entered the library. A practiced pro, she sat down at the computer terminal, hands poised over the keyboard. The screen blinked, waiting for her to enter a command.

Where should she begin? What should she search for? Where would she find the answers to the question that weighed on her mind: How deep was the shit she was in?

She'd start her search with a broad subject term. According to Rob's fax, the SwampLand bulletin board service had gotten busted for maintaining kiddy porn on its computers. Alison typed: "Subject = Computers and Pornography."

The computer returned hundreds of cites, too many for her to examine. Apparently, computer porn was a hot topic. Tightening her search parameters would narrow down the results. She added "and Crime."

Just typing in the word "crime" made her feel guilty for investigating the matter. She looked around the research library to see if anyone was watching her. Was she paranoid? Or embarrassed? Maybe a little of both.

As if sensing Alison's floundering, the computer prompted her to search for "Computers: Crimes and Criminal Activity."

"Okay, whatever you say." Alison rephrased her search request.

The "Crimes and Criminal Activity' area offered scads of possible subtopics she could explore, ranging from "Criminal Cases" to

"Hackers" to "Legislation." Scanning further down, she came upon the heading "Pornography." Bingo. She printed out the cites and pulled the relevant disks before heading over to the CD-ROM readers she'd nicknamed the Big Guns.

One cite on the pornography list sounded exactly on point: "Bulletin Board System Clearinghouse for Pornography." Excited that her legal research was off to a good start, she loaded the CD and skimmed the article, eager to glean information that would shed light on her legal problem. Her possible legal problem. No need to jump to conclusions.

The piece talked about an internet provider's liability for maintaining pornographic images uploaded by users. Not relevant. She hadn't uploaded any file to the BBS. Certainly not porn. She carried on. The next article discussed balancing users' rights of free speech against a network's right to screen email and delete offensive materials.

Close, but no cigar. Maybe she should hire a lawyer. For a quick consultation. But those free initial chats often snowballed into hefty legal fees, fees which could easily wipe out her stash of yen.

She could call a friend from law school, ask them to do her a favor. Not for herself, of course, but for her cousin's brother-in-law's next door neighbor's kid who had joined a BBS that was being rated by the Feds.

She was probably overreacting to Rob's melodramatic fax. He could always get to her with his smartass sense of humor. Researching the law was what she did. Maybe she'd reach a point where she wanted to contact a lawyer. But for now, she'd keep things to herself, gather more information, then figure out her next steps.

If she could get her hands on Lexis, her legal research would be a breeze. Alison remembered from her law school days the wealth of legal-related information a person could summon up with a few pithy key words in a Lexis search. Save-A-Tree couldn't afford the pricey online legal database service, and neither could she.

Alison returned to her list and slogged through the citations. More free speech stuff. More service provider responsibility stuff. Alison was yawning when she came upon a cite that jolted her wide awake faster than the first rumblings of an earthquake. "Federal Liability for Maintaining Illegal Computer Software." Hello! Just what she was looking for.

Alison pounded in the commands to see the entire article. The computer screen flashed: "Material not available at present location. Available locations: TLRC."

What was TLRC? Alison shrugged and continued laboring through her list. More law suits about privacy rights. Another promising cite referred her to TLRC.

She copied down the acronym and carried it to a reference librarian.

"May I help you?" the librarian asked.

"I was on the machine over there," Alison gestured to the Big Guns, "and this came up in response to my inquiry. 'Available locations: TLRC.' Can you tell me what that means?"

"Of course. That's the library of the Tokyo Law Research Center. TLRC."

"Can I get a copy of their material here? Like an interlibrary loan." If she couldn't get the information she needed — and fast — maybe it was time to call a lawyer.

"I'm sorry, but we don't have trading privileges. It's a private library. For attorneys."

"Can I use it as a visiting foreign lawyer?"

The librarian's eyes widened for a moment. Alison was familiar with the look of incredulity. It wasn't the first time someone found it hard to believe she was an attorney. Maybe she should ditch the jeans and the North Face hoodie. Or maybe they should open their minds.

"I'm not sure of their policy," the librarian said.

If what Rob wrote in his fax was true — and not an ill-timed April Fool's joke — at this very moment the Feds were trying to track Alison down as a criminal conspirator in an internet kiddy porn ring. The TLRC legal research center might have restricted entrance rules, but she'd find a way to get in. Even in her jeans and hoodie. Having the FBI on her butt was a great motivator.

"Do you know where the library is?" Alison asked.

The librarian drew a quick map and handed it across the desk. Alison looked at the sketch, surprisingly detailed with bilingual street names. She didn't know the area, but she would find the TLRC. Hopefully, before the FBI found her.

She hailed a taxi outside the American Center, showed the map to the driver, and was whisked off across town.

Alison didn't need a map to recognize the Tokyo Law Research Center. Massive Corinthian columns flanked stone steps leading to entrance doors of grand scale. "Enter, ye who dare," the doors challenged. Legal buildings looked the same wherever you went. Edifices whose solidity and strength were designed to reassure as well as to intimidate.

Alison pushed open the weighty doors and was greeted by a silence befitting a catacomb. Even though she tiptoed through the entrance hallway, her footsteps echoed off the stone walls. Proceeding up a short flight of stairs, she arrived at the research center's main reading area.

Multivolume sets of legal treatises, the hallmark of every law library, lined the walls of the cavernous room. Scholars seated at study tables hunched over weighty tomes. A faint smell of bookbinding paste laced with mildew hung in the air. Considering the overall ambiance of dreariness and sterile erudition, Alison was certain she was in the right place.

She approached a woman seated behind a polished-wood counter. The woman stared into a computer monitor while jabbing her index finger at the keyboard. Her speed of attack was impressive.

Alison smiled and tried to invoke the right phrase. "*Eigo ga dekimasu ka*?" Do you speak English? The woman didn't reply, but her finger kept up its assault on the keyboard. Maybe she hadn't understood Alison's wobbly Japanese. She tried again. "*Eigo ga*—"

"Can I help you?" The librarian frowned at her wristwatch before looking up at Alison.

An English speaker. Alison gave silent thanks. "I was doing some research at the American Center library, and it turns out that the material I need is only available here."

The librarian's eyelids fluttered. Maybe a dust mote from the ancient law books had lodged in the woman's eye. "This library is not open to the public," the librarian said. "I am sorry." She returned to her one-finger punching at the keyboard.

Alison bit the corner of her lip. If she had on a power suit instead of her going-to-the-car-wash jeans, the librarian might be treating her differently. "I'm a lawyer. A *bengoshi*. From America. I don't want to borrow any books, or anything. I need to look up some articles. It's really important, and I can't get this information anywhere else."

"The Research Center is only open to members."

Alison tried to stay calm, but somewhere back in America an overzealous prosecutor with conspiracy on the brain was ready to implicate her in all sorts of criminal deeds. She needed information, and she needed it now. It was time to cut through the Japanese red tape with a little American-style ingenuity.

"Actually," Alison began, "I'm doing some legal research for Lauren Lipton at the American Embassy." Since she was telling a lie, might as well make it a whopper. "Here's her number. You can call her." Alison had committed the embassy employee's contact information to memory ever since she'd helped Alison with immigration advice. It never hurt to have a friend at the embassy. She wrote down Lauren Lipton's name and the embassy phone number and hoped that the librarian wouldn't feel the need to call.

"And I've got my bar card," Alison said. "State Bar of California." She combed through her wallet searching for that hard-earned piece of plastic hidden amidst the random assortment of junk she'd accumulated. Visa, Nordstrom card. Currency exchange receipts, taxi receipts, a picture of Charles, someone's business card she couldn't read. Why didn't she ever clean out her wallet? AAA card — a lot of good that'd do her here. Voilá. Her bar card, barely distinguishable from the other scraps in her wallet.

The librarian took the card from Alison and examined it as if it were a hundred-dollar bill she suspected was counterfeit. She turned the card over before pushing it back to Alison, along with Lipton's embassy phone number.

"What information are you looking for?" the librarian asked.

Alison exhaled. She pulled out the pages of cited articles that had referred her to the TLRC library. The librarian read through the list, stopping to peer up at Alison over the pages of the cites.

"I see you were using the CD-ROM reader at the American Center. We have a similar reader here, but our discs include legal sources. Enter the same cite numbers at our machine, and you'll be able to see your articles. The reference room is through the door and to the right." She pointed to an arched doorway in the rear of the reading room. "But first, you must sign in." She gave Alison a clipboard. "And be sure to sign out when you leave. The Research Center closes at five o'clock." The librarian checked her watch yet again. "You have forty-five minutes."

Alison signed the visitor ledger and hurried off. Only forty-five minutes to find out if she was likely to land on the FBI's Most Wanted list.

The reference room straddled a crossroads of library technology. A handful of digital terminals sat next to card catalogs and hand-cranked microfilm readers. The information-retrieving devices of the TLRC's quaint reference room couldn't compete with the high-tech gadgets at the American Center. Not surprising. The TLRC didn't have the CIA's budget backing it. But what the TLRC did have was the information Alison needed to assess her potential criminal liability. She collected her disks and seated herself at the CD-ROM reader.

Given her limited time, Alison pulled up every cite that referenced the TLRC and printed it out. Articles about online systems and pornography. Printed. Websites and free speech. Printed. Anything and everything that might shed light on her predicament. Reading could come later.

Alison checked the last citation off of her list as the frenzied printer wheezed to a stop. She stacked the heap of pages into a pile then tapped the edges on the desk to neaten them. She had hours of reading ahead. But if she were lucky, somewhere in the reams of disorganized papers, she'd discover a gem that would help with her legal analysis, that would help save her butt. Flying blind, but it was the best she could do. Or was it?

Alison sprinted out to the reference desk. The librarian was still pecking away at her keyboard.

"Excuse me, but by any chance do you have access to Lexis, the legal database service?" Alison held her breath.

"Yes, we do, but the center is closing in ten minutes." The librarian's purse sat on top of her desk. She was packed up and waiting for the five o'clock whistle to blow.

"I'll only be a minute. And I'm sure the American Embassy would appreciate your cooperation." Desperate times called for desperate bull-shitting.

The librarian's eyes flickered open and closed. The nervous habit was a tell, and Alison seized the opportunity to exert nonverbal coercion. She leaned across the desk in what she hoped was an intimidating stance. Apparently, her strong-arming worked because the librarian's eyes focused, and she said, "The Lexis terminal is through the rear door in the reference room. But remember, we close in—"

"Ten minutes," Alison said. She waved her thanks and took off. The clock was ticking, and the librarian was unlikely to cut her any more slack.

Alison wasted precious minutes trying to get her bearings on a database system she hadn't used since law school. She fumbled around with the Lexis commands until she found legal news organized by topical search words. Perfect.

She entered: "Federal Crime and Computer Bulletin Board System." Hundreds of hits on that one. She had to tighten the focus. "And Software," she typed.

Out spewed cites to articles about bulletin boards being shut down for child pornography, hate mail, scamming credit card numbers.

Alison sat back, satisfied, watching the articles scroll out of the screen until she caught a glance at the last headline: "Hacker Charged for Illegal Exportation of FYEO Encryption Software."

What the hell? FYEO was the encryption software she'd downloaded from SwampLand to keep that cyberfreak asshole out of her life. Had she dug herself in deeper as a criminal conspirator by downloading FYEO?

Alison didn't get a chance to read the article before the reference librarian appeared at her side.

"The research center is now closing," the librarian said. Alison could tell from the fresh lipstick the librarian wore that the woman must have Big Plans.

Having spent an exasperating afternoon running in circles, Alison had finally found an article that was on point. Scarily on point. But she needed access to the high-powered Lexis database to read why some guy — she assumed the hacker was a guy. It could well be a woman. A woman like her — was being charged for messing around with the FYEO encryption program. Rob's fax took on a new urgency. This was no April Fool's joke.

Arms folded across her chest, the librarian hovered. Alison considered trying to coax the librarian out of a few more minutes on the Ferrari of legal databases, but thought better of it. She might be spending a lot of time at the Research Center, and it would be smart not to piss off the woman who held the keys.

"You will have to come back tomorrow." The librarian switched off the room lights while Alison was still sitting at the terminal. The librarian might be a jerk, but at least she'd said that Alison could come back.

Tomorrow. How could Alison could wait until tomorrow, sleep until tomorrow, pretend that things were normal until tomorrow? And what if tomorrow was too late?

Alison signed the visitor log, gave a little bow to the librarian and walked down the stairs to the exit. But at the last minute, in a move worthy of a quick-footed offensive receiver on a football field, she cut over to the women's restroom, shutting the door behind her. She stole into one of the toilet stalls and bolted the lock.

The five o'clock song rang in the streets. She listened to employees going home for the day, feet lumbering down the library's steps, colleagues chatting, the building's weighty doors closing with a thud.

How many people worked at the library? How long would it take for them to vacate the building, for the coast to be clear? Alison decided to hide out for fifteen minutes. She didn't have a watch, but she could guess the time based on the quieting of the library. Hopefully that would be long enough for the TLRC personnel to assume that all visitors had long ago cleared out.

The restroom door burst open. Alison leaped up on the toilet seat so that whoever had entered couldn't see her legs under the stall doors. Crouching low in her hiding place, Alison was glad that the toilets were Western style with a seat to stand on and not one of the hole-in-the-floor squat toilets. She was also grateful that Japanese people closed toilet seat lids. Why hadn't the custom rubbed off on Charles?

Through a crack in the stall door, Alison spied a woman fluffing her hair in the mirror. A sickeningly sweet floral fragrance wafted through the air, and Alison pinched the tip of her nose to suppress a sneeze. The woman dabbed at her face with a handkerchief and added lipstick before closing her purse and leaving.

Alison's knees burned and she was losing her balance. But she should stay put a little longer. A few more minutes. Just to be safe. She tried some yoga breathing to pass the time, but it was impossible to execute a deep belly breath with her thighs jammed against her chest.

Legs wobbling, Alison hit her physical limit for perching on a toilet seat. She stepped down and stretched.

Had she lost her mind? The Japanese had a relaxed sense about security and locking up, so she thought she could get away with it. If someone were to find her in the library's restroom after hours, she could explain that she had a touch of upset stomach. But if she was going to go after the information that she needed, that she had to have, and she got caught—it would be hard to explain that she was creeping around the research library after hours because of acid indigestion.

She strained to detect any subtle sounds, any indication that library staff were still roaming the premises. She heard nothing. It was time to make her move.

Alison emerged from the stall, eased open the restroom door, and surveyed the scene. The library's interior had felt catacomb-like by day. Now, with lifeless corridors and windows lit by fading sunlight, the empty structure looked like an abandoned cathedral.

Alison slipped off her shoes to muffle her footsteps and ran back up the stairs to the reference room. She prayed that the library was hard-wired into the Lexis database so that she wouldn't have to log on or know a password.

Alison tapped the keyboard, and the terminal prompted her to enter a query. Prayer answered. She typed in the last search she'd used and pulled up the article that had seized her attention and induced her panic.

A federal grand jury in San Francisco, California, is considering whether Samuel Newman violated federal laws banning the exportation of weapons. According to the Federal Bureau of Investigation, Mr. Newman threatened national security by posting data encryption software on the internet, potentially enabling hostile foreign governments and even terrorist organizations to use the software.

Pursuant to the Export Administration Act and the Arms Export Control Act, jointly administered by the Departments of Commerce, State and Defense, encryption software is subject to strict export controls.

```
Cryptography is included on the list of weapons that
could compromise the country's security and cannot
be exported without a license. The software posted
by Mr. Newman, called FYEO, an acronym for "For Your
Eyes Only," was not licensed for export.

Mr. Newman's lawyer stated that her client could
face a prison sentence of up to fifty-one months.
```

Prison sentence? No way. It was those kiddy-porn pervs on SwampLand who needed to be locked up, not her. But if some gung-ho prosecutor was going for a conspiracy charge, all bets were off. She'd be standing shoulder to shoulder with the porn freaks as they were all roped together and marched into the courthouse in one convenient conspiratorial lump.

Alison tried to take a deep, relaxing yoga breath to slow her racing pulse and focus her mind. She closed her eyes, but instead of seeing her happy place at the top of the mountain in Lake Tahoe, she saw an orange jumpsuit with her name — no, her number — imprinted on it. Forget about the yoga breath. The threat of prison was all the focuser she needed. Alison opened her eyes and prepared to defend herself the best way she knew how — rigorous legal analysis.

Why had SwampLand been a target of the Feds? Rob's fax said it had to do with kiddy porn files found on the BBS' computer. Pornographers preying on kids deserved to get locked up. Let the prosecutors have at those abusive sicko pervs.

But the prosecutors were talking conspiracy theory, which meant that they were casting a wide net, trolling for child pornographers and any other miscreants that might get hauled up in their catch. As a card-carrying member of the SwampLand BBS, Alison would have some explaining to do.

Without even breaking a sweat, the Feds could see from the Swamp-

Land user logs that she'd downloaded FYEO, the same software described in the news article. The same software she and Kiyoshi had been using to protect their conversations from the prying eyes of the creepy cyberfreak. The same software that the U.S. government had categorized as a weapon. And although it appeared that encryption software wasn't exactly illegal, exporting it without a license was.

By downloading the software in Japan, moving the digital bits from the U.S. to Tokyo, had she exported a weapon? She wasn't a criminal. Certainly not an illegal arms dealer. Was she? And if it weren't for that pervert freak online who kept harassing her, she wouldn't have gotten into any of this mess. She'd only been trying to defend herself, but now she could get disbarred. Or worse. Where was the justice? That cyberfreak was the criminal, not her.

With answers leading to more questions, Alison wondered if she were up to the research task. Maybe it was time to call a lawyer. Just for a quickie consult. A hypothetical. *My cousin's babysitter's aunt downloaded some software that might implicate her as an international arms dealer...*

Alison printed out the article along with a host of related cites. The printer, an old-fashioned dot matrix, shimmied as it cranked out pages.

"*Ola*! *Dare desu ka*?" a man shouted from the hall.

Alison sat erect in her chair.

Footsteps, slow, then increasing in speed, grew louder in the corridors.

"*Ola*!"

Party over. It'd been easy — too easy — to sneak into the library after hours to do some serious lawyering on Lexis. Now she was busted. The librarian who'd told her to come back tomorrow wouldn't be as accommodating after hearing about Alison's exploits.

The last of the articles was churning out of the printer as a man in shirtsleeves and necktie rushed into the room. Alison was glad she didn't understand what the man was saying. He wasn't happy. No interpreter needed.

"I was just leaving." Alison stepped into her shoes, grabbed her printouts and ran for the main entrance. The man continued his angry tirade as he followed her and shooed her out the door.

43

Alison flicked on the reading light in the back of the taxi and dove into the printouts she'd gathered at the law library.

Even from the limited material she read, things didn't look good for the home team. The government had used conspiracy theory arguments to haul in BBS operators and users. RICO came up often as the favored means of prosecution.

RICO. Shit.

Alison put down the papers and chewed on a cuticle. In the hands of skilled prosecutors, RICO had long since moved from its original purpose of bringing down "racketeer-influenced and corrupt organizations," aka, the Mob, and had morphed into the Godzilla of all conspiracy laws. Alison had never understood how such a Draconian federal statute was even constitutional.

The RICO act's concern with organized crime carried with it an equal lack of concern for individual due-process rights. The darling of prosecutors, RICO was severe. When skillfully invoked, it enabled them to cast a net — a driftnet — that was as far-reaching and merciless.

If SwampLand was an enterprise engaged in a pattern of racketeering activity, as was all-too-broadly defined by the statute and interpreted by the courts, she could be subjected to RICO's harsh judgment. And SwampLand would be added to RICO's ignominious hit list along with Mafia families, the Hells Angels, abortion clinic demonstrators and even some Catholic bishops.

If the Feds were going after the SwampLand BBS under a conspiracy theory, when Alison downloaded the contraband FYEO encryption software and, making matters worse, emailed a copy to Kiyoshi, a foreign national, she'd clearly joined up with the co-conspirators.

She doubted whether she could untangle her knotty legal problems relying on CD-ROM readers and sneaking onto Lexis terminals. The smart thing to do would be to call a lawyer. But maybe she was jumping to conclusions. Why waste money on unnecessary legal counsel? Not unless and until her situation became a present issue.

She could lay low, like Rob had suggested. He was right — she was all the fucking way on the other side of the fucking planet. Laying low held a certain appeal. Head in the sand worked for her.

She was keen to warn Kiyoshi about what was going on, what muck she might have dragged him into. He might even have some idea about how to fix things. Assuming he still wanted to talk to her.

The cab pulled up in front of the house, and Alison, lost in thought pondering her options, sprang out of the taxi and dashed toward the front door. The cabbie yelled in that international language, universally understood. She'd forgotten the fare. With profuse apologies in English, Alison paid the driver, adding a big tip, which he pocketed.

Entering the front door, she saw the living room flooded with lights and Charles' shoes in the *genkan*.

What rotten timing. Tonight of all nights, when she urgently needed to get online, Charles was home early. She kicked off her shoes, put on slippers and went to the kitchen for a glass of merlot.

"Charles?" she called. There was no answer. Alison poured herself a tall glass of wine and walked into their bedroom. From behind the bath door, the gurgle of the *ofuro*'s jets stopped. Charles stepped out of the bathroom, towel tied around his waist. His chest and shoulders glowed with a moist sheen. Did he realize what a knockout he was? Of course he did.

"Hey, Alicats." He bent over and kissed Alison's head.

"You're getting me wet." Alison flicked water droplets off of her hair.

Charles chuckled and walked to the kitchen bar. "How's your day?" he called.

"It was OK," Alison said. Other than the fact that I'm wanted by the FBI and they could be arresting me at any moment." Alison drank some of her wine. "Why're you home so early? Are the markets closed?"

"Department party. A *bonnenkai*."

"*Bonnenka*i?"

"For the end of the year. You forget everything bad that happened during the past year to get ready for the new year. Didn't I tell you?" Charles brought his drink back to the bedroom.

Alison could think of a whole lot of things during the year that she would just as soon forget. Like her looming legal problems. Which could easily become Charles' legal problems. Even though their relationship had become more stress-fueled sex than romance and roses, he had a right to know. Just like Kiyoshi did.

"There's something I need to talk to you about Charles. It's important."

"Sure thing, Alicats. Calendar it for tomorrow. Soon as I get home." He toweled off and stepped into his briefs.

It wasn't fair to let Charles go off into the night without knowing about the snarl of problems she'd created. "We should talk now," she said.

"Can't. Gotta get dressed."

Alison swirled her glass and watched the wine's honey-like drips slide down the crystal. Why shouldn't Charles enjoy himself? Tomorrow she'd drench him with a splash of cold reality about what she'd been doing and how he could get roped in. He deserved his party. Her confession could wait.

And with him out of the house, she'd have a chance to alert Kiyoshi about the stormy legal clouds gathering on the horizon.

She drained her glass, refilled it, and joined Charles in the bedroom to help him get dressed. And hasten his departure.

"Need a hand?" She hoped she sounded eager to be of assistance rather than eager to see him out the door.

"I'm all right. No, wait." He pulled down a satin bow tie hanging on the back of the closet door alongside a tux. "You tie it better than me."

Alison took the bow tie from Charles' outstretched hand. He stood before her with arms at his sides like an obedient schoolboy. Alison flipped up his collar, circled the satin fabric tight around his neck and pulled, adjusting the bow. "Perfect. For a fancy party."

Charles turned his back to Alison and zipped up his pants. "I know, they're overdoing it. It'll be a snooze."

"I'm sure it will." She flopped on the living room couch and turned on the evening news. The coverage was focused on the English teacher from Canada whose body had been recovered from Tokyo Bay. The police wouldn't comment on the cause of death. Gruesome news grabbed the headlines, just like in the States.

"Hey, Charles! They found the Canadian woman."

"What?" Charles called from the bedroom.

"The missing English teacher. From Canada. They found her body in Tokyo Bay." How could a young woman — a young *gaijin* woman — end up a corpse in the water? Alison hugged a throw pillow to her chest.

"Raw deal," Charles said.

He strolled into the living room. Double-oh-seven-suave in his tux, bow tie and cummerbund. "How do I look?"

As if he didn't know. With those shoulders, Charles could wear a pickle barrel and be ready for the cover of *GQ*. "You look great." Alison caught a whiff of his aftershave. Lagerfeld. She'd given it to him for Valentine's Day.

"You smell good, too."

Charles pecked her cheek with a kiss. "Don't wait up."

She hadn't planned to.

With Charles gone, Alison had a chance to get in touch with Kiyoshi. Rob had intimated that the matter was best not discussed by phone, so she unpacked her computer gear and set up shop in the study. If things went her way, she'd be able to catch Kiyoshi online. And because it was a new, untested toy, Alison turned on the Tracer device in case someone was trying to eavesdrop on her modem line.

She logged on. The familiar voice of World NetLink welcomed her and announced that she had new mail.

She opened her one piece of mail and saw that it had been sent anonymously. Again.

WELCOME HOME! DID YOU MISS ME!! I MISSED YOU. MY FRIENDS SAW YOU IN HONKON. THEY THINK YOU ARE VERY PRETTY AND CHARMING. TOO BAD YOU DID NOT MEET. THEY HAD A PRESENT TO UPLOAD ON YOUR COMPUTER.

Alison's fingers tightened around her mouse. That damn bastard was the reason she was in the fucked-up legal mess she was in. His unrelenting taunts, obscenities and threats. He invaded her privacy with reckless abandon, like she was his toy, an amusement to be trifled with. And now that she'd taken action to defend herself, she could end up losing her law license. She could end up in a prison cell. All because of that psycho online pervert.

She wished she could bring in the authorities to get rid of the guy. But with the pile of legal shit that Alison had innocently stepped into, she didn't know who the authorities would be more eager to pick up: the cyberfreak or her, the cryptographic terrorist conspirator.

But she'd deal with him. For all the torment he'd caused her, she'd find a way to heap it back on him. Somehow, she'd find a way. And payback would be sweet.

Alison broke from her reverie of revenge and refocused on her task at hand, letting Kiyoshi know that maybe he should think about possibly contacting a lawyer. Perhaps. As a bearer of conditional bad news, she felt like she was asking him to consider getting tested for some sexually transmitted disease, which he may or may not have contracted from her.

But he needed to know and had the right to know. She sent out an online page for Kiyoshi, and he responded.

```
"Hi, Kiyo! Glad I caught you."
"Hello, Alison. How are you?"
"It's been a horrible day."
"What happened?"
"It's about the encryption software we've been
using."
"It's working fine."
"We have to stop using it."
"Why?"
"Please, trust me. We can send regular unencoded
email and chat. OK?"
"The guy will be able to intercept our messages."
"I'm running software to try to track him down."
"What software?"
"I don't feel comfortable talking about it online."
"Then let's talk on the phone."
"I feel even more paranoid on the phone. Wiretaps,
and all."
"So what do you want to do?"
"Let's cool it with the encryption software. I'll
find our annoying friend and turn him over to the
police."
"I told you to let me handle him."
```

Alison slumped back in the chair. Her bones were heavy with the weight of taking care of everything by herself, of being paranoid and afraid by herself, of being on the lookout by herself. Why not let Kiyoshi deal with the freak? After all, what could she do? As a foreigner? On a semi-tourist visa? Not speaking Japanese? And an alleged felon subject to extradition?

```
"You win. If I get a lead on the guy, I'll give you
all the info."
"You've got my cell phone number. Call me if you
need me."
```

Why hadn't she told Kiyoshi the whole story? Why hadn't she prepared him for the fact that she might — they both might — need some heavy-duty legal intervention? She was such a wimp. Afraid that the news might scare him off.

"Everything's so fucked up." Alison pounded the table with her fist. "So. Damn. Fucked. Up."

Uncontrollable tears of frustration escalated into ragged sobs. She'd been stupid and naive to think that she could defend against the online predator. Using a bunch of equipment she'd acquired from sources she knew were marginally legal, at best. Now she was fighting a strong current, hoping to stay out of jail, hoping not to implicate Kiyoshi and Charles. She might have fucked up her own life, but they didn't deserve to get sucked up in her whirlpool.

Exhausted and spent by her outburst, Alison took rhythmic yoga breaths to calm her nerves and clear her thinking. She needed her cool, rational lawyer mind to assess the extent of her problems and devise a strategy.

Blithely logging onto World NetLink as a newbie had landed her in a world of trouble. But maybe now, wizened and battle-scarred, she could use the network to help get herself out of trouble. World NetLink was a diesel-fuel clunker compared to the horsepower of Lexis, but she should be able to ferret out some useful legal information. Encouraged by having a plan of action, meager though it be, she returned to her computer.

Alison combed the law and legislation section of World NetLink. In the chat room, people posted questions looking for free online legal advice. She saw listings for the full text of the Constitution, the Code of Federal Regulations, and the U.S. Code. But there was nothing to shed light on the law she needed to know.

Alison decided to give it a rest for the night. Another glass of wine would help. As she prepared to pack up her gear and exit the system, something caught her eye.

The red light on the Tracer box was blinking.

44

It took a few seconds before Alison realized the significance of the Tracer's flashing light. She had company. Nearby. And not the kind of company that rang the front doorbell. It was an uninvited guest, eavesdropping on her modem line. It was him. And he was close.

"You bastard!"

She leaped from her chair and dashed to the *genkan*. At last, she was going to catch her stalker in the act and unmask his ass. Kicking off her slippers, Alison grabbed an umbrella for a weapon and bounded out of the house.

Whoever was tapping her computer transmissions was nearby. Within one hundred meters, according to what Jed had told her.

She prowled up the street, peeking in the bushes and windows of her neighbors' houses. She saw no one. Heard no one.

Alison jogged to the end of her street, guessing the intersection to be the outside of the hundred-meter perimeter from the Tracer device. She saw nothing suspicious.

How had she thought she could find the guy by running into the street like a loon? And if she saw him, what would she do? Bludgeon him with her umbrella? He could be anywhere, could be anyone. It was stupid to think she could find him.

She turned to walk back home when the shadowy figure of a man sprang from the shrubs across from her house and tore down the street.

"Hey, asshole! Stop!" Alison broke into a run in close pursuit. The guy made the corner and headed out onto the main street.

Alison followed. The busy intersection was crowded with salarymen returning home from work and housewives shopping for dinner groceries. Alison tried to figure out where the guy had gone, which of the many faces she saw was his, but to no avail. He'd vanished.

"Leave me alone, you asshole freak! Leave me the fuck alone!" she screamed at the swarming intersection. Faces turned, heads ducked, eyes peered at Alison, her bare feet, the umbrella, her lack of coat.

She could read the glances of the passersby: "Another crazy *gaijin*..."

45

The receptionist at Morgan Sachs looked up from the romance *manga* comic book she'd hidden under her desk. Two men had stepped off the elevator and were headed her way. It was unusual to see visitors to the trading floor this early in the morning. The market was just opening. This was the time when she usually got in her best reading.

She tried not to look annoyed at being interrupted by the men, one Japanese and one white. An American, the receptionist concluded, judging from his pallor, his height and his girth. She prided herself on being able to tell the different Caucasians apart.

The Japanese man walked over and spoke to the receptionist in a whispered voice. The receptionist flushed red, stood and bowed. She bustled off through the doors leading into the trading floor, leaving the lobby reception desk unattended.

Within minutes, she scurried back, trailing behind a rotund Japanese man. His suit's lapel sported the firm's logo pin. Through blubbery downturned lips, he introduced himself to the uninvited visitors as the Managing Director in charge of Morgan Sachs' Tokyo office.

The three men huddled in the lobby. Eyes narrowed, the Managing Director wiped his balding pate with a handkerchief. He asked the men a question. Hearing their reply, he bowed deeply and retreated back through the doors to the trading floor. When he returned, he had an irate Charles in tow.

The American man took the lead. "Mr. Gordon. I'm Fairfax from the U.S. Embassy, and this is Saito-san with the Tokyo Police Security Bureau. We'd like to have a word with you."

Charles looked down on the men and gave a strained smile. "Sorry, gentlemen, but I'm in the middle of a very busy workday."

Fairfax shrugged. "Sorry, Mr. Gordon. But our very busy workday trumps your very busy workday."

"What's this about?" Charles crossed his arms.

"Let's find a room, and we'll tell you all about it." Fairfax nodded at the Managing Director, who'd been easing his way out of the discussion circle.

Taking the cue, the Managing Director spoke up. "Yes, please follow me." He showed the men to a small conference room off of the lobby.

"Call me if I can be of further assistance," the Managing Director said before shutting the conference room door behind him.

01110011 01101111 01101101 01100101

Temples throbbing, Alison greeted the morning with a regrettable headache. Had Charles returned from his company party? The pillow on his side of the bed looked freshly plumped. Maybe he'd come home, slept and was back at work. She wasn't sure. A deep sleep induced by the bottle of wine she'd polished off single-handedly made her pretty much oblivious to Charles' comings and goings. She hadn't intended to drink so much. But after spending a panicked day trying to assess the legal morass she was sinking into and then chasing that cyberfreak Peeping Tom down the street, a nice zin had been just the thing.

Alison groaned out of bed. She was still in her clothes from last night. After a toothbrushing, a shower, a steaming cup of Nicaraguan and an aspirin, the day had potential.

In the clear light of morning, she realized that she'd overreacted to the news in her brother's fax. Sure, the Feds had busted the SwampLand BBS, and she was a member in good standing of said BBS. But the FBI was rooting out child pornographers. All she'd done was download some encryption software from the BBS. And the software itself wasn't even illegal. Not exactly.

If that damn cyberfreak hadn't made her so jumpy and jittery, she would've realized yesterday that she had nothing to worry about. No one with the FBI would be interested in what she was doing in Tokyo.

But her nerves had been on edge. Not just because of the Swamp-Land mess, but also because she couldn't shake the feeling that that cyberfreak was spying on her. His undetectable presence was all too insulting, too intrusive, and — she had to admit — too frightening a menace in her life for her to be able to ground herself and think clearly.

When under attack by an off-tilt predator, a rational person wouldn't grab an umbrella and go chasing the guy down the street. A rational person would call the cops and get a restraining order. Did they have restraining orders in Japan? Her logical, lawyerly, reasoning mind had given way to primal self-defense.

She had to keep her wits about her. What wits she had left.

Alison finished her coffee and lay down on the carpet. She hugged her knees to her chest to coax the morning stiffness out of her back. The ringing phone interrupted her yoga stretch.

"Hello?" she said, too tired to venture forth with the Japanese greeting "*Moshi moshi*," which was likely to invite a wave of incomprehensible verbiage.

"G'morning. Phillip Fairfax here," a man's voice said. Alison exhaled. He sounded like a native English speaker. Lucky for her. "I'm with the U.S. Embassy, and I'm looking for Mizz Alison Crane."

46

The embassy. Looking for her, calling her at home. Not good. Not good at all. The FBI's dragnet for members of the notorious SwampLand BBS had reached across the Pacific. Or was she being paranoid? Maybe it was a coincidence. Maybe they were calling about her visa problem.

Alison faltered for a second, trying to figure out how to respond to that guy, swallowing the urge to say, "This is Alison Crane speaking." She needed to tease out some information first.

"Alison's not here right now. May I tell her what this is in regard to?" Alison held her breath.

"It's about her friend Mr. Gordon. Ma'am, who am I speaking to?" The voice dripped with an unmistakable Texan accent.

They were going to out-polite each other. "I'm Lauren Freeman. "I'm visiting from the States." Freeman? How did you come up with that name? Must be a Freudian slip.

"Mizz Freeman, I'm working with the U.S. Embassy. We'll be coming by your friends' house later this morning. We—"

Coming by the house this morning? Alison's stomach tightened like she was bracing for a punch to the gut. She had to get in front of this catastrophe, head them off at the pass. "Sorry, but I've got to go out, and Charles — Mr. Gordon, is at work."

"That's all right, ma'am," Fairfax said. "We have authorization to search the premises. We can let ourselves in."

Let themselves in? Alison's heart beat in double time. What kind of fishing expedition was this guy planning? Rob had warned her that the Feds were moving quickly to bring in SwampLand BBS members. Now the officials were coming for her, and she was officially fucked.

Alison cleared her throat. "I don't mind staying until you arrive. When should I expect you?" She tried to sound sweet and innocent. Or at least sweet.

"We'll swing by later this morning, Mizz Freeman." Fairfax hung up.

Alison froze, immobilized, cotton-brained, body unresponsive. Panic time.

Snap out of it, Crane! Go! Do something! But what? She chided, goaded and shook herself mentally as she struggled to jump-start her synapses.

Charles. He'd know what she should do. He hated being disturbed during trading hours, but this was an emergency. And it was his house they were searching.

She dialed his work number. An unfamiliar voice answered. "Gordon-san is out of the office. May I take a message?"

"No. Thanks."

How strange that Charles was out of the office when the market was open. She called his cell and was sent to voicemail. Where the hell was he?

Charles was unreachable. The embassy would be arriving any minute to search the house. And in searching the house they'd find her computer. And in searching her computer, they'd find weapons-grade encryption software. In the house that Jack built.

Alison's breaths shortened as anxiety squeezed her rib cage like a vise.

First, they'd arrest her, then they'd deport her. Getting deported would be bad, but getting disbarred would be worse. She could hear her colleagues snickering as they pored over the "Ethics Violations" section in the monthly *Bar Journal*. "Alison Crane, environmental lawyer and activist, having been convicted of illegally exporting munitions, has been disbarred."

"Okay, Crane. Keep it together," Alison mumbled, saying the things she wished a good friend was saying to her. "You can deal with this. No need to be arrested. No need for disbarment. You just need to do a little housekeeping, a little cleaning up."

"The embassy's coming. The guy who called is probably with the USIA. Damn CIA lackeys. They'll be looking for the encryption software. That has to go. What else? Encoded messages you and Kiyoshi shared. Log onto World NetLink and delete them. Fast. And that Tracer box — lose it. And floppies, all the floppy disks. You don't want to have to explain your unusual collection of software. It's not kiddie porn, but it's all got to go. And there's not much time."

Alison booted up her computer and, with trembling fingers, clicked on files. FYEO, PeepHole, FireAx, the connection information about the SwampLand BBS that got her into this mess in the first place. She dragged the incriminating evidence to her computer's trash and deleted the goods. In a millisecond, all of her hard-acquired software vanished. Her computer was clean and pristine. But she had more work to do.

The floppy disks. It was easier to re-initialize them rather than erase their contents.

She lined up her pile of floppies and inserted the first disk to obliterate its data. The computer buzzed, wheezed and hummed. The red light on the disk drive flashed on. Alison chewed on a cuticle. The red light flashed off. Wheeze. Alison's heart pounded in her solar plexus.

She ejected the floppy from the computer's drive, shoved in the next disk from the stack and hit the button to initialize. More buzzing, more humming.

The computer was taking way too damn long. And those CIA henchmen would be arriving any minute. The last thing she needed was to get caught in the act of erasing contraband software. That, alone, would be reason enough to deport her.

Alison dashed into the kitchen and snatched a government-approved clear plastic garbage bag from under the sink. She rooted through the recycle bins and stuffed the bag with rotting persimmon peels, empty Merlot bottles and a grease-soaked Domino's pizza box.

She unplugged her cherished laptop, her window on the world and the repository for her Green Space research. Why hadn't she backed up her latest work? Too late now. She swaddled the laptop in day-old newspapers and tucked it in the middle of the rubbish.

Next went the floppy disks and the Tracer device. A sprinkling of soggy coffee grounds topped the garbage. She cinched the bundle tight.

With marking pen in hand, Alison debated what name to write. Autographing your own garbage bag. How did the Japanese come up with such an asinine law? She started to write "Gordon" but decided against it in case the embassy maggots went digging in the trash. In the end, she signed "Yamada," the only name she could write in passable Japanese characters.

After checking to see if any cars were coming, Alison bolted out to the corner and added her garbage bag to the mound already stacked for the day's pickup. She worked her sack into the middle of the heap so that her kindergarten-level handwriting wouldn't be immediately apparent.

Her dirty deed done, Alison returned to the house, washed her hands and did some deep yoga breathing to steady herself. Finishing the last complete breath, she remembered. She'd loaded her software on Charles' computer, too.

She hurried into Charles' office to discard the files she'd squirreled away on his hard drive. He'd never suspected that she had dared to use his forbidden computer. And now he would never know. She erased all traces of her misdeeds, including the FYEO encryption software. All was neat and tidy. Purged and sanitized.

Alison returned to the living room, sat down and waited.

01100011 01101111 01101111 01101100

A fist pounded at the front door. Nerves strung taut, Alison jumped at the sound. Whatever happened to ringing the doorbell like normal people do?

"Just a minute." She took one more deep breath before walking to the *genkan*.

Peering through the peephole in the door, Alison saw three men. Two white guys and a Japanese guy. Fairfax must be the older of the white guys, she guessed. The other white guy looked like a young punk. Maybe an intern. She cracked open the door.

"Good morning, gentlemen." Alison smiled, gracious as all hell.

"Mizz Freeman," the older white guy said, "I'm Fairfax." As she suspected. "We spoke on the phone. I was looking for your friend Mizz Crane."

"That's me. I'm Alison Crane. How do you do?" Alison said, keeping cool as a can of wheat tea in a Tokyo vending machine. "I'm awfully sorry to have to ask, but would you mind showing me your ID, please?" Anything to stall for time, to give her brain a chance to catch up.

As if they were used to being asked, the men flipped open wallets with what looked like official picture identification cards. Alison made a show of examining the proffered evidence. Not that she'd know if the IDs were legit or not, but it was worth going through the motions, keeping the guys on their toes.

Fairfax stepped up. "Your warrant." He shoved a piece of paper through the opening in the doorway. Alison took the document and examined it. She could read the date and recognized the kanji characters for the address of the house. Stamped with two red seals, the search warrant looked authentic. Not that she would know if it were fake. Why hadn't she called a lawyer when she had the chance? Now matters were spinning out of control, and she was on her own.

Alison held the paper in her fist and opened the door. "Come in."

As the men walked through the *genkan*, Alison glanced past them down the street to see if the garbage truck had come yet. It hadn't.

The men were already in the house before Alison saw that they hadn't taken off their shoes. They should know better. But what the hell.

Shoes in the house were easily the least of her worries. Alison followed the men into the living room.

Fairfax turned to her, and said, "This is Saito-san with the Police Security Bureau, and Peterjohn from the NSA's cyber group."

"NSA?" Alison asked.

"National Security Agency," Fairfax said. He spoke to her in the patient tone of a nursery school teacher.

"I'm in NSA digital," Peterjohn piped up. "Computer stuff. We get farmed out to State and Commerce when they don't know what they're looking for." He shot Fairfax a fleeting sidelong glance.

"I see," said Alison. She sized up Peterjohn. He looked to be late twenties, tall with arms that protruded well beyond the cuffs of his suit. He shifted his weight from foot to foot while staring at the floor. Only Peterjohn carried a briefcase.

"How can I help you, gentlemen?" Alison asked. "Would anyone like some tea? Coffee?"

She needed to take control of the situation to discourage the men from being overly meticulous in carrying out their mission. All three men declined and set about their business.

Fairfax and Saito took themselves on a quick reconnaissance tour around the house. The two men conferred in hushed voices, then spoke to Peterjohn. The computer nerd nodded and, toting his briefcase, marched into Charles' office.

Fairfax and Saito left Peterjohn sitting at Charles' computer while they surveyed the house, room by room. Alison trailed behind, an insipid smile plastered on her face. She kept a keen eye out for things the men were especially interested in, things that they took extra time examining. The men opened closets and pulled out cabinet drawers, but nothing seemed to be what they were looking for. What the hell were they looking for? She was thankful that she'd had the good sense to ditch her notebook computer and get it off of the premises before the embassy's bloodhounds had arrived.

After a cursory search, Fairfax and Saito returned to Charles' office, where Peterjohn was at the controls of Charles' computer.

"How's it going, Pete?" Fairfax asked.

"Some real interesting stuff here." Peterjohn didn't look up from the computer. "He's got a hot patch into the website."

Fairfax whistled. "Some nerve, that guy."

Hot patch? Alison ached to understand what they were talking about.

"Yeah, but he left the door open. Wide open." Peterjohn ejected a disk, pulled another floppy out of his briefcase and inserted it in the drive. His fingers danced a rapid-fire quickstep across the keyboard.

"I got everything we need. More than enough, but give me a minute," Peterjohn said. "I want to take a look at his trash."

Alison stiffened like she'd been touched by a live electrical wire. What did he mean, "Look at his trash?" It didn't sound good. Not if it meant what she thought it meant.

With rapt attention, the men huddled around the computer screen like hungry beasts preparing to go in for the kill. They didn't notice Alison as she eased in closer to get a better view of Charles' monitor. The screen read "Trash" at the top, but was filled with a directory of file names, sizes and types. All were ostensibly deleted files. But, instead of being dead and gone, the zombified files were immortalized on the computer.

"Well, well, well, what have we here?" Peterjohn said, relishing the moment like an adolescent boy sneaking a peek at a centerfold. "Look what our friend dumped from his computer this morning."

Alison's eyes followed where Peterjohn's finger was pointing on the computer screen. The screen read:

```
FYEO 156.8 MB Deleted 09:23
```

Fairfax turned to Alison. "Of course you don't know anything about this, do you, Mizz Crane?"

Derision oozed from Fairfax's eyes. She could almost hear him thinking, "dumb broad."

"Do you know anything about this?" Fairfax said.

Alison's cheeks grew hot. "About the computer?" she said. The wobble in her voice surprised her. She cleared her throat.

"No, this file that was deleted." Fairfax pointed to the screen. "FYEO. For Your Eyes Only. It's for encrypting messages. That means putting something into secret code. Do you know about this file?"

The man was insufferable. Alison resisted the urge to tell him where he could put his secret code. But she was in a serious jam. Maybe his patronizing blind spot might work in her favor.

"Uh, — no, not really," Alison said. "Charles doesn't like me to touch his computer. He uses it for his work. It's his precious little jewel." She remembered how she'd felt about even approaching his sacred computer a few weeks ago. Was it only a few weeks ago?

"Then how was it that this file got erased today?" Fairfax punched the screen with his finger. "Deleted this morning."

Alison crossed her arms on her chest. She was seriously treading now. She remembered an invaluable lesson learned in law school: When in doubt, improvise. "I — I don't know how that happened. Maybe—"

"You know, Phil," Peterjohn spoke up, "Gordon could've gotten in from a remote site. He has this machine wired. Online all the time. He could've accessed this computer from anywhere, could've gotten into the system and deleted the files himself. Maybe he even had a hot key with a cyanide pill."

"Cyanide pill?" Saito asked.

"Yeah, it's a kind of program where the computer destroys certain files if a key is hit. And the files are gone." Peterjohn snapped his fingers. "He could've done any of that stuff from any phone anywhere."

Alison resumed breathing. Bless you, computer nerd. Bless you.

"Okay, let's pack up and ship out," Fairfax was back in charge again. "You boys load up the computer and let's haul it on outta here. And you,

Mizz Crane, I have to ask you to stay in town for the next few days. Your boyfriend's gonna need a whole lotta help."

Alison nodded, wordless with confusion. She sent the crew on their way and closed the door behind them. She took a deep yoga breath and collapsed on the living room couch. Her boyfriend was going to need help? Why hadn't they arrested her?

She rubbed her eyes as if to clear her vision and heard the grunting of the garbage truck lumbering down the street. Alison jumped off the couch, bolted outside, and from the arms of the trash man, rescued her own precious little jewel.

47

Alison stretched out on the carpeted living room floor and, reaching for the remote, set the control to maximum heat. Time. At least she'd bought herself a little time to think. The warming carpet melted knots of tension from her lower back.

Alison rolled onto her stomach and pushed up into at downward dog yoga pose. The pose was supposed to clarify thinking, among other benefits. Her ears pounded with the surge of blood moving through her inverted head.

The embassy was pursuing Charles. For something she'd done. Charles knew nothing about the encryption software on his computer, let alone the SwampLand BBS. She couldn't hang back and let him take the blame. It wouldn't be fair.

But she didn't want to come forward, hands in the air, confessing to the authorities what she'd been up to. It was the right thing to do, it was the ethical thing to do. And yet … throwing away her entire legal career, losing her status as an attorney. Possible jail time? And who knew what else might be meted out by a flawed criminal justice system that was especially harsh on African-Americans.

The embassy had targeted Charles. They were sure they had their man. She had no choice. She had to come clean. He wasn't the criminal. She was.

Arms trembling — because of the intense yoga pose or because of the realization of what was to come — Alison lowered herself to the carpet. She felt calmer knowing what she had to do, bitter though the decision be.

But first, before turning herself in, she needed to explain to Charles. To apologize for screwing up so spectacularly, for involving him in her series of ill-informed choices.

Alison picked up the phone and punched in Charles' number at the office. She was doing the right thing. He shouldn't be taking the heat for her. The truth would out eventually anyway. And the authorities looked favorably on people who cooperated with them. At least that was what they said.

An operator picked up Charles' extension.

"Charles Gordon, please," Alison said.

"I'm sorry, but Gordon-san is out of the office."

"Would you tell him to please call Alison. It's urgent."

The operator hesitated. "Uh, yes, ma'am. I'll—I'll leave a message," she said.

"Remember, it's urgent." Charles still wasn't in the office. In the meantime, until he returned, Alison had matters to take care of.

She dusted the crud off of her computer and set up on the dining room table. She knew she had a guardian angel because the floppies she'd thrown out with the computer all reloaded smoothly in her machine. Plugging in the Tracer box, just in case, she got online to send unencrypted email messages while she still had a chance to use a computer. While she still was a free woman.

Rob–

Good to hear from you the other day. I already had some visitors come by my house who were interested in my little problem. I'm on it, so don't worry. I'll call you when I'm in the clear.

Next, to Kiyoshi:

```
Hello, Kiyo—

There's so much I want to talk to you about, I wish
you were online now. Things have taken an unexpected
turn. I'll tell you about it at 5.

Don't forget, no special software.
```

Working through her list of things to do before she turned herself in, Alison relaxed with a sense of productivity. Her Zen calm in resignation was shattered when her computer emitted a trumpet herald, and a message blasted on her screen.

```
HELLO HELLO HELLO!!!! I THOUGHT YOU DIDN'T LIKE ME
ANYMORE! I CAME TO VISIT YOU!!!! YES YES YES!
```

Dammit, that cyber-creep was back. Alison cursed the jerk to the high heavens before remembering that she'd reinstalled PeepHole with FireAx on her computer. With that powerful combination of software, she had a chance — maybe her last chance — to expose the guy and find out who he was before she pled guilty and faced the music at the embassy.

She typed a new unencrypted email message to herself which she knew the freak would intercept. All part of her plan to lure him in.

"Hello, my mysterious friend. Let's go to a private chat room. Meet me in CHEZ ALI in 2 minutes."

If she could engage him in a direct user-to-user chat, then PeepHole, with a boost from FireAx, could pick up a full reading on who the guy was. That was how it was supposed to work. In theory. No matter, it was her only shot.

She created the chat room and dared the door to open. It did.

"I KNOW YOU LIKE ME!!! I LIKE YOU TOO. WHAT ABOUT A DATE??"

A date with the pervert? The thought nauseated Alison. She needed to stay focused on her plan. Keep the guy online, keep him talking, expose his ass. Would PeepHole work in an instant? Or was it like a phone trace in the movies that took a while to get a good read? Alison didn't know. She'd better keep him talking to her for as long as she could bear it.

"I wanted to meet you yesterday. That's why I came running after you."
"NO, I ALREADY MEET YOU."

What was he talking about?

"I don't think so. I haven't had the pleasure yet."
"YES!!! I MET YOU AT YOUR PARTY!! I GAVE YOU A GOOD NIGHT KISS."

Alison shuddered. Too eerie. But she needed to keep at it, keep him online.

"A kiss? We haven't even been properly introduced. What's your name?"
"NO NAME. DAREMO IS MY NAME. NOBODY. SOMEBODY. I KNOW YOUR NAME ALI. ALISON CRANE."

He knew her name and way too much else about her.

"Do you live in Tokyo, Mr. Daremo?"

"I CAN SHOW YOU PLACES YOUR BOYFRIEND DOES NOT KNOW. SIT ON SOFA AND FEEL GOOD WITH ME."

Her boyfriend? What did the pervert know about Charles? She'd done an excellent job of getting Charles entangled in all of her mishaps. He'd be thrilled.

I WANT TO HEAR YOUR VOICE. DO YOU SING?"

Sing? What's he talking about? The guy was beyond weird. Enough already. Alison closed the chat room.

Who was her perverted friend? She wanted to find out his name, his real name, the creep. Spying through the PeepHole, who could she see?

Alison's fingers fumbled with the mouse and miss-clicked keys in her eagerness to know the true identity of her online tormentor.

The PeepHole log read:

```
12:08
Recipient Name: TokyoAli
Registered as: Alison Crane
User Computer Identification: Alison Crane
Logon Point: 8132345-2348
Message Sender Computer Identification: ERROR 26
Sender Name: ERROR 26
Registered as: ERROR 39
Logon Point: 8135795-4007
```

Alison recognized the logon point after her name. It was her home phone number. That meant that even though PeepHole didn't provide a registered name for the geek, it offered up his logon point, the phone number he was calling from.

Alison raised her fists in the air. "Gotcha!" She copied down the number for the logon point on a memo pad. It was a good start.

Now that she'd found the bastard, what to do with him? She could expose him online, report him to the World NetLink authorities. Or, now that she had his number, she could run FireAx, get into the system he was calling from and poke around. But then what? Would he just disappear and leave her alone? Or would he be pissed and provoked and worm his way into her life even more?

The irony of her situation was almost laughable. At last, she'd found her anonymous stalker. She assumed she'd found him, she corrected herself, not wanting to believe everything she read online. Especially online. But now she didn't know what to do with him.

The access logon phone number was a start. She could pester the freak with crank phone calls. Dial the number, wait for him to answer, then hang up. Other than that, she didn't have any great ideas. But she knew someone who might.

Alison emailed:

```
Hey, Jed – Missed you at my party. Hope you can make
it next time. Meanwhile, I've got a question. That
guy I was telling you about who kept busting into
my email. I found out his logon point of access. No
name, just a phone number. Any suggestions on how to
deal with him?
```

As Alison was typing, she realized that the freak could probably read the email after she sent it. She trashed the email and logged off.

Her pile of *meishi* business cards had multiplied in the dark of night. But at last, she found Jed's card with his phone number. She dialed and hoped Jed would answer.

"*Moshi moshi.*"

"Jed? It's Alison Crane. We met at Kinokuniya, and—"

"Alison! What's up? You're not calling to return my computer, are you?"

Hearing the down-home friendliness of Jed's voice made Alison smile. "No, I love it. No complaints."

"Cool. How's the software working for ya?"

"That's why I'm calling. I've been running PeepHole, like you suggested. And I think I caught him. That guy who's been harassing me online."

"Fucking A! Now you can one-up that bugger."

"The problem is I don't know his user name. Only his logon point of access."

"You know where he's calling from, but you don't know his user ID, right?"

Not sure that's what she meant, Alison said "right" anyway.

"No sweat. It'll take a little more doing, but you can get in the system logs and find out who sent mail to you. You got the time, destination and system. You just need some software. It's called—"

"I can't, Jed. No more software." Alison's breaths shortened. "Isn't there any other way?" She ran her finger along her thumb nail, searching for a rough edge.

After a lengthy silence, Jed inhaled audibly through his teeth. He must have lived in Japan for a long time to have picked up the habit. "You got the report from PeepHole? Read it to me," he said.

Alison recited from the PeepHole log.

"It said 'Error 39' for registered name?" Jed asked.

"Uh, yeah."

"Error 39. Got it. I'll call you back when I get something."

"Oh. Okay." Her stalker had taken the bait and she was in hot pursuit. But now all forward momentum had come to a screeching halt. There was nothing she could do but wait. And she detested waiting.

As if Jed could read her thoughts, he added, "I can call you back in — I dunno — half an hour?"

"You're a lifesaver, Jed."

"All in a day's work. Happy to help. Damsel in digital distress and all that."

Alison sat and waited. And waited. She hated waiting. And as she sat, her thoughts turned to Charles. Where could he be? She decided to try him again, to let him know about the visit from the embassy. How would he take it? Not so well. Those CIA minions were all assuming that he was the one who had been a part of the porno pirate board and downloaded the encryption software. And exported it. No, Charles wouldn't take it too well.

The ringing phone startled her. Her heart pounded, and sweat tickled at her armpits. Was it Charles? The embassy? She might have sophisticated privacy-busting software on her computer, but she didn't even have basic Caller ID on her phone. Alison held her breath and picked up.

"Got the goods." Jed said.

"Great! Who is he?"

"How 'bout you meet me? I'll tell you everything. Shibuya, at Hachiko. In an hour."

"Hachiko? What's that," Alison asked.

"The dog. In Shibuya. Ask anyone. See you in an hour."

01110011 01110000 01101111 01110100 01110011

A crowd of people huddled around a bronze statue of a dog at Shibuya station. Alison had told the taxi driver that she wanted to go to Hachiko, and he'd dropped her off here. Apparently everyone knew about Hachiko. Everyone but her.

It was easy to find Jed among the waiting masses. The fluttering flag with a psychedelic peace sign was a dead giveaway. Following the beacon, Alison walked through the crowd until she saw Jed, flag mounted on his wheelchair.

Cheeks red with cold, Jed cocked his head when he saw Alison. "Let's go inside, warm up." Jed rubbed his hands together and blew into them. "Follow me." They jostled their way through the intersection of overlapping crosswalks and rode the Prime Building's elevator down to the basement.

Bistro-sized ramen restaurants lined the subterranean floor. The garlicky steam from a thousand bowls of ramen warmed Alison's bones and reminded her that she hadn't eaten since her breakfast coffee.

Jed pointed to a tiny shop at the end of the row of eateries. There was only one customer inside. "This joint's my favorite," Jed said. They sat at the counter, and Jed raised a finger to summon a server. "You want a beer, some noodles?" Jed asked.

"Yeah. Sure. Whatever." Alison tried to control her impatience. She was keen to hear what Jed had learned about her stalker, but she was also hungry.

Jed ordered, and soon the server brought two mugs of Asahi beer followed by bowls of thick noodles submerged in a milky broth. Fatty slices of pork and a brown-rimmed hard-boiled egg, cut in half, floated in a pool of oil.

Alison was hungry, but she wasn't sure she was up to having her first meal of the day consist of a greasy assault on her palate. She picked up a tidbit of seaweed and chewed on the edge. A little heavy on the salt, but surprisingly tasty.

Head lowered so close to the bowl that Alison was concerned that his beard would dip in the broth, Jed noisily slurped up a mouthful of noodles. A wheezing asthmatic would have been quieter. He paused to wash the ramen down with a swig of beer.

"Your friend's handle is 'Daremo,'" he said.

Daremo, Daremo. Where had Alison heard that? She remembered. The cyber-freak himself had told her online. She'd overlooked it in his crude, lewd babbling. "Daremo?" she asked.

"Yeah, you know, 'nobody.' In Japanese. He wants to keep a low profile." Jed laughed. "And the system he's calling from is an original logon point. My guess is that he's a SysOp on his own network."

"What does that mean?"

"Just guessing from the echo log I got, but I'd bet this guy's running his own operation."

"Can you explain? In a way I can understand." Alison drank her beer. Its hoppy bubbles cut through the salty oil slick coating her mouth.

"He probably has a computer or two set up and runs his own BBS network. That's how he can access other computers directly, scramble the source ID. Kinda tricky, but nothing too major league." Jed popped the half-egg in his mouth and knocked it back with beer.

Runaway noodles escaped from Alison's unsteady chopsticks and splashed back into her bowl. She was done. Eating wasn't worth the struggle. She parked the chopsticks on the rest. "You said the guy can get into other people's computers?"

Jed nodded. "The dude's a SysOp — a system operator. He's got powers beyond a mere mortal. He can read everyone's email, look over their shoulder, even send software files. All anonymously."

"Oh." Alison said. She didn't understand the how's, but she was glad that Jed did.

"You've gotten off easy," he said.

"Easy? The asshole's been stalking me, threatening me. I wouldn't call that easy."

"Yeah, but some of these guys — and I should say some of these gals, too — can get into other systems and take over. With the right software, they can screw with your files and not even leave a trace. Not unless there's a good firewall."

"That's great information, Jed, but what can I do to get rid of the creep?"

"I've been thinking about that. A coupla things come to mind. Just a second." Jed nodded at the server and held up his empty glass. Alison was ready to buy him a keg if it meant he would sit still and talk to her. The server brought Jed a frothy new mug and took away his empty.

Alison drank her own beer to control her agitation. "You have some ideas about how I can get rid of the guy?"

Jed smiled and lifted one eyebrow. "Ah, yes. This is the fun part. Now that you know who this joker is, you can put a kill on him."

Alison coughed and beer dribbled out of her nose. Pulling a tissue from her purse, she wiped her face. She hoped she hadn't heard what she'd heard. "Kill him? I'm not—"

Jed shook his head. "Jeez louise. What kind of person do you think I am? A kill's a call block. It blocks email from a user ID."

Alison exhaled. She was so in over her head. "Is it hard to do? To put in a kill?" Saying the words made her feel prickly. What would the Bar Association think?

"You're on NutLink, right?" Jed asked.

Alison nodded.

"Tell them what I told you, and they'll set it up. They don't like to advertise the service. Scares the users, makes the network look bad."

"I didn't realize it'd be so easy. I'll send World NetLink an email right away."

"Hold on. The kill's just for starters. Kindergarten level. If you really want to stick it to that guy, I got some other ideas you might want to hear."

"I'm all ears."

"Your guy's firewall isn't for shit. That's how I could get the dirt on him so quick." Jed grabbed chopsticks in his right hand and a soup spoon in his left. With the urgency of a beached fish gasping for breath, he inhaled the last of his ramen.

Alison looked at her bowl, brimming with fugitive noodles floating in puddles of grease. She poked around with her chopsticks searching for a morsel she could get a firm grip on.

"What's a firewall?"

"A firewall? You build it into your system to guard against intruders. Keep the bad guys out, only let the good guys in. A system safeguard."

With the focused determination worthy of a Cirque du Soleil balancing act, Alison landed some noodles in her mouth. Things were looking up. "So you think the jerk's unprotected? Even with a firewall?"

"He's got a firewall, but it's dated. And a crappy firewall offers all kinds of opportunities for fun."

"So what does that mean for me?" Alison drained her beer.

Jed spoke to the server who then deposited a plate of plain noodles on the table and a foaming mug for Alison. Jed dumped the noodles into his bowl, stirred them into the broth and slurped.

"What can I do to get rid of the guy, Jed?"

"You could pop into the guy's network, deliver a little present — a Trojan horse, a worm, a virus. Drop off the package then back out quiet as a ninja."

"Trojan horses, worms, viruses. Speak English, Jed. Not techno-talk." Alison sat back in her chair and pushed away her ramen bowl.

"OK. A Trojan horse. Think Greek mythology. It's an innocent-looking program that visits a remote system, slips by the gate, then wreaks havoc. Worms, viruses. They work kind of the same way."

Alison closed her eyes, struggling to keep up. "So one option is sending the creep a horse or a worm, or something. How do I do that?"

"You need some software for hacking into systems. It's illegal as all hell, but it's effective. Called FireAx."

Alison's eyes flew open wide as Jed's words sent shockwaves through her brain. "Illegal as all hell." Alison was in it deep. Landed smack in the middle of quicksand with both feet and was sinking fast. But it would be unthinkably stupid to risk running any funny software again. Especially since the embassy officials were breathing down her neck.

"Fireax? I think I've heard of something like that." She didn't add that she'd purchased the software in Hong Kong and had used it to snoop around Green Space's BBS network. "But I don't want to mess around with trying to score illegal software."

"I've got a copy of it," Jed said quietly.

"Let me think about that one, Jed. Any other ideas?"

"There is one more possibility." Jed took a toothpick from the dispenser on the counter. "Elegant in its simplicity. Hardly high-tech. More like a drive-by shooting. Easy to execute, virtually no way to see it coming. Or to guard against it." With one hand held up to conceal his mouth, he picked at his teeth. Alison could tell that he was enjoying the build-up.

"All right, already! What is it?"

"You might want to take this guy out altogether. With a mailbomb."

Alison couldn't believe the conversation she was having. Plans for bombs? Kills? If this ramen joint was being bugged, she and Jed were in for it. But then, again, she *already was* in for it.

Alison leaned closer. "I hate to even ask, but what's a mailbomb?"

Jed broke it all down for Alison, describing the what's and how-to's, while Alison took careful notes. At the end of his explanation, she set down her pen. "That sounds perfect, Jed. And like you said, elegant in its simplicity."

48

It was a few minutes before five, but Alison couldn't wait. She got online, hoping, praying that Kiyoshi might be there early. She paged him, and her prayers were answered.

```
"How are you Alison? The email you sent to me was
strange."
"My whole day has been strange. That guy was online
again. He's probably reading our chat now. I'd
really like to talk to you but not by computer. Can
you call me?"
"Sure. Right now."
```

They closed their computer chat room, and Kiyoshi called Alison on her cell phone.

"What's going on, Alison? Are you all right?"

"Yes." She was relieved to hear Kiyoshi's rumbling voice. "Truth is, I don't really know. The embassy was here today searching the house. It was like a police raid."

"What were they looking for?"

"That software." She didn't want to get too specific over the phone. "They brought in some young techno-nerd who was going through the computer files. They said they found what they were looking for, and then they left. I feel uncomfortable talking about this on a cell phone."

"You can tell me the details later. But you're lucky they let you keep your computer."

"Actually, they were searching Charles' computer. You know. My friend."

"Right."

"Kiyoshi, I can't get in touch with Charles. I think he's gotten into trouble for what I did. I've got to go forward, tell the authorities about what I've done."

Kiyoshi was silent for a moment. "Are you sure that's what you want to do? Couldn't they arrest you?"

"Maybe. Probably. But it's not fair to Charles if I don't turn myself in."

"They wouldn't be able to prove anything against your friend, would they? He didn't know about the software you were running."

"I know, but they have what we in the law call a *prima facie* case. In other words, it looks pretty bad for Charles."

"You need to consult with a lawyer, someone who can straighten this out for you. Call my friend Sasaki. He's a Japanese *bengoshi*, and he's licensed in New York and California, too."

"Great. A triple threat."

"I'm serious, Alison." Kiyoshi told her the lawyer's phone number, which she scribbled on a Post-It note. "Sasaki. He's good, he's in Tokyo, and he has powerful friends in the diplomatic community."

"Kiyoshi, this is a nightmare. I'm starting to lose it. I don't know if I'm doing the right thing. It's hard to think straight."

"I can come to Tokyo tomorrow. We can visit Sasaki's office together."

It'd be so wonderful if Kiyoshi were there with her. Someone to help her figure things out, someone who understood. But her misadventures had ensnared Charles in what promised to be a legal nightmare, and she didn't want to drag Kiyoshi further into her quagmire. "Thanks, but

I'll muddle through this somehow. What's the worst that can happen? Extradition? Disbarment? Prison? Really, no big deal."

"Call Sasaki, Alison. Understand?" Kiyoshi ordered.

"Yessir!" Alison said, trying to make light of her predicament. "I'll call."

Alison hung up. The public address speakers quieted with the last tones of the 5 o'clock song. It took Alison a few delayed seconds to realize that she'd not only heard the song from outside but also through her cell phone. From Kiyoshi's end of the conversation.

Alison called his cell phone but there was no answer. She logged back online, looking for him, but he was gone. What was going on? Kiyoshi had offered to come to Tokyo tomorrow, but was he already in town? If Kiyoshi was in Tokyo now, why hadn't he said so?

She looked at the Post-It note with Mr. Sasaki's number, picked up the phone and dialed his office. While the phone was ringing, she hung up. Who was she kidding? She was a co-conspirator in an international cyberterrorist group trading in illegal weapons. For starters. There was nothing Sasaki or anyone else could do to help her. She was doomed and her fate irreparable.

Alison slumped on the sofa, her gaze falling on the olive trees across the street. The darkening sky mirrored her gloomy thoughts.

After minutes of catatonic inertia, Alison roused herself. "Here goes nothing," she said. She dialed the U.S. Embassy, half hoping everyone was already gone for the day. Unfortunately, someone answered the phone.

"Mr. Fairfax, please." Alison wasn't looking forward to talking to that sneering little misogynist who was running the investigation at the embassy. Her heartbeat fluttered, and her armpits itched. She waited. Maybe Fairfax had gone for the day.

"Fairfax," barked a voice, military in its attack.

Alison took a deep breath and plunged right in. "This is Alison Crane. I met you this morning at my house—"

"Mizz Crane. What can I do you for?"

"Uh, it's about—" she paused to try to produce some saliva. "It's that there's some information you should know. I mean, there are some things I'd like to explain, and—"

"Understood. Why don't you swing on over to my office?"

Fairfax was probably merrily dissecting the computer hard drive, bit by byte. Happy as a dog with a bone. "I can be there in an hour."

"Room 367. I'll leave your name with the guards."

"I'll be there soon, Mr. Fairfax."

"No hurry. At the rate we're going, I'll be here spending the night with your boyfriend. But don't you be getting all jealous, now."

Damn! They already had Charles! Why hadn't his office told her that Charles was being detained by the embassy? Maybe she should call Kiyoshi's lawyer.

Alison contemplated what she was going to do with her last hour of freedom. She knew she was doing the right thing by giving herself up, but she wondered why she didn't feel better about being noble. Or at least being honorable. Or maybe just being chicken.

But before she turned over her new leaf, before she resumed a life on the side of truth and justice, she considered the one last thing she had to do. One last little nasty — maybe illegal — deed. After that, she'd change her ways, get back on the straight and narrow.

Considering the mountain of charges she was likely facing, her last little deed would hardly matter. Except to her. And it was like her aunt used to say: If you're going to go crazy, you might as well lose your mind.

Following the instructions she'd gotten from Jed, Alison got back online, pulled up a few files and punched in some commands on her computer. In the end, she had composed the file. Her love letter to Daremo.

She would send Daremo this one little message, meant especially for him. Maybe it wasn't nice, but she wasn't feeling nice. Not today. Not with what he'd put her through. And now she was in a shitload of trouble — maybe even going to the Big House — only because of efforts she had taken to protect herself from Daremo. No, she'd send the message, which carried with it her impassioned feelings for him. And then she would come clean with Fairfax.

Alison was poised over the keyboard, about to enter the Send command to post her message to Daremo, when she hesitated. Hovering mid-air over the keys, she wavered. As much as she wanted to hurt him, hurt him really bad, she knew what she was about to do wasn't right. And knowing it wasn't right but doing it anyway would mean that she'd have the criminal *mens rea*, the guilty mind, that could land her butt in jail for a long, long time.

She logged off, packed up her computer and headed out to her inevitable Day of Reckoning at the embassy.

49

Shiny barbed wire fortified the perimeter of the U.S. Embassy grounds. The complex looked like it would be better situated in a war zone than one of the poshest districts of Tokyo. She knew that once she crossed the line and turned herself in, she'd be in custody. And then what? She didn't want to speculate what her future might hold. But she had to go through with it. For Charles' sake.

Like a prisoner walking to the execution chamber, she forced her reluctant feet to approach the embassy. At the gate of the citadel, she presented herself and gave her name to the Marine guards stationed at the entrance.

A guard checked a clipboard hanging in the entry gate. Satisfied with Alison's bona fides, he searched her computer case before escorting her down two long corridors and up an elevator. The Marine handed her over to a man dressed in a suit. A civilian, Alison guessed. The man took her to a small conference room where he left her.

The room's fluorescent lights emitted an annoyingly loud hiss, and their harsh illumination stung Alison's eyes. She parked her laptop on the table, wiped her sweaty palms on her jeans, and sat down. With hands folded in front of her, she waited like a guilt-ridden young girl at a church Sunday school.

She thought of the many days that lay ahead of her, days she would spend alone in a small room. Alone, that is, unless she had a cell mate to keep her company.

Alison's nervous thumb found a hardened cuticle, which she gnawed on. She noticed another cuticle and bit it clean, as well. She was working on a third finger when the door opened and in walked Fairfax.

Alison rose to her feet as if called to attention.

"Sit down, Mizz Crane." Fairfax tossed a folder on the table and sat. "You want some water? Tea?"

This must be the good cop/bad cop routine, Alison deduced. She wondered when Fairfax's evil twin would burst through the door for hard-core grilling. "Yes, I'd like some tea, please. With milk, if you have it." What a stupid thing to say. This ain't no tea party, honey.

Fairfax reached over to a telephone on a side table and pressed the intercom. He told the person on the other end to bring in a cup of tea.

"Yessir, Mr. Fairfax, sir," a man's voice replied.

Jeez, even the coffee-getters must be Marines. She was surrounded by military men who were experts at interrogation. Her stomach knotted up with tense anticipation of the cross-examination she'd be subjected to. A cup of hot tea would definitely help her queasiness.

Fairfax rocked back on the hind legs of his chair and laced his fingers behind his head. Alison noticed dark circles under his eyes that she hadn't seen that morning when he'd been combing through her house.

"What did you want to talk to me about, Mizz Crane?" Fairfax twisted his mouth into something like a pleasant smile. His effort produced an awkward contortion. Smiling didn't sit well on Fairfax's face.

If the good cop was trying to kill her with kindness, who knew what the bad cop had in store for her? Alison considered picking up her computer and leaving. Fleeing might buy her a few more days of freedom.

While she was a still a free woman, she'd have a chance to see Kiyoshi. She could use her one-way ticket back to the States. She could visit her brother, go hiking in Point Reyes, get a mud bath. Simple pleasures she had looked forward to now felt as distant and improbable as a death-row inmate's fantasies.

Fairfax's laser-focused gaze locked on Alison. "You said you had something you wanted to tell me. What is it?" he asked.

Alison's shoulders drooped with the weight of resignation. What the hell. This was no time for wistful longing for friendly visits and nature walks. This was time for action. She had made the decision to spill her guts to Fairfax. Alison took a deep breath and began spilling.

"It's about that software you found on Charles'—Mr. Gordon's computer. It's just that — you see — actually, that wasn't his software," she began, not knowing exactly where the beginning was.

Fairfax sat forward. "What are you saying?" The tea arrived, and Alison burnt her tongue taking a sip before proceeding.

"To tell you the truth, I'm the one who was online and downloaded that software. It wasn't Charles. It was me. I have my own computer. Look." She unzipped the case to her PowerBook.

Fairfax whistled. "Very pretty."

"I have an account on World NetLink, and Charles doesn't even know about it."

"Let's keep it our little secret then." Fairfax's wink felt as condescending as a pat on a puppy's head.

Alison bit her lower lip. The jerk was insufferable. She was trying to come clean, but he just wasn't getting it. She'd have to explain again.

"Mr. Fairfax, I used to use Charles' computer, before I bought my PowerBook. Some of the software I downloaded when I was using Charles' Mac was still on his machine when you took it. It was my personal software, things I downloaded for me."

"I get it now." Fairfax wiggled his eyebrows. "You were on Gordon's computer and had a little rendezvous," Fairfax scratched the air making that annoying little quotation mark gesture, "with an online friend," he scratched again. "And you didn't want Gordon to find the messages. No problem, he hasn't seen the computer files since we took the machine. It can be our little secret." Fairfax winked at Alison. Again. She valiantly controlled her impulse to punch him out. The last thing she needed would be an assault and battery charge added to the mix.

Alison tried to return Fairfax's gaze, lock him in a stare-down, show him that she was a woman to be reckoned with. But her glance ricocheted off of his bulletproof face and landed in her lap. She'd been alpha-dogged. This was his show, not hers.

"Mr. Fairfax. I'm afraid — I'm afraid I'm not making myself clear. What I'm — I'm trying to say is that I'm the one who downloaded the files. The ones you found this morning. The encryp—encryp—"

"En-cryp-tion," Fairfax offered slowly as if Alison were not a native English speaker.

"Yes. I'm the one you should be arresting. It was me, not Charles. Me. You've got to let Charles go. But I'm not going to say anything else until I can speak to my lawyer."

Fairfax grinned and broke into song. "Stand by your man," he crooned.

Alison listened, incredulous. The guy wasn't taking her seriously. Was it so unthinkable for him to imagine that a woman could be behind the cybercrimes he was investigating? She reminded herself to never underestimate a man's ability to underestimate a woman. Especially a Black woman.

"I want to call my lawyer," she said.

"Much obliged for your offer to help, Mizz Crane, but I can't let you go on with this cockamamie story. We've got everything we need against Gordon. An airtight case. You're free to go."

"Airtight case?"

"Yeah, with some help of our friends at MITI —"

"MITI?"

"The Japanese Ministry of International Trade and Industry. They helped us tie Gordon to the Yamada-gumi."

"The Yamada what?"

"They're a powerful yakuza group out of Kobe. You know the yakuza — kinda like the Mafia back stateside. MITI has been trying to nail the Yamada clan for years."

"But what does Charles have to do with any of that?" Asking the question, Alison's stomach turned leaden.

"The clan's heiress apparent is Yuko Yamada. She and Gordon have been running some pretty slick deals. International bank fraud, to be exact."

Charles? Bank fraud? With Yamada-san? Was that a mild earthquake making her feel unsteady on her feet or had her world turned upside down?

The embassy had misconstrued Alison's digital misadventures and had built a trumped-up case against Charles. How could she tell them that they had arrested the wrong person? "You're making a terrible mistake, Mr. Fairfax."

"We've been tracking your boyfriend and Yamada for a while now. They were using some damn save-the-ozone front for laundering money out of Tokyo and a whole bunch of no-tell banks in the Pacific Rim. We've got evidence of trades, dummy corporations, holding companies. There's no mistake."

Fairfax opened the folder on the table and spread out the contents, a stack of glossy black-and-white prints. The images were blurred, but Alison recognized her face and her travel clothes in Hong Kong.

She snatched up a picture that showed her being tackled on the street when she was looking for Green Space's branch office. "Who took these?" she asked. "Who was following me? I want to call my lawyer."

"Like I said, we've been working on this for a while. Do you know what was on that disk, the one you were carrying into Hong Kong for Yamada?"

"Sure. It had information about donors for Green Space. Her environmental group."

Fairfax chuckled. "It had information, all right. Encrypted passwords for offshore accounts Yamada and Gordon set up. They liked to have the crypto keys delivered by hand. No paper trail that way."

Alison crossed her arms. "I don't believe you," she said.

"I'm sorry, Mizz Crane, but Gordon and Yamada used you. You were their mule."

The embassy had jumped to conclusions. The wrong conclusions. "I don't know what Yuko Yamada is up to, but I'm sure Charles had nothing to do with it. They barely knew each other."

"Oh, they knew each other. Rather well, in fact." Fairfax reached in his jacket pocket, took out a microcassette recorder and hit the play button. Two voices — Charles and Yuko Yamada — issued from the electronic device.

"*Right there. Yeah, that feels really good.*" No mistaking it. That was Charles all right. Alison could hear muffled noises, sounded like kissing.

"*Are you sure it'll be all right?*"

"*What?*"

"*Giving her the disk. Won't she suspect something?*"

"*Alison's so eager to get a job with you she'd do backflips. Nothing to worry about. Now bring that sweet pussy back here.*"

Fairfax turned off the cassette.

Alison covered her face with her hands. Her cheeks burned with embarrassed rage. That asshole! That goddamn asshole! Here she was trying to save Charles' butt, even turning herself in to protect him. And all the while he'd been selling her down the river while fucking Yamada. They had Alison jumping through hoops like a trained dog. Yamada might dress in Chanel, but she was just a skanky bitch.

Alison was all too aware of her own faults. She'd come to the embassy to turn herself in after breaking who knew how many laws by downloading software she knew was questionable. And after her steamy fling with Kiyoshi in Hong Kong, she couldn't hold herself up as a standard of moral virtue. But she'd never used another person— especially a person she claimed to love—to carry out a scheme. An illegal, RICO-worthy scheme.

Alison exhaled loudly over a slow breath and lowered her hands. "What happens now?" she asked.

"Gordon's not stupid," Fairfax said. "He confessed."

"Confessed?"

"Yes, indeedydo. They had quite an international network. Computerized and nut-hard to trace. But your little boyfriend left his electronic bee-hind bare. No protection, no firewall. Cocky SOB. Once we had his computer, we could source out his whole organization."

Alison tasted her tea, which had quickly turned lukewarm. Charles had always wanted it all and had a way of making things happen. Alison liked that about him, his resourceful confidence. But to stoop to criminal plots with Yamada? And use Alison as a pawn? The bastard deserved whatever was coming his way. "What's going to happen to Charles?" she asked.

"Gordon's singing like Tweety Bird, naming names, trying to cut a deal. He's going home, for starters. Folks at Justice have some business to take up with him."

"What a mess he's gotten himself into." Alison dragged her computer case closer and propped it in her lap. Part shield, part security blanket, the computer provided a comforting weight. As awful as the day had turned out to be, she was thankful. No one was asking about her online association with the SwampLand BBS or any of the encryption software she'd downloaded. It looked like she'd dodged a legal bullet.

But no thanks to that online creep. The freak had tormented her so relentlessly, had unnerved her so completely, that she'd resorted to drastic measures to take back her privacy and reclaim her life. How was she to know that with a simple download of encryption software, she'd joined up with a band of online weirdos trading kiddy porn and cyberterrorists exporting illegal software? She'd been acting in self-defense, but she'd come uncomfortably close to being arrested and doing time. All because of that demented digital pervert.

Charles was getting his comeuppance, but what about the cyberfreak? Alison had had the perfect opportunity to deliver her devastating email to him, but decided it was the wrong thing to do. But now, more than anything, she wanted to see justice done. And if she could give justice a little nudge, all the better.

"Mr. Fairfax," Alison began. "There's something else I should tell you."

"What's that?"

"Charles didn't talk too much about his work, and, to tell you the truth, I didn't understand much when he did try to explain what he did." She hoped she wasn't laying the dumb blonde act on too thick. She was far from blonde. And she was tired of being dumb.

"International finance is complicated and confusing," Fairfax agreed. He reached across the table and patted Alison's hand. The jerk.

"I remember that one particular person kept calling Charles on the computer. Email and stuff. Charles said the guy was his system operator, or something like that." Alison paused for a pensive moment. "Once when I was on Charles' computer, a message came through from the guy. I wrote down the email address so that I could tell Charles. Let me check if I've still got it."

She flipped open her computer and went through the motions of pulling up files. "Found it!" Alison wrote down the IP address of her stalker and pushed the information across the table to Fairfax. "I'm not trying to justify what Charles did, but it's not right for him to be taking all the blame if there are others. You might want to talk to this guy, too."

Fairfax looked at the address. "I'll give this to the boys to run a finger on. If it's local, and it looks like it might be, we can bring him in. And thanks, Mizz Crane. You've been the model American citizen abroad."

If he only knew the half of it.

Fairfax buzzed through the intercom. "I need Peterjohn," he said. In moments, the lanky computer nerd Alison recognized from the search party going through her house that morning appeared. "Pete, run this. See if you can find out who's behind it." Fairfax handed Peterjohn the IP address.

Peterjohn studied the paper. "I'm on it," he said and left the room.

Let loose the hounds! Alison smirked, knowing that the U.S. Embassy could hunt down the cyberfreak with more digital prowess than she could ever manage. And if the embassy enforcers paid him a visit, he might think twice before messing around with her.

Alison put on her coat and slung her computer case over her shoulder.

She was eager to take her PowerBook and leave the embassy grounds before her lucky streak turned. But before she headed out, there was one more matter she wanted to take care of. "Mr. Fairfax," Alison said, "can I see Charles?"

"No can do. It's not standard procedure."

"I know it's not how you usually do things, but Charles is my boyfriend. My fiancé, actually. Or he was. Just for one minute. Please."

Fairfax squinted at Alison and his face stretched into that uncomfortable smile. "I'm an old softie when it comes to the ladies. Come on now, just for a minute," he said. "It'll help you get over the sonuva ..."

Fairfax placed his hand in the small of Alison's back and guided her to a room down the hall. Two armed Marines stood posted outside the door. The Marines stepped aside to let Fairfax and Alison enter.

The room, windowless and dimly lit, stank of stale coffee and perspiration. Charles sat slumped in a folding chair at a metal table strewn with empty Styrofoam cups. He looked up, his eyes brightening at the sight of Alison.

"Alison!" Charles walked over to her and gave her a big bear hug, hanging on to her like a drowning man clutching a life preserver. "I'm so glad you're here, Alicats. They're really trying to stick it to me," he said, almost whimpering.

Alison returned Charles' hug. She whispered softly in his ear so that only he could hear, "Charles, Charles, Charles." She rocked him gently, back and forth.

"Alicats, the firm doesn't want to know me. They aren't sending any lawyer, no help, no nothing. I love you so much, Alicats. And you're a lawyer. Hurry, get me out of here." His grip on Alison's shoulders tightened.

"Oh, Charles." She broke away from his embrace. In his eyes where there was usually an imperious assuredness she saw dark pools of fear. He needed a lifeline, all right. But he'd have to cast somewhere else. "Charles, I can't believe what's happening to you. It's really horrible.

And you're right. You do need a lawyer. A really good one. But, you know what? You can't afford my hourly rate."

Alison nodded to Mr. Fairfax who escorted her out the room.

As Fairfax and Alison were walking through the halls of the embassy, Peterjohn appeared from around a corner.

"Phil! Phil! Wait up!" Peterjohn called. He bounded down the hall to catch up with them. "I fingered that address. His name's Daisuke Sogo, and he's in Akihabara. 3-14-2 Akihabara."

"Good job, Pete," Fairfax said. "Get two of the boys and let's head out to Akihabara, take a look at the guy's operation. And get on the horn to our friend at MITI. This might be the guy he's looking for."

"You got it," said Peterjohn.

Fairfax walked Alison back to the main entrance of the embassy. "We all owe you a debt of gratitude, Mizz Crane, for all your help and cooperation," Fairfax said. He extended his hand.

"No, really, Mr. Fairfax. I just believe in seeing justice done."

"A lot of people in your place would have tried to cover up or hide the evidence. But you're a good girl, and you did the right thing."

Alison bristled at the "girl" part, but she managed to bite her tongue rather than bite his head off. There was no need to antagonize Fairfax as long as he had his pit bull Peterjohn who could go fetch electronic evildoers with such ease. Fairfax's "good girl" could be his next target if she didn't keep her head down.

"I'm glad you have the matter resolved now," Alison said. "But what will you do with Mr. Sogo?"

"Assuming he's a Japanese national, we'll have to work with the locals, 'course. But they've been on this with us all along. And if your guy's a link on the AsiaNet gang of hackers, well, the Japanese have been trying to shut AsiaNet down for months."

"Why? What do they do, AsiaNet?"

"Just your garden variety misfits. Like to mess with folks online, worm into their systems. But their new thing is server attacks. Take down an entire site like that." He snapped his fingers. "Bunch o' losers. Not All-Americans like you, Mizz Crane."

"Good luck, Mr. Fairfax. It's been my pleasure to help." She smiled a smile that didn't reach her eyes and waved goodbye.

Alison passed through the embassy's guard checkpoint and out onto the streets of Tokyo. If Fairfax only knew what she knew. But thank God he didn't. Crusty old fart.

Alison caught the first cab she could hail at that busy hour. "Akihabara," she told the driver. "3-14-2 Akihabara."

50

Rush-hour traffic clogged the intersection, and grid-locked drivers flashed their headlights in frustration. Alison chewed her lip, trying to stay calm. She'd wanted to hightail it to the cyberfreak's place before the embassy apprehended him. But at the pace traffic was moving, the show might be over by the time she arrived.

The cab driver, equally aggravated over their slow progress, whacked his steering wheel and drove off of the main artery onto the side roads. But the alleys were engorged with the flow of early-evening pedestrian traffic. The cabbie fought his way through human bodies and bicycles and ended up back on the main thoroughfare not much farther along than where he'd turned off.

As the cab limped along, Alison's cell phone rang.

"Alison, it's Kiyoshi. What's going on? I called the lawyer. Sasaki. He said he never heard from you." Kiyoshi's low voice sounded angry, accusatory.

"I'm on my way back from the embassy, and there wasn't any problem. Except that they've arrested Charles."

"What?"

"Apparently, he's part of some online money-laundering operation. With your old pal Yuko Yamada."

"Yamada-san?" Kiyoshi clicked his teeth. "Doesn't surprise me. Not with her family ties. Does your friend have an attorney?"

Alison smiled. "Kiyoshi, you're sweet to be concerned about Charles. I wish I could say I shared the sentiment. But, frankly, when it comes to Charles, I don't give a damn." And saying it, she knew it was true.

"So you're not in any trouble?"

"I met with the same guy who searched the house this morning, Fairfax. He wasn't interested in anything I had to say. So now I'm in a cab on my way to visit a friend. Someone you know."

"Who?"

"Our friend from online. That anonymous jerk. I found out his name. And his address. He lives in Akihabara, of all places." She felt smug with the information.

"You're not going to see him alone."

"No, the cops are on their way. But I want to have a ring-side seat when they get there and bust his ass."

"That might not be a good idea. He could be dangerous. You don't need to go to his house and—"

"Kiyoshi. The guy has been like a blood-sucking tick that's burrowed under my skin, into my life. I'll stay out of the way and let the cops do their job, but I want to see his face. Watch him go down. After all the shit he's put me through, I'm looking forward to it."

"He might try to—"

"Your signal's breaking up. I'll call you tonight when I get home. Bye." She disconnected before he could further try to dissuade her.

The cab turned onto a murky narrow street and stopped at a two-story building. A bicycle missing a tire leaned against the front railing. Laundry left to dry still hung on the line even though the sun had long since set. All in all, a depressing little abode.

A shabby metal sign with peeling paint was posted in front of the apartments. Even though she was a mediocre student of Japanese, Alison could read the building's name, written in the simplified phonetic *katakana* syllabary used for foreign words. She sounded the words out. "Fo-Re-Su-To Ma-N-Sho-N."

Forest Mansion? Alison glanced over the dreary pre-fab structure.

Dream on. She paid the driver, grabbed her computer, and exited the cab.

Alison stood alone in the noiseless street. She thought she saw a cat crossing in front of her. Or was it a rat? Not waiting to find out, she scrambled up the steps of the apartment building and hid in a dark corner under the stairs to the second floor.

Here she was at last. The home of the bithead goon who had invaded her privacy, spied on her most intimate moments, shattered her confidence and turned her days into living hell. Tonight he would be unmasked.

With the blood thirst of a mob gathered around the gallows, Alison's pulse quickened at the prospect of watching justice be done, up close and personal. And the embassy guys, the deliverers of justice, would be arriving at any moment.

But where were they? She checked her watch. She'd assumed that they'd left the embassy about the same time she had. Certainly they would have been able to cut through the traffic tangle she'd encountered.

An arctic wind disturbed the trash in the corner of the stairwell. Alison's shoulder ached under the weight of her computer case, but she didn't want to set her PowerBook down on the ground. Not with the rat droppings and cigarette butts.

Maybe she should call Fairfax, ask what was keeping them. But Fairfax wouldn't be expecting to find Alison on the scene. She'd gotten off scot-free after her soul-baring visit to the embassy. No need to put herself in their line of sight now. She'd have to be patient. The cavalry from the embassy would be arriving soon.

But while she was waiting, why did she have to stay in hiding? The apartment complex wasn't exactly abuzz with activity. If she was quiet and careful, she could do some advance reconnaissance. Check out the freak's home turf, just as he had surveilled hers. It would feel so good to put one over on the guy. Let him be under the microscope for a change.

Kiyoshi was being overly cautious in warning her not to go to the guy's house. It wasn't like she was planning to go knock on the geek's front door. And any minute now, the cops would be there to arrest the pervert.

01110100 01101111

The flashing light in the corner of his computer screen alerted him. Something — or someone — had set off the motion-activated security camera outside his apartment door. The sex fantasy chat was going strong, and he hated to be bothered.

Ever since that door-to-door newspaper salesman had banged at his entry and ruined a recording session, he'd disconnected his doorbell and hung a "No Soliciting" sign at his door. Why didn't those sales maggots fuck off and leave him alone? Couldn't they read?

He zipped up his pants and shoved his gun in his waistband. What worthless asshole had interrupted his private time and killed his erection? He switched his display to look at the feed coming from the camera.

A small figure was sidling out of the camera's frame. But it didn't look like a salesman. Big tits, long legs and a well-rounded ass, it was a woman. A *gaijin* woman.

He froze the image to zoom in for a better look. An electric surge reinvigorated his dick. It was her. At his apartment.

How had the foreign bitch found him? He was a master of online anonymity. No one was better. And he'd completely covered up his digital tracks.

But here she was, scratching outside his door like a hungry alley cat. Arriving at his apartment like she had been invited. Typical American bitch. So damn pushy.

She should know better. Hadn't he taught her that he was the one who dictated when they met? His terms, his schedule, his satisfaction. He'd have to remind her who was in control, teach her a lesson. Aggressive little cunt.

He logged off of the sex fantasy chat, and, using his computer mouse, adjusted the angle of the security camera.

Now she was standing in the front of the apartment building eyeing the units in the complex. She looked like she was lost, unsure which way to go. He watched her through the camera feed as she shifted her computer case from one shoulder to the other before walking up the stairs to the second floor.

He would teach her an unforgettable lesson, and he had to work fast. From his gear bag he quickly assembled the preparations.

He would teach her, and she would learn, that he was the composer, the arranger and the conductor. He would orchestrate her moaning to a rhythm he set, a tempo he'd command. She would pleasure herself to please him. Masturbate when he told her to, orgasm if he allowed her to. He would record it all, and from her panting, her screams, her whimpers and her climax, he would create a work of genius. The masterpiece of his collection. His dick ached in anticipation.

Soon. Very soon. But where was she now?

Through the camera feed he saw her walking back down the stairs.

No! She was leaving. That part wasn't written in his score. At the bottom of the staircase, she looked at her wristwatch, paused, then turned around. As if lured by the pull of an intractable beam, she moved toward him.

The sign at his front door read "Do Not Disturb," but this was one interruption he would welcome.

01110110 01101001 01110011 01101001 01110100 00100001

Alison stepped out from under the staircase and examined the Forest Mansion complex. Two floors of apartments, two units on each floor. An outdoor walkway connected to the door of each apartment. Your basic motel architecture. Alison studied the four units in front of her.

Some of the apartments seemed to have the names of the occupants posted on the door, but the names were written in kanji beyond Alison's reading ability. And Alison realized — too late — that she'd forgotten the weirdo freak's name. Peterjohn at the embassy had said it was Sogo something. After all the trauma the pervert had put her through, she couldn't remember his name. But one of these apartments was his, and she'd be damned if she couldn't figure out which one.

She was a trained professional with an analytic lawyer's mind. It was time to be logical, systematic. Eeny, meeny, miney, mo.

On the first floor, two units. One had the evening laundry out. Looking at the frilly clothes hanging up, Alison decided a woman lived there. The other ground-floor apartment was dark. Maybe her guy? She couldn't definitively rule it out.

Alison tiptoed up the stairs to check out the two units on the second floor. In one unit she heard a television show with an overly cheery host and maniacal laughter from a studio audience. She also heard a baby crying. Probably not her guy's place. Her guy wouldn't be anybody's idea of Father of the Year. She moved on to the other upstairs unit.

The second unit had a sign on the door that Alison couldn't read, but two names seemed to be listed. A couple? Joe Sato and Mary Sato? A stack of three dirty ramen bowls were piled outside the door waiting for pick up from the restaurant that had delivered the food. Three bowls meant three people. Alison's gut feeling told her that her friend lived alone. He certainly wasn't one-half of any couple. Pass. Must be an apartment on the first floor.

Alison crept back down the stairs, aware of the fact that Fairfax and his entourage would be arriving momentarily. She'd better pick up the pace of her surveillance lest the embassy squad catch her in the act of snooping.

Only one unit remained unexamined. The dark apartment on the ground floor. There were no telltale signs giving her a clue as to who lived inside. The unit felt anonymous, generic, unremarkable. Process of elimination. This would have to be it, she deduced.

No lights on, no sound, no movement. It looked like nobody was home. She'd take a glance to see how the guy lived, observe the beast's native habitat. Just a quick look, and then she'd retreat to her hiding spot under the stairs and wait for Fairfax.

She inched up to the apartment window and peeked in. The blinds were shut but angled in such a way as to give her a partial view. Alison couldn't detect anything inside other than a gray-blue light emanating from a far corner. A television?

She positioned herself at another vantage point. Peering through the blinds, she could make out two computer monitors. The electric glow of the monitors silhouetted a person sitting in front of the screens. Daremo.

So there he was in his lair. Seated in front of a computer screen, head profiled against the light of the monitor. The very position where he regularly tormented and teased her.

Alison had expected to feel rage at seeing the freak, to feel a rush of righteous anger unleashed. Instead, she observed him with the clinical detachment of a pathologist. He had no idea what was coming, that his minutes as a free man were dwindling. But Alison knew, and the knowledge soothed her.

Daremo — Sogo — would soon be arrested. Exposed, uncloaked and naked. His torturing of her would stop. And she'd know that she was the one responsible for bringing him down. Rough justice.

Alison turned and began retreating to her lookout under the stairs when Sogo's door blasted open. Hands clamped down on her arm and yanked her inside the apartment.

51

"Let go of me!" Alison fought to wrench her arm out of Sogo's grasp. He twisted her arm in its socket and dragged her inside his apartment.

Thrashing in protest, Alison banged her left knee against the door jamb. Her heart pounded like a jackhammer, and she barely noticed the pain splintering through her leg.

How could she escape from the clutches of this madman? "Help! Somebody, help me!" Would anyone hear her cries? If they did, would they understand English? Most importantly, would they bother to come to her aid?

Sogo booted the door shut and hauled Alison up the step of the *genkan* entry and into his flat.

Immobilizing Alison's arms, he used his shoulder to switch on an overhead fluorescent light.

For a hellish eternity, he'd been a stalker without a face. But now Alison saw him. Deep-set eyes, long straight nose. Surprisingly good-looking. For a nutjob. And that face was familiar. The recollection crashed into Alison's awareness.

"I remember you, you pervert! You were at my party!" Alison tried to break free from Sogo's vise-like grip. "Help me! Somebody call the police!"

"Shut up. No one can hear you," Sogo said. "And you're hurting my ears."

Alison studied the walls and ceiling of the apartment and saw that they were lined with thick corrugated foam tiles. Hollering for help wasn't going to do her any good.

Sogo bent down and pulled coaxial cables from an open storage bin. He wrapped the cables around Alison's wrists and knotted the cords taut.

Alison kicked the Sysop. The thick sole of her winter shoe made a solid hit to his shin. He scowled, and pushed her so hard that she fell to the ground. Before she had a chance to sit up, he'd tied her ankles with another coax cable. Alison struggled, trying to loosen the restraints, but she was bound up tight as a calf at a rodeo.

Her best-laid plans had gone way, way awry. All she'd wanted was to take a quick peek inside Sogo's apartment before the embassy arrived. Now, as a nosy trespasser who'd been outed, she'd landed herself in the makings of an International Incident.

What did Sogo's twisted mind have in store for her? Looking at her bound limbs, she knew she needed an escape plan. Alison was no Houdini, but she remembered a lesson she'd learned at law school: When in doubt, keep talking.

"I don't know what kind of sick game you're playing, but the cops know all about you. They're on their way over here. Right now. You better let me go."

Sogo sniggered. "Really? I'm sure they'll want to know why you were spying on me." He chuckled as he unclipped the strap on Alison's shoulder and set her computer case on a table.

"Me spying on *you*? Are you kidding me? You're a fucking electronic Peeping Tom." Alison rolled to her side and pushed up on her elbow until she was sitting.

"You *gaijin* think you're so clever. My security camera recorded you hanging around outside my door."

Alison jerked at the cables. "Untie me. It'll look better for you when the cops get here if you aren't holding me captive."

Sogo grabbed Alison's arms. "Get up." He hoisted her to her feet. Keeping a firm grip on her combative hands, he reached out and stroked

Alison's hair. She jerked her head away from his touch, but he grabbed a handful of her curls and yanked her toward him, crushing her against his chest.

Sogo buried his face in Alison's hair and inhaled. "Coconut. Nice. I like this hair. Unusual color. Even for a foreign bitch."

His fingers inched inside Alison's pants and flirted with the skin of her pelvis. Alison squirmed at his groping. "Is your hair down here the same color? The same as your head?" Sogo said. "I want to see. Take off your pants."

"No!" The word shot from Alison's mouth like a spew of vomit. She didn't have an exit plan, didn't know how to escape, but there was no way she was going to strip off her clothes for this freak.

"You don't understand," Sogo said. "I'm in charge here." He stepped away from Alison, reached under his shirt and brandished a handgun. "Take off your pants. Now." He nudged down Alison's waistband with the gun's muzzle.

Alison's breath caught in her throat. Blood pounded in her temples. Kiyoshi was right. The guy was unhinged. And now he was armed. And rapidly proving himself to be dangerous. Not to mention stupid, concealing his gun with an inside-the-waistband carry. If there were bullets in the chamber, he could shoot his own dick off carrying that way. It would serve him right.

Maybe there weren't any bullets. Sogo probably didn't plan to shoot her. Just scare her. He'd certainly accomplished the latter. But Alison didn't want to further antagonize him. She'd have to cooperate if she wanted to survive until the embassy arrived. Where were they? Had they gotten lost?

"I can't take off my pants like this." Alison held up her arms. Sogo pointed the gun at her while he untied the cables with one hand. She kicked off her shoes, slid out of her pants and faced the guy.

"Now your coat and sweater," he said. Alison did as she was told. Shivering in her bra and underpants, she folded her arms across her chest. Alison ground her teeth as Sogo's eyes crawled over her body.

"Come here!" Sogo gestured with his gun. Alison shuffled forward. "More." She moved closer. His body odor reeked of mildew and bay leaves. Where the hell was the embassy?

Sogo spun Alison around so that her back pressed against his chest. His warm breath tickled Alison's neck. He held the gun to her stomach while he caressed the curve of her breasts. Creeping fingers slipped under her bra and rolled her nipple.

"Stop it!" Alison tried to break away but Sogo jabbed the gun barrel into her ribs. Molten tears of fear and anger threatened to flood down Alison's cheeks. She closed her eyes and took a cleansing breath. There had to be something she could do, some way to wake up from the nightmare. "Stop it," she said. "Please."

"We're not finished, yet," Sogo said. "We haven't even started."

Stripped down to her underwear, Alison stood trembling — whether from the cold or from the fright of being held at gunpoint, she didn't know. Probably both.

Sogo snatched a microphone from a table loaded with computer parts. He also picked up something that looked like a purple banana. On closer observation, Alison realized that the banana was a dildo. What the hell was going on?

He brought the gear to Alison. "This will be really easy. I want you to play with yourself. Pretend I'm your boyfriend. Tell me how good it feels." He extended the dildo for Alison to take.

"I'm not touching that thing." Alison's upper lip curled in disgust. Who knew where that dildo had been? What crevices — whose crevices — the sex toy had explored?

"Take it!" Sogo thrust the dildo at her and dragged it across her lips. Alison wiped her mouth with the back of her hand, but Sogo poked her with his gun. She took the dildo and held it at arm's length, dangling it from two fingers as if it were a dead rat.

"I heard you, TokyoAli. I saw you. You and your boyfriend fucking," Sogo said. Alison couldn't help but notice the bulge in his pants.

"You like it rough," he said. "I like it rough, too. We have a lot in common." His teeth gleamed in a lustful grin.

"We have nothing in common," Alison said. "You're a goddamn freak."

Sogo's eyes flared in rage. Alison swallowed dry saliva. It could be suicidal to provoke an unstable psychopath. Especially an *armed*, unstable psychopath.

The anger washed away from his face as quickly as it had appeared, and he seemed back in control of himself.

"I'm going to record you now." He pressed a button on a shoe-box-sized machine and held the mic up to Alison's mouth. The gun remained leveled at her chest. "Play with your pussy, make yourself come. I heard your orgasm, that scream." His gaze drifted far, focusing on a horizon only he could see. "I have to record it. That scream."

What an idiot she'd been to deliver herself to Sogo's front door, to get ensnared in his perverse game of abuse and degradation. He had a gun. She had nothing. But if she wanted to get out alive, she'd better think of something. Fast.

Her hope that the embassy would show up and save her faded. They were noticeably, tragically, absent. She'd given Fairfax Sogo's address — all the same information she'd gotten from Jed.

Jed! That was it! That was the plan. A Hail Mary of a long-shot plan, but it just might work. And it just might keep her alive. If she could play it right.

Alison raised her hands in surrender and forced a laugh. "Hey, I came here to meet you, face-to-face. You don't need that gun."

Sogo wagged the microphone in Alison's face. "I'm recording," he said.

She tried to take a deep breath, but terror gripped her rib cage. Her breathing shortened and stuttered. This was no time for stage fright. The show must go on. And she had to give the performance of a lifetime. Her life might depend on it.

Alison tilted her head and made an effort to smile. "I was thinking about you—" She ran her tongue around her lips.

"So I wrote you a little message." Alison dragged the dildo along the inside of her thigh. "I'd wanted to share it with you online—" Her hips swayed in seductive figure eights.

"But I can read it to you now."

Sogo's gaze followed her fingers, which were stroking between her legs.

Eyes half-closed, Alison purred with pleasure. "I'll read you the message," she said. "It'll make me come, and I'll scream. Loud. The way you like it." She traced the sex toy along her throat. "I just need my computer. The message is on it."

Sogo blinked. He looked at his gun and back at Alison. And blinked again. He lowered the microphone.

Holding Alison at gunpoint, he marched her to the table, unzipped her computer case and booted up her Mac. "Read it," he said.

Alison's computer waited dumbly for her to do something. Do something. Do anything!

"The message is on World NetLink," she said. "I need to connect my modem—"

He poked her with his gun. "You think I'm stupid?"

Alison's heart hammered in her stomach. She hoped he wasn't so stupid that he was jabbing her with a loaded gun. She took a breath. On with the show.

She pulled down the waistband of her underpants and massaged the dildo across her labia. She had no concern about the germs. Germs wouldn't matter if she was dead.

"I'm getting wet. Let me get online to read you the message. I'll scream. Good and loud."

His pinched brow registered his internal confusion, the quick mental calculations of what he should do.

Sogo thrust a cable into the back of her computer, punched in a phone number and nodded.

Alison smiled. "Give me a minute," she said.

Logging on to World NetLink, she browsed for the message she had prepared for Sogo. Earlier at her house, when she had the opportunity to send it, conscience-stricken, she had hesitated. But this time there was no delay. She pulled up the message and hit the Send button. The message was signed, sealed and instantaneously delivered.

In the corner of the apartment, a computer monitor beeped and flashed that he had mail. Then another monitor squawked and flickered. The computers announced, "You've got mail! You've got mail! You've got mail!" like a scratched record caught in a skip. The email poured in.

Sogo dashed to his computer and entered commands, but the keyboard was stuck. No commands went through. He tried another keyboard. No response. One of his monitors shut down while another computer announced mail. And more mail. An endless torrent of mail. He set his gun down and pounded out keyboard commands to defend against the attack on his network.

"A little mailbomb just for you, asshole! Kaboom!"

Alison couldn't wait for the embassy. She had to take a chance — maybe her only chance — now. While Sogo hammered at the keyboard, she lunged for his gun. Sogo careened around and glared at Alison who was now holding the pistol on him. One finger on the trigger, the other hand steadying her aim, Alison sighted down the barrel.

"*Konoyaro*!" Sogo charged toward her.

Alison squeezed the trigger.

A bullet zinged over Sogo's shoulder and lodged in the heart of one of the server computers.

She squeezed the trigger again. Sogo fell to his knees.

She squeezed again. And again.

The bank of server computers exploded in a tangle of twisted metal and broken shards of plastic.

She fired until there were no more bullets.

"Put the gun down," said a man's voice behind her.

Alison wheeled around. In the doorway to Sogo's apartment stood Kiyoshi. He wielded a pocket knife.

"Are you all right, Alison?"

"What are you doing here?"

Kiyoshi knelt down to examine Sogo's prone body on the tatami mat floor. After a quick inspection, Kiyoshi stood up and kicked Sogo's leg. Sogo grunted and turned his back to Kiyoshi.

"You've got to get out of here, Alison. I'll talk to you later, but you need to go." He gathered up Alison's clothes and handed them to her. "And give me that." He reached out for the gun she was still holding. Alison surrendered the weapon, took her clothes from Kiyoshi and quickly dressed.

Curled up in a fetal position, Sogo lay moaning on the floor. Kiyoshi growled at him, and Sogo immediately was silent.

Alison zipped up her computer case. "Kiyoshi, what's going on? Are you—"

"Not now. I'll take care of things here, but you've got to go."

Charles had fed her a steady diet of lies and deceit. Sogo had toyed with her like she was his marionette. And now, Kiyoshi, a person she trusted, was not the person she thought she knew. She was tired of playing the dupe, and she wasn't budging, not without some answers.

Alison closed in on Kiyoshi, stopping when her nose was inches away from his. With hands on her hips, she stood planted.

"Who the hell are you, Kiyoshi? Tell me. Tell me the truth."

She heard distant sirens, the two-tone whine, which made her think of air-raid warnings in old war movies.

Kiyoshi's eyes glanced toward the apartment door. "There's no time. They're on their way and you don't want to be here when they arrive. I'll explain later, but you've got to go. Please."

Alison locked Kiyoshi in her gaze. Lines of worried tension ringed his eyes. She was livid that Kiyoshi had misrepresented who he was, but something in her still wanted to trust those velvet brown eyes that looked at her with such tenderness. And Kiyoshi was right. She didn't need to be present center stage when the embassy arrived.

With a final glance at Kiyoshi, she hitched her computer case up on her shoulder and raced out the door toward the main thoroughfare. The sound of sirens grew louder. Alison flattened herself against the wall bordering the narrow street as two vehicles sped by.

The cars stopped at Sogo's flat and a crew of uniformed Japanese police got out. Kiyoshi met the men outside Sogo's apartment and exchanged words. The officers bowed to Kiyoshi then stormed inside the door.

Careful to stay out of sight, Alison eased closer to the Forest Mansion apartment building. Peering from the shadows, she watched the commotion outside Sogo's flat.

Siren wailing and lights flashing, a minivan arrived at the scene. From her hiding spot, Alison saw Fairfax, Saito, the computer nerd Peterjohn and some other men jump out. Kiyoshi greeted Saito, and the two conferred before Saito introduced Kiyoshi to Fairfax.

"Thanks for calling Saito-san with the heads-up about Sogo," Fairfax said to Kiyoshi. "We're expanding the scope of our investigation, and Sogo's name keeps popping up."

"Glad I could help," Kiyoshi said.

"Sogo's been a naughty boy," Fairfax said. "Messing around in a lot of stuff he shouldn't have."

"We got some echo logs of online chats between Sogo and that dead Canadian girl they found," Peterjohn said.

"Where's Sogo now?" Fairfax asked.

"He's being detained inside."

"Was there anybody with him?" Saito asked.

"No," Kiyoshi said. "There was nobody."

Fairfax turned to his men. "We're going to pay the suspect a little visit, boys. Pack up his gear."

Fairfax's crew invaded the SysOp's apartment, edging past police who were marching a sullen and handcuffed Sogo out the door. The

SysOp paused near the building's stairs, threw his head back and yelled. "TokyoAli!"

Kiyoshi approached Sogo and glared at him with a withering gaze. He slugged Sogo hard in the gut, and the SysOp doubled over. "You didn't know her, Sogo. *Baka*!"

Fairfax's brigade paraded out of Sogo's apartment with a procession of computers, hard drives and discs, which they loaded in their minivan.

"Seems he had quite an operation going on," Fairfax said. "We were lucky that Crane girl got a bead on him."

"Lucky, right," repeated Kiyoshi.

"Thank you, Fairfax-san," said Saito. "The Bureau's cybercrime specialists will meet you at the embassy, and you can get started examining Sogo's gear."

"Roger that." Fairfax saluted from the window of the minivan and sped off with his men.

Saito clutched Sogo by the shoulders, shoved him into the backseat of the car and slammed the door. The car rocked from the impact. Saito bowed to Kiyoshi then got in the police car with Sogo and the officers.

Sirens quieted, the car slipped off, and a restrained SysOp faded into the anonymity of the Akihabara night.

Alone in the dark street, Kiyoshi scanned the shadows. After a minute, Alison appeared from behind a tree in the next-door lot. Kiyoshi smiled when he saw her. "I thought you might still be here," he said.

Alison's face was stony with contained anger. "Who are you, Kiyoshi?" She set her computer on the ground and crossed her arms. "Who the hell are you? Really." Alison's rage burned through the dimness of the night.

Kiyoshi's smile dissolved, and he lowered his head. "I'm sorry, Alison. I'd wanted to tell you."

"Tell me what?"

Kiyoshi rubbed his hands together and shoved them in his trouser pockets. "Alison. Please try to understand. I've been working with MITI, the Ministry of—"

"I know who they are. But who are you? Some kind of cop?"

"A cop?" Kiyoshi's smile returned. "No. What I do for MITI, I guess you'd call information gathering."

"You said you were a businessman in marketing."

"I am. And in my work I meet lots of people, companies, go to trade shows. Sometimes the government is interested in what I've seen. That's all."

"Are you talking about corporate espionage? You're some kind of spy?"

"If I were a spy would I have tried to save you with a Swiss Army knife?"

Alison couldn't help but smirk. "Hardly James Bond."

"That's what I'm trying to tell you."

"But how do you know Saito? I heard him greet you by name. He was one of the ones searching my house. With that jerk Fairfax. I thought they were going to arrest me."

"Saito's the Police Security Bureau liaison to the American Embassy. We've worked together before. When you said that you'd left the embassy and were on your way to Sogo's, I was worried. I thought that if anybody could find out where you were headed, it would be Saito. I didn't know that they were investigating Sogo separately and that he was involved with the Canadian."

"The poor girl." Alison's hand went to her mouth. "Why didn't the cops know about Sogo sooner?"

Kiyoshi shook his head. "A missing foreigner. It just wasn't a high enough priority."

"Until she turned up dead." Alison snorted.

"I told you to let me handle things, Alison. I didn't realize you'd make a personal visit to Sogo's apartment."

"And I told you I could take care of myself."

"So I see."

"What's going to happen to Sogo?"

"Since he's a Japanese national, Saito's Bureau will be interviewing him first. Then they'll probably turn him over to Fairfax. The Canadians will want to talk to him, too."

"I'm glad I had a chance to hit him where it hurt. He deserves everything coming his way."

"Yes, but you've got to tell me. Where'd you learn to shoot like that?"

Alison shrugged in aw-shucks modesty. "We lawyers have to know how to protect ourselves. Mostly from our clients."

Kiyoshi laughed and coughed. "It was a good thing you missed your target."

"Who said I missed? I got exactly what I was aiming for." Alison blew on her index fingers and pocketed her pistols in an imaginary holster.

Kiyoshi stepped closer and put his arms around her. "So did I," he said. He kissed her on the neck and stepped away.

"I've got to get back to finish with Sogo, but can I see you tomorrow at five?" he asked. "I want to start again with you, Alison. To do things right. Will you give me a second chance?"

Kiyoshi's eyes, usually animated and dancing, were motionless with vulnerability as they pleaded with her. Alison's chest tightened and a rush of warmth flooded her body.

"Tomorrow at five?" She looked up as if trying to recall her schedule. "I'm not sure if I'm free." Alison picked up her computer case and smiled. "I'll send you an email."

The End

Acknowledgments

I woke up one morning after a particularly cinematic dream. Sitting at the keyboard, I pounded out a movie treatment which became Tokyo Firewall. Lots of people helped.

I've got the world's best siblings who each — in their own special way — encouraged me to get the book out. Freda, my precious oldest sister who I miss every day, was my first beta reader and returned my manuscript pages covered with sticky notes, red ink, and highlighting. Joyce was my self-appointed publicist, and Edward composed a score for a trailer before I'd even finished writing.

Thanks to Mary Ann Zimmer who championed the embryonic novel; Vero Angriman and Marissa Marchese whose enthusiasm refueled mine; Ashley Forson and Kieshia Divers were insightful sounding boards; and Reshauna Striggles who only sees silver linings. Rafael Andres generated cover designs with impressive creativity and patience; Julie Mianecki and Monica James provided eagle-eyed editing and proofreading.

I offer a bear hug of gratitude to Leigh Jackson, Arden Kass, and Carol Baker for their support, creativity, and nudging.

Most of all, I'd like to thank my ever-supportive husband, Tetsuki. His belief in me makes all the difference.

Please join my mailing list at elizabethwilkerson.com to stay in touch. And let me know if you found the Easter egg!

— Elizabeth

ELIZABETH WILKERSON was one of Silicon Valley's first cyber lawyers. She lived in Tokyo where she practiced securities law, studied Butoh dance, and founded a company to present African-American culture to Japanese audiences. A native of Cleveland, she graduated from Harvard and holds JD and MBA degrees from Stanford.

Get in touch at www.elizabethwilkerson.com.

Made in the USA
Middletown, DE
15 November 2018